DAGENTYR TRIED TO STARE STRAIGHT AHEAD

But he could not. Curiosity was too strong.

There were several women on the wall very close to him; he could not tell which one was Helani. Then a woman detached herself from the others.

Dagentyr felt his pulse quicken. She came closer until she stood in front of him. Her watery laugh caught his ears and he heard her say, "Do not be so shy, warrior. Let me look at you. I am tired of everyone treating me as if I had the evil eye. Look at me if you like." Her voice was liquid.

Her eyes caught his, grabbed them. Stunningly dark and large, they were outlined in black and stood out against her pale skin. Her cheeks were high, smooth, and led to a delicate mouth with gently rounded lips. The face was set in a shaded grove of jet-black hair. The gown she wore was long but bared her willowy arms and her breasts.

Toying with her shawl, she let its tasseled ends dance playfully over the pink circles. Perspiration formed under his helmet, and his legs tingled and were numb.

BEWARE THE HORSE

L. F. LUCKIE

TOR

A TOM DOHERTY ASSOCIATES BOOK
NEW YORK

BEWARE THE HORSE

Copyright © 1989 by Lorenzo Luckie

A TOR Book
Published by Tom Doherty Associates, Inc.
49 West 24 Street
New York, NY 10010

Cover art by Maren

ISBN: 0-812-58526-7   Can. ISBN: 0-812-58527-5

Library of Congress Catalog Card Number: 88-51006

First edition: February 1989

Printed in the United States of America

0   9   8   7   6   5   4   3   2   1

For my parents and grandparents,
for their support in the bad times
and their joy in the good

Chapter 1

The stone slid smoothly across the bronze, wearing the edge sharper with each pass, scraping out a sound that woke the birds in the trees. They blinked dumbly in the half-light of dawn, twittering uneasily at the group of men who waited in the clearing, wrapped in their dirty, woolen cloaks.

As he sat waiting, Dagentyr drew his eyes away from the dark trees, held his sword up to the young sky and studied its shape against the pallor. He pulled his thumb crossways over the edge several times, shook his head, and picked up the stone again. He licked it, and ran it the length of the sword, but Targoth turned round on the tree branch where he sat as lookout and threw a twig at him, gesturing hotly for quiet. The twig startled him and caused his thumb to slip along the blade. He cursed, then suddenly amused, giggled at his own clumsiness. Targoth must be as jittery as I, he thought.

Around them, shadows were being born after a secret nighttime of waiting. The men were swallowed up in the deep woods, in the first stirring of leaves and animals. They felt it, shared it with the forest, those anxious moments that marked the beginning of a new period of light and life. They felt part of the awakening and at the same time were aware that they were out of place, intruders travelling in a strange realm not their own. It made them fearful and their nerves tingled. The trees, though they were like any others, seemed different. No one knew where the obscure forest pathways led, what creatures had made them, or if they had been trampled by the feet of men. Reflexes and tempers were quick. Sounds that went unnoticed in their own forest made them grab for their weapons and thrust their shields up for protection.

Placing his bleeding thumb to his mouth, Dagentyr leaned back against an oak and watched the sun struggle up through the grey, humid air. He mused that as soon as it cleared the top of the hill, it would collapse and roll down into the valley like the yolk of an egg gone bad, making the streams run thick and putrid.

As he watched, the scenery sharpened from its nocturnal blur and took form gradually. The distant hills over which the sun rose lost their dusky appearance. As the dark green of the wooded areas and the soft mossiness of meadows began to brighten, the men in the clearing looked up and ceased to huddle beneath their cloaks. The sun caused their spearpoints to gleam and brought a warm glow to the metal of their swords and axes. Little by little, the mottled patterns of their cowhide shields soaked up the light until colors were apparent— black, white, rusty brown. At their centers, menacing bronze spikes protruded. Some shields were decorated with embossed discs of bronze, others with totem animals of bronze or copper in fierce, swirling designs. The sunlight was caught in the wings of copper-red hawks, in the beards of demons or the open mouths of snarling, metallic wolves.

Their edginess dissipated as they were able to recognize each other by faces, and not by hushed voices. Breathing came at a more relaxed pace as the light burned the forest spirits into mist. With the easing of night's tension, the men got up from their waiting positions and walked about to stretch their legs, but even in the daylight they were alert. If their weapons were not already in their hands, they drew them. Everything was done in careful silence, and Targoth kept his lookout in the tree. There were many bands of roving warriors in the forests, spurred to action by the same calamity that had drawn them far away from their home. The villages were starving, or soon would be. An evil had infested the land, a sickness.

Dagentyr noticed the men forming into groups according to tribal faction. It was a bad thing to have the warriors divided. There should be no trouble between those of the same village; it made fighting difficult when you knew the man at your back could not be trusted. In the din of battle, men did not always see which blow dropped a comrade, or whose hand held the sword. Men whispered and cast scheming, uneasy glances. Dagentyr felt their eyes. He was the son of a great war leader. The eastern tribes were encroaching, spreading their rule by war and by stealth. He spoke for the men who wished to stand and fight. There could be no submission for them. Dagentyr and his men knew the easterners must be stopped. He tapped the sword against his leg in irritation. As if the sickness were not enough, he thought.

Taking his cue from the others, he dropped the stone, and stood. He was of medium height for his people, but lean and muscular, so that if seen by himself, he looked as tall as any man in the village. The hair on his head was thick and brown, worn shoulder length and swept back over the ears. He ran his hand over his short beard and frowned, causing the characteristic pensive furrow to appear between his eyebrows. The frame of hair and beard surrounded a face whose features were strong, almost stern. His eyes were ice-green, matching the streak of sweat-induced patina from his bronze earring. The muted jade trail ran down his skin almost to the bottom of his neck. He did not like the rain and did not bathe often; water rinsed away much of the stain's intensity. Months went by before it returned to the way it had been before.

Since the morning was heavy with chill, he tossed the tail of his woolen cloak across his chest and shoulder. He wore it over a plain woolen, knee-length tunic, cinched at the waist with a woven cord from which hung his food pouch and wooden scabbard. From ankle to knee, his legs were wrapped in wool and leather. Shoes of soft hide hugged his feet, and when he moved in the forest he made no sound.

He adjusted the chin strap of his leather war cap, and with the sword still in hand, walked quietly across the little meadow to the base of the lookout tree. "What do you see?" he asked quietly.

Targoth shifted on the branch, scratched his thigh where the bark had left its imprint, and looked down. "Nothing but smoke and the tops of trees. I can't see the village, but they have the fires going."

Galmar, who had been peering through the bushes, turned his head, topped by the great horned helmet, shushing them through his luxuriant, grizzled beard. They quieted, and Targoth moved his gaze back out over the forest.

Dagentyr muttered under his breath. Clavosius, high chief and war leader of the tribe, usually led the cattle raids into strange forests, but this was a scouting party, not worthy of his attention even though the situation in the village was urgent and grave. And so he sent Galmar, his brother, as head of the group. He led only by his right as brother to Clavosius, for he was much older than the rest, and weak. Many times, Dagentyr and the others had come to his aid when sword or shield became too heavy for him and he gave in to his enemy's blows, puffing and snorting like an old boar. When they returned from battle, he would greatly exaggerate his exploits and puff with pride as though he were king of all the land between the rivers. The bronze-plated leather jerkin pulled at Galmar's shoulders as he stood, watching the woods grow light. He shuffled his feet nervously, wishing for the familiar feel of a war cart beneath them.

Because the sickness had ravaged the country-side, there were no horses in the village of Fottengra, and the cattle were few. In a matter of days they had shown the signs—lethargy, bleeding, confusion. Then they died, fell over with heaving convulsions and died in the fields and pens. Goats and sheep were falling ill now, all the animals were. The priests drove them through smoke from the sacred fires, and blew horns, and made offerings. Still they died, and the evil had gotten worse. Two children had fallen sick and perished. The gods were not pleased.

Dagentyr looked at Galmar and suppressed a chuckle of irony. The old man was incompetent, lazy, in the way, yet today he knew he must fight to keep him alive, if for no other reason than to spite Vorgus, the schemer and traitor.

At the side of the clearing, Vorgus crouched near a stump and sprinkled ochre on a small statuette while he chanted softly in his own dialect. He was the largest of them, bare-chested, kilted. His blond hair fell loose down his back and his thick beard picked up sunlight like twisted gold wire.

A rustle in the undergrowth attracted their attention. Molva was so startled that he aimed his bow in the direction of the noise. When Sem and Arvis

gave the bird call, parted the bushes, and stepped
into the clearing, he blew his breath out through his
mouth, wiping sweat from his fat forehead with his
hand.

Arvis and Sem went straight to Galmar and
spoke in quiet tones.

"Four huts, women and children, youths, one or
two old men. We saw beasts—goats, pigs, and
cattle," Arvis said.

"Warriors? Guards?"

Sem nodded. "In the fields and working on the
palisade. It's a small homestead, a new one. The
defenses are unfinished."

"And how many men are there?"

"Six, perhaps seven."

Dagentyr nodded with satisfaction. They could
strike.

"Horses?" Galmar asked his usual question.

"Only one or two," said Sem.

"Our luck is the dung of pigs! The sickness must
have spread here, too. Pickings are no better here
than on our side of the river. We might as well turn
back now, go home and tell what we have seen."

"What do you mean?" said Dagentyr. "What do
you mean, things are no better? These are the first
horses we've seen." He assumed a hopeful tone.
"Don't forget the women and children. They can
always be used. Besides, two horses and a few cows
are better than none. We came here to find cattle
and sacrifices. This is a plum ripe for picking.
There are hungry people in the village. You heard
what Sem and Arvis said. It is a new homestead;
there are few warriors. We could strike now, quickly, let surprise carry us." He worked consciously to
sound convincing.

The other warriors nodded.

Galmar shook his head. "We are only a scouting
party. It's too dangerous. We could return here later
with the rest of the warriors but—"

"What are we scouting for? Horses, cattle. They're here and we can take them." Dagentyr shrugged vehemently. "Their palisade isn't even finished. There are only four huts. We can strike and be gone easily. That way the journey will have been worthwhile."

"I don't know. We stand to lose . . ."

Dagentyr saw the old man's courage failing. "What do we stand to lose? If we do not bring back horses, and cattle for food, our people lose. The sickness will win. It will have beaten us. Then the eastern men will move in," he added.

"Raiding has not been good," said Targoth. "Clavosius has been displeased. This would be a way to improve his mood."

Excellent, thought Dagentyr, knowing well that Galmar wanted very much to improve his brother's mood. He continued. "What will Clavosius say if we go home with bad news and no loot to make up for it? Let us fight. We're anxious for battle." It was, he was certain, a statement true of both factions.

Vorgus looked up and took interest in the conversation.

"We are a scouting party," complained Galmar.

Dagentyr waved his protest out of the way. "We are warriors in need of cattle and horses. These will be the first horses in Fottengra since the onset of the sickness, and you will have led the group that brought them back." Galmar's eyes brightened. "Keep one of them for yourself; it is your right. You could be one of the few men in the land between the rivers to own one. We should not go back with nothing."

Galmar squinted, and sighed at the thought of returning through the fortress gate empty-handed. "All right. Take all the animals you can and search the huts. The women, children, and youths are to be taken alive. Grab what you can and be quick. We must be quick." He coughed, cleared his throat with a sound like a man walking in thick mud, then moved warily into the brush and creepers, signaling for the others to follow.

Targoth dropped from the tree branch. When he had picked up his axe and shield, he went to Sem and put his arm around him with a clap of approval. Sem smiled at the attention from his older brother and they moved off together, nodding at Dagentyr.

Vorgus stood, and streaked his chest with ochre. The applying finger moved daggerlike and laid out gashes that seemed to bleed gold. In the bustle of men leaving the clearing, he came up to stand in front of Dagentyr. "It is good that you convinced Galmar that we should fight today. It means that you remembered what I told you. You have seen the way and have given me the opportunity I spoke to you about. The old one dies today, in the fight. I will see to it. You will say and do nothing. The men who side with you will do nothing. But, tell me this. What about later, when it is Clavosius's time?" He spoke softly and leaned in close. His hot, invading breath hit Dagentyr in the face and caused him to clench his fist tighter around his sword hilt.

"I was truthful in what I said just now. There was no deceit. I convinced him to fight because I think it is what we should do, not because of anything you said. And he will not fall in the fight. I will see to it."

"You defy me?" Vorgus's face hardened into an ugly parody of the demon on his shield.

"I'd as soon take a knife in the back, or die in bed like a woman as side with you, pig. You're alive and where you are only because of the old chieftain's weakness. You're an outsider, like the eastern tribe you come from. An entire race of outsiders." Dagentyr lowered his voice further. "What if I went to Clavosius and said, 'Your adopted son plans to kill you and rule the village in your place under the protection of his friends, the eastern men. He has never respected you as a father and hates you for your love of him. I know because he has tried to draw me into his plot!' What if I said this, Vorgus?"

"He would not believe you."

"Because he believes only you?"

Vorgus grinned triumphantly. "Yes." He eased his chin toward Dagentyr like a lure, inviting a blow.

"Then he is his own undoing, but I won't go in with you or the eastern men, and you will not succeed."

"You speak dangerously, like a man who wants death."

"I speak the truth." Dagentyr walked by him and picked up his shield from beneath the oak. The way Clavosius believed Vorgus's lies astonished him. The fool doted on his foreign son and never knew. He remembered how his own father had been passed over for the chiefdom, years ago, in favor of Clavosius. It had been a narrow decision. The warriors and elders were divided still. Clavosius had begun to court the easterners because they sent him lavish gifts, and because he was afraid of them.

A curse came to his lips, aimed at Vorgus. He smiled grimly, realizing with satisfaction that he was the main obstacle standing in Vorgus's way. It was more satisfying to know that Vorgus realized it, too.

He glanced at Molva, who had gone to the side of the clearing to urinate. Arvis whispered, "Hurry, cousin," and waited at the meadow's edge. Dagentyr waved him off and watched him go through the leaves toward the village, then he said to Molva, "If you didn't piss before every battle, you'd wet yourself like a child."

The words pricked Molva like the point of a spear, and the sweat trickled down his face and made him miserable. Dagentyr was about to laugh, but he felt Vorgus's hand on his shoulder and heard his strangely accented voice filled with malevolence. "Leave Molva alone. Go with the others and think about my blade striking out for you in the confusion."

Dagentyr regarded the blond giant with cool hate, tightened his grip on the shield, and crossed the shade-spattered meadow into the forest. The last of the men were pushing out through the branches.

Vorgus made a motion with his head for Molva to follow, then left. Cinching his tunic, Molva took his weapons, walked quickly to the edge of the clearing, and disappeared through the hole made by the others.

They made their way through a short stretch of thick woods. A tiny stream ran sluggishly into the valley. The men followed it. When they passed by groves of oak, the dark shades of their garments blended in with the forest, and they were hidden like chameleons.

At a place where the stream narrowed, they jumped it, and ran, crouched over, up the side of a small slope. Just before they reached the crest, they stopped to muffle the click and rattle of their battle trappings, then went up slowly and stealthily to kneel, and peer down at the village.

The hamlet lay in a large open space at the edge of the forest. Meadows stretched up into the woods like velvety harbors, and fingers of trees extended into the valley as if to rip them away. The place was no more than four log huts thatched with branches and grass.

Women sat by small fires. A small boy ran by, chasing a dog. One woman worked in a garden patch. She put her hand to her back as she stooped, digging at the weeds with a stick. An old man sat by the door of a hut, singing to himself. Another man, with flowing grey hair, spoke to a young boy. His voice came and went on the fresh morning breeze that stirred the hem of his cape.

There were men working in the tiny fields on the far side of the village. Two others toiled to fit another log into the half-built palisade around the huts.

"We strike quickly before the men can act," said Galmar. "Kill them first, all of them. We wait until the plowmen are at the far end of the field; it will give us more time. If your judgment about this has been bad, Dagentyr, may you fall today!"

"You, of all people, should say a charm that I do not."

Galmar gave him an uncomprehending stare and then looked away. The oxen pulled the plow slowly down the furrow. When the row was done, the plowers stopped, turned, and began the next, heading away from the raiders. "Soon now," said Galmar.

Quietly, Dagentyr went to each man he knew was his. "Help me see that Galmar lives. Stay close to him."

The oxen had stopped again. Galmar called to the gods at the top of his lungs, and the others added their voices to his. The men stood to their full height, shrieking war cries and beating loudly on their shields. They swung their weapons over their heads.

Molva nocked an arrow into his bow and sent it flying into the grey-haired man's chest. The boy cried out and ran into one of the huts. The women saw them and turned over their cooking pots trying to escape. Two scampered into the huts. The rest went straightaway into the forest, shrieking. One ran from her dwelling carrying a baby and dashed into the woods.

The young men at the palisade ran to get weap-

ons but were killed before they reached the huts.
The band of maddened men running down the hill
engulfed them.

Dagentyr checked over his shoulder to see where
Vorgus was, then cursing himself for cowardice, he
fell back behind the others to be next to Galmar.
The old man looked puzzled but grateful, and
pointed to the fields, dispatching men to kill the
plowers and take the oxen.

The cries of the victims were distinguishable
from those of the attackers by their shrill note of
panic. Arvis shouted in Dagentyr's ear, "Get something for us. Go on! I will watch Galmar for you."

He nodded, ran to the nearest hut and found it
empty. As he turned to go to the next, he saw that
Vorgus had the woman in the garden by the hair
and was hacking her with his axe. She screamed,
and tried to ward off the blows with her hands. The
first axe stroke hit her palm and split her forearm
like a dry stick. She made a noise like a bull when
sacrificed, a horrible bellow that hurt the ears, then
slipped back into her throat where it turned
guttural. Another cut hit her in the neck, and she
was quiet, but Vorgus continued to shake her by the
hair like a wolf when it sinks its fangs into prey. He
shook until her hair started to pull away from the
scalp. The woman slumped against him, and
greased by her own blood, slid down into the
weeds.

Dagentyr swore at the waste of a valuable woman. He had seen Vorgus take pleasure in this before.
For an instant their eyes met. Vorgus knew he
would not get to Galmar without an open confrontation. In frustration, he gave the woman's corpse
another brutal chop.

Going to the second hut, Dagentyr tore away the
door flap and stepped in. A girl hid among the
shadows at the rear, and whimpered. She saw him
and clawed at the back wall, breaking the family

pottery with a loud crash. He stepped toward her, but a young boy jumped out from the darkness, swinging a stick. Dagentyr was caught off guard and the stick broke across his shoulder. Gritting his teeth against the pain, he rammed the boy with his shield and slammed him against the side wall. The woman made a run for the door, but Dagentyr recovered, tripped her, and she fell forward. He grabbed her by the arm and jerked her to her knees, dragging her out the door. Arvis ran up from another hut and helped him tie her with a thong. The dog nipped fiercely at Arvis's legs. Its bark was a high squeak of confusion and fear.

"Who is with Galmar?" Dagentyr asked.

"I have been until now. It is all right. Haltivos is with him," Arvis said breathlessly.

Remembering what Galmar had said about youths, Dagentyr went back in the hut, but the bronze spike on his shield had pierced the boy's chest. He lay bleeding on the dirt floor, among the broken pots. His mouth was open and a sluggish trail of saliva dripped down his cheek. The breaths he took were like those of a sick animal, and the spike had torn a lung, for the wound gurgled like a brook. Dagentyr shook his head. A sense of inexplicable weakness seized him. For an instant, the pain in his shoulder worsened as if it knew his name.

He checked the hut. The surviving jars were all empty. Finding nothing of value, he left. By the time he walked out the door, the boy had stopped breathing altogether.

Sem had a woman in his arms, wrapped in a fur to keep her from fighting, and Targoth followed with a child slung over his shoulder. It pounded his back and pulled at his hair. Cursing, he beat its legs with his axe handle to make it stop.

Men were torching the houses with brands from the cooking fires. Arvis lugged the other woman to where Galmar stood on the slope, directing the sack and wiping the sweat from his face with his cloak. Haltivos stood three steps away.

Dagentyr turned to another hut. Men rushed past him carrying loot and driving animals before them. Before he could enter the dwelling, he saw a dark-clad figure dart into the bushes. He followed at a run.

The crashing footsteps ahead of him dragged through the undergrowth. Dagentyr's heart pumped faster. His arm was afire with the desire to strike, and kill. He let out a piercing war call to the frightened quarry. Then he saw the figure. It was that of a man, leaning against the base of a tree, breathing heavily. When the man saw the warrior he yelled pitifully and threw a rock. It bounced off Dagentyr's shield, and as the man rose to run again, Dagentyr rushed in and kicked him in the groin. The man was lifted off his feet and into the tree trunk, headfirst. The rough bark goudged his head as he fell, twitching and vomiting.

"Please don't kill me," he managed to whisper. "I am valuable, I am—"

Dagentyr had raised his sword to give a killing stroke, but hesitated. "Why?" he yelled, then pulled the man up by his tunic front. "Why are you valuable? Speak up, speak up now!"

"The animals, animals . . ."

"What is that? What about animals?"

"Horses. I tend cattle and horses. When I see to the horses, if they are taken ill, they do not die. I have made the sickness pass us by!"

That was valuable, if he spoke the truth. Not knowing why he chose to be merciful on such unlikely testimony, Dagentyr tied the man's hands with his belt cord and pulled him hurriedly through the vines and leaves, back to the village.

The houses were burning well now. Dry roof thatching crackled, exploding into flame. The old singer still leaned against the door frame, his skull

split. A burning log had fallen across his lap, and
smoke filled his mouth instead of song. The dog
was silent, nowhere to be seen. Men were already
skulking back into the woods with what they had
taken.

Vorgus was empty-handed. The fur of his leg-
gings was stiff, and heavy with clotting blood. He
was red from the knees down, as though he had
wrapped his legs in the pelts of freshly skinned
animals. He leaned over to wipe at the gore with his
cloak.

Sem trotted off with his woman while Targoth
dragged the child away by one arm. It whined and
rubbed the welts on its legs. Molva held the end of a
rope that tethered two pigs. He tugged frantically to
keep the frightened creatures from running away
with him. Arvis saw Dagentyr and helped him drag
the man. They heard a sharp whinny, and two men
rode the horses through the smoke. Their hands
were buried deep in the shaggy manes, and their
scabbards beat rhythmically against the animals'
flanks.

"The men of the nearby hamlets will see the
smoke," said Galmar. "If they come while we are
here, we'll be outnumbered. We should be gone
already. Faster! Back to the clearing."

When they returned to the glade, Galmar
stopped long enough to take a brief look at the
spoils. "Goats, pigs, oxen, cattle, two women, and
one child. Ah, I forgot," he said with pride, "two
horses. No youths? No sheep?"

"Remember, Galmar. I took one of the women.
Let Clavosius keep that in mind when the distribu-
tion is made," Dagentyr said. "This man is mine as
well."

The old war leader frowned at him and began to
cough and wheeze. "Why did you take a man alive?
They are of no use except for sacrifice."

"I believe he is valuable."

"Bah, valuable in what way?"

Dagentyr shrugged, thinking, I'll not tell you, you old fool, for if he speaks truth he is a prize worth keeping secret.

Galmar squinted his eyes into wrinkled slits. "He's shaking. What's wrong?"

He looked. The man was short, thin, and his head tilted and swayed erratically. The mouth opened uncontrollably now and then as the head moved. His features were like wet potter's clay, changing shape spasmodically. On his chin the beard grew sparsely, barely covering the drawn face, which was young, but creased.

"I don't know." Dagentyr nudged him with his sword.

"Maybe he's possessed by spirits or has a catching sickness. Perhaps the horse sickness can be passed to men." Arvis's voice was tense and worried. They all stepped back quickly. "Kill him, Dagentyr, quickly, or we'll be possessed, too."

Dagentyr recoiled and said a charm against evil.

"No! The evil is trapped within him. He contains it. He hurts no one. Don't kill him. It will only anger the gods and release the evil against us." It was one of the women who spoke up.

Dagentyr stepped toward the man. "Does she speak the truth?" He gave what Dagentyr took to be a nod. "Are you a sorcerer or ghost conjurer?" The head swung a negative answer. He looked at the faces of the other warriors and made his decision. "I believe the woman. I'll keep him." He was not sure that he did believe, but would chance it.

"No. Keep him away from us. The woman may lie or be a sorceress herself. He could bewitch us all. Kill him!" said Galmar.

"I won't go back to Fottengra like a beggar. The animals and captives we've taken are few." He threw an accusing look at Vorgus. "You have your horses; give me what I want. I won't be laughed at because you're all frightened like children."

Galmar jutted his lip out. "I'm scared of no man alive! Take care what you say to me. Keep him, then, but watch him closely. If there's any witchery on the trip home, he dies, demons or no demons, and you go back empty-handed. On now." An owl hooted nearby and its night call was eerie in the light, falling across their hearts like a shroud. "Move quicker, quicker! The spirits may not leave this forest in the daytime." He turned, went to the horses, and rubbed a friendly hand over their long necks. Then he took the lead and started home, handing his shield and spear to his weapons bearer. The others took their spoils and followed behind him.

Dagentyr said to his prisoner, "Go in front of me, strange one. I've enough danger behind me as it is."

Chapter 2

The rest of the day turned bleak. A thin gauze of clouds spread across the sky in streaks. By the time the group paused at midday to make sure of its bearings, the overcast was so dense that light found it hard to get through.

All during the morning they had moved at a quick pace, seeking to travel as much as possible in patches of forest that lay along their way. Over open areas, they hurried, feeling exposed, and naked to attack. Even Galmar drew energy from their urgency and moved like a much younger man. He went in front to assure the way, then would fall to the rear to watch and listen with Arvis, who led the group that lagged behind to warn of followers. The spryness he showed now never appeared before battle, just after, when there was booty to parade in Fottengra. Once during the trek, he slipped on a slick spot on the trail, and the weight of his helmet carried him over sideways into a patch of ivy that covered him till just the bronze horns protruded from the leaves. The others were too preoccupied to notice.

Targoth and Sem prodded the women relentlessly with their spears and kept up a constant stream of threats and curses to keep them moving. One carried the child in her arms, and she swayed dizzily with the strain and fatigue. She did not faint; Targoth would not let her. At the times when she wavered, he slipped his arm around her waist and gave her water, not out of kindness but out of need to keep her going.

In their hurry, they did not stop to eat. The child became hungry and cried. Its first wail sliced through the silence, and they all ran as fast as they could to the next concealing stand of trees.

Galmar came panting back to where the women stood, anger filling his eyes. The beard danced savagely as he spoke. "Kill it! It'll be nothing but trouble. If anyone is following, they will hear. We'll be finished. Kill it now!" He pulled his sword from its scabbard and set the blade to the child's throat, elbow bent for a vicious downward stroke.

"Wait." Dagentyr spoke in an urgent whisper. "We can't afford to lose anything. Kill it, and it's one less thing to take back. That's good now, but not after we get home. Should we cut the animals' throats too just to save ourselves the trouble? The child would be useful and pleasing to the gods as a sacrifice, but not if we kill it here."

The woman who held the child looked up in horror. Dagentyr turned to the other one. "Rip a shred from your skirt."

With a puzzled look, she stooped and tore a strip from the bottom of her long woolen skirt. Dagentyr took it and wadded it up, then stuffed it into the child's mouth. It still cried, but in a muffled way. When they had travelled on for a while the child slipped into sleep from lack of air, and exhaustion. The stuffing was removed.

Dagentyr dropped back to walk with Arvis. In front of them, Molva and Vorgus herded the goats and pigs. The two men prodded, and pulled at the ropes, and sometimes, in desperation, slung one of the creatures across their shoulders when it went too slowly.

Dagentyr's captive did no better than the beasts. His walk was crooked, slow. One foot dragged. Several times, Dagentyr followed the herdsmen's example, pulling him by the rope around his neck then nudging with his sword. "I'll take Galmar's advice and kill you if I have to," he threatened. "Hurry! I won't put you over my back and carry you like a pig. Walk!"

Yanking on the cord, he quickened his step, forcing the bound man to stumble on as best he could. Arvis laughed softly at the outburst. Dagentyr turned to him and gave an exasperated shrug.

The forested hills rolled on, unending. Far away, the horizon pressed itself up against the sky. They journeyed carefully, for in the woods nearby thin stems of smoke rose and flowered.

They had seen larger villages here, fortified ones, and wished to avoid them. Galmar turned, and signaled for stealth. Targoth and Sem drew their daggers and put them at the women's throats. Dagentyr let his man feel the swordpoint at his back.

They pressed on, climbing the slopes until the muscles in their legs ached. Vorgus, who was carrying a goat, let out a grunt of breath with each step. The sword was getting heavy in Dagentyr's hand. The arm that pulled the captive burned inside. Galmar was now in the middle of the pack, unable to set the leading pace. He shivered at the long shadows and repinned his cloak closer about his neck.

As the light came to an end, the group trudged up a wooded rise and paused at its peak. Beneath them was a shallow depression glowing pale in the spent sunlight. Soft grasses spread out to both sides. Patches of dark clover and pink wild flowers spot-

ted the green smoothness. There was a small lake
pressed like a thumbprint into the earth. Grey
clouds, reflected from the sky, filled the lake, dappling the surface like curdled milk. At the crest of
the rise on the far side, the forest started again. The
trees formed a palisade that followed the horizon.
From farther down in the hollow, the droning of
bees filtered through the grass to lull their ears.

They stood and breathed in the scene like air.
Bodies exhausted from a long day of hard travel, no
food, tension, went loose, and the descent was easy,
refreshing.

Varza and Marnusat collected the water skins
and went off toward the lake to fill them. Their
happy voices receded until they were lost in the dull
hum of the bees.

The woman with the child raised her head for the
first time and glanced at the lake, the grass, and the
flowers. The day's terror had not been forgotten,
but the surroundings eased the heaviness from her.
She was less afraid, thankful at least that the night
would not be spent in deep woods filled with
wolves, and ghosts that would touch her in the
blackness. Even the surly Vorgus was pleased at the
sight. He nodded his head repeatedly as he looked,
and muttered things to Molva.

Dagentyr liked the spot. It was beautiful, and
thinking in a more practical sense, he realized it
was a useful place, a good site for a village. If
Fottengra became too large and pressure from the
easterners too great, a colony would have to split off
to settle elsewhere. This place seemed as likely as
any. There was the lake for water, and grazing land.
Trees for building and fire were close at hand. A
spot to make a man smile. Sleep would be good
tonight.

Halfway up the opposite side of the hollow was a
small grove, placed like an afterthought. They

climbed, making for the long branches newly covered with the silvery-jade leaves of spring.

When they reached the trees, Galmar gave the signal to stop. Breathing heavily, he let his swordpoint slip to the ground and steadied himself against one of the grey trunks. He spoke in between gasps. "We'll stay here. Make a fire quickly, over there, but make it a small one and see that it cannot be detected. Tie the women and animals to that tree. Dagentyr, the man sleeps apart, not with us. Take him away and watch first. Where are those two with the water?" He looked expectantly toward the lake and eased himself to the ground. Above him, the cicadas began to buzz.

Dagentyr shook his head and shoved the prisoner to the edge of the grove. "You're more trouble than I expected, holding us up all day long and now making me keep first watch."

When he had tied the man to the base of a dead tree, Dagentyr gave him some dried pork from his food pouch. Setting down his shield, he removed his leather helmet and raked his fingers through his wet hair. His mind ached like his body, for sleep and home. His thoughts walked the streets of his village as he picked up wood and built a fire of his own.

Varza and Marnusat returned with the skins, giving them to their owners. Galmar took noisy gulps. "It took you so long to get here," he complained. "Take first watch with Dagentyr." The two looked at Galmar, dumbfounded. They were Vorgus's men and were used to favored treatment. Their eyes stayed unpleasantly long in Dagentyr's direction.

A chuckle came from Dagentyr as he gave the captive water. He spoke secretively. "Listen to that. Old Galmar drinks like a cow and moos out his bad leadership the same way." The man's eyes were

closed. A nudge from Dagentyr's foot woke him.
"Stay awake. You'll sleep when I say so."

The women sat close by where he could see them.
One still held the child and swayed back and forth,
wide-eyed, sobbing. She would not eat or drink.
Opening its eyes, the child looked around. He grew
nervous when a goat sniffed at him, but the woman
struck the beast's nose. It bleated and joined the
rest of the animals, grazing near a rotting stump.

Darkness came suddenly. There was no vivid-
ness to the sunset, no glow. The thick clouds
prevented it. The night did not sneak in behind
layers of pink and amber. It dropped from the sky
and pressed down on the leaves. The whole land-
scape sagged as if heavy with soot. The air stirred
slightly, rippling the meadow like the folds of a
cape cast off by a giant. In Fottengra the guard at
the gate would be lighting the torches. Cooking fires
would flare up in the houses, sending glimmers of
light out through the tiny chinks in the walls.
Clavosius would be sitting in his hut, sipping warm
mead from a cup while slaves placed roasted meat
on the hearth.

Up in the grove the breeze swirled through the
trees, bringing with it a chill and the smell of water.
It felt cold to Dagentyr as it blew against his damp
hair, so he covered his head with his cloak and went
to find more wood for his fire.

Targoth had built a fire in the other half of the
grove, around which the others sat. Molva and
Vorgus sat close together, huddled in one cape.
Galmar still sprawled under the tree, away from the
fire, the water skin in his hands, head back, mouth
open, snoring to rival the wind. The helmet sat
awkwardly on his brow. Varza and Marnusat mumbled under their breath as they took up their posts
near the animals.

"After the first watch is done, who then?" asked
Arvis.

Vorgus tilted his head up at him. "I will, and Molva after me."

Molva looked at him with tired eyes that pleaded for rest and no responsibility, but Vorgus did not see.

"That's enough," Dagentyr called from his side of the grove. "Arvis, watch with Vorgus, and Sem, you stand guard with Molva."

Vorgus started to protest, but instead, clenched his teeth and let the issue pass.

Dagentyr turned his attention away from what went on with the others. He arranged himself comfortably at the foot of a tree by his fire, across from his captive. Seen through the flames, the man's twitchings were even more grotesque. The red glare gave his face highlights that accentuated the contortions. The whites of his eyes caught wisps of flame and sent them hurtling back.

Sitting with his legs pulled up, Dagentyr rested his sword across his knees. "We must be fair about who watches," he said, "but even more importantly we must be careful. For each one of Vorgus's followers on watch, we must have one of our own. If we did not do this, it would be easy for them to murder us in our sleep and say that we fell in the skirmishing." Realizing that the man would not be aware of, or interested in, the struggle in Fottengra, he moved on to other things. "You know, if not for you, I might have been able to skip watch altogether tonight. I'm tired, but I have to sit here and watch you and listen to the old man snore and the women weep. Who are you, strange one? Are you really as valuable as you say you are? What is your name? If I have to stay awake, so do you."

The man shifted his position a little as though the flames Dagentyr saw him through were becoming uncomfortable, starting to singe. He did not speak.

Dagentyr gave the sword a quick thrust in his direction and spoke harshly through his teeth.

"Talk to me!" The man drew back and turned his face to the tree. "You can just as easily go to the priests." He saw the man's head nod, and he lowered the sword. "What are you called in your village?"

"Ruki." The lips moved exaggeratedly, slowly. The sounds they made were long sounds, slurred as with mead, or loss of blood, sounds like women mourning.

Dagentyr became thoughtful. He hadn't noticed the odd quality of the voice when he had captured the man. It took him by surprise. It had spoken only one word tonight, but he did not like the sound of it. He took a few breaths before he continued.

"Are you trying to bewitch me with incantations?" The man shook his head. "Ruki?" A nod, no words. "What are you, a feared warrior?" He chuckled at what he thought was a joke. The captive's face didn't alter, and the breeze ate Dagentyr's words. "What are you that you know how to dispel sickness? How do you do it if not by sorcery?" He felt himself tense as a protection against the voice. He knew the question couldn't be answered with a nod.

"I have knowledge, of herbs, treatments. The animals know me; they trust me. I spend time with them."

"Do you speak with them?" he asked fearfully.

Ruki's eyes narrowed. The heat had begun to make them water. "No." He looked at the man who, from his point of view, sat wrapped in a fiery cloak, brandishing a glowing sword. He talked through a beard of flame, and his words burned, picking up heat as they crossed.

When the voice ended Dagentyr was relieved. He thought of another question. "Why are you like this? The woman mentioned demons. Why were you not left in the woods when you were born if your father and mother knew you were cursed?"

"Yes, cursed. That's what they say, but not like this from birth. In my twelfth summer. It happened then. The village men were afraid and wanted to kill me but the shaman stopped them. He said that there was evil in me, and killing me would only release it to harm others. So they let me live, out of fear. I began to spend my time with the beasts."

A gust of wind beat through the trees and hit the fire, putting a spray of ash and twigs into the air between the two men. The smoke left its vertical channel and washed over Dagentyr. It stung his nostrils and made him gag. He held back the coughing until he thought the eyes would pop from his head, then he coughed in quick, sharp bursts. The fire was nearly blown out, but the wind passed. A couple of jabs with the sword, and extra fuel started it crackling as before.

Dagentyr wiped the water from his eyes. "I could be asleep, but I have to stay awake and eat smoke." His tone was acid. "You're supposed to be a good thing for me, Ruki. It seems that the omens are turning bad; for me or you, I don't know. You'd better have the knowledge you say you do."

In the other camp circle they were all asleep, lying as close to the fire as they could. Dagentyr thought he could hear them breathing with one long sigh. There had been no stories told tonight or mead passed around. Everything was quiet. Gods! Dagentyr thought, and took a huge chestful of cool air to keep himself awake.

"I don't know what I'll do with you, Ruki. Perhaps if you are as good with beasts as you say, I'll keep you. If not, I may give you to the priests or my wife. Neither is pleasant. Maybe you could ease Gertera's urges. She gets none from me, you understand." He laughed. "You'd probably disgust her."

His troubled thoughts took over, banishing his
apprehension of Ruki for the moment. He spoke
almost as if to an equal. "She's a sickly, clinging
thing. She was my father's wife after my mother
died and was no older than I when they were
joined." He stared into the embers and pressed his
lips together. "A skinny, weak girl with breasts like
stunted acorns. She wraps round my life, binds it
like a greedy, choking weed." The fire seared his
eyes, so he looked straight up into the black sky,
watching the phantom lights that lingered. "She
was passed on to me when my father was killed. It
is the custom. She's mine to take care of, my
inheritance. I'd give her back to her family but for a
promise to him that I would not."

He remembered himself suddenly. Leaning in to
the man as far as the fire permitted, he whispered,
"The priests or Gertera. Either way is bad for you,
so cure my animals, Ruki."

The captive's eyes had closed again and his chin
rested on his chest. Dagentyr placed the flat of the
sword blade on Ruki's arm. The cold metal jolted
him awake. He would have shrunk back into the
tree trunk if he could have. Dagentyr saw him
cringe through the flames. The illusion made him
smile.

"From where I am, slave, you sit in fire."

The captive's face, for once, stayed immobile as
he watched the man with the flaming sword. His
answer plodded through the air.

"You also, warrior."

Chapter 3

The watch went slowly. Ruki fell asleep and now even the sword would not wake him. Dagentyr got up several times and gathered more wood, passing the time by thinking of Kerkina, who was his wife in his heart. As he was starting to doze, he heard a twig snap. When he got up to check the area, he found nothing, but Galmar's cloak was thrown open and his body quivered with the chill. Dagentyr covered him up and returned to his place. Varza and Marnusat whispered but said nothing to him. Soon after, Arvis came and told him to sleep. He drifted off as soon as his head settled on the earth. There were no dreams.

A murmuring sound woke him. The eastern half of the world was already purple, and a star was dimming out behind strips of cloud. Rolling stiffly to his other side, he saw Vorgus talking quietly to Ruki, offering him water and stroking his hair. It made him angry and alert. He threw off his cloak, stood, and moved his hand to his dagger, all in the same move.

"Go away, big man. He'll have water. You don't have to feel any concern. Go and care for your friend. He's the one who'll need it. Change his clothes. He's sure to have wet them during the night."

Vorgus stared at him. They faced each other for a while and then, taking a last look at Ruki, Vorgus strolled away. Dagentyr continued to watch him from the corner of his eye. At the edge of the grove, the easterner drew his dagger, made a slashing movement across his throat, and grinned.

The others were up and gathering their things. Galmar hobbled around the dying fire, trying to get his joints warm. "I feel like I've slept on ice. We leave soon."

Dagentyr untied Ruki from the tree and helped him get to his feet, wondering if a forest demon had crawled into Galmar's chest during the time he was uncovered, ready to steal his life. "You must watch out for Vorgus," he told Ruki. "He's not one of us. He was brought back as a child from some raid or other, from the east. He'll be trouble now, more so than usual; he likes you."

Dagentyr turned away. He could just barely see the lake shining between the trees. There was sunlight now, clear and golden. The water sparkled like a gilded field of grain. The ghost of the previous day had dried up, shrinking back from the sky, exposing bright blue.

As Targoth and Arvis roused the women and got them to their feet for the day, Dagentyr gave Sem temporary charge of his prisoner and walked down the hill to where the reeds and cattails swayed at the edge of the water. The air was pure and cool to the skin. He felt younger when he breathed it. Dew soaked his shoes. When he walked through the tall grass, he kicked up a spray that landed in tingling droplets on his knees.

He skirted the reeds and came to the side of the lake where water met ground in a stony shallows. The other men were here, dunking their heads beneath the surface and drinking their fill. Going to the edge, he dipped his hands in and splashed the icy water sparingly on his face. It was an ointment to him. He drank deeply, washing away the taste of sleep.

Sem waved to him, and whistled. He waved back and headed for the cattails to relieve himself. Stepping through, he saw Vorgus on his knees by the shore. With a thick stick held between his hands, he pinned a small frog to the ground and pressed till his arms quivered. The frog's mouth opened wide as the weight crushed it. Its abdomen split, spilling its insides onto the ground. He threw the stick over his shoulder carelessly and looked thoughtfully at the frog, satisfied, as though he had cast bones and seen a good sign. Dagentyr thought his presence had gone unnoticed, but Vorgus turned to him.

"It will be like that for you, little man. Your mouth will open, and I'll mash your guts out as you squeak at me to stop." He picked up the frog by the foot and flung it at Dagentyr. It missed him, landing in the water. Vorgus's voice rose in pitch and the muscles tightened around his mouth. "You should not get in my way, or Molva's. His way and mine are the same. I'm a man who takes what he wants. If your prisoner has caught my eye, stay back. You've disappointed me too many times already."

Dagentyr moved a step closer to him. "It's my purpose to disappoint you. You're a sweating sow, grunting in your stinking pen of treachery. The whole village marvels that Clavosius cannot smell the stench."

Vorgus drew his dagger and made a quick lunge for Dagentyr's face, but he misjudged and his thrust went high. Ducking underneath it, Dagentyr stamped his foot sideways into Vorgus's shin. Vorgus yelled and hit the ground on his side.

Dagentyr drew back from him and slipped out his sword. He felt lucky to have it. Evenly armed, he knew he would be at a disadvantage.

The ground by the water was wet and slick. Vorgus had a hard time standing up, and when he lunged again, his footing left him, and he fell to one knee. Dagentyr had been waiting for him to stand, and as he did, slashed crossways where he expected the other man's midsection to be, but as Vorgus slid down again, the blade passed over his head, lopping off the cattails behind him. The other men at the lake noticed and crowded near, calling to the men in the grove.

The sword was knocked from Dagentyr's hand as Vorgus jumped at his legs and toppled him. He landed hard on his back and the wind left him. The easterner was on him quickly.

He grabbed at Vorgus's hands to stop the inevitable thrust. The cool edge of the blade cut his fingers as he fumbled madly. With a quick movement like a convulsion, he wrenched his head sideways. The point of Vorgus's dagger hit the ground beside his ear and sank to the hilt. Vorgus had pinned his left arm, but with his right, Dagentyr reached down with desperate speed and tore his own dagger out of its sheath. Vorgus tugged his from the earth.

They were both ready to strike. Vorgus aimed for the larynx; Dagentyr was poised to drive his blade through the ribs. Neither hit. An unseen blow struck Vorgus and rolled him away. Dagentyr struck vainly at nothing. Arvis and Galmar stood over them, apart from the ring of onlookers. Arvis held the shield he had used to give Vorgus the shove. Galmar shook with anger.

"Idiots! We're out here, who knows where, with enemies all around us, watching maybe, and you two are trying to kill each other. Get up! Kill each other later when the spoils are home, and we're

home. More of this and I'll kill you both myself."
He drew his sword to give emphasis to his words.

Vorgus and Dagentyr looked at each other, then
at the old man, his sword shaking like a useless
appendage. Dagentyr lowered his head to Galmar,
got his sword, and left, fist tightly clenched against
the blood running from between his fingers.

There were many cuts, some deep. His wrist was
gashed, but not badly. Arvis helped him bind his
hand. He wound the cloth in and around, again and
again, pulling hard to stop the bleeding. When
Dagentyr winced, he would ease the pressure a little
and go more carefully. Tying the ends of the
bandage in a knot, he shook his head and said,
"That's the best I can do. You need to salve it when
we get back. Some of the cuts are deep, and it will
take time to heal." He looked into Dagentyr's face.
"You're lucky you're still alive. I thought the least
he would do was slice off an ear, or your nose. It
was madness to fight him."

"I had no choice."

"Then your mistake was in not killing him. You
with a sword and he got the better of you. You were
careless."

Dagentyr nodded. He knew Arvis was right. "I'll
get the chance again," he joked, opening and closing his fingers painfully.

"We must tell Galmar and Clavosius of Vorgus's
plot," Arvis whispered. "The time has come when
we can do nothing else."

"No, cousin." Dagentyr took him by the shoulders and flinched at the pain in his hand. "We can't
do that. You know Clavosius is suspicious of me.
He will not believe. It will only make him think that
we are trying to make trouble. It would go badly for
us. But you are right about one thing, a move of
some kind must be made soon."

"Why won't Clavosius believe you?" Arvis
asked.

"He sees ambition in me."

"If that were reason enough, then no one in the village would believe you." Arvis smirked.

"I do not hide things well. I speak out. Many times I speak first. Clavosius cannot forget who my father was and their struggle. He is in danger from Vorgus but can't see it. He is letting me block his view of it."

"Have you told anyone but me about what Vorgus plans?"

"No, I've kept it silent. Those who know will be in danger, too. There's no point in exposing all those who are with us."

"What are we going to do?"

Dagentyr stared straight ahead, perplexed. "I must think. I don't have an answer now." He looped the cord that held his prisoner around his arm, and picked up his sword with his good hand. Already, the bandage was soaked, and the whole arm throbbed. He tried to ignore it, but every surge of pain sparked his hate and vaulted his mind toward the next encounter with Vorgus. He wished it to be soon and in the open, for when they returned home, there would be many times and places that daggers could stab secretly and unexpectedly. It was Vorgus's way.

The journey continued more pleasantly than before. They moved at a good pace, but not with the previous urgency. The sun glowed all morning, interrupted occasionally by patches of cloud that brushed by. Dagentyr forgot the pain and became cheerful in spite of the slowness of his captive. Ruki walked better, perhaps because of the night's rest. The men had lost some of their fear of him, and no one stared as before. They had too much on their minds to notice the little man. There had been no witchcraft and they were becoming convinced of his harmlessness.

Ruki was too out of breath to speak as he dragged

his way along, but Dagentyr spoke to him nevertheless, encouraging him as he would an ox tired with
a day's work. He exchanged glances with Vorgus
several times. The big man would look back at him,
trying to hide the fact that he limped from
Dagentyr's kick, and show his yellow teeth like a
dog, or glare from under his brows as if he were
studying. Dagentyr mirrored each expression.

Molva noticed it all and sweated even more as he
drove the animals. His forehead wrinkled up as he
looked at Dagentyr, then across at his friend. After
the fight his eyes had been wide. He stuck close to
Vorgus. Now, he watched the play between the two
men, thinking of the same dark corners Dagentyr
did, and the same knives leaping out. Only the
hand that held them was different.

"I'd give up my sword for a cup of berry wine
right now," said Targoth as they went along. The
dark green slopes unfolded before them. Their feet
brushed with a hush over the forest floor. "I
wouldn't mind," he continued, "if the division of
spoils were fair, but we know how it will go. My
share will be next to nothing. You can be sure that
Clavosius will keep the horses." The metal-plated
cap sat heavy on his head. Perspiration crept slowly
up the leather in little peaks. Dagentyr, who had
moved close behind, overheard, and tapped
Targoth's shoulder.

"The more you complain, the worse it will seem.
Talk to the women if you are bored."

Targoth gave the bedraggled women a glance and
looked at Dagentyr flatly. "One of them's yours,
isn't she? A replacement for the one you have?"
The corners of his mouth turned up sarcastically.

"I'll give Gertera to you then," said Dagentyr.
"Weaves without fault, easy to please, loving." He
felt his stomach go sour as he spoke of her. He gave
Ruki's cord a tug in annoyance.

Sem's long, blond moustache gleamed in the

sunlight when he spoke. "What happened back at the lake?"

Dagentyr shook his head.

Targoth snorted. "A fight that's been long in coming." He raised his shoulders in a sigh. "Life is difficult. No man needs to be in a position where others envy him enough to wish him dead, or kill him themselves so they can replace him. Be careful, Dagentyr. You've tried to kill a man"—he checked to see if Vorgus was listening, but Molva held him in conversation—"a man who sits close to the chieftain. You'll be lucky to eat with the dogs at the next feast." His face, usually immaculately shaved, was dark with stubble. He looked uncomfortable with it and rubbed his cheeks. When he noticed Dagentyr watching him, he dropped his hand, embarrassed at his obvious concern for his appearance. Sem broke in.

"If you want my advice, you'll kill him as soon as we get back, discreetly, though."

"What do you think, Targoth?" asked Dagentyr.

"I think something must be done, but I cannot say what. It seems as though you are the one who must make that decision. We are with you, whatever it is."

Sem grunted agreement and went back to eyeing the women.

Dagentyr placed the butt of his sword between his captive's shoulder blades and pushed. It sent the man forward, swinging his bound arms from side to side in spastic arcs.

The blow made flickers of light dart across Ruki's vision as he desperately put one foot in front of the other, praying for balance. His head felt so light, he thought it would leave his shoulders and go bouncing among the high branches. Fear kept him conscious, fear that if he fainted he would simply be killed. The journey had been one constant misery. The rope rubbed his neck raw, and his back and

buttocks ached from the constant use of Dagentyr's
sword as incentive to go faster.

In a small way he was thankful. He was alive and
had not been seriously hurt. He had settled for
small happinesses all his life. It was no different
now. The blond giant stared at him frequently.
Dislike rose instinctively in him, and Dagentyr's
warning made him shudder. Fear was rolling in his
bowels, but hopelessness helped negate it. His
people, and all men, were nothing in the face of the
forces that pushed them through the world. The
gods left and the crops, without the blessing of rain,
died in their furrows. Lightning and fire destroyed
whole villages and could not be stopped. Other
men came, taking and doing what they liked, going
away afterward like the wind. Men were part of the
world, a force as unpredictable as the others, and as
overwhelming. He was caught up, lost, as if a huge
gust had wrenched him from the ground and tumbled him to some other place.

Early afternoon saw Galmar raise up from his
slouch long enough to order a halt, giving the
animals and men a brief rest. He was the only one
who required it. Since they were in thicker forest,
the going was slower, cooler in the heavy shade.
Ruki gave up the struggle and let his knees buckle.
The fallen leaves and soft forest mulch felt good.

Dagentyr unwound the cord from his hand. The
bleeding had stopped, but it had swollen badly. The
bandage was caked and black. He sat down and let
the arm hang limp on the cool earth.

Ruki moaned and worked the bindings at his
wrists. They had loosened, and chafed the skin.
The sweat burned the irritated flesh. Dagentyr took
his dagger, reached over, and cut the bindings.

"If you try to get away, I'll kill you. It's that
simple. Understand?" Ruki nodded, mumbling
thanks more from habit than gratitude. "Take off
the noose, too, and give it to me," he added. "I

can't go on dragging you." His hand was feverish
and had given him a headache.

Arvis suggested leaving the wrappings on until
they reached the village. "Gertera should be able to
bathe it for you and apply herbs," he said. "Let her
at least do that."

"You are beginning to sound like the old
woman."

"You should listen to the old woman sometimes.
She knows many things and is very wise."

"Wise even when it comes to Gertera? Her
sympathy seems misplaced to me. She bore my
father. Can she have forgotten that?"

"No, she has not forgotten. Have Gertera see to
this."

He agreed reluctantly and turned his attention to
the women. The prettier one was talking shyly to
Sem, raising her eyes at intervals to meet his. She
was not beautiful, but her features had a softness;
they went well with her long brown hair and dark,
trusting eyes. She was small and slender. She is the
lucky one, he thought. Clavosius will like her, sleep
with her occasionally, and keep her in the household in spite of the fact that she is rightfully mine. I
may put up a fight for her, but I will lose. If
Clavosius does not keep her, whoever he gives her
to will take her gladly. I should let Vorgus kill
Clavosius, the pompous simpleton.

The other woman sat, still holding the child.
Everything she had in life had been taken from her
but the orphan, and she had it because no one else
cared. At times she looked at it as if not knowing
what to do, then she would sing to it, and cry. She
was not much older than the soft-eyed girl, but
looked matronly. She was not pretty or even pleasing. As he watched her he became sad. She'll go to
the priests, with the child, then to the earth.

The soft-eyed girl laughed demurely at something Sem told her. The woman with the child

raised her head. Her lips started to say something, didn't. She looked at the thing in her arms.

The pretty one's thoughts adjust quickly, Dagentyr reflected. She will come to like Fottengra. Hadn't Gertera adjusted quickly from his father to him? He felt his dislike of the cow-eyed girl growing and asked Ruki her name.

"Edalia," he said.

Dagentyr said the name over a couple of times. If he had been near her, and alone, he would have struck her. "She's the one with a future," he told Ruki.

Ruki heard through a haze of exhaustion. The words made his eyes open. "Do I have a future?"

"That depends on you."

"Let me go." Fatigue had induced a calmness in him. He said the words because there was nothing else left against the helplessness.

Dagentyr did not know what to say. It was outrageous. His reply was still in his head when Galmar reluctantly bellowed an end to the rest. Sem helped the women, noticed something odd, and beckoned to the others. Galmar came running back.

"What's the delay? Let's go quickly."

Sem looked at him patiently. He placed his fingers lightly on the child's neck. Targoth caught his meaning and bent his ear to its chest. "It's dead," he said with disappointment.

"What? Well, I told you so, told you it was more trouble than good. Leave it for the wolves and let's move on." He spoke sharply to Targoth. "You must have injured it when you captured it."

Sem took it from the woman and put it on the ground. Her face never moved, stayed as still as stone. Dagentyr tried to read something into her lack of expression, couldn't, and gave up. Ruki got up by himself. The soft-eyed girl stared in horror at the small corpse, and cried.

Bitch, Dagentyr said in his mind, inconstant bitch.

In single file, they walked by as if in respect except that none of the men seemed to notice the body. Their thoughts pushed on ahead, unencumbered by guilt. To be dead was to be forgotten. Targoth was merely puzzled. He didn't think he had hurt it, but he might have been wrong.

The woman's lack of emotion and the child's day-long silence touched a place far back in Dagentyr's brain. Waiting until the last, he knelt by the child and examined its neck. The faint bruises he thought would be there, were. Trying to turn its head for a better look, he found it stiff with death.

She could've done it almost anytime, last night probably, perhaps during my watch. He hoped vaguely that it hadn't been. Very quick, very easy, quiet. A distant sob from the soft-eyed girl pained him with a hint of regret. Children should play and laugh; men should die. It was not a profound idea. He dismissed it.

The child had been spared the ordeal of the ritual. The woman would face that by herself. Dagentyr noticed a spark of admiration in his heart for the homely one, quietly, desperately brave, and now solitary. He would ask to take her in the other's place but knew his request would be denied. She deserved better than she was going to get, better than Cow-eyes. "It's too bad," he announced to Ruki. "I wish she could trade fates with the other." The cripple stared at him uncomprehendingly. Dagentyr brushed himself off, and they joined the shabby procession in its snakelike meander.

Chapter 4

Home. Soon we will be home." Dagentyr spoke to the rain. It had drizzled all during their final night in the forest, making sleep difficult. Now as they approached Fottengra, the drops grew heavier and slapped the ground. The forest was filled with the crash of rain on leaves. Rushing loudly, like fast-moving water over rocks, it assaulted the ears. Dagentyr's heart was beating faster. In a little while they would be breaking into the clearing, in sight of the village.

He knew their return would be a sorry, rain-drenched display, but better than if they had kept to their original scouting purpose and gained nothing. Though they had not brought back much, they had captured a few of the commodities that Clavosius desired most—slaves and horses. He imagined the chieftain scolding them like naughty children gone playing in the mud.

The path they were on was well worn. Up ahead they saw the opening between two old trees that marked the place where the river could be forded. Dagentyr could feel the blood run through him. He had the feeling that if the rain-noise were gone, he could have heard the heartbeats of the others quicken with his, like the pulse of a great animal.

Sem hooted and skipped around childlike as they came in sight of the river, and beyond that, the broad, clear space that surrounded Fottengra, dividing it from the forest. The river flowed in front of them, between the hillocks and away into the woods again, only breaking free here, in this place that floated like a clear bubble in a black pool of trees. Dagentyr laughed and shouted.

There were women at the shallows, fetching water. Looking up from their work, they saw the war party and joined the shouting. Sem waved to them, and two ran to alert the town. Dagentyr watched their wet hair bounce behind them as they ran, long skirts held around their hips to free the feet.

Galmar donned his self-importance instantly, like a robe. He held his hand up in a triumphal gesture and waded into the river. Rain played loud music on the green water. The animals' hooves splashed pleasantly as they crossed, and the foam they stirred up moved on downstream and was destroyed beneath the drops. The water was cold, and as they moved farther across, all other sounds were lost in the splash of rain on river. It was like going slowly to sleep, hearing nothing as the world faded off into unimportance.

Dagentyr put a hand under Ruki's arm to steady him against the push of the current, then emerging from their dream, they were across and climbing the gentle incline of the bank.

Close to the water they saw the first cow. The cattle were dying so fast that the villagers did not have time to burn all the carcasses. The beast was on its side, legs limp and dangling, belly bloated. Thin trickles of blood ran from its nostrils.

The men covered their noses with their cloaks as they passed, saying charms of protection and frightened prayers. There was another cow near the first, visible where its form had pressed down the high grass, and as they looked at the meadow, they saw that there were many, and their spirits fell. A small boy, watching what was left of his sheep, tooted listlessly on a bone flute, hitting random notes. It was a depressing, mournful sound.

Several young girls came up to them, chattering and smiling. They stayed at the men's heels like overfriendly dogs, laughing, and pointing happily at the animals. Their questions came in a continuous, unintelligible stream. They brought fresh water and ran crazily to each man, offering drink. Dagentyr let the liquid run down his throat slowly, savoringly. "Thank you, little one," he said, and handed back the water jar. The little girl who had given it to him approached Ruki curiously, then drew away. She noticed his uncontrolled twitchings and dashed to the rear of the group, hiding behind Vorgus. Her blond hair matched his. He grinned and took the jug.

The girls running up the hill had paused in the lower village to shout the news, and from the clustering of log huts near the water's edge, voices could be heard picking up the excitement and passing it on. In ones and twos people ran toward them. Children stared in wonder at the horses. Though there had been none for only a short while, in that time they had become mythical to the young ones. They were gladdened at seeing them again. The path up the hill was lined with villagers, cloaks pulled over their heads, drab clothing speckled and dripping.

Ruki was drawing attention. Dagentyr tried hard not to notice, but he could see people point, and whisper behind their capes. Old women cringed. There was evil in the village already; they saw new trouble in their midst. The people were frightened, nervous, looking for someone or something to blame, ready to do anything to gain a return of the gods' favor. They wanted no new devilment.

They passed through the lower village where even the dogs sat at the pathside with their masters

to see the war party go by. Their barking added to
the buzz of voices. Dagentyr let his eyes follow the
path ahead, up to the hilly prominence that overlooked the river, where the fortress and upper
village sat. Its high, palisaded walls jutted from the
ridge like the knife-toothed jaw of a demon. Only
the roof of the big hut of Clavosius showed over the
top.

The village was iridescent behind drapes of haze,
dipped in fog and rain mist. Whenever Dagentyr
dreamed of home, it was like this, mysterious,
ethereal, dominant over everything around it.
From the walls, the rest of the earth was a blackness. Dimly, he could make out the figures of the
guards standing on either side of the gate, warming
their hands in the folds of their cloaks.

The women had reached the upper village now.
The guards saw them coming and blew the long,
twisting signal horn. Its somber note drifted across
to Dagentyr's ears. His skin rose in gooseflesh and
suddenly his heart slipped into his stomach. Misery
overwhelmed him. His clothes were wet. Everything he wore was soaked and limp. Their homecoming was tainted by the aura of death and the
stench of carcasses. Much as he tried, he could not
protect his stain. The rain ran down his chest with a
green tinge. It suddenly occurred to him that there
could be no real glory in this day. Soon, it would be
all over the village that he had fought Vorgus and
failed to kill him. His standing with the other men
might suffer. He gritted his teeth and remembered
other parties returning in sunlit triumph. His
shoulder ached and had gone stiff. Blood that had
clotted in his wound found rebirth in the rain.
Drop after drop flowed again, down to his fingertips.

The climb up the path was long, so long. The gate
spilled out people who watched them all the way,
shouting. There were cheers and prayers of thanks

all mingled together and exclamations of happiness at the sight of the animals. Dagentyr kept his eyes on the path, chewed his lip, and was disappointed that the elation he had felt was gone. Now that he had tried to kill Vorgus, Clavosius would hate him even more. In that respect, Vorgus had won the fight. Dagentyr concentrated on the drops pattering on his shield and head, and tried to forget his worries.

With eyes that opened wider with each step, the captive women watched Fottengra unfold in front of them. The fortress crept out of the woods as they ascended, dark and menacing. The sharpened ends of the log palisade bristled from the earth like the back of a boar. Villagers who watched them yelled and taunted. Men looked them over appraisingly, old ones grinning toothlessly, young ones leering. The women and children threw clods of mud at them and cursed. The way was lined with faces shouting death.

When they reached the gate they were ankle-deep in mud. The streets were fetid rivers, smelling of garbage and dung. From all the huts people had gathered, old men needlessly dressed in war gear, babes, women, giggling girls anxious to see the fierce, eligible warriors. They waited in a crowded semicircle inside the fortress gate.

As the men passed through the gate itself, the sentries hailed them and held their weapons high in salutation. There was a sudden silence, and down from his hut, oblivious to the wetness and mud, came Irzag, shaman and overseer of the sacred rites. He greeted them. The gruff voice came from his mouth like awful thunder as he lifted his arms.

"The blessed sun rises, sets, and rises once more in fire! The seasons tumble on as a wheel, bringing endless renewals of spring. The warriors leave, and the warriors return, and the gods watch over the time between."

He drew the sun circle on each of them with the blood of a freshly killed dove and dropped the pale petals of early spring flowers on their heads. His long grey moustache drooped in the moisture, making the creased old face look even more forlorn. Other priests who stood behind him were younger images of Irzag, standing mute and undaunted as the drizzle watered down the blood. To Dagentyr, the poke of the ancient man's dirty fingernail felt like an arrow sinking into his chest. After each man had been anointed, the priests chanted thanks and followed them, with the crowd, up to the big hut of Clavosius.

Galmar was uneasy as he stood at the entrance and waited. He looked at the spoils, taking courage from them, then tiredly let his head droop to stare at the ground. He did not want to be the one to tell his brother the sad news but it was his lot. Aside from the two they had taken, there were no horses in the land.

The hide that hung over the door swung aside and Clavosius stepped out brusquely, forcefully. His hair and beard were red. From his youth down through the advancement of summers its color had never dimmed, and now it flowed downward like a bright burnished flame, defying the face that had withered behind it. Around his neck was a twisted ring of gold. He was dry and comfortable. Keeping beneath the overhang of the hut, he surveyed the warriors, the people, counted the prisoners and animals all in one greedy, comprehensive sweep of the eyes. He forced a big smile, thanked the gods loudly for the men's boldness, and observed the rain pouring from the eaves. Slapping his arms to his sides in disgusted resignation, he pushed through the sheet of water to embrace his brother and the others, exclaiming, "I am pleased, I am pleased!"

When he had congratulated them, he turned and

entered the hut again, giving Galmar a glance. Dagentyr could see Galmar melt under his brother's gaze as if under a great heat.

After Clavosius had gone and his brother had followed him in, the crowd rushed up, wives to their men, children to their fathers. The guards of Clavosius claimed the women and spoils for division later. They would not touch Ruki, and Dagentyr was left with him.

Dagentyr looked anxiously for the face he hoped to see, and did his best to avoid the one he knew would be there, waiting a little behind the rest for the proper moment.

She saw him and filled the air with her praises and ceremonious sobs of joy. Dagentyr could hear her above all the noise of the others. Running, she came to him and embraced him with tears in her eyes, then fell to her knees to clasp his legs in thanks.

"The gods have blessed us both with your return, my warrior and husband. My sacrifices have not been ignored," she yelled, throwing her arms to the sky. Others began to take notice as her voice rose above their own jubilation.

"Lower your voice," he said through clenched teeth. "Don't make a spectacle or, when we reach home, I'll beat you till you drop and send you packing, back to your family." His skin was hot in spite of the cool rain.

"My joy embarrasses you?"

From one of the huts, two women watched. He kissed her hard on the mouth for them. Giggling, they disappeared behind the doorflap, satisfied.

"It overwhelms me, and half the village besides. You're hawking your joy to me like a trader selling his wares, afraid that a poor show on his part will make the crowd go away. You want people to believe that there is something where there is not." He indicated Ruki. "I have taken this man. Do not be put off by him. He is harmless and may have skills that are useful." Ruki stood like an old stump in the gloom. "You've wanted another slave, haven't you?" Gertera made the sign of protection and stared at Dagentyr as if he were a dog that had brought something foul and dead into the house. "Don't look at me as though I've wronged you, bitch! You nag me for a slave. I've gotten one now and it cost nothing but an aching shoulder. Isn't there any joy left over for this? No? I took a woman also." At the mention of a woman, Gertera's eyes became stone. "Would you prefer that I take her in place of the man? I could make her mine in ceremony and let her share my bed. Is that what you want?" She shook her head and began to caress his face. He pushed her hands away. "Don't offer sacrifices for me. Don't whine or plead or smother me in affection and praise." Tiredness overtook him as he spoke. Because of the rain, the people were gone. Gertera was crying. "How is the old woman?" Dagentyr asked.

"She is well, and wished me to greet you for her. There was too much stiffness in her limbs for her to come herself." He nodded. "And will you ask about me?"

"You seem well enough. Let's go home."

Tears continued to stream out of her eyes, but she took his shield and walked ahead of him to the hut. She turned to smile wanly at him, silently asking forgiveness.

"This is my home," Dagentyr said to Ruki. "Now it will be your home. For your sake, I hope you are more at ease here than I." He brushed the bruised petals from his shoulders and watched them wash down the path.

"Two days hence is the day of sacrifice and feast."

Rest, he thought. Let me rest.

The pungent aroma of the salve with which she had dressed his hand stung his nostrils, whetting his aggravation. She had mixed it up quickly, grinding the yarrow and other herbs to a thick pulp. With clever hands, she had rubbed it into his wounds and wound a clean cloth about the hand. It was only natural that she would ask the cause of the cuts. Too annoyed to fabricate anything, he told her the truth.

"I wish you had killed him!" she said.

"At least we agree on that."

"He doesn't even deserve to be a freeman. Now he's a noble and son to the chief." She clasped his hand tenderly to her face. "This will be painful for a while. Healing is a slow thing, and the cuts are bad. You must be careful and pamper it." Nodding nervously, he withdrew his hand. "What will you do now?" she continued.

"I will go on as before, of course. What else would I do?"

"See that he dies!"

"When the time comes for us to meet again, I will be ready. Then he will die."

"If anything were ever to happen to you, I am not sure the gods would spare me from the demons of madness. Oh, please be careful. Don't go about the village needlessly or at night."

"Enough! I'm tired of hearing it. Save your whining for someone who cares. I'm no baby that needs counseling on what to do."

The old woman looked up at him from her bed near the warm fire. He thought he saw reproach in the heavily wrinkled face. Her eyes were dull, getting cloudy; they gave away no emotion. Hers was a face that could conceal anything, yet he had learned long ago to read what others could not see. Behind the face was where he searched. Though she was old and a woman, they could think alike at times. They could exchange glances, and in them,

see the other's mind. And so, he knew that his
grandmother chided him behind the sunken eyes
and the face that said nothing.

He felt abashed, as if they had returned to the
days before his man-training when she had punished him with sharp strokes from a switch kept in
the corner. He told himself it was only because she
was so old, awesome in the dark mystique of age.
Her arm had no vitality in it now. The hand shook,
and she spilled food when she ate. She was, after
all, only a woman.

Sullenly, he went to bed. Later, as her agitation
eased, Gertera slipped from hurt silence into more
trivial talk. She jabbered on about the feast day.

"We must make small sacrifices tomorrow to
insure good fortune. Fate may place you close to
Clavosius at the banquet."

Not much chance of that, he thought. Rest. He
concentrated on not hearing her.

Kneeling down beside him, Gertera offered a cup
of steaming broth. He lay facedown on the bed of
straw and furs. Ruki leaned against the far wall,
collapsed in sleep. Dagentyr let him stay where he
was. It would be better. They could keep an eye on
him. Tomorrow there would be time to move him
into the adjacent hut where the slaves lived. Ruki
would have to be questioned soon about his healing
skills. The other slaves would have to be told to
keep quiet about it.

Dagentyr tried to sleep. Gertera's words were
nothing to him, as vaporous as the smell of soup
that teased his nose. He did not speak. Sensing his
indifference, she placed the bowl next to him and
sat on the floor beside the pallet.

"Do you hate me all the time, even when you are
away?"

He opened his eyes to look at her. Her limp
brown hair had been taken from its net and hung
down around her plain face. He could not give her

the simple answer. It would be better to lie. The truth would bring no end to her wailing. He tried to keep his voice low to keep the old woman from hearing.

"No. I hate you when you force yourself on me like a willing slave girl. You are my father's wife, though I know it slipped from your mind long ago. The custom has given you to me. I wish it were different."

"I have love for you. I have had it since the day your father brought me to wife and I saw you."

"Don't make me angry. You offend the gods with talk of that and dishonor my father's memory!" Her eyes began to glisten. "You are a responsibility I must face; I do not have to enjoy it."

The crying began again.

"I know of this other girl," she said. "The village talks of you. Kerkina, daughter of Lokuos. I know that you are thinking of taking her as wife. Did you think you could hide that from me? If you take her, what will become of me?" His refusal to answer churned her anguish. "There is so much humiliation in this! You refuse to give other people even the illusion that I am your wife!"

Dagentyr flipped over on his back. The walls of the hut were covered with things that were familiar to him, his shield, sword, spear, his mud-stained clothes. Jugs hung from the ceiling by leather thongs. Meat was smoking over the fire. Gertera was a disrupting note.

"If the words people say bother you, it is best to turn away so as not to hear them spoken."

"There are many things that can be done to keep weddings from taking place."

He sat up and listened, for there was malice underneath her sobs. He eyed his dagger on the wall and made sure she saw.

"Pray to the gods that it will happen. I will be angry if it should not, very angry."

"It's true, then. You will take her?"

"Yes, of course I'll take her. Why should I not? It is my right to choose who I want." He reached for the bowl and sipped at the broth, eating the chunks of meat with his fingers. It was good. The warm taste filled his head. The touch of the fur was warm against his naked skin. Outside, the sunset sifted in between the doorframe and the hide that covered it. "I do not know what to say to you, and I don't know why I must tolerate what you put upon me. The gods have tied me to you," he told her. "You will still be of this household. I have promised it. You don't have to fear being cast aside."

"I fear losing you. I cannot share you with anyone."

"You frustrate me so! *She* will not be sharing me with *you*. You are not my wife!"

"I am!" She beat her fists petulantly against the floor and left him. Reclining again, he buried his face in the thick pelt, allowing his mind to darken. As his consciousness winked out, Gertera's sobs faded away and he heard the clacking of the loom as she gave up and worked resignedly at a new cloak. The old woman rustled her bedclothes as she tossed, seeking a position that would give her aching limbs relief. Rest, he thought, and this time, lulled by the rhythmic sounds of weaving, he fell into sleep.

He woke to the dull echoing of thunder and a flea biting his foot. As the fire had gone to embers the hut had lost some of its warmth. Now it was getting cold and damp. No light showed at the door. There was no patter of rain, just darkness and the rumbling in the clouds. The bed was an island of heat and comfort. Gertera moved against him, restless with the noise. He had not noticed when she slipped in beside him. The clothes she had shed lay on the floor in a heap. Silence was everywhere, and the world was a charred cinder.

Pulling himself slowly and purposefully out of bed, he stood up naked in the center of the hut. Chills ran up and down his skin as the cool air stirred him into wakefulness.

Aloneness. That was what gnawed at him whether he was away or home in his own village. The realization swept over him like a shiver. He was helpless and unclothed in a void inhabited only by the god of thunder and himself, and the gods were apart. None could help him, not the woman in his bed, not the chieftain, perhaps not even the gods, but he had the feeling that Kerkina could, or would make the effort. He knew that she would make the void he inhabited less lonely and fill the void within. He would always be alone until he possessed her. Pulling a wolfskin over his shoulders, he moved to the door.

"Dagentyr, where are you going?" Rising up beside the hearth, huddled in her blankets, the old woman pushed a veil of grey hair back out of sight and called to him. He went to her; the voice was weak yet it did not ask, it demanded. To see her easily, face to face, he knelt, and stirred the embers. A fresh wave of light and heat spilled out over them.

"I am going to see Irzag," he whispered.

"It is so late."

She is only a woman. I will go. "I cannot wait. The things I seek to know are pressing, important. They cannot wait, either. I need the priest's knowledge."

"Priest's knowledge." Her head bobbed up indignantly like a bird's. "Irzag knows mystical things. He knows magic. I know life. I can remember Irzag when he was still soiling himself, and when his mother whipped him when he was trouble, as I whipped you. Are these problems that simple wisdom will not solve? Tell me."

"They are men's problems."

The withered hand moved about, looking for the switch as in older days. "Men's problems!"

"Shh, quietly. Do not wake Gertera."

"Men's problems . . . indeed. There are no such things. There are only problems. You are a problem . . . for Gertera. You were sharp. You are a man . . . of course you are a man, haven't I watched you grow into one? But why must you treat her so badly? I should have asked this of you long ago. Your father would not be pleased."

"He would not be pleased to see her behave so openly and falsely. She doesn't think of him anymore. What is she that she can forget so easily? Here is something I will ask of you, old woman; why does she persist?"

"You ask me?" And behind the face she was saying, You should have asked me all along because I know you. I am part of you. I have lived, and I can see your life, can help you live. I am life, and death, and love, the hand that beat you and wiped your feverish forehead until you became a man. "I will tell you"—she held up a skeletal finger, but there was no menace in it—"if you will listen."

He took her hand carefully, wrapped it between both of his. It was so fragile, but its touch made him feel young and old at the same time. She had raised but one finger, and cast a spell out of childhood memory and the comforting orange firelight, out of knowing when he was troubled, out of magic. "I will."

"Gertera is a woman, a wife, but she has no warrior. Men cannot see what it is like to be without and alone. Let me stop you before you speak. You feel lonely, and that is a different thing. I have seen my parents and husband die. I have seen your mother die, and your father. That is alone. I understand Gertera."

"How can you understand, or even tolerate? She was the woman—"

"Of your father, yes. Even so, she was alone because she loved you and did not have you. When your father died, she did not have him, either. She had nothing."

"It is wrong of her."

"Does that make any difference? Think before you answer. Right or wrong will not make the feeling go away. Can you make the feeling for Kerkina go away?"

"No."

"So now you know, then, what it is like for her. And once you take Kerkina, Gertera will not even have the lie that you are hers. A woman with a pained heart can be an unpleasant and dangerous thing. If what you say about Vorgus is true, then you need no more trouble."

"Are you asking me to take Gertera and treat her as wife?"

She sank lower in the pile of fur and wool. "I ask nothing; it is not my place. You are a man with . . . a man's problems. I only tell you what you asked of me." He nodded. "But now that you understand a little, think before you bite."

"You have taken the switch to me again." He stirred the fire for her once more, kissed the wrinkled hand and tucked it back under the cover as she lay down.

"I hope it stings for a long time."

He sighed at the memories she had awakened, then slipped out of the hut.

There was no moon. No matter; he knew the paths well. Splashing through the puddles, he homed in on the shaman's hut like a moth. Pebbles and cold mud against the soles of his feet stimulated him. When he reached the hut, there was no one around. Firelight leaked through holes in the daubed walls and was reflected in the wet ground. Standing at the door of the hut, he called quietly.

"Irzag?" There was no answer. "Irzag. I beg to

speak with you. I know you are busy. Please. It is
Dagentyr." Hearing nothing, he pulled the flap
away and peeked inside. Irzag looked at him intently through the foul smoke of a smoldering fire
where he was burning herbs, feathers, and bones.
He regarded Dagentyr for a moment.

There was a long pause and a peal of thunder.
Dagentyr was about to ask pardon and withdraw,
but in a tone that sliced through the rumble, Irzag
addressed him.

"Enter, warrior. I am busy but there is time. Men
do not ordinarily wander about the night like
shades, seeking me out. You spark my curiosity.
Come in, come in. Old men like me do not sleep as
much as when we were young. There is much time
in the night for thought, especially now with the
sickness and the warlike tribes in the east, but
tonight we may as well fill the sleepless spaces with
talk." His breath blew out to Dagentyr, sending the
smoke swirling into fantastic designs. Dagentyr
swore for an instant that his eyes saw a wolf
devouring a deer in the flimsy vapor, suspended on
a draft of air. A wave of the priest's hand sent both
phantoms spiraling and eddying back into form-
lessness. The apprentice priests slumbered in the
bed, getting brief rest from the festival preparations.

"Say what has moved you here to me," said the
shaman. Dagentyr's lips had just parted when Irzag
cut him off. "Wait. I will tell you." He leaned his
body forward, immersing his head in the acrid
fumes. His long grey locks seemed to blend and
weave into the smoke. He stared at Dagentyr. The
smoke drew lines and shapes about his face, and yet
he did not blink. The whites of his eyes were
yellowish with age, like amber. His hooked nose
cleaved the rising steam, knifelike.

Dagentyr's uneasiness increased. All around
were charms and magic. Bizarre objects hung from

the walls and ceiling along with the familiar things of everyday life. There were skulls of birds and animals, wings of falcons, beads of silver and bone, antlers, boars' tusks. Two human heads, withered and darkened with age, bald scalps worn smooth with handling, lay on the floor flanking Irzag. One still retained its long, full moustache.

"You have come," Irzag said, "to ask for the life of your captive because you think the gods require that it be taken from him as sacrifice. You fear to lose the property you have newly won. Do not worry. The gods require more perfect sacrifices. We do not offer up the cursed or afflicted for fear of causing them anger. Besides, killing him would only release the demon in him to prey on others. Keep him if you like, barter him away. It makes no difference. The woman has been chosen. Clavosius has taken both the women and the horses as his own."

"That is not surprising. I should be grateful to the gods that I am left with anything at all." There was an angry quaver of neglect in his words.

"But you are not grateful to Clavosius?" Irzag squinted up his owl eyes.

"Are you trying to draw me out, old one, into speaking disloyally of the chieftain?" The priest laughed in his throat, but challenged Dagentyr with an absence of speech. "All right, priest, no, not to Clavosius. Those are words from my heart. I'm not afraid to say them. I consider myself lucky to have the captive."

"The ways of our fate are strange, aren't they? Your father was a favored man sitting close to the chieftain, but you in your turn are not, and your father's old rival sits in the big hut."

Dagentyr nodded and waved away the stench of the smoke with his hand. "It was not always that way. When Clavosius was sonless I was liked well enough."

"Were you liked, Dagentyr, or merely tolerated?"

"I do not know, but now Clavosius is between Vorgus's hands and those of the easterners, those who want our land. He sells us all away like animals because the easterners praise him and bring him gifts to hide their purpose." Dagentyr mumbled a curse. "I am not the only man who thinks of the easterners as enemies."

Looking at Dagentyr, Irzag could see the nervous turmoil in his eyes. "It is good to talk of things that bother you, but we were speaking of the captive man. That is why you came?"

"I have come because I am troubled. I have never asked to know my fate as some of the other warriors have. It will be, whether or not I know its nature, but there are bad things unfolding, and I wish to know it now. I want to know which course is the right one." His voice trailed off and he looked at the earthen floor. Irzag blinked.

"Is that what you seek, your fortune?"

"I beg it of you and the gods."

Irzag frowned inwardly, a man whose guess had gone astray of the mark. The thunder was near, rippling the air. "I see then that you are here about more important things than the fate of the spoils. I am glad, for to ask his future is a request worthy of a warrior. It shows his concern and his courage. The future is not always an easy thing to face. All men seek it sooner or later, but some wish to forget the knowledge once it is gained."

"I need to know. I will not back away from it."

"The knowledge cannot be taken away." Dagentyr grasped the wolfskin closer about his torso. "Very well, Dagentyr. The future is shadowy. It cannot be seen clearly, only glimpsed, brought back in bits and pieces, and interpreted. Pieces are all you get. They are all any man ever gets." Once more, Irzag reached for the bag of herbs. Green sprigs sizzled on the flames. "I feel things in the air tonight, Dagentyr. It may be that you have asked at an opportune moment." You *have* come opportunely, he thought, as if you knew of the future that I have seen for you.

From a separate pouch he pulled a small, gilded disc. It hung from a leather thong which he pulled over his head. When he leaned over, it dangled like a live thing bound. In Dagentyr's hand he placed an arrowhead of stone, ancient and waxy-looking. "This point is from long ago. From the time of the ancient stories when men did not know metal. It was dug up when the palisades of Fottengra were first built, and that too was very long ago. The shamans of Fottengra pass it down. It has been so for generations. It has magic."

The fumes made Dagentyr dizzy. Irzag poured water on the embers and mumbled gruffly. The rush of steam made it hard to see. Solemnly, the priest drew the cloak of his garment over his head. Placing one hand over his eyes and the other on the golden disc, he swayed precariously, then steadied upright. There was a crackling of thunder that Dagentyr thought would split the hut open, and when it was over, the brown skull with the moustache spoke.

"Dagentyr . . . warrior, son of Ashak, and Fregga, his wife. You wish to know your fate. Do you seek it?"

Dagentyr's mouth went dry as dust. He pulled back and put his hands to the floor to brace himself. The head spoke to him hollowly, the empty eyes not seeing or caring, the open mouth stiff. Twirling slowly, the disc sent glimmers of light speeding across the dry, leathery forehead.

"Yes, I seek it." Dagentyr's answer was a squeak.

The head continued indifferently.

"Warriors die in the quest for horses and slaves. Few count the winters of their old age. They make their lives good in their youth, so when they die, their ghosts will be satisfied. Do not die unfulfilled. Places of honor and glory are not won by allowing your foe to get the upper hand through carelessness." Dagentyr went red in the face. His folly with Vorgus had been heard of even in the world of the dead. "Listen," the skull rasped. "Men are not meant to die in bed . . . watchful, be watchful, and when your chances come, be bold, bold! Beware the horse, the golden horse! He sees through eyes of murderous hate and cunning. He is hard to overcome, for he knows much and works through deceit. Mere strength alone will not stop him from his work, but he must be stopped. Those who cross him and are not then wise, are soon dead.

"The gods have given some men the power to mold their own future. You are one of them, and behind you is the power of the old ways, the right ways. Ahead, there is only fog. There can be no telling of something that is not yet shaped. Nothing but fog—"

With a coarse laugh that might have betrayed the character of its previous owner, the head fell silent. The sudden quiet stunned Dagentyr. He stared at the head a long time, waiting for more . . . nothing. Again like any other trophy taken in battle, it leered ordinarily, mute, dumb. The shock left Dagentyr slowly. Irzag sat as before, watching him.

"Uncertainty is our lot, son of Ashak. Even to priests the future comes as a tiny flame in a giant wood. It is hidden and easily lost from view." He pushed back the cloak. "Take what you can from this. Ponder."

In the skull's rambling, Dagentyr had heard ominous omens. He realized he was not trained in the reading of signs, but it was clear enough. It was clear to him who must be stopped.

"You have helped me, Irzag. I see meaning in your words."

"The god's words."

"Yes, but what is the bold action?" He paused. A
flash of lightning illuminated the outline of the
door. "Does it involve death?" The thunder followed, and rolled off across the night.

Irzag lowered his head. "Yes. It involves death.
You are the arm of death."

The arrowhead felt cold suddenly, very sharp
and deadly. He put it down beside the fire.

"What is wrong, Dagentyr? Do you pretend that
it never occurred to you, even after this last encounter?"

"I had thought of it. This is what the words
mean? You are sure?"

"I have told you already; why do you ask me
again? Do not let doubt paralyze you. It will make
you a dead man. In your heart you have heard
nothing that you did not already know. What more
assurance can I give you?"

"I said I would not back away."

He started to leave. The old man raised a hand to
stop him. "Wait. You have heard what the gods
have said. Now, listen to me, Irzag, a man. You are
a leader. You have the spirit of a chieftain and the
desire to keep change from ruining us, the desire to
keep our place here and stay as we are. The gods
can do nothing but smile on such a man. To save us
all, you need only take advantage of your opportun-
ities.

"Go alone to the forest tomorrow. The first
blackbird you see, note its flight. An eastern course
is favorable. It will be the sign for action. East.
Make sure."

"I will." He pulled the flap back from the door
and stepped outside.

Now that he was out of the presence of Irzag and
the skull, he breathed more easily. So, the next
move was death. He had suspected it was what he
must do, kill Vorgus. Irzag had told him the right
course. He decided to pursue things and seek the

bird omen. The thunder made him shudder, even in his relief, and made him hurry along the path, home to safety and warmth, wishing despite his hate that he was not the arm of death, and that the right course had been something else entirely.

Inside the hut, Irzag cleared his throat. Leaning back against the wall, he rubbed his eyes with his knuckles, smiled, and reached for a long, quenching drink of mead. He hoped his meaning had been understood. The easterners were enemies. If they were not stopped, the land of Fottengra and the ways of the fathers would be changed.

He had seen the answer. It had been god-given in a dream. He had seen Vorgus, and then Dagentyr. There had been blood, swirls of blackness, then it had cleared and Vorgus was dead. His body, huge and hulking like that of a horse, had been picked up in the talons of a huge crow, and it flew east. He saw dirty gold locks disappearing over the hills, into the sky. Dagentyr must kill Vorgus. He was the hope of the village. By telling the warrior of the sign, he had done as the gods had wished him to. He put his trust in Dagentyr to do the same.

Chapter 5

Early, before Gertera and most of the other villagers had risen, he dressed, bound his legs against the briars of the forest, and took his bow and quiver from the wall. The old woman was awake and watched silently. Gertera roused at his stirring and inquired sleepily, "Where are you going?"

"I am going hunting," he told her as he fitted the string into the nocks. "The meat is low. We cannot take one of the herd, they are too few. Watch them today. Take the new slave with you. I want him to see the animals. Watch him and tell me how he is with them. If he asks to treat them and needs your help, do as he says." Ruki was still lying in his corner with his arms folded around himself.

Before Gertera had time to protest, Dagentyr slung the quiver over his back, picked up his pouch, filled it with food, and left on his way. Morning was tinged with the crispness of rain-washed air. After the skull's prophecies, he had not slept. Giving in to sleeplessness, he had planned to hunt, not caring if he killed any game, just wanting to be alone and seek the bird, find Kerkina, be with her if possible.

Two young boys wearing only capes greeted him on their way to the grazing fields. One or two herdsmen were there already. They looked sleepy leaning on their staffs, annoyed at troubling with animals they feared might soon be dead.

After entering the woods, Dagentyr sat on a rock and ate. Relaxation came more easily in the forest, away, though momentarily, from troubles. Gertera, the skull, Vorgus, the matronly captive, all seemed far away, in a dream possibly, following courses that didn't involve him. Food raised his spirits even more. He set out almost cheerfully for the deeper woods in hopes of finding a deer. On his way, he kept his eyes up, in the direction of the treetops.

All morning long he thought and watched. The beauty of the day had made the problems vanish, but now, angry at being put off, they drilled at him. His memories of Vorgus had blurred, merging over the years into one massive hate. He doubted he would recall any specific incidents that had sparked it, even if he wanted to. It wasn't necessary. Putting a reason to the hate would make no difference. It would remain.

Vorgus wanted the chiefdom. Dagentyr knew it. That in itself would be reason enough to hate him. Their mutual ambitions had set them up as enemies. It was disgusting to Dagentyr that a malicious oaf of a foreigner should take the responsibility of ruling the tribe; he did not belong. I belong, he mused, not that bearded woman. I, son of a great warrior and counselor to the chieftain, aristocrat, not a lout saved from slavery by some whim of the gods. Beware the horse, the golden horse. Shaking his head, trying to dislodge the unpleasant thoughts, he walked on.

The gods gave him a pheasant before noon. He shot it cleanly as it opened its wings to fly. As he moved to claim the bird and retrieve the arrow, he passed near the carcass of a young fawn killed by

some forest predator, half-eaten then left. The
scavengers had moved in. As he walked by, there
was a flurry of wings and a loud, croaking birdcall.
A lone crow, feasting on the remains and startled
by his approach, leapt up from the fawn and flew
straight up. Then with another annoyed cry, it
veered away to the west, following the river toward
the big water.

He watched it sail away over the leaves and felt
the beads of cold sweat begin to spot his forehead.
"West," he grumbled, and moved on hesitantly to
get his kill. What did west mean?

With the pheasant in his hand he felt more
confident. Good hunting was always a lucky omen.
Reassuring himself that the bird's flight would
prove a fortunate sign, he returned to the forest
outskirts near the village, whistling as he went.

Pausing at the same rock where he had eaten, he
looked expectantly over the valley. He could see the
river curving nearby and the women collecting
water in large jugs. His burden of troubles lightened
as he saw them. The nerves in his hands came alive
with a jolt like lightning. Some of the women had
shed their clothing and splashed playfully in mid-
stream. Among them was one who seemed more
watchful, alert, apart from the others. Bare from
the waist up, voluminous skirt bunched up in her
hands, she waded in to her knees. She was detached, participating in the festivity but not allowing herself to get fully lost in it, never losing her
perception of the scene around her.

Her hair sat pulled up and netted at the back of
her head. It was russet, and when the sun caught it,
it was very red. The water made her slender body
shine, as with oil. Drops, gleaming like electrum,
beaded her breasts and shoulders. From the sound
of her laughter, faint, but magnified by Dagentyr's
imagination, he could envision her smile, see the
way the long, straight nose dipped at the end when

she spoke, feel the way the innocent eyes, green like his, probed him, searched him out even in his sleep.

Hesitating as she filled the water jars, the girl looked up at the village, then at the forest. Feeling his heart surge, he stepped unobtrusively from the cover of trees, and she saw him.

She stood still for a moment, went to the bank, donned her short jacket, picked up her jars, and said her good-byes cheerfully, inconspicuously, looking over her shoulder and waving. Her walk was light and happy. None of the other girls had seen him and they were so engrossed in frivolity that they didn't see her now as she ignored the path home and made her way into the woods.

It was like a mask had been removed. The water jars nearly tipped over, so carelessly and quickly had she set them down. The casual air fell away. She tripped running to him.

"Dagentyr!"

He put his finger to his lips for quiet, dropped the pheasant and the bow, and embraced her.

He whispered excitedly, "This is why I went out today." He drew her still closer and they kissed.

"I wanted to meet you as you returned," she moaned disappointedly. "We heard the trumpets, but I had to stay away. I watched from a distance. It would have been difficult"—she smiled and pulled herself closer to him—"to keep what I feel from showing through, and with Gertera there . . . I don't want to confront her, and I would never shame you." She spoke in a rush of excitement, not stopping to breathe.

"My shame lives with me."

Her head dropped to his shoulder.

"You must not talk of her that way. It makes me feel guilty. I know how much she hates me."

"Kerkina, let's not talk of her at all. You are what I care about. My despair of her lifts only when I see you. I know that my future includes you. It should not include Gertera, but Irzag said nothing of it. I wish now we had spoken less of horses and more of what future there is for you and me."

"What does Irzag say? When did you talk to him?"

"It isn't important; the time I spend with you is. A warrior's problems do not concern women."

"They do if he is her warrior." Her hands were cool, still moist with river water. There were tiny drops on her forehead. Where her body was wet, the jacket clung. "I prayed for your safe return. I do not know whether my prayers or hers brought you back, and I don't care."

He placed his hand over her mouth. "Please, please."

She nodded assent. "Did the raid fare well?"

"No." He snickered sadly and shrugged, leaving out any inkling of what he knew she must be aware of.

"Even in the short time that you have been home there has been talk, talk of you and Vorgus." Her eyes took on a frightened look. "I love you, but I wish you were a more careful man. Much worry will come of this. I do not know why you do these things. My father says you are in danger. Why do you behave so recklessly?"

"It is an affair you do not understand. You worry too much. None of that concerns us now. When I am with you, all the problems are brushed off as easily as dust off a cloak. At least wait until you are my wife to be so fearful."

"But what if he tries to kill you?"

"Then he will die!" he said angrily. The vision of the bird flying west struck cold, irritating doubt into his brain. "You are not to think of it. Laugh, laugh when I am around you and look at me with a smile on your lips. I like you calm and peaceful. A mighty warrior's woman is proud and dignified. What pleasant face will I ever see if not yours?"

Lovingly, she caressed his neck, stroking his faded stain wistfully. The torrent of russet hair fell past her shoulders as he undid her corded hair net. The forest floor was damp and cushioned, sinking beneath them as they lay back. It smelled ancient and deep, old as the world itself. Whatever problems I have will wait, Dagentyr thought. The blackbird's flight became meaningless. He was aware of nothing but her. He lost himself in the feel of her skin, in her eager, encircling arms.

"Go away, you silly, ugly old cow. Go, and leave me alone." Ruki said it low in his garbled, drawnout manner. With indifference, the cow walked past him, intent on a thick clump of grass not more than a man's height from where he sat. Suddenly aware that the other animals, like this one, might be wandering, he stood and made a quick check of the general area. The beasts in his charge grazed together in a bunch in front of him. A speedy count gave him reassurance.

Why should I worry, he chided himself. There are other slaves to do the watching besides me. Nevertheless, feeling foolish, he counted again. They were all there. Only the one stubborn creature defied him and chewed rudely in his ear. If the situation were not so new and full of despair, he would have laughed, but although a long night's rest had allowed him to look on his condition with more detachment, it was still nothing to be laughed at; ripped from his home, watching another man's cattle, still in danger of losing his life. Soon, too soon, they would find out that he had lied. He knew nothing of preventing the animal sickness. The lie had come to his mind quickly, easily. His physical weakness had shown him the necessity of quick thought. His end had been postponed. Now he would have to work harder at whatever else he was put to, to show that he was useful, to soothe the angry outburst that would come when the next cow died. He had examined the animals. All were beginning to show signs of the illness. He could recognize it at least, but did not know why his village had been spared. Which cow will be the next to fall and cause my death, he wondered idly.

He was aware that his epithet to the cow might just as appropriately have been lavished on the woman who now owned him. The small bud of what was left of his sense of humor blossomed briefly. Distorted chuckles rose in his throat. It was difficult to conceive of her as his owner, difficult to conceive of her as anything but a two-footed cousin to the creatures he watched. He thought back bitterly to how a nudge of her foot had roused him from sleep. She had said nothing to him and was wary. He had eaten with the other slaves, then she had taken him aside.

"You will help watch the cattle," she had said. "You have tended beasts before, I hear."

He had given her a verbal answer that had made her flinch and call on the gods. Thereafter, he had made do with exaggerated nods and shakes of the head in response to her questions. It would be better not to upset her. He had surmised that she was temper-prone. He did not wish to be beaten or punished for her own frustrations.

She had helped take the beasts out to pasture, prodding them with a long staff. Keep your eyes on the stick, he told himself, and he made sure he was well out of reach at all times.

Before long, she had become bothered by his presence and went to the river to fill the water pots and seek gossip. He had told her also that he needed certain herbs to help the sick animals and described a blatantly imaginary concoction. As she left she threw him a glance that betrayed her fear that if left alone, he would run. Putting her worry underfoot, she tramped away, refusing to look back.

He knew a better chance for escape might never come and that a decision to stay might doom him, but quick action was not his strong point, couldn't be. Dejectedly, he bent his scrawny legs and plopped down. The damp grass smelled strong and steamy in the heat, a brief reprieve from the stink of the dead animals. It was hopeless to run. A cripple would not make it far in the forest, and when nightfall came? The wolves would eat him. Even if he survived, what a simple thing it would be to take half a day and track him down. They would kill him when they found him. He would rot away into nothing on the black earth, like the dead child.

Slavery was not new to him. Servitude to his curse had given him a taste of what it was like. A thing to be laughed at, that's what I am, he thought. Even the other slaves will have nothing to do with me. There is no one like me here, or across that hill, or in the next valley, or the next, or between this place and the big water. There was very little to do about the situation and far less to hope for. Where were all the gods? Surely the deities of his tribe had perished in the raid with everyone else. He contorted his face into a hideous grimace and sobbed until he could taste his tears.

While he sat crying, the cackling of the women at the river took on a different quality. Mournfully out of place in the brightness of the day, the sentinel trumpets vomited a flat note into the valley. There was a commotion down by the water. He stood and made another tally of the cattle, judging whether or not he had a chance of driving them to safety if this was a raid. Women on the bank were pointing and waving; then he saw that there were rafts on the river. They were large for river craft and there were many. Men were poling them upstream. Plumes waved at the tops of their helmets. A few men carried spears and large, oddly shaped shields like two circles placed one on top of the other.

His heart jumped. Was it a raid? The gods had given him enough misfortune without placing him in slavery twice in almost as many days. No, that couldn't be it. No one was hurrying to the fortress. The gates stood open. There was a sense of excitement more than alarm. The rafts turned to the shore, moving deliberately but not with the frantic speed of a raiding group. The armed men in the party removed their helmets and held their weapons over their heads in friendship.

Ruki relaxed and noticed that there were unarmed men in the party as well, and men too old to be warriors. He was confused. Who were they? Then it came to him, traders most probably. He had never seen foreign traders before. His village sat to the side of the main river routes.

They were close enough now for Ruki to see the smiles on the men's lips as the women greeted them, giving them hurriedly picked bunches of buttercups and wild pansies. There were twenty or so men in all, he noted. Their tunics were of a brighter nature than he had ever seen before—white, blue, deep scarlet. These brilliantly clad men carried themselves impressively, but seemed short. Almost haughtily, they looked around, chatting and laughing as they jumped into the shallow water to pull their craft to the bank. "I wonder what kind of place it is they come from that they walk so proudly in a strange land," Ruki said, half aloud. And then the men noticed dead cattle by the bank, and backed away, shaking their heads and sniffing the air nervously.

Another blast of the horns pulled Ruki's attention away to the fortress. Coming through the gate was the chief and a hastily assembled band of retainers and warriors. He noticed a pomposity in the chief as he rode his war cart down the slanting path to the meadow, pulled by the two captured horses. The chief priest, very old, walked beside the cart, keeping pace easily. The village party's bearing was friendly, but arrogant as well, as if to remind the strangers that they were not parading in their own land, strutting for wives and lovers.

The two groups met at the riverside. Clavosius and a man in a white tunic clasped arms in greeting. After much gesturing and conversation, the foreigners began to set up camp on the bank, but farther upstream, away from the carcasses. The chief and his retinue climbed the road home.

Ruki sat watching them unload the rafts. Most of the village women had gone back to their chores except for the flirtatious ones, who lingered, standing in twos and threes, pointing to their favorites.

During the span of the afternoon, awnings were set up on poles and tents were raised. Campfires were built. It was an enthralling thing to watch. Ruki saw a couple of the guards flexing an arm or grinning in answer to the girls' coy behavior. Sitting on a large bundle, a grey-haired trader plucked a lyre and displayed a box of trinkets to a spellbound ring of children. A young village boy with a wooden sword sparred with one of the warriors, who growled and made fierce mock attacks. Gleefully, in the end, the boy felled the man, who played dead so convincingly that the lad became frightened and slunk away. Ruki watched delightedly, stopping only to eat when a slave woman brought food. Later, Gertera ran up the hill to them and shouted what news she had heard.

"They are traders from the big water, and they are so strange!" Gertera told Ruki excitedly, letting her fear of him disappear briefly. "They have come a long, long way. What things they must have with them! I wish Dagentyr were here to see. There are always beautiful things to see and bargain for when trading men come from anywhere. Can't you see how cheerful it makes everyone?" She asked Ruki directly, "Isn't it wonderful?" He bobbed his head up and down like a drowning man. "It is the first time anyone has seen men from the big water. Clavosius has told them to stay and be his guests for the day of feasting. Afterward, they will show their wares. We are lucky to have them stay at all. They fear the sickness. They say they have seen it for the past two days along the river. They want to be clear of it.

"Raiding has been bad. Dagentyr does not have many furs. What will we trade with?" He noticed a gleam in her dark eyes that he knew meant she was considering what his trade worth would be. "Oh, why worry? It will be a happy time anyway, in spite of the bad things. Things will be happy now that the watermen have come."

As quickly as the drape had fallen, it tacked itself up again. She looked at him, half shocked that she had spoken to him so much, dropped the herbs he had requested at his feet, and went off to tell the other slaves.

Men from the big water, here. I suppose it is festive at that, he thought. At least my first day as a field slave has not been boring. He contemplated the small bundle of plants for a moment, then, resolving not to make this his last day as a field slave, tucked them into his belt and set off to do his imaginary healing.

Chapter 6

People were stirring. From all the huts came sounds that meant their inhabitants were up and moving. The chanting of the priests had roused them. The voices had begun as a murmur that floated through the narrow streets of the village as the priests sang the call to the ceremony. They glided past the doorways like specters.

Dawn was not far away. It was still black, but the priests carried torches and the townsfolk who fell in behind them also brought torches till the coming of the sun. As more and more joined the train, it brightened. Like a beaded necklace of flame, the line wound its way toward the gate.

The singing grew louder, swelling with each step. Irzag led, trailed by the other priests. His voice dominated the rest, harsh and commanding. The other voices blurred to form his accompaniment, like a rumbling deep in the earth. He moved with arms stretched upward, face lifted. It was the day of the gods, the day of renewal.

The priests walking behind Irzag carried offerings; pots of jewelry and beads, birds and small animals like fox and squirrel, branches heavy and sagging with new buds, cut flowers of the field in silver cauldrons, bowls of mead and beer. They also

brought a bull bedecked with golden trinkets and a
fine blanket of woven cloth. With the sickness
ravaging the herds, the bull would be a great loss,
but the need was great, and the sacrifice had to
match the need.

The matronly captive walked after the bull, hag-
gard and at bay, guarded by two warriors with
spears. Her hair was entwined with strands of
blossoming vine. Symbols of sun and earth were
inscribed on her face. She wore a gold collar,
hammered thin and molded; nothing else.

As they moved on, priests rubbed pigment onto
her limbs. With berry juice and the crushed buds of
brilliant flowers, they accentuated the curve of her
breasts and outlined the genitals with a broad,
bright streak. Routinely, she was given thinly di-
luted mead which she drank in deep gulps. It was
obvious that she had already consumed much
during the night. Her step was wobbly and unsure.
Each sip tarnished but could not extinguish the
gleam of fear that brightened her eyes.

Dagentyr slept peacefully until the priests blew
on their copper-rimmed bull horns, sending a
sharp, distressing note resounding through the air.
His time with Kerkina had been medicine. He felt
cleansed. When he had returned home, Gertera
had been easier to tolerate. Sensing no anger or
impatience, she had been curious, but too pleased
that they had not argued, to question the source of
his good humor.

He and Gertera dressed quickly. The old woman
was up and alert, peevish that her frailty would not
let her take part in the rite.

"You watch it all and tell me of it when you come
back," she said.

Dagentyr lit a torch from the embers of the
hearth fire and woke Ruki by throwing a cup of
water in his face. "Come with us, Ruki. It is a
special day." Ruki was confused and sleepy, but he
obeyed and followed them out into the street.

Greetings were nodded. An intense undercurrent of excitement ran among the people. From man to man it leapt, catching hold of each as he joined the procession. It was communicable, stimulating; they were intoxicated with it. Drowsiness vanished in its wake, and it quickened their hearts. To Dagentyr, the feeling was akin to that infinitely long instant before he locked with a foe in combat, where the enemy moved at him slowly, every thought spread on his face.

Out they went through the palisade and into the forest, following the trail that would take them to the top of the hill where the gods' grove stood. The camp of the watermen was dark but for one fire where a lonely sentry watched them go in silhouette, grasping his spear harder for comfort at the sight of so many men and the wail of the songs. Sunrise was still only an idea in the people's minds, but the thought sustained them in the forest, and the priests blew the horns all the way to chase away the evil and guide the daylight to where they waited.

Kerkina followed her father and mother in the line. She kept her eyes down, not wanting to see Dagentyr. A simple, unwary exchange of glances might provoke Gertera. In spite of her attempts to think kindly of the woman, she did not like to be near her. It made her uncomfortable, especially when Gertera and Dagentyr were together. Gertera was the thing between them. She was the distance that needed to be overcome. It was Kerkina's worst fear that it would always be so.

The upgrade of the path became steeper and the woods thickened. Feet crunched through the moist forest debris. Sprigs of dried pine needles stuck to clothing, dangling like pendants from the hems of the women's skirts.

Dagentyr watched the matronly captive walk passively at her place in the line. Her head rocked with an almost rhythmic sway. The leaves in her hair trembled, and their waxen gloss was nearly as bright as the burnish on the golden collar. Priests had to support her by the arms. Tired and groggy, near sated with mead, her legs had begun to weaken. The muscles of her body were going flaccid with exhaustion.

To Dagentyr, her warm flesh appeared already dead in the torchlight. She was a painted and baubled corpse, late in dying. It was hard to look at her now without imagining the child in her arms, relaxed with alcohol, decorated, also dead. The gods are pleased by strange things, he reflected.

Ruki's mind was clearing. He jolted awake as he heard the words of the chants, praise to the sun. It was the time of festival, and they were going to the place of worship. Nervous sweat dampened his tunic. Was he to be given? There had been no preparation or warning. He wanted to stop and turn back, but the press of people pushed him on unrelentingly. He lost his balance and grabbed Dagentyr's shoulder to steady himself.

Turning, Dagentyr saw the fear on his face. By the elbow, he dragged Ruki up beside him and bent to his ear. "This is not for you, but for the woman. You are safe," he said. "I bring you because she is of your village. It is right that you be here. Perhaps she will feel better knowing that someone familiar is near." Then he released him and walked on.

Ruki believed, and felt better. Somewhere up ahead, he knew the woman of his tribe marched to the gods. He was ashamed at the relief he felt and thought he would be sick to his stomach.

Dagentyr felt the press of bodies all around him. Heat from torches and men flushed his cheeks. Gertera grabbed his hand in excitement. Around the edge of the grove, the mass of people was formed into a ring. The grove was ablaze with torchlight. In the center stood the god-pillar, weathered and coarse. It had been a log once, like any other log used in the building of Fottengra until it had been chosen, set apart, purified, shaped. The top had been carved long, long ago into the face of a god, a stern god with hooked nose and vague, shadowy features. His head was crowned with a carved cone of flame. It was a face to raise unsure feelings of loathing in each person, a visage that demanded reverence. Incised into the wood beneath the face was the wedding of earth and sun, the consummation of spring. Heaped near the pillar was a pile of wood, layer after layer crosshatched on each other, and a plain, earthen jar.

Irzag grabbed the woman by the wrist, and looking directly into her eyes, led her to the pillar, coaxing her firmly when she wavered. He seemed almost gentle, but Dagentyr saw his fingertips digging into her forearm and knew the grip was like the jaws of a bear, unrelenting and savage.

She looked around the grove, turning this way and that, searching the faces. Dagentyr pushed Ruki forward so she could see him. Her eyes lingered for a moment. A sob tore loose from inside her, and then her gaze moved on. No amount of mead could vanquish her fear now, and with the sun so near, it was revitalized. When she whimpered, Irzag gave a fierce jerk of her arm and pulled her to him. With one hand still clutching her wrist, he moved her closer to the pillar.

Dagentyr scrutinized her. Under the taint of smeared pigment, he could just distinguish the bluish marks that were not the essence of any berry or flower. Irzag had been rough when he had taken her. Irzag was the link with the gods. When she had been bathed and purified, they had entered her forcefully, as Irzag had, having his way while the priests sang and beat drums to veil her screaming. Dagentyr felt pity for her; but fate was unavoidable. She was chosen and honored, fire and fertility incarnate, bride of the sun.

She sweated profusely. Her hair and the vines were limp with it. It dripped between her breasts

and from under her arms. In the coolness of an
approaching sunrise, she was drenched. The corners of her mouth and her chin were coated and
sticky with spilled mead. Her throat rose and fell as
she swallowed dryly. To see her eyes was terrible;
dumb beasts possessed more reason in their gaze
than she did. When Irzag did not compel her to
look at him, her eyes darted from man to man,
helplessly, pathetically. Intoxication blurred her
vision and made her nose run. Cold bark against
her skin caused a gasp as Irzag pressed her back to
the pillar. He outstretched her arms, and two other
priests held her there as the carvings chafed her
raw.

The horns began their music, loud and terrible.
Through the glare of the torches it was nearly
imperceptible, but gradually they all saw it, a lifting
of the darkness in the east. The horns blared
louder. Two priests stripped nude and donned the
horns of bulls. Singing and smearing themselves
with ash, they danced, pounding the earth with
their feet, faster and faster, frenzied.

Trees on the eastern ridge were coming into
focus. The sky was pallid, taking on the bland look
just before dawn where it possesses no color at all.
The woman saw it too, or rather sensed it, for her
back was toward it. She saw all eyes attentive in
that direction and noticed from under her swollen
lids that she could see the faces better, see the
second row of people standing behind the first, and
just barely, the third behind that, and the spots of
light that meant others stood back in the woods,
watching her through the branches. The ache in her
shoulders grew as the priests pulled at her arms,
straining the bones in their sockets. Irzag chanted
monotonously, stopping only to paint a fresh mark
on her or make magic passes over the brazier that
burned at his side.

Dagentyr thought he could smell her through the
closeness of men and the forest scents, could smell

her wet hair and the perspiration-soaked blossoms, and Irzag's hot breath. The pillar looked down on her without pity.

In the face of her fear, the people grew expectant. As she squirmed against the pillar and cried out at Irzag's touch, they tensed, and murmured low to themselves. The torches sputtered in a dialogue of their own.

The horned priests neared collapse, spinning wildly with hoarse outcries, limbs taut, demons in the intangible blue light. The bull grunted nervously.

From a pouch of skin, Irzag took a cymbal of bronze. Green and old, it hung from a chain. With a mallet, he struck it over and over. It rang like the crash of a hundred swords in war. Other priests took rattles of gourd or copper, and raised the din to a deafening pitch that the sun himself must have heard. Everyone's breath came fast, geared to the mad banging and clamor.

The singing was a throaty roar. The multitude looked at each other with fear. Dagentyr checked the trees to see if all the spirits of the wood were dangling there, screaming with cold, stinking mouths. Gertera clutched at his wrist. Children and young girls covered their ears. The priests were hard-pressed to keep the bull under control.

The sky turned pale yellow, then blue. Irzag turned quickly from the woman, gave the cymbal to a helper, and from under his cloak, drew the long dagger. Its handle was worked in gold and silver. At the woman's arms, the two men got a better grip and braced themselves.

Dagentyr's head felt like it would burst. The throbbing noise of the instruments kicked his insides. He felt molded to the others around him.

Irzag removed the collar from the woman's neck and handed it away. As it was taken, she shivered, and moaned long until she ran out of breath. Half the sky was light.

"The sun!" A woman in the crowd yelled it. "The sun, look!" Irzag tensed. The crowd picked up the woman's call. "The sun comes!" Dagentyr shouted it. "The sun!" His head felt light.

It was only a gleam as the edge of the orb rose over the eastern hills, and its rays spread out starlike. Every horn and gong sounded in a great climax of noise.

Irzag raised his arms high and screamed, "The sun! Take what we offer!" Like a beast, he leapt at her and wrenched her head back by the hair. The dagger moved like lightning across her throat. In one move he cut her deeply from ear to ear and planted himself with his arms overhead, gripping the dagger like life itself as she spurted blood in his face.

Her eyes showed only momentary surprise, then her tongue protruded and she gurgled a brief cry. Gritting their teeth, the priests held her. The dirt and leaves at her feet shot into the air as she kicked frantically. The wound gaped and closed. The symbols in yellow and blue and green dissolved in a wave of crimson that ran down the front of her body. The crowd cried out in cackling unison to give her death sound that she could not. Ruki turned away, put his palms against his ears and started to gag.

Cheers greeted the sun. Mothers held their children close and angled their heads away. Bad fortune could make any one of them a spouse of the sun at some later time.

Loss of blood from her head was rapid, and her lids drooped. Her violent fighting became only an impotent and slow writhing. Putting a bowl at her throat, Irzag collected the red flow. The dirt and grass at his feet were stained and slick. Horns, bells, and song had all stopped. Attention was on the woman, her life draining slowly into an earthenware dish.

As the light became greater, her eyes rolled up

unseeing, showing the whites, and the two priests lowered her to the ground, still and quiet.

With blood, Irzag colored the wood. He ran his dipped finger along the carved grooves until the stick figures of the spring wedding were clothed in red, vibrant life. The horns began again as he worked, and bells too, tinkling flatly. The two dancing priests stood still and panted. Irzag moved away from the great pillar, anointed his assistants, then the bull. Turning again to the woman, he pointed a red finger and they lifted her high in the air and carried her to the pyre, stretching her out upon it. Irzag closed the cloudy eyes with his fingertips. Cut branches were laid over her like a blanket. Under a cover of leaves she vanished bit by bit. Nature hid her lovingly on the logs, and claimed her.

The brilliant circle of the sun was up past the horizon. Irzag took a torch from Clavosius and threw it on the bed of branches. This was the time, and Irzag beckoned to them. From the edge of the clearing, those with torches walked forward intermittently and threw them on the pyre or stoked them underneath. Dagentyr released Gertera's hand and went to the pyre. He set his torch at her feet, saw the flame eat the feathery cushion of leaves, and went back to his place.

When all the torches were thrown on the fire bed, Irzag lifted his face to the rising flames. "Fire of earth and fire of sky! Merge and become one for us, your children. Set the mantle of richness upon the world. Protect the beasts, for they are our life. Drive away the pestilence that threatens them. Quicken the fruit upon the trees, the child within the womb. Let all be fertile, whether woman or forest creature. Give us abundance, and smile fondly on this patch of forest."

At the end of the prayer, the bull was driven through the smoke of the cleansing fire, and led away to be slaughtered and prepared for the evening feast. The people began to drift away in the same way they had gathered, going back to the village, the women to make small sacrifices for fertility, the children to play, the men to ready their goods for trade.

The warmth in their cheeks cooled as they went away from the bright flames that climbed higher than the trees. Only Irzag stayed, watching the fire destroy the pyre and the woman. Other priests ministered to the pots of offerings to be buried with her. She would be placed in the woods in a secret spot, safe in her urn, surrounded by beads, berry wine, and gold. As if ashamed to be rivaled by such a puny blaze, the sun climbed higher. Irzag was pleased, and stared at it briefly, then lowering his head he stayed motionless as the people walked away.

Left with Gertera and Ruki, Dagentyr lingered for a moment, then started off with them at his side, ambling in silence. They could still feel the presence of the gods in the oily black smoke and the smell that hung on their clothes, in the warmth of the sun, in the awakening of the forest, and in their own wordlessness. No one looked back to the crackling flames.

Ahead, on the trail home, Arvis waved to them. He stood to the side of the path with his young wife, Milandi. They acknowledged each other and proceeded in quiet until they had left the grove far behind.

"Greetings, Dagentyr," said Arvis, "and Gertera."

"Greetings, cousin of my husband," she replied, relishing the chance to publicly use the word "husband."

Milandi regarded Gertera coolly, sarcastic mirth dancing in her eyes.

Dagentyr greeted them both. "Happy feast day, cousins, prosperity and fertility." He emphasized the last word and smiled at Milandi. She blushed. Gertera's face went hard.

Milandi answered, "And to your wife also." Her smile to Gertera was overexaggerated, sharp. There was an embarrassing silence. Arvis broke it diplomatically.

"Milandi, go and get ready for the trading. Paint yourself and make your face beautiful. You and Gertera can gossip to your heart's content on the way back." His attempt at joviality failed. "Go. I wish to talk to Dagentyr. We'll meet you at the gate later and go to the watermen's camp." Milandi nodded.

Dagentyr spoke to Gertera. "Go along. Have the slaves ready my trade goods. Tell the old woman about the ceremony. Ruki, go also and inspect the animals. They'll stay penned today; we'll not drive them to pasture. Give them food and water. Milk the ones that need it. Do it quickly, then help Gertera carry my goods."

Ruki was roused from his stupor and he nodded, knowing it was the last day there would be any animals left to worry about.

Before Gertera could make a spectacle of their parting, Dagentyr left, going with Arvis into the forest to take the long way back.

"Come on, Gertera. We'd better hurry. They'll want food when they get back." Milandi got no answer, so she shrugged, and trotted on down the path alone. Stamping her foot and giving Ruki a threatening glance, Gertera followed.

Arvis broke an elder twig between his hands. "The household guards of Clavosius told me he is angry. Vorgus will try to make the most of it. Clavosius may even confront you with your actions, tonight at the feast. Whether you started it or not will make no difference. What will you do?"

"If he confronts me with the incident, I will tell Clavosius of the plot."

"You yourself said he will not believe you."

"I know that, but soon we'll not have to worry about Vorgus. Irzag told out my fortune. It is intended that I destroy him. The words were veiled, but I know what is meant by them. The bird omen was wrong, but I don't think that I, or any of us, can afford to wait. In the end, it is the only thing I can do."

"Then you will kill him? What will Clavosius do?"

"He will do nothing, because he is nothing without Vorgus. Few are happy with the chieftain, but he has power because people fear Vorgus and the easterners." Dagentyr pulled his beard thoughtfully. "There are enough malcontents to sweep him away if he tried revenge."

"You hope that there are." Arvis snickered and threw the two halves of the stick away.

They walked down the side of the hill. Through the trees, they caught glimpses of Fottengra. The sun-bleached thatch of the houses reflected the light warmly, and the river sparkled. There was movement in the camp of the watermen.

"Irzag says it is my fate," said Dagentyr. "I must take advantage of my chances. I am reluctant to do this but what else can I do? The gods have said it should be. Will you be with me? If we wait too long, Clavosius may do away with us. Vorgus would be happy to do it. This last confrontation may be the thing that tips the chieftain's decision against us. The eastern men are close, hungry for our land. If Vorgus becomes chieftain, they will know that they have a friend and will come in hordes."

Arvis sighed. "Yes, I am with you whatever happens, but I am not as certain as you are about Clavosius. He is a pompous old dolt, but he is the chieftain. Are you sure he will let death go unpunished? If you are wrong, our lives will be worth nothing."

"It will be all right. Without Vorgus he will be lost."

Arvis looked around cautiously and sat on a fallen log. Fottengra was spread out beneath them, full of life and motion. "All of this worries me, Dagentyr. What a risk you are taking. I think you underestimate Clavosius's love for Vorgus. We may suffer; those we love may suffer."

Dagentyr began carving little marks into a tree with his dagger. He could read the disquiet beneath the surface. He sensed that Arvis indeed feared. "It is Vorgus who is our real enemy. It is he who rules the chieftain's ear. If he is gone, there is no danger. Trust in what Irzag has said."

Arvis shrugged. "I have not had the benefit of hearing it from Irzag himself. Not that I disbelieve you, but you may have interpreted the words the way you wanted to."

"No, there is no mistake."

"I worry not so much for myself as for Milandi, and it has put me on edge. I worry about her without me."

Dagentyr scratched his neck. "The gods smile on brave warriors and glory and spoils taken in their name, cousin. They do not smile on worriers."

Arvis laughed uncertainly. "You are right. We need to do something to soothe their long and dour faces, and be men again. A destiny without glory and spoils isn't worth having."

Dagentyr sheathed the dagger after wiping the blade on the skirt of his tunic. He loved Arvis even more for his brave words, spoken in spite of his fear. "That's the cousin I know. Enough of this. We'll talk again tonight. I'm hungry for food and for haggling with the watermen. I hear their camp is a strange and wonderful place, and they will not be here long."

Arvis nodded and they both laughed and continued their climb down the hill to the village.

Chapter 7

All over the village there was a bustle of activity. The women had primped themselves after the rite, as painstakingly as time permitted, donning their best jewelry, and shading their eyes with color. They painted their lips with berry juice. Men combed their beards and strapped on swords. Laden with bundles or leading slaves, they spilled out the gate, across the field to the brightly colored canopies of the watermen. A light morning breeze stirred the fringed tassels on the awnings. The eligible girls scurried like chickens, pushing stray wisps of hair under their nets and practicing winsome looks.

Dagentyr wolfed down some cheese Gertera had ready for him, and they met Arvis and Milandi at the gate. Ruki was nearly buckled under the weight of a bundle of furs. He leaned painfully against the gatepost in a desperate attempt to ease the load. Dagentyr was so amused that he shook with mirth at the sight of the skinny little man whose head peeked out from the bushy heap of pelts. They all laughed, and slapped their thighs.

"Give them to me." Dagentyr took the furs from him with tears of laughter in his eyes. "If we wait

for you to right yourself again, we'll waste the
whole day." Ruki didn't join in the jollity but was
relieved to be free of the bundle. Together, they all
walked to the strangers' camp.

There was something special about the day. The
scent of new spices brought by the watermen was
tantalizing and exotic. They themselves were colorful and strange. They stood behind their
wares, walked among the people to encourage them.
Their tunics were fine, the fabric smooth. Unusual designs bordered their bottom hems and
the short, open sleeves. A few of them wore
beards. The guards carried their huge bullhide
shields with swagger and were bare-chested for
what might prove to be a warm day. Short kilts covered their loins, and their bodies had been rubbed
with oil. At the tops of their metal helmets, horsehair plumes waved, dyed different hues. Men
and women alike stopped to appraise the strange
warriors.

"What about it? Do you think you could beat one
of them, single combat, armed evenly?" Arvis
pointed to a thick-bodied man with arms like tree
trunks, who guarded a table covered with rich
lengths of fabric.

Dagentyr shook his head. "I don't know. He's
big, but probably slow, just like that hulking horse,
Vorgus. On the other hand, if his fight is as good as
his appearance . . ." He shrugged.

Arvis smiled and went to the shade of an awning
to unroll his bundle. Dagentyr lingered a little
longer, looking at the brawny guard, who noticed,
and returned a stern expression. The man frightened Gertera, and she pulled at Dagentyr's arm. He
hefted his bundle back on his shoulders and went to
a canopy where a lean, grey-haired trader hawked
arms. Gertera wandered away, disinterested.

The weapons drew the men like flies. Spread on
the ground was a white cloth, and on it lay daggers,

swords, axes, scabbards. On the best ones, scenes of
hunting, strange animals, and warriors fighting
were inlaid in gold and silver. The metal-covered
scabbards were stamped with spiraling designs,
birds, beasts. Men passed the swords from hand to
hand, testing the blades. No one had seen anything
so fine before. Peering over each other's shoulders
they exclaimed loudly, clicked their tongues, and
anxiously asked the trade price. Sitting on a stool,
the trader pulled long faces and shrugged. He spoke
the language brokenly and held up fingers occasionally as he rubbed the furs or held bits of northern
amber up to the light with cold scrutiny.

Dagentyr knelt and picked up one of the swords
in its scabbard. He drew it out, savoring the sound
it made. It was polished smooth and oiled. From
hilt to point it tapered evenly. The grip was of wood
riveted on with flat-headed silver nails. It had a
pommel of worked bronze and felt good in his
hand, even through the bandage. He liked it. When
he swung it through the air quickly, it made a
swishing sound that excited him. Sharp and keen,
the wicked edge took the hair from his arm when he
drew it up gently.

"You like it?" a voice asked him.

Dagentyr turned around. The skinny trader was
bickering with another man. Behind him was a
short, slimly built man in mid-years, with curled
brown hair and beard. His upper lip was shaven,
and his eyes were pale and piercing. Dagentyr
thought of the neutral sky just before the sacrifice.
The man's tunic was white, belted with a bright
scarlet sash from which hung a dagger whose
pommel was of gold.

"It is a very fine blade, worthy of a prince, I
would say," the man continued. "You do like it,
don't you? I am Astekar, leader of this expedition.
Perhaps we can talk about the weapon. You have
something to give me for it?"

"Yes, I do like it, but it does not look good for cutting." Dagentyr was surprised that the man spoke the language so well. It sounded different, though, like sparkling water. The accent was rippling, and passed lightly over the harsher, guttural sounds.

"It is meant for thrusting more than cutting, but it does that also. It will hack muscle from bone or limb from body, and what more does one ask of a sword?"

The words of praise for the sword pleased Dagentyr. What an honor it would be to own such a fine weapon. He slashed it through the air playfully, stopped suddenly, and sobered.

"What will you take for it?"

The man shrugged. "What have you got?"

"Furs. I have furs of wolf, rabbit, fox, very thick and warm." The man motioned for him to continue, so he squatted and untied the cord from around the bundle, spreading out his skins. Choosing a red fox skin he was proud of, he handed it to the trader and stood up, beaming. "Soft, isn't it?"

The man gave no reply, but rubbed his hands over the skin, then again with his eyes closed. He lifted it in one hand. "It has a nice color, thick." Dagentyr grinned proudly. "Are all of your furs this good?"

"All of them. How many for the sword . . . and the scabbard, of course."

The trader did some quick figuring in his head and knelt to look through the rest of the pile. "More than you have, I'm afraid. Perhaps we could trade for cattle as well, but no sick ones. I'll touch no animal that has the sickness."

"Cattle?"

"It is a princely sword. They do not go for nothing."

"My cattle are few. I can give none of them."

"Your cattle are dying, then?" He knitted his

brow at the unwelcome reminder that he was in a
cursed land. "Well, slaves then?"

"They are needed for the cattle."

"None to spare? A nice brooch for your woman,
then, or a small jug of grape wine."

Dagentyr hesitated. "Grape wine?"

"Ah, you've never tried it?" Dagentyr kept silence. The trader raised his eyebrows in amazement and ducked into a tent not far away. He
returned with two small earthen jugs and a cup.
From the jugs, he mixed wine and water, and
handed the cup to Dagentyr. "Drink."

He drank a big swig and hummed in satisfaction
as it burned its sweet way down. "It is good. So
strange. You will give this to me?"

"For something in return."

"How many furs?"

"Wine is very dear in your land. Ten, of my
choosing. If you were willing to give cattle or slaves,
we could talk more of the sword, eh?"

"I'll keep the wine." Dagentyr fought back the
longing for the sword. To give cattle would be
foolish. He had few enough as it was, and those
depended on Ruki.

"Still no? Think of the fear and admiration you
will strike into your enemies when you slice off
their heads with a blade such as this, kissed by Ares
himself." Dagentyr did not know this Ares, but
Astekar spoke the name with force and awe.

"Dagentyr!" It was Gertera. "Come and see! A
bolt of cloth like pink wildrose, fit for the wife of a
high chieftain. Bring your furs!" She came running
to where he was. Ruki followed at a safe distance.
"Come, Dagentyr, quickly!"

Astekar smiled knowingly.

"Quiet, woman. Not now."

"But you have a sword already." He ignored her
and busied himself with holding the weapon up to
his eye to judge its straightness. It was, of course,

perfect. "Oh, please, Dagentyr! Even Truda, wife of Clavosius, has no cloth like it. It is a sunset woven by the gods for mortals. The man told me so!"

Dagentyr felt as he had when returning from the raid. He could imagine all eyes turning toward him. He looked around. Everyone was so involved in the barter that none noticed him, or her.

"Please, Dagentyr. I will make you so proud of me in such a magical cloth!" The shading over her eyes merely made them small, weasellike. The rain-heightened color of her cheeks was wrong, unnatural. He relented grudgingly. "All right. Take what you need and let me be." Anything, he thought, if you will leave me alone. He called to Ruki. "Take these over to where your mistress says, then carry the cloth for her."

Ruki walked haltingly to the furs, tripped over one of the cords securing the awning to the ground, pitched forward, and fell flat on his face. Astekar laughed heartily. Dagentyr shook his head in disgust, and after a few moments, while Ruki struggled madly and comically, he grabbed Ruki's tunic and pulled him to his feet.

"Quite a funny fellow," said Astekar. "He is your slave, I suppose?"

"Yes," answered Dagentyr.

Astekar eyed Ruki up and down like a pelt, with a smile still on his face. "Is he this funny all the time?"

Dagentyr shrugged. "He is like this all the time."

"Does he know how to make music?"

"No. He tells me his skills lie elsewhere."

"I like him. He might, given the proper training, naturally, make a good buffoon. At great feasts he would be an entertainment. An affliction is an asset for that kind of thing. Does he speak?"

"Yes." He paused. "In a way."

"Have him sing a song for me."

Dagentyr could not understand. "Why?"

Astekar was surprised. "Because I may want to buy him from you. I deal in slaves as well, as I told you. If he is funny enough, he will fetch a good price elsewhere. A foreign buffoon from outside the Pillars. I could even give him as a gift to my prince, who has been in need of mirth lately." Stepping past Dagentyr, he went to Ruki and made him open his mouth. "His teeth look good enough. You say he twitches like this all the time?" Dagentyr nodded. Astekar planted his fists on his hips. "Sing," he commanded. "Something sad."

Ruki looked over Astekar's shoulder at Dagentyr, then at Gertera, still in a frenzy to get her cloth.

Dagentyr spoke. "I see no harm in it. Sing for the man."

Ruki felt the tears coming to his eyes in anticipation of his humiliation. To refuse would worsen his position; one of the cattle was showing all the signs of imminent death. Fighting the lump in his throat, he opened his mouth and began.

Astekar roared. The man at the arms tent roared. The sullen guard roared. Ruki's voice rose and fell, finding no note or finding them all at the same time. The words were lost in his uncontrolled and tremulous caterwauling. He howled like a drunken dog. He did not get far. Laughter obliterated his song.

Astekar was rubbing the tears from his eyes and slapping his thighs merrily. "I like him!"

Ruki hung his head. His arms shook so much that he could not cover his ears effectively against the laughter. He hated it. He hated them.

"If he could be trained a little, if he knew some stories, with a lyre in his hands he might be worth a fortune." Astekar addressed Dagentyr. "I'll take him from you."

Dagentyr was uncertain and surprised. "I don't know. He's . . . valuable."

"Indeed. I know he is. That is why I want him."

"No. I mean in another way."

"He is?"

"I can say no more. I do not wish to sell him."

Astekar saw a hopeful look in Gertera's expression and played upon it. "I'll give you the whole length of cloth for this slave."

Gertera clapped her hands together and jumped in the air. "Take it, Dagentyr! Take it! Please. We're better off without him. Oh, please. Come and look at the cloth. Come and feel it. It's worth it. What a trade!"

He cut her off with a gesture and spoke to Astekar. "I might consider this, the sword and the cloth for the slave . . . and the wine." The sword seemed magical. It was eating away at his resolve to keep Ruki and save what was left of his herd.

Astekar put up his hands. "Ah, now there's too much. You're trying to get the best of me. If I let you do that, then the others might try to take unfair advantage as well. The cloth for the slave."

Gertera bit her lips. Ruki was still trying to hide himself with his hands and did not catch the conversation.

"If he's worth so much to you, why not take my offer?"

"He's a risk, looks frail, might die on the journey. A trader takes a chance when he buys slaves."

"I cannot give him up, then."

"Ah, here comes your chieftain."

Through the crowds, Clavosius rode with his retinue. Galmar and Vorgus were behind the war cart, herding a long line of slaves for barter. Each slave carried a bundle of valuables—furs, amber, mead, beer. Vorgus strutted and was liberal with the lash. Clavosius recognized Astekar from their earlier meeting by the river, and came directly toward him. Astekar greeted him, and they clasped hands.

"Hail again, Clavosius, chieftain of the land

between the rivers. I see you have brought much with you."

"I have come to steal you blind, trader," he said good-naturedly. "These men, taken in battle, were to be sacrificed, but they can be put to better use by trading."

"I hope you will not drive a bargain like this warrior who hopes to ruin me." Clavosius glanced disdainfully at Dagentyr, who lowered his head in greeting. There was cold silence. "I was trying to buy this slave, but he commands a steep price," said Astekar.

Clavosius jumped back into speech. "Really? This man, the one that they brought back? Why is that so?" He looked at Ruki in amazement.

"He is very funny and could bring a high price if properly trained, but I am afraid I shall not be able to afford him. I am told by the warrior that he has some other hidden value, as well. It's a pity. He might be fit for a king's household."

Clavosius raised his bushy red eyebrows and straightened indignantly. "If he is so worthy, he shall perform for me tonight at the feast of spring." Astekar regretted his words instantly and gave a casual nod. "I am anxious to see him. I am a king after all, no less than any other. He shall come, Dagentyr; you shall bring him."

Dagentyr saw Vorgus smirk. He pursed his lips while gathering himself. "As you wish, Clavosius."

"Good!" he rumbled. "Maybe we will learn of this hidden value. That settles that. Show me your wares, trader, and only the best." Saying that, he motioned to Vorgus. Galmar and the other retainers brushed past Dagentyr, nearly knocking him over. Vorgus stepped on his foot as he went by. Dagentyr burned. The sword he held took control of his emotions. He slashed it through the air. Vorgus heard, and wheeled around. Dagentyr coolly examined the blade again. Never taking his eyes off Dagentyr, Vorgus shoved the butt end of his

spear into a slave's stomach and roughly dragged
the man away as he gasped for air.

Astekar watched detachedly, taking it all in like
an omniscient being. He yelled to the man in
charge of arms. "Lemnias! Go and fetch our best
wares. Bring wine also!" Clavosius was already
inspecting the weapons. Astekar slapped Dagentyr
on the back. "Think quickly about what I offer,
warrior. We will only be here until tomorrow, then
we head for home. There is much evil in this land."

Dagentyr stared after Vorgus. "Yes, trader, there
is."

"The whole length of cloth. Think about it. You
still want the wine, no? Good. I'll take my furs
then." The trader stooped to choose the pelts he
wanted. Dagentyr held out his hand.

"Oh yes, the wine." He gave the jug to Dagentyr,
who heard Gertera's broken sob.

"Is it your purpose in life to cry? Get the slave to
take the rest of the furs, and if it is enough, buy
your cloth. Stop weeping." He turned to speak with
Astekar, but the trader was already haggling with
Clavosius.

Gertera went to Ruki, slapped him across the
face, and told him to get the furs and follow her.
The slap stirred him to quickness, and they disappeared in the crowd.

Young village boys were running foot races
through the crowd while the little girls cheered
their favorites. Everywhere, people sat gloating
over their new purchases, eating, drinking, gaming.
Men wrestled and had mock combat.

Dagentyr took a great swallow of undiluted wine
and made his way to another canopy that floated
colorfully against the vivid blue sky. As he moved
closer he could see that men were selling female
slaves. The women stood in the center of the
traders, undraping themselves on request as the
watermen studied them, noting the fairness of a

particular head of hair, the sparkle in a particular pair of eyes. When each woman had been appraised, a trader would nod or shake his head, then motion to the next.

Dagentyr thought of going to the slave tent and taking a closer look, but halted his step. In the crowd of men and women lingering in the shade of the awning, he saw Kerkina. A shining copper comb adorned her hair and she had stained her lips dark. Her gestures were happy and animated, sending the polished metal pendants of her girdle spinning. She and her mother were admiring a new bracelet on her slim wrist while her father watched the bargaining attentively.

Dagentyr did not want to take his eyes from her. Prudently, he forced himself to check the place where the cloth merchant was. Amid all the people, he could see Gertera with the pink cloth draped over her head and shoulders, skipping back and forth, running her fingers over its length lovingly. Her spiraled ankle rings jingled as she moved. Soon, he knew she would come to him and praise his generosity, and wind the cloth playfully about his head, laughing, and thanking him.

Kerkina and her family had seen him. They left the slave tent and approached him, nodding a greeting. He nodded back and held out his hand to Lokuos. Kerkina's father halted and wished him a happy feast day. Kerkina did not speak. The women sensed that they were not to hear, and moved out of earshot.

"Lokuos, I would talk to you. Only a moment now, but there is more I would ask of you later, at a better time. I think you know what I will ask for."

Lokuos planted one hand on his hip and another on Dagentyr's shoulder. "I do know, Dagentyr. Kerkina speaks of nothing else, hopes for nothing else."

"I am happy for that."

Lokuos took his hand away and moved it to his belt. His eyes darted down and did not meet Dagentyr's. "It must wait," he said.

"Wait?"

The older man nodded irritably. "Yes, it must wait."

"Is it Gertera you worry about? Do you have fears for your daughter's standing in the household? The woman is my father's wife. I do not lie with her as a husband lies with his woman. I'll treat Kerkina as my first wife; she will *be* my first wife."

"No. Don't be angry. There is no trouble there. Nor is there any with you. I know you and I knew your father. He was a good and noble man, as are you. You are courageous."

"Then what will keep us waiting?"

"I said you were good and courageous. I did not say you were popular, or safe. The power in the tribe hates you. I'll not give away my daughter into danger."

There it is, he thought. Vorgus again. "I understand. And if the danger were removed?"

"It's another matter then, another time, but I don't see—"

"A good time for a wedding?"

"Yes. It would be." Lokuos nodded, perhaps in enlightenment, smiled agreeably, and raised his hand in farewell. Dagentyr glanced at Kerkina and his eyes told her it had not gone well.

Now more than ever, Vorgus had to die. He flushed with anger to think that Vorgus could threaten his life and happiness in so many ways. He whispered, "Not for much longer. He will not keep Kerkina from me. No misguided bird will stop me. When the sun rises tomorrow, there will be no Vorgus."

Chapter 8

Dagentyr was getting drunk, not calmly, but vengefully drunk with each huge mouthful of meat and cheese that he washed down. The wine jug was nearly empty. He and Arvis had drained it. Arvis sat next to him fingering his cup nervously.

The jug sat in Dagentyr's lap, fiercely guarded. It sloshed feebly when he moved, as did his stomach. His blood was warm with the alcohol. Everything was confusion, loud voices, powerful smells of cooking food and hot bodies, drunken laughter. The air was blue with wood smoke.

The coarse log walls of the chieftain's hut were hung with shields, spears, and quivers of arrows. Around the circle of seated guests, slave women came and went with trays of wild pig and fowl, jugs of mead and beer, meat from the sacrificial bull, honey cakes with hazelnuts and acorns.

His mouth felt dry, so he raised the jug to his lips and sent another swallow down to his fiery insides. He looked around the circle and contemplated his place in it. It was the farthest away from Clavosius and the places of honor. Arvis looked like a disappointed child as he peered into his cup and took the slaps on the back from the lesser warriors.

Dagentyr fumed. Fifteen nobles sat on the floor, feasting, and of them, he had been considered the least important. It was a grave and intentional insult, more humiliating than being left out altogether, for this way they could see his reaction, savor his misery. Soon the wine would be gone. He called loudly for mead, and a slave girl hurried to refill his cup.

Away from the circle of men sat Ruki, knees up, head drooped. He did not respond when the passing slave girl kicked him out of her way.

Dagentyr was surprised how quickly fear and disgust could turn to scorn. He leaned out and nudged Ruki's foot with the jug. There was no reaction. Shrugging, he dropped the jug next to him and said, "Take it," then wiping his greasy fingers on his tunic, he reached for a loaf of coarse bread. He cut a large slice with his dagger, dipped it into his mead, and ate it hungrily. Gesturing with the knife, he spoke quietly to Arvis.

"A great feast, isn't it, cousin? A brilliant feast with much honor and favor bestowed on our best warriors. See how they sit in splendor, there next to the chieftain. We should be honored to be here at all." His tongue was getting thick and numb.

Amused, Arvis snickered and emptied his cup. "I told you it would be so, Dagentyr. Here we are, humbled and insulted while the village horse's ass, a lesser man than we are, pats the chieftain's back and surveys the hall as if it were his own. We're not even men anymore." His insistent banging on the floor with the cup soon brought the girl scurrying with more beverage.

Dagentyr looked across the circle. Lokuos eyed him sadly and expectantly. Suddenly he felt shamed. What would Kerkina's father think of a man who suffered insults and did nothing to avenge them? What would the warriors think?

Between his fat hands, Clavosius tore a hunk of

bread. His red beard was flecked and dirty with bits of goat cheese and congealed grease. Next to him, Galmar was pitched over sideways on the floor, sleeping. He pulled at the wolfskin he had been sitting on and covered himself.

At Clavosius's right, Vorgus drank from a golden cup. He and Astekar, the trader, talked and told stories. They were much alike. When they were not occupied with conversation they would look over the hall at the men. Dagentyr could see Vorgus make silent, mental calculations on which warriors would back him, which would not, which would have to be killed. His touch on the golden goblet was like a caress.

Astekar's bearing was always that of a slave trader. Every man that entered his field of vision became a list of attributes, a thing, a commodity, whether slave or freeman. He was disturbing. They sat like gods incarnate over the rest, different in their appearance but ominously the same beneath.

Clavosius fawned over Vorgus like an overindulgent mother. The best portions of the meat were his, the ripest and sweetest fruits. The most comely slaves served him.

Puffing his chest out proudly, Vorgus nodded at each thing the chieftain said. Many times during the evening he had looked at Dagentyr and opened his mouth wide as if laughing. His followers were easily recognizable; they jested more loudly, laughed harder.

Vorgus pushes me to the limit this time, Dagentyr thought. "Arvis, men cannot take such insults and do nothing."

Arvis stared absently into his cup. "We might as well join the women and learn to weave as be here and bear this. I am very drunk, Dagentyr. I have consumed much mead and little food. If I were not afraid of toppling over, I would go now and stick my blade into his reeking guts." He wiped his nose and swayed precariously in his cross-legged posture.

"Shh, be still. Guard what you say."

Clavosius straightened at his place. "Quiet! All quiet! Entertainment, that's what we need. At the gathering of a great chieftain there should be entertainment! Let's have a tale of men, great deeds, war." He chuckled brusquely.

Too brusquely, Dagentyr thought, and his manner was too solicitous. It was obvious. In spite of the veneer of good fellowship and drunken camaraderie, he was tense. The whole room was uneasy except for Astekar.

Dagentyr looked about him. The men of his following were cautious, not nearly as drunk as they were at other feasts. They were quieter, listened more, and kept their hands close to their sides, in easy reach of their daggers. Sem did not joke as usual. Targoth was dead silent.

Are you frightened of me, Clavosius? What tales has Vorgus told you, that I am not to be trusted, that I plan to kill you in your sleep? What lies make you so afraid? Coward, Dagentyr thought, foolish old coward. He belched, disgusted, but ripe for a story.

Herkin, an older warrior, pushed himself to a standing position.

Clavosius sat with his hands on his thighs, satisfied. "So, you'll tell us a tale, Herkin?"

The man nodded. Coughing momentously, he got the attention of the company and launched into his saga. He told tales well, and at feasts was invariably called on to recite stories of heroes and monsters. He and Dagentyr's father had been friends. Dagentyr could recall the times long ago when he had feigned sleep and listened to Herkin and his father swap their stories of hunts and wars.

His tale now was a mighty one, filled with magic and battle. In the clear space around the fire pit in the center of the ring, he moved and gesticulated. His imagination turned posts into trees, ordinary kitchen utensils into golden treasures. In the dim hall, his words painted scenes that all could share as the warrior-hero slew beasts and men, and outwitted spirits, collecting much gold and fame.

No one made any noise. Dagentyr's heart quickened as he heard of the hero's great deeds and then he fell into despondency as he compared them to his own. Someone, once, had done great deeds and had not borne insults.

Herkin was masterful, and his audience was attentive. They laughed at the bawdy jokes, and as quickly as the outbursts subsided, were caught back up in the telling.

At the climax of the story, the hero destroyed his archenemy in battle. Herkin drew his dagger and slashed madly at the air for emphasis. It startled everyone. All over the room, daggers came out of their sheaths, and Vorgus's people stood, thinking this the cue for the others to fall on them in ambush. There were exclamations of surprise. Vorgus's man next to Dagentyr nearly knocked him over in his rush to get to his feet. In turn startled, Dagentyr's men drew weapons.

"Stop it! Stop it!" Clavosius shouted.

Vorgus was standing, ignorant of what to expect, surprise plain in his eyes.

There was a hesitation, just a small one. Everyone halted and looked toward Vorgus, then Dagentyr. Flustered by his error, Herkin fought to regain his composure.

"Finish your story, Herkin," Dagentyr said, and calmly, slowly, as if in perfect keeping with his pantomime, the storyteller exaggeratedly lowered his blade and slipped it back in its sheath. The hero of his tale was victorious. Herkin never let a crowd get the better of him.

He waited still as stone. The others slowly mimicked him and put their weapons away. One by one, they sat down and allowed themselves to breathe again. There was silence for a moment. Suddenly, timidly at first, there was cheering, and shouts for more. Soon the whole room roared. Clavosius beat his leg with his hand, relief gushing out of him. Those around Herkin offered him drink to wet his throat so he could go on. He just held his hands in the air and shook his head, taking the mead and the slaps of approval. Vorgus did not cheer, but the muscles of his face relaxed. Astekar smiled non-committally.

The man next to him looked at Dagentyr and grinned. Dagentyr let his mouth grin in answer, and his thoughts cursed him—disloyal bastard, dung-eating son of a pig. As if they had been brothers, Dagentyr gave him a firm pat on the shoulder.

During the continuing clamor over Herkin's story, Astekar rose and addressed the chieftain.

"Hold! Silence!" Clavosius exclaimed. "The waterman wishes to tell us a story of his land."

"Yes," they all shouted. "Let's hear! Quiet!"

New interest was suddenly aroused. A new yarn from a faraway place was about to be unfolded. Even though he did not particularly like the waterman, Dagentyr found his attention drawn away from his hate and humiliation, outward to the small man in the white tunic who stepped into the center of focus.

"My story may not be as exciting as the other you have heard, or as long, but I know it will be new and fresh, full of things with which you are not acquainted." His tunic grew orange as he paced closer to the fire pit.

"Generations ago, many generations of our fathers before now, there was trouble in the realm of the gods. The lord of heaven, Teshub . . ." He noted several blank expressions and questioning whispers. His mind searched for words that would clarify. "Teshub rules the skies, and when he is angry the skies roar and flash with terrible light which he hurls with a mighty arm, for the lightning is heavier still than the heaviest sword or shield."

Now they knew who the god was, lord of thunder. To add effect, Astekar threw an imaginary thunderbolt at one of the warriors and then flexed his arm, grasping the muscle firmly with the other hand. They laughed and then nodded gravely. The group was warming to Astekar and his tale.

"Teshub was firmly enthroned in the skies, and his power was great. He had usurped this throne from great Kumarbis, father of the gods, and he held his power with firm, brazen fists, and storms danced in his eyes.

"Far below, Kumarbis walked the earth and sulked, and brooded. He said, 'I will raise up a son, mighty and wise, to challenge the storm god. He will fight at my side and we will drive Teshub from his place of power.' When he had said this he fastened on the sandals of the winds and flew across the great water, and there, in the middle of the sea was a huge stone. A cleft ran down its middle. Kumarbis rested upon the stone and fell into a deep sleep. In his sleep he dreamed and became aroused. He took the stone as a man takes a woman." He winked and did an obscene acting-out of his words.

They were involved now and shouted at him, "What then?"

"The rock grew, swelled, gave birth, spit forth a man, huge, of stone, son of mighty Kumarbis."

They called in surprise, "A man of stone? Ha! How so?"

He waved for quiet. "Kumarbis saw that he had a son, child of his loins and the stone. He called him Ullikumis. 'We will fight the storm god together,' he cried, and his son rose up, taller and taller. His head brushed the clouds. He parted the clouds with his hands like a man parts the web of a spider.

"And Kumarbis rode on his son's shoulder in his bright armor of gold. He shouted his war call while the man of stone waded the ocean and shook his fists through the high clouds, knocking on the dome of heaven.

"The messengers of Teshub flew to him and begged him mount the storm chariot and take up his weapons. 'Who is there to be afraid of? No man or god can threaten me!' His laughter blew out the black, swirling clouds. The air became cold and windy." The men seemed to scoot closer to the fire, as if they could feel the mythical breezes.

"Kumarbis gave the command, and Ullikumis reached up a mighty hand and shook the throne of the sky. Teshub tumbled on his rump and called in anger and fear for his horses and his bolts of lightning. Ullikumis flicked him away with his finger as a man waves away a gnat.

"Kumarbis laughed and the stone man laughed. Teshub had the chariot brought, donned his armor, took up his quiver of lightning death and drove at the head of a great storm to do battle.

"They fought till men on earth thought the ground would split. There was darkness when the sun should have shone. Day was black; the world shook. The dark clouds blazed with Teshub's fire, but his lightning landed harmlessly on the stone man. The storm horses wearied. Teshub's arm wearied, drooping with the weight of his weapons.

"Ullikumis plucked him from his chariot and said, 'I will crush you now, little storm god.' Teshub was afraid."

The threat echoed familiarly in Dagentyr's head. He found himself in sympathy with the usurper Teshub.

"Quickly, Teshub sent a messenger far away to seek Ishtar, goddess of love, with news of his plight. When she heard, she changed into a beautiful, bejeweled dolphin and swam to the battle site, where she became woman and goddess again."

"What is a dolphin?" one noble interrupted.

"A huge fish," Astekar replied. He shook his head at the inelegance of the translation. "The goddess called, 'Man of stone, is your heart also made of cold rock?' Ullikumis set Teshub upon a cloud and stooped to stare at the goddess of love. She began to dance for him. She whispered enticing words of love into his huge ear. She removed her garments and danced on and on.

"Kumarbis was enraged and called to his son to continue the fight, but Ullikumis would not listen, so entranced was he.

"Teshub saw his chance and sneaked away. He rode fast and far, beyond the land of the gods to the place where the cleaver was kept, the cleaver that was used to separate heaven from earth. He plucked it from its resting place and galloped back to do battle. He thundered down on his foe. Ullikumis still watched Ishtar and did not see. Teshub wielded the cleaver and struck the man of stone."

"What happened? Go on!"

"The earth split, belched fire and smoke. There were harsh clouds on the horizon, and a great wind blew at mortal men's clothing as they stood and gaped at the fight. It was a hot wind that stung their eyes. In the red light they saw the sea crawl back from the shore as the earth swallowed the stone man and the ocean with him. Fish were stranded, dying in the wet sand. Ships sat on the rocks. Then in the ruddy twilight, the great wave came."

"What is a wave?"

He searched his brain. "A great flood. The water that had gone suddenly came back all at once as the earth spit the ocean and fragments of the stone man out again with fire and steam. It rushed in on the

land like a huge wall made from the ocean. It was as
tall as the tallest three trees put on top of one
another, and it fell on the land. It washed away
villages and boats, men and cattle, goats and forests, and when it left, it pulled what it could out
with it. The pieces of the stone man fell over the
earth, and my people took them to rebuild the walls
of their ruined city. They made them high, as high
as the wave, so they would have no fear of such a
thing again. And Kumarbis still sulks."

He folded his arms smugly to indicate he was
finished.

The men cheered but not as loudly as for Herkin.
Herkin's tale was as familiar as the woods around
them, as the feel of their weapons. The waterman
brought a tale of mystery, difficult to understand.
They were stunned.

Dagentyr closed his eyes and tried to imagine
walls as high as trees and made of stone! It disturbed him.

Astekar grinned, shrugged, and accepted the cup
that Clavosius offered him as he went back to his
seat. Seeing him drink, Dagentyr was reminded of
his own cup still gripped in his hand, and he
emptied it in a gulp.

Vorgus sat as composed as ever, not allowing
himself to be impressed. In his eyes was a jealousy
and hatred of the things he had heard described.

More food and drink were brought out.
Dagentyr's throat was thick and hot so he called for
water and let it wash away the burning sensation.

Arvis had been silent through the stories and
now turned to Dagentyr. "I don't know what to
make of it. Such a strange story. I have heard of the
big water, but hearing him speak of it, I cannot
think of a thing so huge." Dagentyr did not know
what to make of it, either.

Vorgus was whispering to Clavosius. The chieftain's face came alive with recollection, and he

yelled, "Dagentyr! You have brought us entertainment tonight!"

"I'm sure it will be small compared with the entertainment that you have provided." He allowed sarcasm to enter his voice. "I have merely done as I was told." He was playing with fire but was too drunk to care. He got up, grabbed the front of Ruki's tunic and hauled him up still clinging to the now empty wine jug. There was a ripple of laughter.

Clavosius said, "Come up here, slave, and make us laugh."

Dagentyr gave him a push and he went into the circle slowly, evoking howls simply by the way he moved.

Astekar leaned in and spoke to Clavosius.

The chieftain grinned. "The trader tells me you sing. Give us a song now like you did for him. Sing about . . . love, that's good, love and robust women, and mighty prowess on the hay mats!"

They hooted and jeered, and threw pieces of food at him.

He probably doesn't know any, thought Dagentyr.

Surprisingly enough, he did, and he sang a song of love but not a bawdy one, more like a lullaby. It was tender and all the more poignant for the way it was sung, almost a desperate pleading accompanied by the slaps of chicken bones against his body. His eyes were closed.

For the first time, Vorgus looked like he was enjoying himself. He laughed out loud with the rest of the men. He threw a cup at Ruki that bounced off his head with a rattle and made him drop the wine jug on his foot.

The song ended. Ruki stopped, and fell, gripping the foot in pain. It was screamingly funny. The room went wild. Dagentyr couldn't laugh. He didn't know why.

It was just the beginning. Ruki was given a wooden knife, a bowl for a helmet, and was made to fight one of the best warriors in the house. He was forced to serve, and spilled a whole tray of food. Ordinarily, a slave who had been so clumsy would have been beaten, but they just laughed, and smeared him with the mess. Some of the men made him drink an entire cup of mead at one breath and nearly rolled on the floor when he stumbled over to the hearth to vomit.

At length, Vorgus stood up. Wiping tears from his eyes, he spoke to Clavosius. "Have I been given my share of spoils from the raid?"

Clavosius looked puzzled and obviously nervous. "No. You have claimed nothing."

"Then I claim it now. I claim the buffoon as my spoils. My standing entitles me to choose over Dagentyr."

Astekar was stone and watched the goings-on as if from a distance. The other warriors were becoming interested.

Chuckling in understanding, Clavosius agreed. "Then he is yours. I give him to you as your portion."

Vorgus sneered triumphantly.

"He belongs to me," said Dagentyr.

Vorgus ignored him. "Thank you, Father. I am grateful."

"He is mine. He belongs to me!" He would stand it no longer. I won't be a coward and backstab you, he thought, I will be man enough to kill you now, in the open.

Vorgus seized his opportunity. He stood angrily and leaned his huge frame toward Dagentyr. "Do you presume to go against the commands of your chieftain? Who are you but a small man sitting far away?"

Arvis tensed.

Dagentyr went on, trying not to let his approach-

ing rage show. "I presume to say that he is mine,
gotten fairly, and I intend to do with him what I
please and not what someone else pleases, you
hulking son of a village whore!"

They all gasped. There were outcries.

Vorgus drew his dagger and leapt out, sending
cups and bowls of food topsy-turvy.

Dagentyr was up and pulled his blade in the
painful grip of his right hand. "I'll kill you here and
now. No wrong-flying bird will stop me."

"No! Stop them! Guards!" Clavosius was in a
panic.

The two men at the door left their places and
hurried to break them up. One stepped in Vorgus's
way and both went sprawling. The other pushed
Dagentyr up against a wall and held him there with
his spear.

Dagentyr could have killed him easily; the man
was unprepared and had forgotten his shield. One
thrust would have done it, but he would not. His
quarrel was not with the guard.

Seeing them both immobilized, Clavosius
jumped to the center of the room to stand between
them. "This will stop. Vorgus, return to your place.
Guards, throw Dagentyr into the street. The slave
shall be given over as I have said."

Dagentyr thought desperately for some way to
save the situation. Now, confront him now. Tell
Clavosius of the plan. "Lord Clavosius, wait. There
is something you must know. There is a plan to kill
you. Certain men, many of those here, would be
happy to see you dead, and if you do not listen to
me and believe what I tell you, you will be dead.
Your own son will kill you!"

Clavosius's face went bright red, his eyes bulged.
"What! What good do you hope to do for yourself
by telling me such filth! Lies! Plan, yes I know of a
plan. Vorgus has told me, and he has told me whose
plan it truly is, yours. You are the traitor here, the

viper, the liar! And tomorrow the elders will be gathered to hear of your falseness and know why I will banish you from here. Banish! Hadn't counted on that, had you? But they will see, and then you will be gone from here, forever!"

"Banished? Me, driven out? You coward. You aren't sure enough of yourself to have me murdered, are you? There would be trouble, dissent. Banishment is much safer." The sides of Dagentyr's vision were blacking out, closing in on him in rage.

"Take him out now. I want no more trouble."

Vorgus leered at Dagentyr, then at Ruki. "Molva," he croaked, "take the slave away to my hut and watch till the feast is over, then I will take charge for the night." He sat down again, staring malevolently.

Tiredly, knowingly, Molva took Ruki away.

Dagentyr moved away as the guard motioned with his spear. As he approached the door, the girl with the cow eyes passed with a pitcher. She looked at him unconcernedly, secure in her new position. With the back of his hand, he struck her across the face and sent her reeling against the wall. The pitcher crashed to the floor and broke.

Chapter 9

Ruki did not know how long he had been lying by the fire. The revelry was still going on; he could hear it. His body was all pain from being kicked and pushed. He felt bruises, aches, hatred, and shame. He was stiff. The fire felt good. He thought of rolling into it and being consumed by a blinding heat. It would not pain him any more than what he already felt. Life would hold more of this in store for him if he stayed here, and worse. Every day would be a repetition of what he had already been through, and he would finally die, maybe old, maybe not, with the same aches and hatred and shame.

He had resolved when he had first heard it mentioned, that he would not go with Vorgus. It hadn't taken much pondering. He had prayed that Dagentyr would be successful in his fight to keep him. It was disgusting to pray for one master over another, but there was no better choice. When he knew that he was lost, he had decided to die.

The fat one, Molva, was asleep by the door, limp arms resting on the ground, palms upward. His chest rose and fell heavily, slowly; his head was down. Through slitted eyes, Ruki watched him until he was certain that he was asleep. The sword and the slave were unguarded.

A hand's length at a time, fighting all the way to keep silent and resist the spasms, he began to crawl from the warmth of the fire to the cold sword. Slowly, and then forcing himself to go slower still, he crept up, eating the dirt of the floor, wincing as it scratched his face. The man slept. By the gods, he was nearly there, and still the man slept. What if he actually managed to grasp the sword; could the shaking hand plunge it deep enough, quickly, painlessly? He didn't want to linger for the pleasure of his tormentors. A hurried and botched cut across the wrists, the throat? His guts turned over.

Inches from his grasp was the handle. He reached for it, and his hand swung uncontrollably and brushed the sleeping fingertips. Nothing, no awakening, just an involuntary closing of the hand.

Then, he was there and the smooth sword grip was in his hand. He began to pull it toward him and heard the scrape as it dragged across the floor. Carefully, he took it in both hands, got to his knees, and placed the hilt against the ground with the point wavering just below his heart. He leaned on it. It was so sharp! He drew away and fell back.

He was a coward. He did not want to die like this. But the hate! In a madness of frustration, he grabbed the sword as it should be held. Unsteadily, he got to his feet. He was unsure where would be best, but picked a spot midway down the rib cage and fell with all his weight.

The hall had been stuffy and hot. It was more pleasant outside, better for thinking. Walking the mead from his head, Dagentyr had done much thinking.

His recollections were vivid. Vorgus staring, Clavosius in a panic, the awakened Galmar looking scared and befuddled, the guards at the gate whispering in astonishment at his ejection from the hall. It had all gone wrong. Another confrontation, another draw with no other result than a worsening of feelings between factions, and banishment.

Perhaps the omen had been right. The bird had flown west and this was not the night to move. There is one thing that has come of this, he thought. I will feel no more remorse or hesitation. When I kill him, it will be with pleasure.

His feet carried him through the streets, away from the noisy hall. The hand was bleeding again, but he ignored it and went on walking, breathing the crisp air. The stars were bright, and an orange moon hung just above the western hills. Just when he had paused to catch his breath, he heard the scream, high-pitched and loud.

Forgetting everything, he ran in the direction of the cry with his dagger drawn. On the path outside the hut of Vorgus, he rushed headlong into a dark shape and knocked it over. He blinked, striving to see better in the darkness.

The slave fought madly to get to his feet and run. Dagentyr crouched, and pointed the dagger at him. "Stay there against the wall. Move and I'll kill you."

Ruki plastered himself to the outside of the hut, panting.

Still pointing the dagger in his direction, Dagentyr moved closer. Molva lay half in, half outside the doorway, his head and torso sticking into the street. Firelight from inside the hut sparkled in his open eyes. The sword handle was stuck between two ribs, and the ugly point protruded out the other side. Already, blood was beginning to puddle in the dirt.

The slave rolled his eyes and whispered harshly and desperately. "Let me go, please."

Dagentyr looked at the fear in the man's face.

The slave did not belong to him any longer; why should he care? He had earned freedom. Looking at Molva, he thought fleetingly of Vorgus, and imagined his anger when he found his bedmate dead and his slave gone. He lowered his dagger.

"Go, get out." The slave stared in disbelief. "Go on. The guards at the gate will be here soon. They must have heard the scream. Go behind the huts quietly and when you see the gates unmanned, sneak out as best you can. Hurry up. If they catch you, this never happened, and I will kill you myself to prove it to them." He turned and moved to the body, hearing the soft shuffle of feet as Ruki made his escape in the night. He realized it was not wise for him to stay either, and then it was too late.

"Dagentyr!" The guards from the gate had recognized him. They had alerted the hall, and men were coming up the path, weapons drawn. The street began to burn with the light of many torches. Clavosius walked behind the two guards, Vorgus behind him. Women, frightened by the scream, heard the voices and were brave enough to stick their heads from the nearby huts.

When he was close enough to see the body, Vorgus broke through the others and ran to kneel over it.

Clavosius approached. "What has happened here, Dagentyr?"

"I heard a scream and ran to see. When I got here I found things as you see them. There was no one here. The slave was gone." He knew things were bad. Even the men of his group looked perplexed and doubtful.

"No!" Vorgus got up from his kneeling position. Emotion clogged his voice and thickened his accent. "You killed him with his own sword as he slept, and then you freed the slave because you hate me. To get cowardly revenge on me, you came up here like a fox in the night and murdered Molva!"

Dagentyr swallowed hard. "That is not true. The slave must have done it and then run away. To get revenge, I would not have killed Molva, I would have killed you."

"You expect us to believe that?" He towered over Dagentyr, tears in his eyes. "You!" He shook all over. Molva's blood was bright on his hands, warm and red in the torchlight. The one word was all he needed to say.

There was total silence as Vorgus's cry died away. In that time, Dagentyr realized that he was not believed, not by the chieftain, not even by his own men. Clavosius beckoned to the guards.

He still had his dagger in his hand. If he fought, he could call on the others to join him, but it would mean that some of his friends might die. Worse, they might not succeed. The gate guards were Clavosius's men. The numbers were not in their favor and his followers' confidence had been shaken. His own had been hurt by the bad omen. There was another choice. It would keep him alive, and them.

With his forearm, he shoved Vorgus aside and bolted through the two guards into the crowd. They hadn't expected him to run. He prayed that the others believed him enough to let him go. Swinging the dagger while he ran, he saw the crowd part for him.

Vorgus recovered quickly from the blow and followed at a dead run. Dagentyr could hear his screaming and Clavosius's shouted orders.

A spear struck the ground at his heel and another flew over his head and glanced off a hut in front of him, then the street curved and he was out of sight. He would have to make it out the gate and into the woods where he could hide. His pursuers rounded the bend behind him.

He looked back over his shoulder and stopped. Arvis had run ahead of the press of men and stood

in Vorgus's way. "Run, Dagentyr," he yelled, then
Vorgus caught up with him.

He made a slash, and Arvis sprang back to avoid
it. The street was narrow and he fell against the
outside wall of a hut. Vorgus charged in, pinned
Arvis's sword arm against the wall and butted his
head upward.

Arvis's skull slammed back onto the logs, and
then Vorgus's sword was through his middle.

It was so quick that Dagentyr could not believe
his eyes. There was no time to think, only time to
see Arvis slump to the ground, then Vorgus's
screams started again. His followers joined him in
the chase and Dagentyr knew that he had diso-
beyed an omen. The bird had flown west, and
everything was doomed.

He ran again, fighting the urge to turn back. He
told himself, Keep going. If you turn, you die.
Escape and you live to seek revenge. Live and you
can still kill Vorgus. Your hand is useless. If you
stand and fight, you will be slaughtered before you
can redden your own blade.

He made himself run faster, as fast as he could,
down the street, the men shouting behind him. The
gates were ahead and open, unmanned. He sped
through a newly assembled cluster of people who
had gathered to wonder at the noise, and through
the portal. He hoped the crowd would give him the
time he needed.

As soon as he was outside he made straight for
the woods. The muscles in his thighs were tighten-
ing, and his lungs hurt, but he had to go faster, put
as much distance as he could between himself and
his pursuers. Give yourself time, he thought. Had
Kerkina been in the crowd? He decided not to
think, and ran.

The woods were pitch-black. It was demon time.
The spirits would be abroad. Cries of alarm came

from the village, but they seemed far away. He
listened hard as he ran. He was outdistancing them,
or perhaps not. They had stopped to regroup, arm,
and find more torches. Only a desperate man would
enter the forest at night without one.

He stopped. From branches and thorns, his legs
were crisscrossed with scratches. The hand bled,
still clenched around the dagger handle. He gasped
for air. If he could travel along the river to hide
himself, then cross to the woods on the other side,
he would be in safer country. The farther away
from Fottengra, the better, but where after that? He
couldn't go to the other villages of the tribe. They
would know of him soon, and he would be caught.
Despair took hold of him; there was absolutely no
place to go.

"Courage, you idiot." He spoke aloud to himself
and the sound of his own voice in the blackness
made him feel better. He could survive in the
forest, then return in secret and kill Vorgus. "You
must get out now and make plans later." With a
bracing gulp of air, he changed directions and
headed to the edge of the wood.

There was still noise in Fottengra. They hadn't
started after him yet. As far as he could tell, the
valley was quiet. It seemed as though he had been
running for days. Dim fires flickered in the
watermen's camp. The village itself was out of
sight. He saw no one.

Running fast and low to stay beneath the level of
the tall meadow growth, he fled toward the river,
and then it was as if a hand had reached out of the
earth to clutch his ankle. The way was blocked, he
tripped, went tumbling over. A surprised yell escaped from his mouth as he fell.

A rush of terror was near to engulfing him. He
fought, cursed his outburst, forced his eyes to open
and confront his demon. There was a black shape

in the grass beside him, a great, dead, black mass. The putrid smell of rotting flesh was overpowering. His fear eased. He turned in revulsion from the cow's carcass and ran on.

When he reached the riverbank, he slid down on his seat and splashed knee-deep in the flow. He stopped, listened. A group of men was moving up into the woods where he had just been. Hazarding a peek over the bank, he could see the torches. Another group split off and veered in the other direction, to the north, where he had met Kerkina. Time to head upstream, away from the village.

He stopped himself. That's what they would be expecting him to do. Perhaps if he headed toward the village he could reach the watermen's camp and use it as a screen when he made his dash for the woods across the river. Indecision was deadly. If they sent a party across the ford to the other bank, he would be trapped.

He went as quickly as possible downriver, cursing the noise his feet made as they plowed through the water. Every few paces, he stopped to listen and place the location of the search groups in his mind's eye.

He was unsure how much time he had until dawn. Once the sun came up, he would be finished. He had lost track of time, but the east was still black. There was no sign of daylight. Ahead, the awnings of the watermen were barely distinguishable. He could just hear the crackle of the fires and the intermittent words of confusion from the sentinels. Not too close, he thought.

He found a place where the bank sloped up gently, and squatted down, dripping and cold, ready for a mad, clawing swim and a final sprint across open country to the trees.

"Warrior."

He nearly cried out in his surprise. His heart made the climb into his mouth. Wheeling around,

he leveled his dagger and stared, ready to strike and
flee if he could only see who it was that had spoken.
"Up here, up here, quickly." It was Astekar.
"Come on," he whispered hoarsely. "Hurry. I'll
hide you. Come, I have no reason to betray you.
They'll be here soon but they won't search us.
Don't stand there; there's no time, come!" There
were torches flickering upriver. The ford, thought
Dagentyr in horror. Astekar glanced over his shoul-
der. "Hurry!"

Dagentyr took the hand offered him. He hadn't
realized that the little man was so strong until he
felt the tug that helped him up the slope. They were
behind one of the tents, shielded from sight of the
village. Astekar hurried him beneath an awning.
There were large bundles and sacks stacked about,
cargo ready for the next day's loading.

"When you were thrown out, I begged permission to leave the village," Astekar said. "You never
know what happens in a strange land. There are
many dangers. You are lucky I was alert and
happened on you." He spoke while pulling furs
from a large sack. "Here, get in. I'll cover you up
with furs and then we'll pack you up tomorrow
when we move on. Stay quiet, and whatever happens, don't move or give yourself away until I come
and take you out. Do you understand?"

He was still stunned by it all. "Yes, I . . . thank
you. Why should you help me like this?"

"There's no time, come, give me that." He took
the dagger. It was stuck to Dagentyr's hand with
dried blood; pulling it away hurt. "We'll tend to
that later. Get in." He parted the opening for
Dagentyr, who crawled in and settled himself in a
ball among the furs. Astekar threw some more
skins on top of him and pulled the drawstring tight.

The sack smelled bad, but the pelts were soft and
warm. His tired, aching muscles needed rest.
Everything had happened in a whirlwind around

him. He let himself be sad now that he was safe, sad for Arvis, his cousin. He was not sure how he would do it, but he would kill Vorgus.

The air in the bag was stuffy. He was drowsy and confused. Why had Astekar taken his dagger? Clutching his injured hand to his body for warmth, he stayed alert until fatigue and spent nerves forced him into sleep.

"Let no one near, but more important, do not let him out. If the savages come and want to see inside, fetch me and I will handle it. Guard well. We break camp at dawn." Astekar spoke to the man he had placed at the canopy. The guard nodded. The chieftain of the watermen tucked Dagentyr's dagger into his belt and returned to his own tent.

Chapter 10

The early morning noises of men breaking camp did not wake him. He slept in complete mental and physical exhaustion through the loud calls and orders of the traders as they saw to the boats and the dismantling and packing away of awnings and cargo. Only when he felt himself lifted off the ground did he open his eyes and begin to wonder what was happening.

The air in the bag was stifling. Every muscle was aching and cramped from his escape and the long night in a huddled position. He expected to feel the dagger in his hand and then remembered that the trader had taken it.

The bag was rocking slowly from side to side in rhythm to the steps of men. It hung on a stout pole which two watermen supported on their shoulders as they carried it to one of the rafts. Dagentyr heard the voices now and recognized one of them as Astekar's, chiding the men to be careful.

He stayed motionless in the sack, hardly daring to breathe, wondering if the carriers knew he was in the bag or if Astekar had kept the secret to himself. The noise and confusion were subdued, muffled by the fur all around him. With an unceremonious plop, he was set down on the raft.

What had been comfortable warmth during the night was now unbearable heat, and now that he was awake it didn't take him long to realize that he was hungry, very hungry. To take his mind away from his stomach and the sickening closeness of the bag, he thought of his predicament and what he might do to solve it.

Clearly, his chance meeting with Astekar was the best thing that could have happened. He had a safe hiding place, and what was more important, safe passage away from Fottengra, out of reach of Vorgus and Clavosius. That was the good of the situation. It did little to relieve the bad.

It was unfathomable, the thing that had happened to him. In the space of half a day, he had lost whatever position he had and become a hunted outcast. There was still time to go back and put his case before the elders and priests, but he knew he would stand no chance with Clavosius and Vorgus talking against him.

Whatever happened, he knew Kerkina would understand that he hadn't killed Molva, but something told him that she would spend the rest of her life without him.

There was a thunderous outburst of farewells, wishes for a safe journey. The raft creaked and lurched forward as it was pushed out into the current.

Dagentyr felt the craft turn and gain forward speed as the men with poles started to guide it along. He was only vaguely aware of where he was headed. The old, the safe, the familiar were left behind. Cursing his bleak thoughts, he promised himself that he would be back to the woods near Fottengra soon. In spite of that, he imagined the worst, saw himself mercenary to some tribal chieftain closer to the big water, standing watch over his

cattle and women, while in Fottengra his own
name, which had been on everyone's lips one
spring evening, was quietly forgotten.

It was not much to look forward to, but he had
escaped death. Plunder was plunder whether here
or at the world's edge. There were women everywhere; green eyes and auburn hair were attributes
that many of them could claim. He didn't believe
any of it. His stomach ached with hunger and
despair. With each moment, his realm receded, and
he could not convince himself that the future held
anything but empty space and questions.

For what seemed like forever, the boats floated
their way west, sleepily down the valley of Fottengra, past the small hamlets, past fishermen and
women rinsing out clothing, westward on the river
that served as the main trade passageway from the
coast to the interior. The people greeted them as
they had when they had first come this way, giving
them food and drink, but the rest stops were not
long. Astekar was eager to clear out and, with as
much speed as possible, meet with the small flotilla
beached on the bleak and stony western shore.
They had seen enough of the river and the dark,
smelly villages full of savage people.

Dagentyr could tell, even in his hiding place, that
it was nearing midday. It became even hotter in the
sack. He was wringing wet. The ache in his stomach
was more acute, gnawing away, making him want
to retch even though he knew there was nothing to
bring up.

As they travelled down the waterway, poling
between the sand bars, choosing the deepest channels they could, he became brave enough to worry a
hole in the bag with his cloak pin, put his eye to the
frayed cloth and peek out. The light hurt his eyes,
but the faint breath of fresh air was sweet.

He was on the edge of the raft next to the water.
An instinctive ripple of fear passed through him.

He tried to draw away. He could see the bank going
by, lined with weeping willow and river grasses.
Twigs and leaves floated along, rolling and swirling
in the eddies and currents. He watched the debris
until the motion made him dizzy, and sick to his
stomach again.

After calling for a halt sometime later, Astekar
swung himself over the side of the raft. Wading to
the shore, he then moved back to inspect the rest of
the boats as they landed. He checked the slaves,
making sure that the women's wrists were not being
cut by the ropes and giving a few halfhearted words
of encouragement and comfort.

He had taken only the best; beautiful women,
and strong young men chosen for the mercenary
companies. They were valuable and a prime concern in these days, with the Ahhiyawa roving up
and down the coast. Each spring saw the calming of
the winter storms, and with the good weather came
the sails of the Ahhiyawa on the horizon. More and
more often they came, and in greater numbers,
even daring to attack the city. His master's latest
folly with the Ahhiyawan woman would bring
trouble on trouble. The city depended in part upon
mercenaries to help dispel the threat, for although
the city was rich, it was small in the face of the
barbarous invasions in the north and the continual
pirating of the Ahhiyawa.

The slaves were given water, and the guards
stopped to eat and take long pulls at the wineskins.
Astekar went from boat to boat, man to man,
checking the ropes and lashings, whistling to himself and addressing the warriors.

"Don't tell me you have sore feet, Melawos.
We're going by boat, not walking." He spoke to a
burly man who sat rubbing his toes.

"It's the god-cursed toes. They swell and itch in
this damp and cursed place. They're as red and raw

as meat. My shoes won't dry out and it seems to make them even worse. This miserable forest doesn't agree with me. I'd rather spend my life at sea and never see land again than be lost in this place waiting for a crop to grow or a calf to drop."

"You've lost sight of the good life. There's security in settling down."

"Bah!"

Astekar laughed and continued on his tour. He gave Dagentyr's raft a friendly kick and motioned for two guards to open the sack. The drawstring was untied, the sack spread, and there was Dagentyr, head poking up through the fur. The light dazzled him and confused him enough to stop his sudden urge to run.

"Ah, warrior. I see you are still with us—hungry, I would imagine." Astekar had food and water brought back for Dagentyr and had the two guards help him out of the sack.

His legs were weak and cramped. The men held him up as he walked shakily off the raft. He did not particularly like the way they grinned at him, or the revelation that they were not the least surprised at his being there.

Astekar went on as he watched Dagentyr eat. "Well, I think we're far enough away for you to come out. There won't be another village for a ways yet. No one will recognize you there, will they?" Dagentyr shook his head. "Good."

The bank was cool and shady. Out in the river, a dead tree stuck its branches up through the surface, and the water gurgled and rushed around them.

With his mouth full of food, Dagentyr tried to speak. "I thank you for this. I am safe because of you. I owe you my life."

"Yes, you do, but we won't talk of that now. I'm sure you'll repay the debt." With that, he gave a quick move of the head in Dagentyr's direction.

The two guards were on him instantly, one at

each arm. A third ran up and put the point of a spear at his belly.

"Melawos," said Astekar. "Release the other one."

The footsore man popped up and went to the raft. There, he found another sack and tugged at the drawstring. Ruki stuck his head out, panting, near collapse. He stayed with his eyes closed, enjoying the ecstasy of fresh air and was startled when he finally saw Dagentyr between the two watermen.

"This one's all right too, a little worn out maybe," Melawos said.

"Good. Tie up his hands and feed him. He'll ride in the raft with me. I think there's room. Take the warrior and bind him with the slaves for now. Show me your hand, warrior." Dagentyr held out his wounded hand. "Is it your sword hand?"

He swallowed the lump of rage in his throat and answered. "Yes."

"We can't have you damaged. Take him to Zaris and tell him to treat the hand. A fighting man who can't pick up a sword isn't much good. You'll be all right, warrior; we'll take good care of you. I saved your life and now you can repay me by coming with us to fight. A fair trade, isn't it? And how fortunate too that the buffoon came my way. Such luck! You see, I got what I wanted in the end. All of it."

"You can't do this to me, trader. I'm a free man. I have a destiny to fulfill in my own place!"

"No more."

"There is a man who must die!"

The guards took him away. There was only time for one move. Summoning everything he had, he threw his arms outward and wrenched himself free. Melawos swung his spear squarely across Dagentyr's kidneys before he had time to break into the undergrowth. Instead of walking to Zaris, he was dragged, coughing and out of wind. A short while later, the boats resumed the voyage, with one addition to the group of carefully picked men and women.

Day went quickly. In his dumbstruck state, Dagentyr sat with the others, not noticing the change in the angle of the sunlight or the approaching chill in the air. The trees went by, one by one, identical to him.

There was nothing to think about, no plans to make. Everything was in the hands of the gods, those whose omen he had ignored and who had repaid him with despair. There was a shadowy apprehension in his mind about what would happen to him, but he was sure that it was like the place he was going, far away and indistinguishable.

Camp was made in an open space beside the water with the smoke of a village sneaking into the darkening sky not far away. Provisions were available there, and protection in case of trouble.

The prisoners were fed again and given cloaks of wool for the night, and a fire around which to sleep. The women were separated from the rest. Their bonds were loosened so as not to mar the skin; Astekar was very careful with his goods. Two guards were posted to watch the men as they sat around the fire. To keep themselves alert and amused, the watermen conversed continuously.

Astekar came by to talk to the prisoners.

"You will all be treated well and win honor in battle. There is opportunity for wealth and for pleasure, and to raise your position. The future that awaits you in Trusya is much more favorable than what waits for you here, especially you, warrior. I have noticed your spark. You have courage. You, and the rest of you"—he indicated the others—"have been given a great chance to be men. Don't feel sorry for yourselves because you leave this land behind. You are warriors, aren't you?" Expecting no reply, he went away.

When he had gone, their bonds were checked for the night. Lying on his side, Dagentyr listened to the babble of the guards. Some words every now and then seemed understandable, and a phrase here and there, but the effort it took to try and keep up with the conversation was too much. He abandoned the attempt. Even if he had wished to talk to the slaves, they would have given him no answer. They regarded him as an outsider. The ragtag men looked at him sideways and were glad of his misfortune.

"You're the one they were looking for, aren't you?" Someone lying next to him asked the question. He was young, scarcely approaching the threshold of manhood. Dagentyr thought he looked familiar and noticed that his hands were not bound.

"What difference does it make?"

"None. The night is long. I asked merely to talk. I'm tired of listening to these two." He was a sandy-haired youth with blue eyes that twinkled with obstinate determination. "If you wish to dwell on troubles rather than talk, it makes no difference to me. It sounds as though we'll be in each other's company for a long time. It would be a bore to spend it all in silence. I'd be happy if I were you. I'd rather win honor in strange foreign lands than watch over Clavosius's cattle all day."

"You know Clavosius? You are of the village, then?"

"Not really. I am from the east. My father is important in our tribe. I was sent to learn to be a man in your village. An exchange of sons, for friendship."

"Listen, eastern boy. It's easy to dismiss someone else's problems and prattle on like an old woman, wise in the workings of the world. Save your wisdom and wind for someone else. Tomorrow will be even longer than tonight, so why don't you rest and leave me alone."

The other men chuckled.

The boy blushed at the rebuff but talked on.

"You've had enough adventure in the last day to last a while." Dagentyr smiled in spite of himself. A man's disaster was a boy's adventure. Why not talk of it? The stranger's tone was not unfriendly.

"So it seems. And who are you?"

"I am Bolgios, until recently shield bearer to Clavosius."

"Ah. That's where I've seen you, then."

"And you are Dagentyr."

"Dagentyr, son of Ashak, warrior to Clavosius." He noticed the snide expressions appear on the others' faces. "Until recently."

Bolgios spat distastefully. "Clavosius is no longer my chieftain. I am my own man."

"He let you go?"

He shook his head excitedly. "I came on my own. Clavosius never noticed me before, he will not miss me now. The trader convinced me to come."

Dagentyr nodded knowingly. "I have been convinced, too."

"How exciting it must have been."

"Not very exciting to be hunted like an animal and then betrayed into this. You're addled in the head if that's your idea of excitement."

The guards mimed for him to be quiet. Bolgios lapsed into silence and Dagentyr was grateful for the break-off. Testing his bonds, he found them tight. He looked again at Bolgios twiddling his thumbs.

"Bolgios," he whispered. "Your hands are free. Help me. When everyone is asleep, roll next to me, as you would by accident. It might be possible to untie me without the guards noticing. Give me the chance to get away."

Suddenly he was hesitant and unsure. "I don't think I can."

"What do you mean? You must try."

"They would punish me, wouldn't they?"

"How do I know what the foreign ways are? Do it."

"I can't!"

"Not so loud."

The guards had noticed something odd in the conversation or their behavior. One of them wrinkled up his face in deep thought and then went for Astekar. The trader came to where they were lying.

"I see. You're right. Tie this one up, too. We wouldn't want you to change your mind about going, boy, or the warrior's, either."

Escape was hopeless. Even if he should somehow get free, the others would give him away. They would hate to see their justice undone.

"I'm sorry, Dagentyr," whispered Bolgios.

Eventually the sentries ran out of talk, and everything became hushed in the darkness. He tried to sleep, but could not. All night long his head ached with all that had transpired. When he had relived his past three days a thousand times, he thought of escape, formulating endless plans. Beside him, Bolgios snored contentedly under his blanket while Dagentyr watched the guards change watches once, twice, and saw the day replacing the night.

Chapter 11

It was not his desperate situation that made the time go on forever; it was the monotony, the sameness of each day, the stomping around the fire and the rubbing of numb feet each morning as the ropes were undone, the days of travel on the river broken only by stopovers in villages that were all beginning to wear an oppressive air of familiarity. Like a recurring nightmare whose action was always the same but whose setting changed subtly with each dreaming, the days began to pile up, and Dagentyr felt the weight of them. He had been gone from Fottengra for many days, yet he could not pick any day from the rest and say that there was anything about it that distinguished it from any other on the journey. Only that first day of flight stayed separate in his mind. Come what may at the edge of the great water, he was ready for it.

If he was right in his thinking, then Bolgios had asked him yesterday if he knew where they were bound after they reached the big water, but the youth had asked so many questions, Dagentyr could not be sure that he had not asked that particular one days ago. He had snapped back a vague answer about stone walls as high as trees and fallen into an irritable silence.

He was speaking more to Bolgios these days. At the start of the journey he had felt different, apart. When speaking to the group, Astekar had always saved some remark especially for him—"Don't worry, warrior. Think of the evil fate you left behind." Now he was lumped with the rest, no special words were reserved for him. The other men only grunted in monosyllables when he spoke to them. Bolgios was the friendliest. During days when the only different thing was who he was put next to in the raft, he began to look forward to the times it was Bolgios; then there was talk. Gods, how far had he fallen, actually looking forward to boyish drivel? But there was nothing he could do. He either got Bolgios's outpouring or the cold silence of the others. To keep his sanity and keep himself from brooding, he chose the first.

Ruki was seldom seen. He always rode on the lead raft with Astekar, who had already begun to train him in the lore and ways of Trusya. Dagentyr considered Ruki much better off than himself, being able to spend the days in drill and practice that kept boredom away.

It had begun to rain. The slaves sat with their capes and blankets pulled over their heads to shed the lazy drops. Dagentyr, who usually despised the rain, was pleased; it was a change.

The forests had thinned out into grassy fields and plains. Yesterday and today the air had gotten heavier and wet. A tangy smell of salt came on the breezes that always blew east. The river opened up, became broader. Astekar ordered the rafts along with impatience.

The rain stopped as the voyagers landed. After the rafts were unloaded, they went on foot over a series of small, sandy hillocks. Then there were tiny fields where new shoots were just sprouting up through the sickly soil. Heads turned, and the men and women at work in the fields ran to speed news of their arrival, while others came to speak greetings to them.

Not again, Dagentyr thought. The scene was familiar, old. Every other day, they camped on the edge of some farmstead, and it was always the same. A group of goats ran bleating through their ranks, and a laughing boy with a fur thrown over his shoulders chased them with a stick.

He was at the end of the line with Bolgios, and together they heard exclamations of surprise and awe that came from the women at the head of the file as they reached the top of the next rise. The others, in an anxious rush to see whatever it was, pushed forward. Dagentyr was dragged along, fighting to keep his balance. As they mounted the crest, there it was.

"It's incredible, Dagentyr! I've never seen anything like it," Bolgios said, sighing.

Dagentyr's heart was beating faster, and he turned his head from left to right and back again, mouth agape, cowed and dumbfounded. As far as he could see, to the clouded and ominous horizon, there was only water. The sun sent brilliant rays through the breaks in the clouds to shimmer on the rippled surface that extended, it seemed, to the limits of the earth. Directly in front of him, the hill sloped down to a marshy and rocky shore where the waves lapped up over grey sand. The sounds of the breakers and the gulls were crisp in the pure air. Down below, he saw Ruki staring in amazement. The captured warriors began to talk excitedly to each other.

The train turned and followed the shore. Ahead were the huts of a shoreside village, hiding among rocks and mountainous piles of discarded shells and fish bones. It was uninteresting. The big water held their gaze, and they stumbled along, unable to

take their eyes off it, not caring that they stubbed
and bruised their feet on the stones or lost their
footing in the deep sand.

When they finally reached the village, they were
shocked again, for pulled up on the beach, near the
huts, were the ships of the watermen. They were big
and dark, rising at prow and stern, fitted with a
single mast midway on the deck. A small, hide-
covered enclosure shaded each stern. They dwarfed
the river rafts they had just left and instilled fear
and apprehension about the journey to come.

Dagentyr clicked his tongue at sight of the ships.
"Look, Bolgios, that pole at the center. I've heard
that on the big water, men use the wind to make the
boats go, with huge pieces of cloth on trees."

Up from the boats were tents like the ones the
watermen had pitched at Fottengra, and one, set
apart from the rest, was colored dull red. The
watermen's camp was large, and there were men
everywhere, tending to the boats, polishing weapons, cursing the rain-doused campfires.

At the edge of the village, Astekar halted. The
curious people gathered as always, eyeing the captives, giving refreshment to the guards and traders.
The headman of the village stepped forward and
took Astekar's hand in welcome, then joined his
people again to stare at the slaves and heaps of
goods.

A group of girls with necklaces of shell tittered.
Dagentyr gave them a fierce scowl that only made
them giggle harder, and point. He noticed that the
guards and traders were instantly at ease, pleased to
be at the end of one journey, back near the boats
and the sea that were home to them. They breathed
deeply, loving the sea air, and smiled at the female
slaves and village girls with renewed interest.

Astekar gave orders to disperse and settle everything in, then walked to the crimson tent. Before he
got there, the flaps were thrown aside, and a young
man stepped out. A servant came with him holding

a basin and a razor. At his appearance, the guards brought their spears to salute.

Seeing the man, Astekar approached. Though his shrewder self always advised distance in his dealings with the prince, he could not escape the old feelings of affection. Surrendering to them, he bowed his head deferentially.

The man wiped his face with a cloth, and spoke. "Astekar, my old friend! I thought you'd never return and I'd have to spend the rest of my life on this disgusting little stretch of sand, for by the gods, I couldn't sail without you. I'd be lost without your counsel."

"My lord Parush does me honor. Truly, I am glad to see you again."

Astekar bowed somewhat formally, and then they both laughed and embraced. The prince was young, with a head of long brown hair falling loose over his shoulders and back, and fine carved features. He was not overly tall, but even so stood taller than Astekar. His kilt was blue and his upper arm was encircled by a band of gold. He gave the cloth to the servant, and patting Astekar on the back, approached the dispersing trading party.

"I see the trip has been successful. I wish now I'd gone with you, no excitement here. I know every woman's face in this village by heart, and all those for several leagues up and down the coast. I swear if I eat another shellfish, it will poison me."

"You should have come, my lord. Was that not the purpose of this voyage, adventure? We are, after all, the first men of Trusya to venture outside the Pillars." With a swaggering stride, Parush went to the captive women and drew aside their hoods, one by one, pursing his lips and nodding in approval. "Feel free, my lord, to examine them all," cooed Astekar. "I try as much as I can to copy your taste in these matters though I lack my lord's discriminating eye for the fine points."

Parush was amused. "Not such a discriminating

eye when it comes to a woman's heart, eh? Oh, I pick a pretty face or a pleasing mouth better than most, but I couldn't choose a beautiful soul if the kingdom depended on it." He ran his finger down one girl's cheek and raised her face with his hand under her chin. "You do well, Astekar, very well." Turning to the male slaves and cargo, he said, "I trust that everything else was chosen with the same care, and concern for a good bargain?"

Astekar drew himself up with mock dignity. "My lord puts up with me because I do my job well. I get the best for the least and I can turn a profit anywhere, Knossus, Alasiya, or here on the fringes of the earth."

"That you can. Come, I'll inspect all this later. It can wait. We must talk and drink. Oh, Astekar." He pulled the little man aside and spoke confidentially. "The girl, third from the end. Tell Vilarimon to have her cleaned up, robed, and sent to me at dinner. And pull a couple of the males out for some competition with our men. It will be good for them to fight, release the tension, drive away the monotony. We'll give them a celebration. Pick the savages you think will do best. Give extra wine to all the men, and starting tomorrow, pack the goods into the ships. This place begins to depress me. I'm eager to be home. Now that you are back, there is nothing to stop us from leaving."

"Are we not to have a few days' rest at least?"

"No. Now that you are here, I want no delays."

"It will be as you say," he mumbled tiredly. "I have a surprise for my lord which it will be my pleasure to give to you tonight as you dine."

"Excellent. I am in need of surprise."

The servant held aside the flap, and they disappeared within the tent.

Dagentyr understood none of the conversation but guessed from Parush's whispered words and the look in his eye where the pretty, blond-haired girl would be tonight. He tried to size up the man he had just seen. Pampered, egotistical, wealthy, these he was sure of, but he could tell no more. He reserved judgment for later and took the meeting in stride, as he had learned on the journey.

The leader of the guard pushed them on, speaking gibberish. He had forgotten they could not understand him and became exasperated when they returned his orders with blank stares. He fell into a ridiculous and lewd pantomime indicating who should go where.

Bolgios laughed, unable to help himself.

The guard slapped him across the face. Bolgios was stunned. The others mumbled their dislike of the guard.

"Enjoy the adventure," Dagentyr said to him as they were marched away.

The camp was a busy place even at night. Preparations were being made by torchlight for the starting of loading on the morrow. The ships were made ready to take on cargo and loomed up menacingly like wooden beasts in the wavering aura of the driftwood fires. In celebration of the caravan's return, goats were killed and roasted whole. The salty air enhanced the aroma of the cooking meat, making the familiar seem rare and exotic. Extra wine was given to all, and the sailors sang happy songs as they toiled on the boats.

The slaves were put under a windbreak that took the edge from the cool air blowing from the sea. They were all fed well, given extra cloaks, and wine. The drink brought back foul memories for Dagentyr, so he drank little. Bolgios recovered from his humiliation with characteristic verve and was as good-natured and outgoing as ever.

The other men were loosening up with the good food, and wine, and the security that came with ending a difficult leg of their journey. Everyone gave thanks to the gods for surviving the trip and considered that things might not have turned out so badly after all. Their treatment was good, and from the appearance of the water prince and the wondrous ships, there was gold, wealth, and power to be had in this land across the sea.

After the meal, while the dogs picked at the remains of the goat carcasses, and the watermen sat sated and belching round the fires, Astekar and the leader of the guard came to the windbreak. The trader looked the group over and picked his teeth with a fish bone.

"Well, I don't know. What do you think, Tuwasis? The one with the long moustache looks healthy, and the one in the back, blue-eyes there, what do you think of him?" Not waiting for an answer, he switched to the language of the tribes. "You. Do you know how to use a sword?"

The man nodded eagerly. "As good as any man, better!"

"Good. And you, droopy-whiskers, how about you? What's your weapon?"

"I know the axe best."

"Interesting. You two stand up. Now a third."

The guard interrupted. "I think the young one here in front might do well." He pointed an antagonistic finger at Bolgios.

"The boy? He's young, inexperienced. What could he do?"

"He should start to fight now. There will be no favoritism in Trusya. It might do him good to be put in his place."

Astekar was unconvinced. "I don't know. Maybe the warrior here instead."

"No, his hand, might injure it again. I'll tell his match to go easy with the youth, bruise him up, no more. I tell you what; I'll fight him myself."

Astekar sighed. "I think I see. Can you fight, boy?"

With unnecessary bravado he replied, "Of course. I am Bolgios. I am feared in the lands of my people, and the heads I have severed are as numerous as the stars."

Astekar looked bored.

Dagentyr spoke up. "He is a shield bearer. I am a warrior. I use a sword well. I know how to fight."

"I picked this one well, Tuwasis. Luck was with me."

"I can fight!" Bolgios tried to stand. "Let me fight. I'll show you."

Astekar shook his head. "No. I'll—"

"Give the boy a chance. A few knocks on the head won't hurt him." Tuwasis spoke reassuringly.

Astekar looked at the bandage still wrapped around Dagentyr's hand and relented. "Very well. Give him a sword then, and make sure he knows which end to hold. Find an axe for the whiskered one. Bring the others along. They might enjoy this, too."

They left, and other guards came and escorted them to the largest of the campfires. Around it, grouped in a circle, was the entire population of the camp and more than a few of the village men and girls. The listlessness of the repast had been replaced by eagerness for the fight. Once again passing around the wineskins, the watermen were rowdy and loud.

Inside the boundaries of the circle were Bolgios and the other two captives, untied and armed. On the other side of the bonfire were two watermen stripped to their kilts. Dagentyr met Bolgios's eyes for a moment, shrugged, and sat down with the others as he was instructed. From the doorway of the scarlet tent, Astekar and Parush watched. The prince kept one hand on the waist of the frightened girl and the other around a silver goblet.

Tuwasis shouted for quiet. "We're going to see if my lord Astekar has been lucky in his dealings! Amnas will fight the blue-eyed savage first!"

A cheer went up for Amnas, a dark, wiry man,

and Dagentyr saw the crowd hold up fingers and argue among themselves, wagering on their favorites, yelling encouragement. "Show him who's best, Amnas! He won't look so good with only one blue eye instead of two!"

Tuwasis called them to the center. "All right. No kills, remember that." He poked the savage with his finger for emphasis. "Are you ready?"

"This is only for sport, barbarian!" called Astekar.

Tuwasis jumped back and crouched on his haunches. The swords met with a crash. The two men circled, each sizing up his foe. The waterman jabbed several times and then lunged in deep. Blue-eyes sidestepped and swung, the blade cutting the air with a slither. He then tried a lunge of his own which Amnas parried, then they were clenched together. In a spray of sand they fell to the ground, wrestling, rolling over and over. The savage got his feet into the other's stomach and pushed him away so that he went sprawling, and all at once they were both on their feet again, cutting and thrusting viciously.

Through the murmurs and cheering of the crowd came the grunts of the combatants and the striking of the swords. The waterman was obviously disappointed that the contest was not as easy as he thought it would be. His self-confident air had vanished and was replaced by caution and determination.

Amnas crouched as if to lunge again and instead swung his foot up and sent a cloud of sand into Blue-eyes's face, making him stagger back, hands to his eyes.

Amnas hooked his foot under the dazed man's calf and tripped him to his knees, swinging the hilt of the sword into his head. The pommel hit with a thud, and Blue-eyes fell back unconscious.

"Well done, Amnas," they cried with relief, not

having expected the savage to put up such a good fight. The relief showed in Amnas's eyes too, and he raised his hands in the air to acknowledge the cheers. Astekar clapped his hands together, more for the loser, Dagentyr thought, realizing the man was a good fighter, worth the price. Wagers were collected, and Tuwasis brought the next two into the circle.

The second contest was different, sword against axe. About his ability with the axe, the moustachioed one had been humble. He used it well, but it was not enough. After a few moments the eventual outcome was obvious to all.

The axe was knocked from his hand with a blow to the wrist and he collapsed with the pain. The waterman planted his foot in his rival's chest and shoved him back onto the ground like a helpless turtle. With a mighty swing he brought the sword down, burying it in the sand next to the fallen man's ear.

The watermen whooped and cheered. Tribesmen shook their heads and pulled their beards in dismay. Tuwasis was laughing, and the loser was helped away.

"Come on, Tuwasis! It's up to you to make it three for us!" The crowd was ready.

Tuwasis grinned broadly and stripped off his cloak. He was the largest of the three watermen. He pulled his own sword and beckoned for Bolgios to step up.

"Now's the time, little one. We'll see how you laugh now, won't we?"

Bolgios stepped forward, not comprehending the man's words. Dagentyr guessed their meaning by the tone the guard used. The youth licked his lips and took what he thought was a fighting stance. His mouth was dry and droplets of sweat speckled his forehead.

The men laughed at the ridiculous position he

had taken, and the sound of their mirth emboldened Tuwasis to attack. He rushed forward, screaming maniacally.

Bolgios stumbled back in shock and nearly fell. Tuwasis came off his guard and chuckled, shrugging at the spectators. Breathing heavily, Bolgios stood there, not knowing what to expect.

"Let's get down to it, little one," growled Tuwasis.

Bolgios held the sword in front of him, and the guard gave him a slap across the forearm with the flat of his blade. The sword dropped from Bolgios's hand and his eyes widened with horror. He looked at his arm, and seeing that it was all right, backed away from Tuwasis, around the fire. The waterman followed, taking stabs now and then that kept the boy retreating steadily. They were approaching the side of the fire where Dagentyr sat watching.

Tuwasis feinted and plowed straight ahead, knocking Bolgios down with his shoulder. Kneeling over him, the burly leader of the guard struck a sideways blow across Bolgios's nose with his fist, then crowned him atop the head with the pommel of his sword. Tears came into the boy's eyes. Blood ran between his fingers as he clutched at his nose, then he scampered backward on all fours like a crab, desperate to get away.

Dagentyr waited. Bolgios was nearly at his feet. Tuwasis followed him hunched over, brandishing the point of the blade in front of the boy's eyes.

The waterman was almost near enough. He took another step; Dagentyr kicked out a foot and swung it as hard as he could at Tuwasis's ankle. The big man's leg buckled and he fell. Dagentyr struggled to his feet, hands still tied, and before Tuwasis recovered, gave him a sharp kick in the rib cage.

"Not fair!" they all cried. "Show him, Tuwasis. Get up and really show him. Unfair!"

Dagentyr stepped away from the man as he got to his feet.

"You whoreson. I'm going to take your ears off and feed them to the pigs," rasped the waterman. He mimed the action viciously.

"Watch out, Dagentyr!" Bolgios yelled in a thick, nasal tone.

Tuwasis lunged, and Dagentyr hopped away and held his hands up in front of him, the leather cords still tight. Setting himself solidly, legs apart, he confronted Tuwasis, held his gaze unrelentingly.

The guard stopped, lowered his sword, and hesitated. Suddenly, he lifted the weapon high, gritted his teeth, and brought it down between Dagentyr's wrists. Bolgios gasped and covered his eyes. Astekar had started to shout but breathed easy now; the cool facade returned. The leather cord, cut cleanly, fell away in the middle, and Dagentyr unwound it, and the bandage, and rubbed his wrists.

"Amnas! Pick up the other sword and throw it to the barbarian." The others were surprised. "Do as I say!"

Dagentyr caught it handily. He flexed his hand a couple of times and then wrapped his fingers around the handle. For the first time, he was glad for the long journey that had given the hand good opportunity to heal. Though the hand was stiff, the feel of a sword was stimulating.

"I'm still going to take your ears, bumpkin," said Tuwasis.

There was a murmur in the ranks of the barbarians, and the men who had refused to talk to him on the trip began to call encouragement, not loudly but audibly. The watermen noticed and cheered louder to drown it out. Village men whispered to each other and cheered for the eastern tribesman to put the overbearing foreigner in his place. The egotism and haughtiness of the watermen had annoyed them these past months; they were eager for satisfaction.

Tuwasis sank into a crouch. They circled, looking for weakness. The guard's breathing came painfully. Dagentyr felt elation. After the weeks of boredom he was alive again and keen. Tuwasis made a thrust, recovered, and aimed a downward cut at Dagentyr's shoulder. Dagentyr blocked and the sword rang in his hand. Immediately recoiling from the blow, he slashed at his opponent's face. It was enough to move the guard back, put him on the defensive.

Dagentyr was quick, cutting again and again, then he faked for the shoulder. Wrenching his body sideways to avoid the stab, Tuwasis exposed his torso. Dagentyr swung and opened a gash from armpit to nipple.

The waterman began to lose his composure. Grabbing the wound, he smeared bloody hand prints down his midriff.

Not letting up, Dagentyr pushed in again. His cuts were blocked, but more weakly. He could feel his advantage.

Tuwasis slashed high to put Dagentyr's blade up for the block, then he swung low, missed, and carried his arm too far across. Dagentyr kicked him in the stomach. He fell clutching it with his free hand.

"Get up, big man. Stand up and show us what you can do now. Come get my ears."

He stood slowly, stunned. He could understand Dagentyr no better than Dagentyr understood him, but the phrase, uttered with its guttural sounds through clenched teeth, was heavy with meaning. He tried to swallow and found he couldn't.

Dagentyr lunged. Speed was the key. He slashed crossways, opening his chest on purpose for Tuwasis's thrust. It came. He ducked under the

extended arm, driving his elbow into the sore ribs.
It knocked the wind from Tuwasis, and he went
down. His weapon dropped to the ground. Shoving
it aside with his foot, Dagentyr grabbed him roughly under the arm and dragged him facedown
through the sand to where Bolgios was. He threw
the guard over on his back, put his foot to his
throat, and tossed the sword to Bolgios.

"Take his ears." Bolgios was slow to react and
just stared at Dagentyr. "Come over here and cut
his ears off!"

Bolgios took the sword, and keeping one hand to
his dripping nose, stood over Tuwasis and let the
blade fall next to his head so he could feel the cold
metal on his skin.

"Cut them off! Do it!"

"No! Stop him. I yield. Get him away. By
Teshub, I yield," Tuwasis shouted hoarsely.

Dagentyr turned to Astekar. "Does he say that he
surrenders? If so, tell him to yield to Bolgios."

"Tuwasis! He wants you to yield to the boy!"

There was silence. Dagentyr nodded for Bolgios
to go ahead. "Yes! Very well, I yield to the boy!"

"He has done it, warrior."

Dagentyr grabbed Bolgios's wrist, took the sword
and threw it aside. He removed his foot from the
waterman's throat and walked away to his place. A
feeling of power grew inside him. He was triumphant, almost happy. For an instant despair was
obscured. He imagined Tuwasis as Vorgus and
imagined he had won.

The tribesmen cheered unrestrainedly. Parush
applauded in the doorway. "Well done, Astekar.
You outdid yourself in your choices. He's very
good, brave, has spirit."

"Yes, he has. He should do well."

"Marvelous. I should try him myself sometime."

"You'd give him a better turn than Tuwasis, I'm
sure, my lord," he said, knowing that the prince

would be short work for Dagentyr. "He's the best bargain of the lot. I must tell you how I got him. It was a night of pure luck. And now, there's a slave I would like to present to you for other amusement, another bargain as good as the warrior, a sweet singer of songs." He motioned for Parush and the girl to go back in the tent and snapped his fingers. From the darkness, a guard pushed Ruki into the light. He was garbed in a tunic of soft green and wore a circlet of silver around his hurriedly combed and perfumed hair. "Come in, slave. It's time to sing for your supper and impress my lord with your training so far."

Chapter 12

Parush fell back heavily against the cushions and let his empty goblet tip downward in his relaxed hand. "She drove me to it, that Ahhiyawan bitch. Did you know that? Drove me out here to this gravelly stretch of beach and these filthy, unwashed barbarians, away from my own home. I shouldn't have let her do it, but I had to get away. I couldn't stand her anymore."

The great amount of wine he had drunk gave energy to his tongue. Across from him, the older man who had heard it all before nodded sympathetically.

"She told me I'm boring." The prince's eyes became soft for a moment, then a new thought revived them to anger. "I wasn't boring at the banquet in Spartusha, no, not then. I was genuinely witty and it wasn't the wine in me. I didn't drink much; I would have been shamed to be drunk in front of a woman so beautiful and regal. I wasn't boring when I went to her chambers that night in secret. She whispered in my ear how brave I was as I led her away to the boat, and she let ringlets of hair brush my bare shoulder as we stood on the deck. I showed her the landmarks of the coast and pointed the directions to Knossus and Mykunai."

He stopped and raked his fingers through the golden hair of the wide-eyed and nervous girl who sat next to him in a pink gown edged with designs in tiny silver beads. A decorated bronze pin held the folds of the gown together at her shoulder. He gave its dangling pendants a tap with his finger. She blushed and lowered her head. "Does this girl understand anything I say, Astekar?"

"No, my lord, I doubt that she does. Perhaps she is receptive to the tone of what you say and catches the bitterness of your words."

"All women should be so sensitive. She's a pretty one. Look at her hair. See how it glints in the lamplight like the border of her robe." Astekar nodded silent assent. "I should have taken this one instead. She has a heart. The Lady Helani would be envious of her. A slave, yes, but on the verge of new things, new sights. Adventure, she would call it. Trusya is like an old rug or sandal now, boring, in need of changing. I am in need of changing. Bitch. She even stops being regal once she's got what she wants."

His brown forelocks hung damp against his forehead. "I know my trouble, Astekar, though you think I don't. In spite of everything, I see her as I did on that warm night in Spartusha, a cool river in the midst of all those steaming men talking so loudly. I could just pick up the slight hint of her scent over the fragrance of the wine. Oh, Astekar, what a bearing she had, what an air! I saw her like a polished jewel, unfit for that boorish husband of hers. She didn't know my language and I knew little of hers, but still, in that hall, she was speaking to me." He gave a great, relaxed sigh, and the goblet clattered to the floor. "I was younger then, and stupid."

Astekar filled his own cup and handed it to the prince. "My lord mustn't consider the journey a waste. Tedious perhaps, but profitable. Didn't you yourself say that you wanted to go so far away that you wouldn't hear her nag—forgive me if I speak too bluntly—farther than any boats of Trusya had gone before, out past the Pillars? Well, we are here and the richer for it, richer in goods, in lore, richer as men."

"Riches." Parush grunted. "Is that all you think about?" He drank the cup dry and belched. Astekar did not answer, but sat back on his cushion thoughtfully. "It's spring already. We're far north. It's fair sailing weather inside the Pillars. Perhaps I was foolish to leave Trusya." Astekar poured more wine for him. "That ass Mensalakus will be up and kicking again. His brother will use the woman as an excuse, just as he has in years past, to stir his southern Ahhiyawan cousins into their pirating ways.

"She thinks it's all because of her. As the Ahhiyawa were drawing into formation outside the city the last time they raided, I caught her going up to the battlements. When I asked her what she was doing, she told me she was going to show herself so that the Ahhiyawan host would see her and be inspired to greatness." He smiled. "Do you know what I told her? I told her that if she set one foot on the ramparts I'd have her disfigured. Then she looked at me with fear, and with hate, more hate than I've seen in any man's eyes. That's when I had to set the guard around her. She's glad to have them now with the people against her."

It was the same story. Astekar interlaced his fingers and studied the face of the prince, the man who had been carefree not too long ago, unburdened except by the foolishness of youth until he had met the she-jackal. Now he was the perpetually sad man whose good-natured facade melted with the wine. Astekar suspected her of being a witch. He had travelled wide, heard and seen many strange things. He did not doubt for an instant the

existence of witches, and marvelled at what a
powerful sorceress she must be who could torment
a man even as he sat with a beautiful woman at the
edge of the world.

"My brother will be at the head of our men,
screaming at the top of his lungs, causing the
pirates to tremble. I swear to you, Astekar, I'll kill
the first Ahhiyawan I see. I swear . . . to redeem
myself." Parush emptied the cup. Astekar refilled it
yet again, and the prince continued. "Am I missed,
Astekar? Put aside your thoughts of riches and tell
me if I am missed in my homeland, or should I stay
here and spend the rest of my days with this
golden-haired creature." He leaned toward the girl
and kissed her. She drew back as much as she dared
but allowed him to press his lips against hers. "I
have been a fool. I lose honor here. My place is at
home. What will the people think? What will
Helani think?"

Ruki watched from his place behind Astekar. He
stood, holding his lyre, in the dim edge of the circle
of lamplight. He had stood for the whole meal
watching the prince eat, and flirt with the girl. The
joking and bravado had faded when the intake of
wine exceeded that of food. Slowly, he seemed to
pay less attention to the girl and rambled at length,
slumping lower and lower. He was not happy, or so
it seemed to Ruki. The prince frightened him.
Outwardly he fought to stay calm, but inside, his
stomach was stone. What must it be like for the
poor girl, he wondered.

"My lord is melancholy because of the wine and
the sound of the sea. Think of the triumphant entry
we will have when we return. They will say, what a
brave adventurer Prince Parush is. He is back from
beyond the Pillars with wonderful things and glorious tales. It will make even the Lady Helani take
notice and be intrigued."

"You're trying to revive me. I thank you for that,

but I am hopeless." His speech was becoming muddled. His blue robe was wrinkled, and stained under the armpits.

Ruki thought the tent a little close.

"The only thing that would make the Lady Helani take notice would be my failure to return. Then she would entrance some other lout over dinner and be off to Aigypta, or Hattus, or somewhere . . . away. Where's the wine?"

"Doesn't my lord think he has drunk enough?"

"No, not nearly enough. Fill my cup."

He obeyed, and the prince took another long drink, then offered the cup to the girl. "Wouldn't you like some, girl? It's sweet and cool, the last of what we brought from home. I'll bet you've never even tasted it." She raised her eyes briefly and gave a shy shake of the head. "Look, Astekar. See how the light changes on her hair as she moves. You can see the little lamp flames reflected in her eyes. Look, when I tilt her head up like this. Blue eyes. You don't find those at home."

"No, my lord."

"Astekar, I—" For a moment he seemed to brighten, faced by the girl's beauty, but it was a short-lived interest. He stared mutely at her and shook his head. "Take this girl away. She is very pretty, and it makes me lonely. In any case, I am too drunk for love. Wait." Taking the cup, he emptied it on the floor. It was silver, worked all over in delicate flowers. He took her hand and wound her fingers around it. "Take this and keep it. Do not let the guards take it away from you. Astekar, she is to have this. Make sure the men know. I'll order a beating for anyone who tries to take it."

Astekar muttered, "As you wish," and clapped his hands. Instantly a guard appeared to take the girl.

As she left, she raised her head and looked

directly at the prince for the first time during the evening. Her expression was unsure but kind. It was the only show of gratitude that she could manage.

Parush did not notice. Already, he had forgotten about her. His gift had been enough to drive her from his mind. He sat with his head on his palm, staring at the ground.

A snap of Astekar's fingers brought Ruki back to his own problems, and he shuffled up beside the trader's seat. The fine cloth of his new tunic rubbed pleasingly against his legs. Perfume in his hair formed a sweet-smelling cloud around his head. His clean-shaven skin tingled. In a sudden rush of fear, he went over in his mind the words to the songs he had been taught. What if he forgot? Would he be beaten, killed? The noise of Astekar clearing his throat distracted him. He went to the beginning and started over.

"My lord is in need of cheering. It was with this in mind that I brought this man. He is good at reviving one's spirits and invoking the god of mirth."

Mirth. Ruki recognized the word, discarded the song he had been rehearsing, and fumbled in his brain for one of the bawdy tunes learned on the journey.

"Ruki is his barbarian name, though it is up to my lord to call him anything he pleases. He is yours. Ask a song of him, my lord, of laughter and gaiety," he coaxed, hoping that the skinny little man would remember his teaching well, well enough to drag Parush from the grasp of the spell-casting Ahhiyawan tart.

"Laughter? I want none of it. You taught him some obscene, beachside song, didn't you, to make a common sailor laugh? It doesn't go well with the lonely wine I'm drinking tonight." Parush watched

Ruki for a moment and raised his eyebrows. "What is wrong with him?"

"Only the gods know, my lord. It's part of his charm; it makes him more interesting. Let me—"

"No."

"You do not desire a song tonight?"

"No. Yes, yes I mean, but a song of love . . . Tell him to sing a song gently, sweetly. That's what I want, a song to fit my mood."

"He is not suited to sweet songs. He is a buffoon."

"I have said what I want! I am master here. I'll not be defied in my own tent. The gods have given me enough of that elsewhere." He turned directly to Ruki. "Sing a love song!"

"Sing a love song for the prince," Astekar translated. "And sing it well." He put a hand in the small of Ruki's back and pushed him closer to the prince. He was obviously disappointed.

Ruki lifted his lyre, and after another remark of forceful encouragement from the trader, he closed his eyes and strummed a clumsy, dissonant chord.

> "Oh, pluck a merry string for me, Ishtar.
> Let fly a shining bird.
> Take to her in a golden vessel
> the fire from my heart.
> It burns too much for me alone.
> Tell her these things I ask of you.
> Breathe for me a wind
> that whispers in the leaves
> and lifts the dark hair
> from a fair and lovely neck.
> Touch her once for me.
> Touch her once for me."

With each phrase, his uncontrolled hand struck another ghastly succession of notes. He kept his voice low to keep from wailing like a dog. He was not quite sure what he sang. Astekar had taught him the words and notes by rote, paying special attention to the proper sounds. "Say the words correctly! Gods witness you're hard enough to understand as it is without that barbaric accent." He had practiced, but now he was so nervous that he lost all thought to inflection and concentrated on not forgetting the words.

As he tweaked the last note, he pressed his eyelids even tighter and waited for a long time. Astekar's breathing was all he could hear, and the rush of the waves on the sand. Was there more to remember? He didn't think so; he had sung it all.

"It's from the land of the Sidonese, my lord. I heard it once and taught it to this man, knowing you might need a song like it one day. You know well that I am never unprepared."

Ruki opened his eyes.

"I see it has done its best for you."

Astekar got no answer. He sat there a moment longer watching the prince snore quietly on his pillows, then put a coverlet across the prince and opened the tent flap.

Curiosity made Ruki speak. "Did I sing it well?"

Astekar sighed, and took the lyre. The prince stirred and settled back again. Saying nothing, the trader scratched his head, gestured for the guard to take charge of the slave, and walked away.

Chapter 13

Turning his head so that his cheek rested on the salt-slimy rail, Dagentyr heaved his guts up into the sea. It was bad with his eyes closed, like being tossed around in a cave, but worse with them open. Then he could see the rigging ropes swaying against the sky, the sail full of wind, the black, foam-tipped waves sliding rapidly past the hull. The men were blurs of motion as they saw to the chores of the ship. Everything together was a dizzying chaos that made him so sick that he fell backward to the deck. With each slap of the hull against the water, he gave a nauseated groan. Next to him, Bolgios kept his bound hands over his mouth and watched through puffy eyes; his nose and face had swollen badly.

Dagentyr felt a slight and sudden pressure on his chest. He took a sharp, startled gasp that only half filled his lungs. The strange animal had jumped up on him and stood poised on its four delicate paws, sniffing at his face. Its long, foxlike whiskers dragged ticklishly across his brow. He held his breath and waited with faint dread for the beast to go away.

It shifted a soft foot and peered at him with yellow eyes, eyes that were wrong it suddenly occurred to him as he met them at close range. The pupils were not round like a dog's, but long, slitted like two evil crescent moons. Sweeping back and forth against the sky, its tail darted with a serpentine life of its own. A warm, pink paw pressed his bare skin.

Away! he thought. Puckering his lips, he blew a sharp breath into the animal's face. It squinted its eyes almost shut, pulled its ears down flat against its head, and raised high on its feet, curving its back like a taut bow. It blew its breath out with a rushing hiss, and the furred muzzle drew back over sharp teeth. Beneath the weight of each paw he could feel tiny pricks of pain as if, somehow, the beast had become instantly clawed.

Dagentyr turned over on his side, and the bow snapped straight. The beast, its resting place up-ended, leapt soundlessly back to the deck in a slow, graceful arc. It looked over its shoulder at him with a face that expressed more contempt than an ordinary animal's should have, and went its smooth way along the deck, tail whipping violently, warning others to stay away.

He breathed with relief, and the sailors laughed. A dark, hairy man knelt on the deck and called softly, holding out a fish head.

"Come, Sekhmet." The animal butted its head against him, took the head and ran to the far end of the ship. "Brave warrior, afraid of poor, ferocious Sekhmet." The sailor shook his head and laughed again. The others enjoyed the joke.

"Dagentyr," Bolgios said through clenched teeth, "I want to die. Every move this boat makes sends the god's own anger through my nose, and I've nothing left to vomit up."

"Quiet. The nose will heal. I've had mine broken too, now quiet. My head throbs and—" He felt his stomach come up and swallowed hard. He gave up the conversation, too sick to care that the sailors still snickered. The water shot spray up over the side. Its coldness felt bracing against his face and helped him to keep his wits.

They were the second ship in line. His position gave him a good view of the lead ship as it plowed up and down the rising waves. It was long, sleek, with a single mast, and billowing from that, a large square woolen sail bearing a once brilliant beast in scarlet, faded now with months of voyaging.

The oars had been used earlier to propel the ship out from the encampment on shore to the good winds, where the sail had filled out. He gave closer scrutiny to the side of the ship that carried him. The strip of planking that contained the oar ports had once been white. It was some off-shade now and peeling. There were faint traces of blue where a curling design had been superimposed, bright at one time probably, but muted with wear to the color of a twilight sky. The ship's sail was plain and dirty.

He was on the landward side. He could see beyond the frightening expanse of ocean to the thin grey strip that was land. It was never out of sight.

Bolgios said, "Dagentyr, if you could get free, then you could jump over the side and swim back."

"And how will I get free?"

"I will help you this time. I promise I will."

"They will not untie you, either. You are as much a slave as I am," he said irritably. He was not much good at reckoning such vast distances. An arrow's flight he could guess to within a few paces; that sort of thinking was useless here. A seagull flew over the ship and headed in toward land. He watched it grow smaller and smaller, and then it was gone. "Besides, it's too far."

"Are you sure? I swam across the river of my home once. That was a long distance."

Dagentyr let his bound hands dangle over the side into the cold water and imagined being immersed in it. There was no deep water near his home. He could swim but not well, and he disliked it, had always disliked and feared it. "I'm sure."

Bolgios didn't mention it again.

They were lying with several other slaves near the captain's cowhide awning placed over the stern as a protection from the sun. They were still tied although it was not really necessary; all were too sick to move. They lay sprawled on various sacks and bundles, clutching their bellies or weakly vomiting over the sides. The guards who watched them had an easy task and sat gambling at bones, oblivious to the moaning of their charges.

"I can do nothing for them, Master Astekar. They've been able to keep nothing down for close to three days. I'm at my knowledge's and wit's end."

Astekar snarled disgustedly at Vilarimon, the balding little man who served as physician to the party. "Slaves and warriors are no good if they're sick or die in the travelling. Call on that puny brain of yours and come up with a concoction that these people can get down and keep down. I've a great deal of time and trouble invested in these folk. I won't see my profit thrown overboard as they die one by one from starvation."

"If you would let me use poppy . . ."

"Only if you prepare it so as not to dull the wits."

Vilarimon recoiled from his words as from the touch of a whip. "As you wish, and couldn't it be arranged for us to land and stay in camp for a day or two so that if I can do nothing here, I will at least be able to get them on their feet for the next stretch of sea?"

Astekar gave his head a shake and looked across the water to the lead ship. The royal standard snapped crisply at the top of the mast. "I don't know. Prince Parush is anxious to return to Trusya. I doubt he will tolerate any such delay. He's feeling the prod of guilt. He thinks he's shirked his duty. When his head is made up it's impossible to talk to him. He gives no thought to the practical end of these journeys; if not for me, we'd all go back poorer than we started. He has it in his head to return, and quickly. However, I will ask him to-night if we can stay in camp a few days."

"I will do my best for them until then." He bowed and scurried away to his mixing bowls and potions.

Astekar wandered to the stern and watched dejectedly as his profits squirmed in discomfort. "Hapsaru!" he called.

The captain, a worried-looking man clad in a white linen kilt, responded by jumping down from the prow platform and joining him in front of the slaves. "Yes, Astekar?"

"The clouds on the western horizon portend a certain storm. It has been so since morning. Was this not supposed to be a short travelling day? The waves grow already. What are the prince's plans?"

The captain shaded his eyes and peered out at the heavy, blackening clouds and the increased swells. "I thought you were the confidant of the prince. His only order to me this morning was 'Tonight we anchor inside the Pillars.' He said no more. His ship gives no signal to head in. I must follow until he raises the pennant if I am to collect my sailing fee."

"Is it not dangerous to be out with ill weather so close at hand?"

"Aye, it's dangerous. I'd have put in for shore long ago, but the stiff wind gives us speed. The Pillars are just visible on the horizon there." He pointed. "We've still half a day's time to reach them, but the storm, it may not let us. There's water in the air already." He sniffed. "We Sidonians trust the seamanship of our Trusian comrades. Is our trust misplaced?" he asked sarcastically. "Mitas! Raise the signal to head for shore. We'll see what answer the prince gives us."

A dark sailor unfurled the pennant and held it up on a pole. Astekar and Hapsaru looked to the lead ship. No sign went up in answer.

Hapsaru muttered his feelings. "We'll be caught if we don't head in soon. As it is, if we go in now, it may catch us on our approach to the beach. Why doesn't he head in? Can't he see? You'll be the first men of Trusya to die outside the Pillars, and us along with you."

"Shall I bring down the signal?" the sailor asked.

"No, leave it up. Perhaps he has not seen."

"Or does not wish to," Astekar added under his breath. He hooked his thumbs in his belt-cord and looked to the six other ships. They were positioned in a line behind his vessel and the prince's. All were waving the pennant. The prince's ship gave no answer. He's a man driven to foolhardiness in everything, he thought.

"Doesn't the man have enough patience to wait out a storm for the sake of his life? Helmsmen! Steer in closer toward shore. Perhaps he'll follow our lead. I want to swim the shortest distance I have to. When you came to Sidon, Astekar, you paid us to sail for you, not die for you."

"You've weathered storms on the Blue Sea," said Astekar.

"Yes, but I've heard the storms outside the Pillars are blown by demons. The storms here would make me glad for one of those feeble blows. What's he in such a hurry to do?"

"Gain glory by killing the first Ahhiyawan he sees."

Hapsaru looked surprised and went back to the prow, leaving Astekar alone. Remounting the platform, he cupped his hands to his mouth, shouting out to the prince's ship and pointing exaggeratedly

at the pennant. The men had ceased their busywork
and watched him, anxious to know the result. A
cloud of spray whipped over the side, puddling the
deck. The rising wind made it difficult to hear.
After several tries and no response from Parush,
Hapsaru again jumped down and spoke to the
crew.

"Lash everything down and prepare for rough
water. He's going to try and beat the storm. Lower
the signal." He nervously fingered the amulet
around his neck and addressed himself to Astekar.
"The slaves should be tied down. If the waves get
big enough, they could be thrown over." He kissed
the amulet.

Astekar shouted to the two guards, who fetched
rope and started to tie them, women first, to objects
on the deck.

"Bolgios, something's wrong." Dagentyr's voice
showed anxiety. "The boat is rocking even more.
Can you feel it? And open your eyes. The men are
worried, afraid, even the trader." He regarded the
black and rainy horizon with trepidation. "I think
there's a storm coming, a bad one. I don't know
anything about storms on the water, but . . ." He
thought of the boat overturning and the mad
struggle to reach the heaving surface. "It's enough
to frighten these men, and they travel often on the
waters."

Bolgios opened his eyes in time to see the pennant cease its helpless fluttering. He had enough
strength to push himself up on his elbows and see
the whitecaps. "The waves are bigger."

"Why don't we go back to land?"

A guard took advantage of Bolgios's upright
position to wind a rope around his waist and pull it
snug.

"I don't think we are going back. They're tying us
down."

"Trader!" Dagentyr called to Astekar. "Trader!"

He did not hear. Again he was engaged in conversation with Hapsaru.

The air whistled through the ropes. The other slaves in the stern were frightened and curious. They began to ply each other with questions. A frothy wave tip fell on Dagentyr and slicked his hair down to his head. He shook the stinging saltwater out of his eyes and blinked in the direction of the storm. It was closer. The distant sheets of rain were almost touchable. He could see the movements of the clouds as they rolled toward the coast. The bumpy grey strip of land seemed a little closer but was still a long way off.

"Have the jars ready," Hapsaru was shouting. "Curse Parush. We're heading in. Steer for shore! Do I have your permission, Astekar?" he added bitingly.

"Yes, head in. I've no wish to end up on the bottom of the sea. The prince will have to take care of himself this time."

A hurried sailor slipped on the wet boards and fell to the deck, cursing. The guard came to Dagentyr and cinched the rope around his chest. He felt it pulled tight as the man secured it to one of the rower's benches.

The prow dropped hard into a wall of water and split it. The cloud of spray hid Hapsaru on his platform.

Dagentyr felt no urge to vomit. Fear had taken over from sickness. He did not like being tied down while other men were free to make a swim for it. One of the women was crying. A prayer from a man on the other side of the boat was almost lost in the angry sound of the oncoming storm.

Another wave broke over the deck. Hapsaru grumbled and cursed his way down the center of the deck. The men were ready with the bailing jars. The steersman braced his bare feet against the deck and put all the strength of his back and shoulders into the rudder. Hapsaru went to him and shouted orders into his ear.

Astekar stood under the awning and supervised the cargo and slaves. The guards and assistants scurried under his words.

"If anything's lost, I'll flay your hides. Check the covers and lashings again!"

Dagentyr yelled at him. "Why are we tied down, trader?"

"So you won't drown, barbarian!"

The words put fear into Dagentyr, they were a confirmation of danger. "Bolgios, we are in trouble."

Closer, the storm was more ominous. Veil after veil of rain fell like as many translucent tapestries. The air was more than moist; it was misty. Cold wind blew from the storm, freezing any feeling of oncoming spring. A bleak, departing winter was reaching his hand backward as he passed, to dip his finger in the confused ocean and stir.

The ship sank into a trough. Dagentyr stared in disbelief at the height of the waves. A swirl of sea foam at a watery crest flew up on the wind and disintegrated. Darkness hid the afternoon sun as the forerunning clouds spread overhead. The coast still stood in sunshine, like the promise of safe landing. Rain beat down on the sea with a waterfall's roar. The black, rolling surface was fractured by the millions of icy drops. A last prayer went up from Dagentyr, and the first torrent of rain slammed suddenly onto the deck.

Bolgios shivered and moaned aloud. "We're going to die, Dagentyr!"

He believed it, but it was not the time to give way to fear. A warrior died like a man. To fall in battle was better, but whatever came, and wherever, he died well.

"No, we will not. Grit your teeth; pull your courage up. We are men!" A cold rush of wet wind hit the back of his head and blew his hair forward into his eyes.

The ship lurched. Astekar reached for a rope and barely averted falling into the benches. Hapsaru was hurled from the platform to the deck. He got up clutching his elbow and ran to the helmsman, who stood with every sinew tensed, blinking cold water out of his eyes. Bravely, a soaked seaman leaned out over the rail and tried to fix the positions of the other vessels. The royal standard stood out straight, the only part of the prince's ship that could be seen as it slipped down a swell. The sailor shouted to Hapsaru the locations of the ships he could see, and by the time he had finished, they were all out of sight in the worsening rain.

Waves were starting to break over the side of the ship.

"Start bailing, bail! I'll not die for that puppy prince. For the shore!" Hapsaru was enraged.

The steersman shouted "Aye," and took his hand from the rudder long enough to wipe his hair from his face.

"Bail, I said!"

The men dipped their jars in and threw the water back to the sea, stopping when the ship rolled, threatening to spill them overboard. The bailers in the prow disappeared in a mass of spray.

Goosebumps covered Dagentyr's arms. With the storm's anger fully on them, the tribesmen were quiet, watching the busy, shouting sailors with hopeful desperation. He tried to close his eyes but could not. Danger held his gaze, forced him to behold its onrush, like the spellbinding eyes of a giant serpent.

Barely visible through the deluge, the scarlet sail beast bobbed ahead. Hapsaru said harshly, "Keep your eyes sharp for rocks!" and realizing there was not much else he could do, grabbed a jar and bailed with the rest.

Astekar still kept hold of the rope. Always detached, he seemed elsewhere as the sea tossed the ship from hand to watery hand. If we go down, damn Parush then! Damn him if we sink. Sweep his bones out over the edge of the world so that even his shade will never see Trusya again, he thought. His facade was that of a man who could leave the danger whenever he wished, leap off the ship, and fly back to shore on the whirling elements. The guards looked to him for instructions that didn't come and resignedly began to scoop water over the side with their helmets.

"Bolgios, are you all right?" Dagentyr asked.

"Yes." His voice was shaky. "It's so cold. Cold makes my nose achey." He was a helpless sight, tied down on his back, soaked, spitting seawater as each breaking wave fell on them. "Great god of rivers, help us if you have any power over these waters."

Assured that the lad was well, Dagentyr rested his head on a spongy bale of furs and stiffened for the next crashing jolt of the hull on the surface. Cold pellets of rain stung his face; the hollows of his eyes were pools. To clear them, he shook his head violently. He caught a glimpse of the strange beast, crouched under a rower's bench, looking small and bony with its fur drenched and spiky. The head with the amber eyes was like a snake's. Land was gone, vanished in the rain. Hapsaru looked for the other boats.

"How many do you see?" Astekar screamed.

The captain shook his head and went back to bailing with savage anger. Droplets hung in the trader's chin whiskers and quivered with the movement of the wind. His hands were growing white around the rope.

From behind him, Dagentyr heard the grunts of the helmsman as he fought with the rudder. The prow slid up a mountainous wave as another, from Dagentyr's side of the ship, threatened to rush over the deck. Rolling precariously, the ship dipped and seemed to glide on its side as the waves tried to destroy it. For a moment, the slaves dangled from their ropes. Astekar's feet left the deck, and he fought madly to keep his grip, his feet kicking air.

The two guards reached for something to hold on to, but there was nothing. Thrown off balance, they fell over the side and were carried away.

Dagentyr saw the wave devour them. Even though his hands were tied, he made an instinctive grab for Bolgios's arm. Crew members clutched at what they could and cried to their gods. Hapsaru made a wild flailing with his arms, lost his footing as the ship careened, and was pitched sideways over the rail. He grabbed at the side and hooked it with the crooks of his elbows as he fell. The steersman leaned into the rudder oar with all he had.

There was panic on the deck. Men shouted as if dying. Hapsaru's arms were still visible, tensed insanely for any kind of grip. Time condensed into a single moment, one heartbeat, one shouted note of men's voices. Dagentyr stared into the water and began to struggle to get free of the rope. The ship groaned. Bolgios cried out. "We're going to tip!" The moment ended as the ship miraculously fell back level and went slicing on.

"Grab him! Pull him up!" Astekar found his feet and rushed to where Hapsaru clung. Confused shouts went up all around. Two men had presence of mind enough to grab his arms and drag him, shaking and coughing, into the rowers' benches.

A man who had seen the guards washed over stayed huddled on his knees, staring straight ahead, mumbling. After an instant he found his voice. "They're over the side! Men over, Hapsaru!"

The cry made all heads turn. Several men rushed to the side, searching the ship's wake. The rain was so heavy, they could see nothing. Hapsaru pulled himself to all fours and did his best to be heard.

"Keep bailing! Go on. The gods have them now; it's too late. Get back to the bailing. Check to see if anyone else is missing. Come, see to these men!" He indicated an unconscious man pinned between benches, and another clutching his bleeding head. "Astekar!" The trader knelt beside him. "This is insanity. He's demon-struck. I'll try to get us in, but I fear that we're finished."

"Hapsaru!" a panting, downcast sailor called. "His neck is broken." Astekar and Hapsaru looked sadly at the limp figure between the benches. The man with the injured head was on his feet.

"Put him in the stern and lay him down."

"Yes, Captain."

"One of my crew and two of your men dead." Hapsaru stood on shaky legs. Again, the ship swayed. "It's the prince's fault. Bail, bail! Can you see land?"

A lookout clambered into the prow platform. "No!" was the cry that came back.

"And the other ships?"

"No!"

"Louder, man. I can't hear you above the wind!"

"I can see none!"

"Bail! By every god you know and by the whores you call mothers, bail!"

They did, furiously. The ropes and mast were beginning to show strain. Even Dagentyr could see that the ship was riding low in the water. Waves that were not dangerous earlier put the men in fear of their lives. Surging rushes of water swept from stem to stern, and back as the ship tipped up and down. The water lapped at Dagentyr's feet. His toes were numb. The rope had to go. He took a deep breath and yelled.

"Trader, come here!" Astekar wanted to ignore

him but came anyway. "You have men to bail that you are not using. Cut this stinking rope and we can help. Cut it!"

A loud crack and the sound of wood splintering punctuated his plea. An immense gust of wind had filled the sail, and the mast had parted. Hapsaru and Astekar shouted warnings, but the mast fell too quickly, driven by the wind, parting its stays like threads. It fell forward, smashing the woodwork of the prow and crushing the lookout beneath its weight. There were horrible shouts from men pinned to the deck, and the screams of those knocked overboard seemed to stay in the air. Half the sail lay on the deck; the other half draped over the side into the water. Under its folds, those who were still alive struggled to free themselves, making weird, globular shapes out of the cloth as they groped. Astekar stood stunned. Then he cut the ropes as quickly as he could. "Up, all of you. There's no time to waste."

Hapsaru called, "Astekar, send them here. Come on, men. Let's get this wreckage over the side." Every available man placed himself behind the mast and put his hands to the hard wood. "Astekar, get them down here!"

Dagentyr didn't understand him, but he knew the situation was desperate. "Hurry, Bolgios," he said.

He went as fast as his seasick legs would take him, with Bolgios and the other men following. Astekar sheathed his dagger and joined them. When Hapsaru gave the signal, they lifted with all their might.

"Heave it up!" The captain's voice was hoarse with strain. Men shifted their feet for more leverage. Cold water leapt over the rail and they tensed against it. A freezing gust came next, and Dagentyr's calf began to cramp. "Heave!"

"Lift, Bolgios." Under the weight he felt weak

and useless. The deck rolled. With a rumble, the
mast fell from their hands and rolled to the side of
the ship.

"Hurry, lift! If it stays where it is, the next big
wave will tip us. Get under it!" Hapsaru screamed.

The hands and slaves sprang to it and squatted,
trying to raise it from the deck. Dagentyr's legs
were stiff. A tiredness born of fear and cold drained
him. He was more tired than on his frantic escape
from Fottengra, but he jammed his fingers under
the mast, crouching, and with the cry "Heave,"
forced his painful legs to straighten. He and
Astekar stood, shoulders touching, and fought for a
better hold. Other men were cutting the sail away
and threw it over the side.

"Up with it!" shouted Hapsaru. Astekar cried
out with the exertion, and along the mast, men
lifted for their lives and puffed with red, distorted
faces; the mast was waist-high. "Get it higher!"
Dagentyr breathed, tensed every part of his being,
and lifted. They had it chest-level. "On my command, heave it together. Now!" Dagentyr yelled
with a final effort, and the mast scraped the side,
sliding into the water like a spear down a monster's
throat.

The naked deck was a miserable sight. Three
men were sprawled where the falling mast had
beaten them to the boards. The lookout's body lay
on the ruined platform, his head rolling back and
forth with the motion of the ship. At Dagentyr's
feet, a man whimpered foolishly and dragged himself to the stern. One leg pushed to help him along.
The other was bent hideously, the knee flexing in
an off direction. Dagentyr tried to shake off the
fatigue. He picked up a loose jar and started to bail.

"Pick up the injured and take them under the
canopy." Hapsaru paced the length of the ship like
a beast chased by dogs. "All spare men bail. Back to
the jars!"

Bolgios staggered next to Dagentyr and dipped a jar into the water. His swollen face was pale. Astekar knelt in the stern, comforting the women, concerned as ever with his goods now that immediate disaster had been avoided.

Bolgios's efforts became more frenzied, uncontrolled. He flung the jarfuls indiscriminately over the side or into the rail where they rushed back down to his feet. Dagentyr stopped work and put a hand on his shoulder. "Stop. Take hold! You're alive. Be the warrior you told everyone you were. Clear your head; find your courage!"

Hearing the admonition gave his own sagging bravery a lift. Bolgios slumped against the side in exhaustion. His breathing came in gasps. Dagentyr began to bail again, keeping a watchful eye on his companion. After a few jarfuls, Bolgios joined him, and worked more steadily, letting his breath escape through his teeth with each dip and throw.

Without its sail, the ship tossed directionless. The bobbing waves swept it in every direction and every conceivable combination of up, down, and sideways. Dagentyr's stomach turned over again at the worsened disorder of motion, but he kept his numb hands at their work.

The rain had stopped, and the wind lessened. Water broke over the deck less often; the dying gale was robbing the waves of their rage. The men were winning their contest against the invading sea. Moans and pitiful curses from the injured stood out sharply against the hypnotic slosh-splash of the bailing. The dead men had been taken to the stern and covered. The women shied away, sat as far off as possible. Hapsaru stood at the fore of the ship, looking again for some sign of the other ships now that the rain had stopped.

As he straightened up to throw, Dagentyr looked for land. Thick clouds and fog had moved in, obscuring everything, but as the ceaseless work went on he was aware of a darkening of the clouds. High above the fog, the sun was setting.

The helmsman was sagging with fatigue, so Hapsaru replaced him, measuring the man's tiredness by his own. He called for a rest. Bolgios dropped his jar and went to one of the benches. Wrapping his cold hands in the skirt of his tunic, Dagentyr sat down beside him. He was surprised that his brief words had worked such a change in Bolgios; although pale and tired, he did not seem terrified as before.

"How are you?" Dagentyr asked.

Bolgios's speech was accented with fits of shivering. "I'm afraid . . . but too tired now to care, very tired. Are we going to die, Dagentyr?"

He searched his mind for an honest answer. "No. I do not think that we are. We are very close to death, but they say it comes when you least expect it. When your power and confidence in battle are high, that's when the sword surprises you. We've been too close for too long, too expectant. The storm is getting no worse. We are meant to die somewhere else."

"I could wish now that I were home, even in the cow pastures of the chieftain, there perhaps more than anywhere else, with sunlight above and earth under my feet." He shivered, sneezed, and held his nose as the blast of air made his head rock with pain. "I was stupid to want to be here." Dagentyr watched the tears fill his eyes, catching the faint twilight. His crying made his nose run bloody. "Why can't I go home? Why do I have to be here? All my words were fool's words. I knew no better, but I do now. I know that—" He lost his voice in sobbing for a moment. "Are you afraid, Dagentyr?"

He didn't answer. It was one thing to be afraid. Men could fight it but not help it. It was another thing to admit fear. A warrior never admitted fear.

He knew that he had been afraid, that fear had made him call for Astekar to cut their bonds. He thought he was aware of fear now, a dull, unobtrusive fear, but it did not control him. And yet, I do not control it, he thought.

"I am tired, too," he said finally. He tried to laugh. An uneasy sound came out, and he looked over his shoulder at the covered bodies. The ghosts of unburied men walked at night.

There was a strange silence as the other men rested, then a long call interrupted it. Hapsaru had stationed men at prow and stern to call through the fog to the other ships. No answer came back but the sound of the waves. Dagentyr sat in the approaching darkness watching Bolgios weep like a girl but feeling no annoyance. This he found strange.

Ruki was of the opinion that what one could not see was less frightening than what one viewed outright. After seeing the storm and the scurrying, fearful men, night was a welcome cover.

It was impossible to stay dry and warm even in the most sheltered corner of the stern enclosure. He hadn't moved throughout the day's madness, had barely shifted position as he watched Parush shout orders like a lunatic, stomping up and down the deck, cursing and defying the storm. The prince seemed to feel a certain glee as he gambled with fate. Tuwasis hopped to his sharp commands, seeing that orders were carried through, kicking the bailers when they were slow.

If he remembered well, Astekar's ship had been directly behind them, carrying his old master. The positions of the ships hadn't changed through the last four days of sea travel. Four days' journey on land was a trifling matter compared to this. It was odd that he hadn't gotten as sick as the others. The rocking of the ship disturbed him little, and at the moment, was almost soothing.

The storm was easing. The prince was grinning broadly like a child who had been mischievous and gotten away with it.

Ruki had never seen a man as intense as Parush when making the decision to weather the storm and travel on. "No! We'll go on as I've said. I want to camp inside the Pillars. Get out those jars and sail on!"

Now, night had caught them on the open sea, and no land was visible. They had gone through the worst of it, it was being said. The ship was doing well, tossing benignly on the still sizable waves. Men were trying, unsuccessfully, to hail the other ships. Ruki could see each unanswered call chip slowly away at the prince's confidence. He had the sick feeling that they were all alone as Parush ordered the signal torches to be lit.

Chapter 14

The lookout was dismayed. It had been there a moment ago, or he thought it had, and when he called, "I can see a light," everyone had gone to the side. They strained their tired eyes in an attempt to see what had roused his attention, but it was not even possible to delineate sky from sea in the darkness. Miraculously, to the lookout's relief, it appeared again, a flicker of light, brief and instantly quenched in the rolling swells. Then, the same glimmer again, and yet another behind it until both were visible together, rising and falling in opposite directions, indicating the prow and stern of a ship not far away.

A cheer went up, and Dagentyr allowed a broad grin of relief to animate his features. Relief was a rush of warm feeling through his body, as if the heat of the other ship's signal torches could warm him across the cold, uneven water.

"Light torches in answer!" snapped Hapsaru, and several men scurried to find something dry with which to strike a fire. The two points of light continued to twinkle in the blackness as their own torches were lit and swung in slow, sputtering arcs.

The distant pinpoints wavered back, and again the men cheered. Seemingly in answer to their massed outcry, the horizon made itself seen, and night gave way before the first hints of dawn.

As it became even lighter, Dagentyr made out the shape of the other ship's mast, standing like a lonely, misplaced tree, and saw the blurred outlines at the rail, reflected images of his own ship's crew. The sail was lowered but the royal standard snapped in the breeze. The prince stood on the stern deck. His blue tunic was streaky and he looked tired, but he waved to Astekar.

Astekar called to the ship, and the prince's voice answered.

"The gods are with us, my friend. I am glad that you are alive and safe."

"It is the same with me, Lord Parush. I am truly gladdened to see you; we are all gladdened to see you!" He was obviously relieved when he heard the prince, in spite of his earlier anger, and he gave a great smile. It was the second time that Dagentyr had seen Astekar let his emotions slip over the wall that held them back.

The time to marvel at Astekar's lapse and bask in the moment of redemption was cut short by an order to break out the oars. Even though the men were like dream figures, slow and blank-eyed from fatigue, they unshipped the oars with speed and strength renewed by the answering of their prayers. The ship itself seemed more buoyant with the sudden, thankful lightheartedness of the crew. The sky was turning to greys and blues. Even the sea was looking less black, though Dagentyr's mind, hardened against it, could not regard it as anything but dark and ugly.

The covered bodies in the stern were insistent reminders that the ship was shorthanded. Dagentyr saw Hapsaru point a finger at him, then he and Bolgios and the other captives had long oars shoved

into their hands and were pushed roughly to the
benches.

He did the best he could, clumsily fitting the
unwieldy oar into the port and imitating the man in
front of him, bracing his feet against the base of the
bench in front and pulling hard, watching for the
moment when the back muscles of the man before
him flexed, taking that as his signal. He had seen
the men at the oars before and knew vaguely the
pattern of pull, release, raise oar, find the water,
pull again. His oar banged loudly into another, and
the man in front turned round to glare at him with
bloodshot eyes, and grunt unintelligible oaths.

Dagentyr was angered and shamed, but rowing
left little enough time to dwell on it. He kept his
eyes to the oar blades as they surfaced, passed
backward, dipped. The cycle repeated itself again
and again. He watched closely, forcing his oar to
duplicate the smooth motions of its fellows. He
ceased to lock oars with anyone; he could feel the
water give way under his pull, hesitantly at first,
and felt the ship moving.

Daylight came on with stark ferocity. The sea
mist lifted. The changing angle of the sunlight
made different shadow plays and contours on his
muscles as they struggled with the oar and caused
the sea to churn alongside. He enjoyed it. It was
agony for a while, for his arms had grown weak
from disuse and seasickness, but the pain was a
good feeling, weakness was not. He pulled on,
picking up the knack of putting his back into it,
pushing with his legs and leaning far back on the
stroke for a more powerful pull.

Bolgios sat on the opposite bench. Already, his
face was contorted with effort. Dagentyr was about
to make a remark, but a drop of perspiration slid
down to the end of his nose, and he realized that his
own forehead was drenched, as well.

He was facing the stern and could not see where

the ship was going, but from the length of time they
had been rowing, he assumed that they were nearing the prince's vessel. The shouts back and forth
were more distinct.

Hapsaru shouted a command, and Dagentyr
ceased rowing and held his oar out of the water like
the others. The ship glided in, losing speed in a
shallow arc as the helmsman turned it about to
come up alongside the other.

"You have lost your mast," shouted the prince.

"Yes," Astekar replied. "Cracked with the heavy
wind. We have men dead."

Parush was silent at the subject he had not
wanted anyone to bring up. He nodded self-
consciously and went on.

"There's a fair breeze heading to land. We'll set
sail and put in for shore. There are many villages
on this coast, aren't there? It should not be hard to
find one. Keep the men at the oars and follow us.
We'll try to hold back for you."

Astekar waved affirmation.

The red sail-beast unfurled itself against the sky;
the sail filled in the moving air. The crippled ship's
crew pulled at the oars. Both inched their way
toward the minuscule line that marked land. Miraculously, they were still in sight of it, and as the
line widened and took on the contours of a land-
scape, four more dull specks of sail crept up to
them and by noon had joined Astekar and Parush
with much cheering and celebration on board all
the vessels. There would be time later to mourn for
the two ships lost. Together they sailed toward the
brown, mountainous coast, in search of a safe
landing.

Dagentyr had been cheered by the arrival of the
other ships, but his hands were beginning to blister,
and his backside was raw and tender from the
splintery wooden bench.

As the afternoon went on, the shore loomed

larger and larger. From the prow deck it was possible to see the white foam of the breakers as they rushed over golden beaches. The water, becoming shallower, richened in hue, and Dagentyr saw his oar blade slice into an ocean that might just be called blue.

The mountains were brown and rust, speckled with the green of shrubs. Shadows cast and broken by the scarified rocks gave them pebbly textures, and the smooth beaches lay beneath them in odd contrast.

They turned east and followed the coast, giving the rowers a view of the land they had worked so hard to reach. Two beaches they passed, and a third, and then from the fourth rose a feeble strand of smoke. Another wisp was seen, and then there were many, and huts, hidden from a distance by their dull coloring. They were of the same square shape as those of Dagentyr's home, but some of the building was done with stone and rectangular blocks of earth. Smooth areas were garden patches and small fields. Other ships were pulled up on the shore. Lines of men passed cargo along the beach. Sacks, bales, and urns stood in orderly rows just up from the sand. Strains of a raucous song sung by drunken men floated from the dark door of a large hut.

The ships drifted in closer and, in ragged order, ran up on the beach, where the crews jumped out to haul them up farther and shore up the sloping sides of the hulls to keep them from tilting. Dagentyr jumped out with the rest, took hold of the rail, and helped the men drag the ship up on the land. The sand was deep and still warm from the heat of the sun. It was ecstasy just to walk on it, and even the unsure footing of sand was better to him than the firm but heaving deck of any ship.

A crowd was gathering round the six new arrivals, men ready to unload cargo if necessary; gawky

local youths; dark men like the crew of the ship that
carried Dagentyr, wearing soft, conical hats, asking
anxiously of the recent voyage; other traders envi-
ously asking what goods were obtained, and for
what price; men selling wine; dark women in gaudy
robes with vivid embroidery along their edges, eyes
thick with paint.

Even as he watched all these sights, he became
slowly aware that he was on land and untied,
almost unwatched. He stole a glance at Bolgios that
said, Be ready. Taking advantage of the hubbub, he
started to move slowly away from the ship, down
the beach. Bolgios worked his way around the stern
and followed.

With a shout, Astekar and Hapsaru jumped from
the boat and pointed to them. Two guards sprang
from the press and raised their spears, ready to
throw. Dagentyr looked down the beach and back
at the spears. His chances were not good. It would
be ignoble to die spitted on the sand like a dying
fish. He held his ground until two sailors grabbed
his elbows and walked him back to the ship, where
he was firmly tied and placed in the stern.

Astekar knelt down before Dagentyr and slapped
him hard in the face with the back of his hand.

"I can guess your every move, warrior. I am not
angry that you were going to run. I expected it.
That's the kind of trait I ordinarily pay highly for,
but you must know how things are. If you try again,
I'll have you whipped and saltwater thrown on your
wounds."

Dagentyr spoke to him from his position on the
stern boards, wishing that words could cut like
bronze.

"If I could kill you now, trader, I would."

"I pay for that kind of spirit, too. Keep hating
me, warrior, and you too, boy." He started to slap
Bolgios but stopped because of the broken nose. He
was amused at Bolgios's exaggerated flinch and

laughed uproariously when the boy gritted his teeth and spat on his tunic. "Good. Some fighting spirit is rubbing off on you.

"Listen, warrior. Do you have any comprehension of how far away from home you are? Let me tell you, it is very far. Escaping now would have done you no good. At the end of this voyage, when we reach Trusya, it will be many times farther still. There is nowhere to escape to there, either. You could wander the country for days, years, and not know a word of anyone's language or see a familiar sight or find anyone who has even heard of the place that you come from. There is no help for you." He nodded at them. "Think about that." He left and walked away to the village.

The village at night was a thing more alive and moving than in the day. Like a huge nocturnal animal that was sluggish in the light, it began to stir with the kindling of the torches, and the loud mixing of many voices and tongues became its inhuman growl. Stars were overhead in a cloudless night sky. A half-moon was shining brightly, putting anemic glimmers on the gently rippling ocean.

Dagentyr had been fed along with the other slaves, the bodies had been taken away, and the ship was empty except for a small group that huddled on the foredeck drinking cheap wine supplied by the vendors, and telling stories. Their dark beards were spearpoints in the rusty firelight. The rest of the men had fires burning by the ships and were cooking meat. Wherever a ship obscured the sand, it was ringed by campfires, for the sailors always lived near their ships. Men would stagger from the fires to the village, where the painted women waited patiently outside the winehouse doors. Later they would come back, share more wine with their fellows, and faint into a sleep or get up and trudge back to the village once more. The noise of their revelry was everywhere. A fight broke out now and then, separating the periods of constant buzz with sharp outcries. Guards had been posted near the ships to protect cargo that remained on board, and they scraped designs in the deep sand with their spear butts, wishing their lot had fallen to someone else, longing for the black tresses of a painted, embroidered woman or a saucy local girl.

The little coastal town was filled with news and gossip of the six new arrivals. The men gathered round the beach fires listened raptly as crewmen from the prince's flotilla went from ship to ship to tell their hair-raising tales of the north country and the storm in hopes of receiving a cup of wine or two in return. In their turn, the listeners told of affairs in the east, of their recent cruises from Knossus or Aigypta. Some of the men knew each other, for the sea routes were crowded places, and they embraced as parted brothers, wept, drank, and fell asleep after exchanging amulets from exotic places.

Not all the ships were from the same land. There were those, set apart a little, that came from the nearby islands to the northeast of the Pillars, or from the northern, barbarian coast. The men were different, the clothes, the tongues, but the subject of all conversation was the six ships that had weathered the squall on the return from the strange and perilous lands near the mysterious Islands of Tin.

The six ship's crews were men with boasts of bravery and important stories to tell. In the exhilaration of their tales, they told themselves they wouldn't have missed the storm for all the gold of the pharoah. It was only later, after the wine left headaches and melancholy, that they stretched out in the boats or on the beach in their rough blankets, clutched at the solid ground like desperate lovers, and whispered prayers of thanks for the gift of safe harbor and strong drink.

Dagentyr and Bolgios paid attention to the nighttime sounds of the town until they became bored and dropped their heads back to see the stars. Being near the village with its reminders of home pained Dagentyr's heart.

"Look there," he said. "That line of stars." He jerked his head in their direction. "They make a picture when you connect them, like a winding snake. It is the snake I see at home, and here it is, following me. There's a comfort in that, I think. It's a piece of home that stays with me." For the whole world, stars unchanging. It was an interesting idea. He held on to the thought for a while, and then put it away.

"Does the serpent have a name?" Bolgios asked, glad that Dagentyr had ventured to talk to him.

"If he does, I do not know it. By his movements, I am told, priests can tell the coming of seasons, and pending pestilence."

Somewhere the star snake was looking down on Kerkina, on a victorious Vorgus, and Arvis's cool, buried ashes. Dagentyr stared longingly at the sky for some moments, then spoke again.

"This must not be the final direction of my fate. My life must come to more than this. There was no mention of this in Irzag's prophecy; it can't be lasting. Events are waiting for me in Fottengra, waiting for me to make them happen. Vorgus hasn't won." He finished in a mumbling manner and stopped, embarrassed for talking to the boy so much. He had been so wrapped up in his own thoughts that the scene had dissolved around him. Bolgios was forgotten, and he lived his labors again. With his last trailing phrase, vivid memory left him. The pattern of the ship's planking came into focus through his misty eyes. The star snake was again over the foreign beach and not over a hidden, woodland village to the north.

Bolgios whispered, "I'll go with you. Please, Dagentyr. Let me go with you when you return."

It was a depressing, false display of camaraderie brought on by shared hardship and loneliness. Dagentyr found himself so self-conscious that he turned away and pretended to sleep.

Bolgios had felt pity to see Dagentyr's jaw twitch and his eyes well up with tears of insufferable rage. Next to the worry of the warrior, his own trials seemed inconsequential. No village was lost nor woman left behind. There was no glory hanging in the balance for him either way.

Coming back from the village, Hapsaru kicked a stone and hopped his way painfully around the fires to his own ship. Getting a foot up on one of the braces and a hand into an oar port, he pulled himself over the side and plumped down on the foredeck.

"Strutting pretty-boy, but I told him. I told him." The men in the prow moved over for him and poured him a cup of wine that he didn't need. "I told him! Went down to the prince's tent with Ketubal, Beyush, and the others after I found them in the dirt of the wineshop floor pounding away at some whore. I knew the way they felt. It's the way we all feel, isn't it?" There were nods and slurred exclamations of approval. We went in and stood our ground, with Astekar there, too. I dislike breaking with him, he's good and would get better trade prices for us, but I told him that no Sidonese captain would sail with him past Ebiosh, we'd take our cut and do the best we could in Knossus or Sidon. I won't sail into Ahhiyawan waters with him, the gods witness it. Only a crazed man would have tried to weather that storm. It was only our prayers and the sea god's pity for fools that saved us. Two captains paid for this folly by going to the bottom with all their good men and bales of fine goods." He spat and rubbed his amulet. The other men fumbled for theirs and whispered to the sea gods.

"I won't get caught in the pay of a Trusian prince. That's all the excuse the Ahhiyawa would need to take everything and leave us adrift with our throats cut. They'd need little enough excuse for that anyway." He nervously slipped the amulet between his thumb and forefinger. "Parush turned red and raved at me that we'd broken the agreement and that you could never trust a Sidonese water-pig to keep his word on anything. I wanted to draw my dagger and have it out with him right there; he would have been happy to. Astekar held us apart and tried to keep him calm. He did his best to convince us to go on, but we were firm. I told him he could hire other captains and crews in Ebiosh. There's plenty that would do the work; the world's populated by fools. Ebiosh is as far as we go, I said, and that's an end to it, and then we left, walked out on the barking pup and went to the wineshop happy men."

"What did he do then?" asked a sailor.

"He fumed and called insults at us all the way, but we'll be rid of him soon enough." He drank his wine noisily. The group clapped him on the back and broke up to tell the men at the fires the news.

Hapsaru plodded to the stern, pulling his oily black beard. His pinecone-shaped cap sat comically askew. He nearly tripped over the slaves huddled in his path.

"Get out of my way, you swine. I am the captain of this ship! I am the captain!" he bellowed, pulling his knife. He growled, showing his teeth, and waved the dagger menacingly, pleased with his bold treatment of a prince. What a story to brag of at home. He had spit in the eye of a Trusian nobleman. There was probably no one on the whole coast from Tyre to Millawanda who had done that. It struck his funnybone. He laughed his way under the stern canopy and fell. The laughter continued off and on until he gave in to the wine and fell asleep.

It started out a sleepless night for Dagentyr. The idea of the same stars over the whole world resurrected itself and intrigued him. If the stars were everywhere might they not provide directions to a ship's captain or an escaped man searching for his village? He resolved not to remain idle in the stern on the next leg of the journey. He would convince Astekar to let him remain at the oars, and he would watch and ask about which stars might indicate which directions. It would be a time to build himself, harden himself, learn. His sore hands told him that it would not be easy, but he would not rot in the stern and let his muscles grow useless. There would be a time when they would be needed. He knew he could not afford to let any opportunity go by. The work would make him strong and quick. The elation he had felt at the exertion of pulling the oar, the deep, painful breathing it took, the sweat, were all things that had to be maintained. He would speak to Astekar. The trader would have to agree for the sake of his cargo.

The last strains of Ruki's song were fading away. It seemed to be his misfortune to always entertain the prince when he was in a foul temper, or inattentive, or preoccupied. It irked him. In spite of himself he was developing a disgusting pride in his new work. To perform and be ignored wounded his ego, a thing that was new to him, for he had not known pride before. He was elevated now; he was a different man, a better thing than he was before. His clothes were provided, and better than the rest. Care and time had been put into his training. He slept, ate, travelled apart from the others. There was a price placed on him for something other than strong muscles and a talent for slicing up men. An art had been given to him to perfect, and he worked at doing just that. No matter that the object of his trade was ridicule and merriment at his own expense. What he did, he would do well. Laughter could be endured for the reward it brought. Never again would he be a target for the chicken bones and taunts from the bearded men he was rapidly coming to regard as inferior.

He had rehearsed his song well. Granted, it was hard to learn with Astekar busy for most of the day with little time to spare for teaching, but he had worked on it for many hours.

Astekar had told him what the words meant in his own language. Ruki insisted on knowing so he could give extra meaning and nuance to the songs. It was another demonstration of the interest and energy he put into his newfound art. Working to tame his unruly fingers to pluck the proper strings had been tedious but had proven worthwhile. The semblance of a melody had come.

The song was a dock ditty popular with seafaring men, the kind Parush had accused Astekar of teaching him the first time he had been presented. It was funny. The prince should have shed tears of laughter, if not at his jerking rendition, then at the song itself, but here he sat staring fixedly out the tent opening at the campfires, rasping his fingernail over the grooved metalwork of his dagger hilt. By Appolos, the god he was told watched over music, it irked him. In his peevishness he plucked a wrong note. It struck a raw nerve inside Parush's head, and he exploded.

"Stop that cursed noise, dunghead! Must you aggravate my soul as these dishonest Sidonese whoregrabbers have done?"

Ruki stopped. He withdrew to a respectful distance and sat down in the shadows to sulk. He had not been dismissed.

The prince thumped his fist on his knee as the sentry announced Astekar. On seeing him, Parush popped anxiously to his feet. "Well, did you find them?" he asked.

Astekar bowed formally, inhibited by the bad tidings that he brought. "Yes, my lord. I found them in the wineshop or at their ships. They will not be swayed. Hapsaru did not lie to you when he said they were all of one mind. None of the captains will go past Ebiosh. Two were reluctant to go even that far."

Parush sat down angrily. "They'll get nothing for this! They broke the agreement. I'll pay them nothing!"

"I have also spoken again with Hapsaru. He was angered, but I told him they would receive only half pay. Forgive me for not obtaining your sanction, but we are badly outnumbered here. Only your ship is manned by Trusians. They, and the guards on the other vessels, are not enough to enforce demands. These Sidonese men would stick together and revolt if we offered them nothing at all. I convinced them that half was fair."

"I'd love to see them all dead. They're causing me delay when I least desire it. Can captains be obtained as easily on Ebiosh as that greasy lout says they can?"

Astekar shrugged. "I assume they can. I will do my best. My lord knows that I have never failed him yet."

"You have. You failed me tonight when you dissuaded me from killing that treacherous pig!"

"My lord knows that is not so. I simply saved you from doing something you would have regretted later on, perhaps after you had been forced to stay here for many months, or had had to leave all your cargo behind, for no captain would have taken you anywhere if you had killed him." His words had a calming effect on the prince. "There is still enough left to bring profit even after the captains are paid off. However, the new ones we pick up in Ebiosh will be doubly expensive."

"It doesn't matter," said Parush impatiently.

"Getting home quickly is my main objective." He leaned back on his cushions, forcing himself to appear self-controlled and careless.

Astekar was not fooled. "That brings me to something else, my lord." The prince bade him sit, and he did so. "When I was in the wineshop I took advantage of the opportunity to ask questions, ask news of home, ask what the Ahhiyawa are up to. Answers can be had easily for a cup of wine. Most of the time sailors will talk freely if there is an attentive ear to listen."

Parush sat upright again, his attempt at nonchalance forgotten. "What did you learn?"

"It is difficult to say. News travels many channels, some slow, some quick. Here at the end of the world it can travel no way but slowly, but thank the gods for luck. There was a captain from a Sidonese ship whose last port was Knossus."

"Knossus?"

Astekar shrugged. "It is the only news to be had. The captain says that a Cretan fleet sits in the harbor but that there are preparations being made for departure. Idomnus is still holding audience, but something is up. He could say no more."

"What did he say of Ahhiyawan shipping or of home?"

"Nothing, my lord."

"Could it be that Mensalakus and Aganon are not satisfied with their pirating and have called on the other Ahhiyawan states for alliance? Is there possibility in that?"

It had crossed Astekar's mind. "Yes. There is possibility in everything."

"Gods! We need to be away, Astekar. We may already be too late."

"There is reason for hope. The captain is only two weeks out from Knossus. He did say that preparations were not hurried. I would think not. Idomnus is not anxious to join in a struggle not

precisely his own, merely to please Aganon and
Mensalakus."

"Trusya is a rich prize, isn't it?" Astekar agreed.
"Reason enough for him to join. Was there other
news? No? Then make preparations to leave as
soon as we can. That oaf Mensalakus's pride must
itch more with each passing season without his
beautiful wife. He'll never know that my folly saved
him from the bitch. How he must want my skin.
How soon can we depart?"

"Soon, two or three days. I'll see that we leave at
the nearest possible moment." He nodded to Ruki.
"Does my lord wish more songs?"

Parush looked up. "No."

Astekar motioned with his head. Ruki understood and left.

The guard outside the tent gave him little notice
as he made his way past. He had seen him come
and go often enough. Ruki gave the lyre an angry
strum.

The air was cold near the ocean. There was not
even the hint of a breeze. It was as clear and
beautiful a night as anyone could have wanted.
What use was anger? Better to sleep warm and
secure in his blanket under the dazzling stars than
waste anger on the prince. He bedded down in
anticipation of the oblivion that brought him his
only true freedom.

Chapter 15

When the sunlight touched Dagentyr's face, he opened his crusty eyes and knew that he had slept after all. It was quiet. The usual dawn scramble to get under way was absent. There was activity around the other ships, but around the six of Parush there was none. Unattended fires had gone out, and the ashes smoked. The men huddled around them were still asleep and the beach was noisy with their snoring. Several men lay in the boat, wrapped in their blankets. Hapsaru had not shifted position. His dagger was still clutched in his hand.

The village was sleeping, too. Its streets were empty for the most part. There were no painted women or wine sellers. A disheveled sailor leaned in the wineshop door and rubbed his back, aching from a night on the floor, and prepared to make the trek back to his ship. In the early morning the sand was more golden than ever. Its surface was pocked and rough with the footprints of men. They held pools of shadow till the sun's angle changed.

Dagentyr had tossed in the night, and his shoulder had stuck out from under the blanket. The chill made his skin clammy. He longed to rub it briskly to bring back warmth and blood, but his bindings prevented it. He was indignant at having to wait for these drunken oafs to wake before he could relieve his bladder. A vision of himself breaking free and pissing on Hapsaru as he slept crossed his mind, bringing a smile. While he waited, he woke Bolgios and told him the plans he had for the trip to come.

"Will he do it, let you stay untied to work the ship?" Bolgios asked.

"Of course. He thinks of his property first. You've seen how the women are pampered. He knows warriors won't be able to fight if they're wasted away and weak. It will make sense to him. If you expect to go with me, you must do the same."

Bolgios frowned. A threatening thought had pierced his skull. "Dagentyr, will we all be expected to fight? Will I have to be a warrior? I'm a—"

"You're a shield bearer."

Bolgios hung his head. "Yes," he said sheepishly. "And I have never even seen a battle. All the time I was with him, Clavosius never went to battle."

"You'd be wise to become strong in case this foreign king wants you to fight. You wanted to, didn't you? There must be a way to guide our journey by the stars. I need to know what it is when we escape."

"Once we are free on the ship will we jump over and swim away?" The mention of swimming irritated him.

"To where? We don't even know where we are. First we must know where home is and how to find it, then we can leave when the best moment presents itself. You and I must learn."

"Do we tell the others?"

"No. They must know nothing."

Later, Astekar made his rounds of the flotilla.

"Get up, you drunken, lazy fools!" Dagentyr heard him say. "Up off your asses and to work!" The previous night's conversation with the captains had sharpened his temper. He jutted his head up over the side of the ship and glared round with eyes that Dagentyr had expected to be puffy and red. They were not. Astekar had foregone the pleasures of port; his vision was unclouded and his tongue was ready. "Hapsaru! Get these sand fleas of yours up and busy." The captain grumbled and rolled to his other side. Astekar climbed into the boat and gave him a kick. "Get up! By the gods, if you'll only take us as far as Ebiosh, you'll work all the way. I'll see to it." Another kick made Hapsaru clutch his thigh and spring up. "Set these idiots to their chores and see to the feeding and comfort of the slaves." Without saying anything more, he stormed off. Dagentyr spoke to him just as he was climbing down.

"Trader!" He knew it was not the best time to ask, but the time of inactivity was over. He was eager to put his plan into effect.

"What do you waste my time with now, barbarian?"

Dagentyr noticed the word "barbarian" instead of "warrior."

"We need to be set to work as well. We grow weak and puny. Is a warrior worth anything if the wind can grab at his shield and blow him away?" Astekar raised an eyebrow. "Set us to the same tasks as these men to strengthen us. When the ship sails again, let us help at the oars. Already I feel my sword arm losing its strength and skill."

Astekar paused long enough to let his face show that he was considering it and disappeared down the beach in the direction of the next ship.

Hapsaru hollered to the men, most of them already wakened by Astekar, and they stretched and went to the water's edge to douse their throbbing heads in the freezing surf.

Guards rounded up the slaves from each ship and marched them away from the village. Astekar went along. The women were stripped and herded into the shallow waves to bathe, and they shrieked at the cold. Dagentyr became suddenly aware of his tunic reeking of brine and weeks of sweat. While the women splashed, Astekar examined the men. He stopped and picked a louse out of Dagentyr's hair, clicked his tongue in disapproval, and ordered the men into the water as well.

Afterward, as they were drying around a fire, sitting cross-legged on the warm sand, picking the lice from each other's scalps (a job Dagentyr thought unfit for a warrior), they tossed their clothes into a shallow tidal pool where the women trampled them clean. Dagentyr leaned over the pool and looked at his reflection. It was different. It seemed leaner, sadder. The hair was stringy; the beard, untrimmed, was losing its shape as it grew. His cheeks, nose, and the top of his forehead were sunburned and garish. The magnificent green stain had been decimated by the storm and recent bath. He made a face and looked like a tousled child playing at ferocity. His double in the water hurt his pride, and he turned away.

Though the garments were a little less rank, they were slightly damp, and full of sand. With the scrape and subsequent itch, Dagentyr was almost sorry they'd been washed. The work they were involved in was hot. Sweat aggravated his chafed skin, so he let the upper part of his tunic fall loose to his waist. Astekar had lost little time in acting on Dagentyr's request. Under the eyes of the guards, he was hauling a heavy water urn to the ship. It was the fifth urn he had filled and hauled, for they were laboring to supply all six ships with fresh water. Bolgios worked too, the weight of his burden bothering him more than it did Dagentyr.

Lines of men stretched across the beach passing cargo and supplies from hand to hand. A new mast was being hewn by a party of men with axes. The toil was hard and the wine vendors were out in droves.

Dagentyr passed the prince's tent on his way from the stream to the boat. Ruki was sitting in the shade with a lyre, fretting over a combination of chords. When the sounds were wrong he would beat his fist into the sand and pluck again. Dagentyr had noticed that Ruki was never bound. Considered harmless, he went about free. Perhaps if Astekar had seen Molva with the sword stuck through his torso, Ruki would have been practicing with his wrists lashed together. Ruki glanced up at him as he passed with the urn. His look conveyed nothing, and he did not speak. Dagentyr trudged on with his load. It was funny to think of slavery as a fortunate thing, but it had improved Ruki's lot. He wore a green tunic now and not the woolen homespun of Fottengra. He lived apart from the rest and kept company with Astekar and Parush. Though Dagentyr considered that he did nothing to earn this, he led a life that was infinitely more interesting than watching Dagentyr's cattle.

I should be hating him. If not for him . . . I should break away from the guard long enough to crush his skull with this urn. Yet Dagentyr could muster no real animosity. If anyone was responsible for his plight it was Vorgus. All his hate was there; none was left for the skinny buffoon.

The amphora nearly slipped out of his hands and he had to let it rest on the sand for a moment before picking it up again. Tuwasis, supervising one of the cargo lines, saw him and came over.

"Pick it up and no shirking, you dung beetle!" He jabbed Dagentyr's ribs with his spear butt and gave Bolgios a thump on the back of the head for good measure. "Astekar isn't here to coddle you now. I'm free to give you what you deserve." He jabbed again.

A plan formed in Dagentyr's mind. He would

turn, drop the amphora on Tuwasis's foot, and when he screamed with pain and let fall the spear, he would snatch it up before the other guards could stop him, and plant it through the waterman's heart. He was only seconds away from implementing his thoughts when his better judgment stopped him. It would be a blunder that could be fatal. At the least, Astekar would realize how dangerous he was and refuse to let him work on the ship. He might never learn the secret of finding his way home. There would be other times to settle with Tuwasis, better ones than this. Waiting was a thing he was learning to do well. He hefted the amphora and did as he was told.

The ensuing night's revelries were less wild than those of that first welcome night in port. The sailors were more quiet and stayed more in their own company than that of the whores. Maybe it was because they were too tired after the day's endless work to do anything but eat and get quietly, warmly drunk at their spots around the fires.

The next day there was silver to be hauled and loaded, for Astekar had taken advantage of the stop to change much of the northern cargo for the local product, gleaming ingots of silver from the brown mountains nearby. It was necessary for guards to patrol near the ships constantly now that the white metal was on board. On these nights Dagentyr would listen to the hushed footsteps of the sentries and scratch his peeling back by rocking back and forth against the boards. The dark-haired, dark-skinned sailors had laughed to see him writhe in pain after the sun had blistered his fair skin. The stupidity of that first long day spent bare from the waist up had been driven home.

When the ships were ready to put to sea, the raging fire in his shoulders still burned. He felt a surge of excitement as they struck the braces and pushed the craft out into the breakers, and as the

ship glided out, he and Bolgios sat at the oar
benches, pulling the vessel out of the sheltered
water of the cove, into the vast ocean. They did not
row for long. The sail caught a good wind, and the
repaired prow furrowed white foam from the sea as
they went. With oars shipped and no work to do,
they were again tied up and relegated to their places
near the stern. Astekar was playing their game but
he took no chances.

The breeze held, and it was a grand view
Dagentyr had as they ran in through the Pillars. He
saw the huge, bleak mountaintop, precipitous and
steep on one side, sloping on the other, rise above
the rail and pass backward until it was out of sight.
He heard the crew chatter as the small fleet left the
great swells and storms of the outer ocean behind
and nosed into the brilliant aquamarine waters of
the Blue Sea, the home sea that they had known
since birth.

Hapsaru seemed pleased at the weather; the sky
was clear with puffs of cloud just floating on the
horizon. The wind blew steadily. The trip to Ebiosh
would be pleasant and quick. He gave his orders
happily from his honored position under the stern
canopy. His crew worked contentedly, enjoying the
weather as much as he did.

Astekar's curt manner warmed. He worked hard
for self-control but was not immune to the good
feelings brought on by home waters and the ever-
nearing prospect of landfall at Trusya. At the times
when only the helmsman worked, he and Hapsaru
would sit under the canopy talking and drinking.

It was a surprise to Dagentyr when one evening
the ships made no indication of heading for shore.
Men lit the torches as they had routinely after the
storm. Torches from the other ships winked back
companionably. The stars came out and Dagentyr
recognized the serpent. Hapsaru stirred himself
from his place in the stern and gazed at the sky. He

went to the helmsman. They conferred, pointed at certain specks of light, and then the captain resumed his seat and picked up his interrupted conversation with Astekar.

Dagentyr's heart leapt. They were finding their direction by the stars! He thought of different ways of asking Astekar how it was done and decided that bluntness would be the best approach. Hapsaru laughed, then both men were silent. The captain stretched out and covered himself with a blanket. Obviously the conversation was at an end. Dagentyr decided to ask.

"Trader."

Astekar leaned his head out from under the canopy. "Yes, warrior?"

"I would ask you a question."

"Ask it." He seemed full of wine and good spirits.

"I would know how the ship is steered with the stars as guides." Astekar was taken aback for a moment. He cleared his throat. "Aha. How do you know that is how it is done?"

"I saw the captain do it. Even now the steersman keeps his eyes on the stars."

"You have more intelligence than I suspected." He got up and stood over Dagentyr. "Why should I tell you this? Would I not be placing in your hands the means of returning home should you escape? A slave is much more obedient when he knows that there is no place to go but where his master orders."

"Do you put so little trust in your ability to hold me captive? Are you not from a land where men build stone walls as high as trees?"

A smile crossed Astekar's lips. "Yes I am, and I am not."

"What do you mean? You said in your tale that you were. Do you practice lying as well as treachery?"

Astekar ignored the insult, leaned back on the

rail, and steadied himself there with his hands.
"I'm going to tell you another story. It's a story
about me. Have you not wondered at the ease with
which I speak the language of the tribes?"

"You speak it strangely."

"It is not quite the same dialect, and I have not
used it for a long time. You see, when I was young I
knew the forests and the fields and the animals. I
was of the tribes, born in the forest. I'm not of your
tribe, of course; my forest lies far to the southeast of
yours, but not far from Trusya.

"I spent my boyhood in the woods, and then I
realized that there was another world outside my
village, something better. The trade goods came up
from Trusya and so did the stories of the city's
grandeur, power. So I left one day and sailed
downriver to the sea and to a new life. And when I
got there, what did I do? I was an ignorant savage. I
did not know the tongue or the ways, and I was
hungry. So I sought to start low but in a high place.
I went to the palace and became a servant . . . a
servant, me. My pride, well, it was injured, but I
worked hard and was lucky. I was of a good age,
they thought, to be a playmate and companion-
servant to young Prince Parush. I was older, but
they thought that would be good. There is much I
can leave out. In time I became his personal
steward, his friend, and I came to be Astekar, the
trader."

"And are you still a servant?"

"It is a question that I have thought much about.
If I am, it is unimportant. I am Astekar the trader
now, Astekar the rich, the traveller. And servant or
not, I do not regret leaving the forest. I was always
intended to be of Trusya. You will have to see the
place to fully understand." He stood up. "What I
am trying to tell you is this. What I left behind,
what you leave behind, is nothing. You have fire
and cunning. You can prosper as I did! Then you

will thank me. I do not think of myself as a servant;
you must not think of yourself as a slave, warriors
are not, in the exact sense."

Dagentyr turned a cold, uninterested eye to the
trader. "You have turned your back on what you
are, and you have ripped me away from what I am.
For that, I will always want to kill you, for you have
no inkling of what you have done to me."

"It will take time with you, but you will see."

"I asked you about the stars."

"As you wish. I will tell you about them not from
friendship or anything like it, or pity, but because I
want you to know that even armed with the knowledge of how to navigate by the stars, you will not
have any hope of escape, much less return, and
because in time, I know you will not want to. I am
that sure of myself." He hooked a thumb in his
belt-cord. "Do you see those stars, there, ahead of
the ship, the ones we steer for?"

"Yes." Dagentyr had to shift against the rail and
strain his neck to see.

"Can you see the picture they make? A bear.
That bright star is its head, that one its tail."

Dagentyr didn't think that it bore any resem-
blance to any bear he had ever seen, and suspected
Astekar of lying, but he listened carefully.

Chapter 16

There were fools in Ebiosh, or so the crews of the Sidonian ships thought, for Parush found eager captains for the last phase of the voyage in spite of the stories they told and the warnings they proffered. Astekar worked quickly to hire other men and ships of Sidon before news of the ill-fated voyage and the prince's erratic behavior became widespread. In the hurry to get out to port and under way again, they did not stay long. Dagentyr was glad. The tiny town was not much different from the one before. The water was bluer, the sand brighter, but the men and women were the same, and as the new ships set out again, he knew that the same drunken scenes would be repeated on the island until the captains and sailors became weary of telling the same stories to audiences that had already heard, and restless for another voyage to a place where their lore was fresh and greeted with interest.

The first time that they had sailed at night, and he had awakened the next morning to see that there was no land in sight, fear, like that during the storm, brought nervous sweat to his face. It was an event that repeated itself, and he became used to it, working at the oars or resting, as the wind dictated, regaining his strength at night and steering the ship in his imagination, keeping his eyes on the Bear, against the day when the knowledge might lead him home to vengeance.

His work on the ship was making him strong. His arms began to thicken and bulge pleasingly from the toil of rowing. Sunlight was putting light streaks in his hair, and his skin was getting darker.

Bolgios, with the flexibility of youth, was growing to like his role as sailor, working with enthusiasm when work was called for and relishing the breeze and sunshine. The sailors seemed to like him and joked with him as much as the difference in language permitted. He was picking up words of their tongue here and there and was making attempts at phrases, another thing given ease by his youth. Two of the Trusians were teaching him to gamble.

When they were well out from Ebiosh, as they steered south to avoid the Ahhiyawan lands, the lookout called back to the stern that there was another ship in sight. It was a lone mast heading due south across their path. Astekar and the new captain exchanged nervous glances and went to the prow. The prince's ship, in the lead, dropped sail and fell back to within hailing distance.

"What do you make of her, Astekar?" shouted Parush.

Astekar and the captain cupped their hands over their eyes and traded a few words. Astekar nodded.

"A small Ahhiyawan trader making for Knossus."

"I knew it! Can we catch her?" He was agitated.

The captain shrugged "of course" to Astekar. A small, heavily laden vessel would be no match for the swift, well-handled Sidonese ships.

"Yes."

"Good. You and I will give chase and take her! It should be easy; he has no wind. The other vessels will follow us at a distance. I told you that I would kill the first Ahhiyawan I saw. I told you!" With that, he yelled an order to his helmsman and the ship veered off to intercept the faint mast in the distance. The other ships were informed, and Astekar's vessel pointed its prow into the prince's wake.

The little Ahhiyawan ship was becoming clearer, for they were gaining on him. The wind was against him, and he was using rowers. The captain and Astekar began barking orders, and every man not involved in the sailing of the ship readied himself for a fight. At such long distance swords and knives would be useless. The Trusian guards prepared their bows and unsheaved a bundle of spears. Astekar ordered Dagentyr and Bolgios freed and gave them weapons.

"Since you two insist on working on the ship, you will have the honor of fighting on it. How are you with the bow, warrior?"

"Better than most," said Dagentyr.

Astekar gave him one, and a quiver of arrows. To Bolgios he gave spears. "Resist your urge to kill me for the moment, warrior. I've left orders that if I am harmed, you'll be thrown overboard."

The ships were almost upon the hapless Ahhiyawan. Confusion and panic were obvious on her deck; the rowers had lost their rhythm. Some of the oars lay unmanned as their owners had scrambled to arm themselves. The sail was being hoisted in a bid to catch the wind and outrun the two attackers. The dull square of cloth started to billow, then filled out, bringing the ship before the wind.

"He's too late," said Astekar.

As the Ahhiyawan picked up speed the oars were shipped, but it was too late. Parush's ship was already alongside, and the arrows began to fly. Dagentyr saw a well-aimed shaft drop the Ahhiyawan helmsman. He let go the steering oar and arched backward into the sea. Another man rushed to take his place.

Dagentyr pulled an arrow from the quiver and nocked it. They would be close enough soon. The ship seemed to fly over the surface even as the blood seemed to fly through his veins. There was bright sunlight and beautiful water and the prospect of battle in a new place, a new way, on a moving ship fast as a horse on a flat meadow. He had not had a weapon in his hands since beating Tuwasis in the fight on the beach. His hands shook with excitement. The thought of being thrown into the water with no friendly spot of land in sight kept him from even thinking of killing Astekar.

The red sail-beast swooped in on the trader on its faded, deadly wings. An arrow whined its way past Dagentyr and dropped the sailor next to him. He could see the archer kneeling by the stern housing to protect the new helmsman.

A guard took the next shaft on his shield. It struck with a hollow thud and imbedded itself in the layered bullhide. Another man ran to the stern to cover their own steersman.

Dagentyr moved to the rail, got as good a footing as he could, and raised the bow, drawing the string and fletching to his ear. The archer in the other ship saw him and took aim. Dagentyr let go and felt the string snap back musically, sensing its sting against his forearm. The archer dropped his bow into the water and slumped against the deck. There was a cheer from the crew.

Bolgios fidgeted nervously and, not really sure of the grip or the target, threw his spear. It arched across the gap between the two ships and landed in the deck, doing no damage. Even so, he whooped and laughed. He had not even expected to be able to throw that far.

There was no time to waste congratulating Bolgios on a useless throw. Dagentyr nocked anoth-

er arrow and looked for a mark. Unarmed sailors
were diving for cover beneath the rail. An enemy
arrow zipped above their heads and through the
sail.

The Ahhiyawans were breaking out the oars
again to use in pushing the prince's ship away and
prevent boarding. As one of the Ahhiyawa bent
over to lift his oar, he turned his back on the
Sidonese ship, making a good target. Before
Dagentyr could fire, a Trusian guard had shot an
arrow into the man's spine. They were close enough
to hear his cry of pain as he fell.

Dagentyr ducked beneath the rail. A spear, slow
compared to the speeding arrows, pierced the air
where he had been standing. In the prow, a sailor
screamed and slumped into the benches. Wild
shouts came from the Ahhiyawan vessel as the
prince's ship rubbed alongside. Men threw ropes
and hooks to hold the ships together, and the
battle-fired Trusians poured over.

Dagentyr stood again. With all the confusion on
the Ahhiyawan deck he could no longer tell who his
targets were supposed to be. Men from both ships
struggled with each other. He could tell no difference between them.

The rain of projectiles from the Ahhiyawan had
ceased. The helmsman was dead at his post. Most
of their crew was dead, killed in the rush of
boarding. There was no more shouting. All decks
were quiet as the haughty Tuwasis lowered the
enemy sail, and then the crews cheered their victory.

Dagentyr lowered the bow. His heart still thud-
ded in his chest, pumping blood and battle lust that
were no longer needed. It was over. He felt unsatis-
fied somehow. One man dropped at long range and
not even the chance to see the look in his eyes.
There should be more.

Bolgios was still elated at his spear cast and the

blessing that none of the flying arrows had hit him in return. "Did you see me, Dagentyr? My throw, did you see that? It was good, wasn't it?"

"Drop sail," their captain ordered. Once done, they drifted, letting the sea take them where it would while they watched the Trusians sack the captured ship.

Parush wasted no time; no sooner had the Ahhiyawan captain surrendered than the men started rifling through the cargo and throwing bundles across to their own ship. The remaining Ahhiyawans were taken to the prow platform where the prince had them killed and tossed over the side. When the exchange of cargo was complete, the Trusians gave a last whoop, and Parush kindled a torch and threw it mockingly into the lifeless, drifting ship.

The other ships of the flotilla arrived. They set sail again and steered east. Dagentyr looked back to where the flames were consuming the ship. Its mast was a fiery tree. Astekar came to take back their weapons.

"Shall I have them bound again, Master Astekar?" asked the guard who accompanied him.

He gave Dagentyr a searching glance. "No. I don't think we need to. Put them back to work, but keep a close watch. They must see that valor has its rewards with us and that brave men who fight have nothing to fear and much to gain in Trusya. Be careful to keep your hate restrained, warrior. The orders I gave about my safety apply for the entire voyage. Do you understand?"

"I already know the rewards a brave man receives at your hands. I also know the terrible rewards of treachery. Do you?" He handed the bow and quiver into Astekar's outstretched hands.

Chapter 17

Spring had come late to Trusya, and the ensuing hot winds of summer had come later still. The signs were everywhere, in the carpet of flowers on the plain that should, during any normal summer, have already dropped their blooms to shrivel in the heat of the sun, in the low level of the river, in the frail but not unpleasantly warm breeze that blew round them as they rowed into land.

The work was not as hard as before. With arms grown strong from much rowing, Dagentyr could toil mechanically and set his mind free to study the sights or daydream. Clear blue water danced along the hull planking with a pleasant, mollifying gurgle. It did not seem like the ending to a voyage, but more like a beginning, a time when truly extraordinary and new visions would become apparent. His curiosity about the future while stuffed in the sack was about to be satisfied.

His own apprehension was lost in the general jubilation of the Trusian men. Those who were not manning oars hopped along the decks chattering and laughing, mumbling thanks to every sea god and slapping each other on the back for a voyage returned home, a voyage survived.

Astekar sat beneath the ship's awning and watched the land grow in front of him. Every muscle and relaxed limb showed his relief. Lightened by pending profits, a comfortable bed for the night, and surcease from pressure, his heart flew high. Ahead was the warming glow of praise and fame. These were minor benefits compared to the profits, but he was not averse to them.

Sidonian sailors and captains shook their heads at the wild antics of joy that the Trusians performed, and allowed a brief thought for home ports that they seldom saw, for they were wanderers. The sea was their true home; any other was strange.

As they approached the headland, they saw the signal fire lit in the lone tower that served as a warning to the city that a ship was approaching Trusya. The port village and the city would know of their coming.

Bolgios was caught up in the excitement and cheered as loudly as any of the rest as they rounded the point, crossed the bay, and came in sight of the beach landing.

Dagentyr leaned far back on his long, leisurely oar strokes and turned his head over his shoulder to see the landing. There were people scurrying on the shore, and other ships being loaded and unloaded. The tiny people in the distance were bent under the weight of bales of goods. They led animals for loading, shouted under canopies as Dagentyr had seen them do countless times, and they came and went by a dusty brown road that wound away from the site over the mounded hills behind the beach.

There were the usual seaside buildings and shelters protecting the waiting goods, wine shops and vendors, hawkers of cheap trinkets and amulets blessed by the sea gods, sailors seeing to the ships or fretting free time away around cook fires by telling their perpetual stories. There were ordinary people come to see the strange ships, the bright sails, and enjoy the cool sea breezes. As always, the painted women with their dark animal eyes mingled with the crowd.

Now the people on land had caught sight of the signal fire and the ships. A general shout went up from them, a shout of alarm. Dagentyr saw all of them drop what they were doing and run toward the hills and the road.

Astekar stood up, concerned.

"Gods!" he shouted. "Captain! Hail the prince and tell him to raise his sail. From this distance they've taken us to be an Ahhiyawan raiding party. They need a sign to know who has returned."

It was done, and the red sail-beast reared up and swayed soundlessly in the slack wind. On shore the clamor died slowly away and then changed. People returned to the beach and gawked at the royal emblem. The dust raised by their flight settled back to earth.

In the lead boat, Parush put on his boar's-tooth helmet with its scarlet plume, and mounted the prow. He cupped one hand to his mouth and called, "It is I, Parush, Prince of Trusya!" Then he waved his arm.

Dagentyr thought it doubtful that the people on the beach had heard from such a distance, but evidently they had seen, and the combination of the emblazoned sail and the proud, plumed figure waving to them was enough. As the ships came closer, Dagentyr began to hear the noise of the waiting throng. He heard it grow and cover the splash of his oar, yet it was a restrained cheering, not equal to the happiness of the Trusians who were returning. It was a tentative greeting; it was not adulation. They rowed faster.

Now he could make out more clearly the details of the scene. There were guards, armed like those on the ships in gleaming bronze, painted women, gaudier and richer looking than any he had seen before. Many people were coming to the beach, over the hills and down the road, raising a new cloud that hid those who followed them. All kinds of people, rich, poor, powerful, insignificant, some hailing the ships for news of loved ones or keeping their cheering respectable for the man standing at the prow of his ship like a young god.

As they upped oars and slid into the sand of the beach, Dagentyr saw the charred ribs of many unfortunate ships burned in some mishap. A broken stump of a mast poked from the surf. Barnacles had already made a home along its length. They stood out like bones in a mud puddle, something ugly and harsh against the bright clothes and gold, the burnished armor and happy voices. The thought was brief. He was out over the side, knee-deep in the water, pushing the boat farther up on shore. Men bounded into the water to help them, and with so many men pulling, the ship went easily and quickly upon the land, and slaves rushed to shore it up.

The prince's ship had landed first, and the crush of people was so thick round it that it was nearly hidden from view. Parush stood in the prow above all the rest, beneath the red sail-beast that Dagentyr had come to equate with the man.

Astekar stood in the prow of his vessel and acknowledged the cheers that greeted him. There was enough praise for all. Those with loved ones in the crowd left their places and ran among the people, seeking them, taking the embraces, the slaps on the back, the wine, the excited questions. Chaos took over the beach as the ships landed one by one. People came down the road in an endless stream or left the road's smoothness and walked across the hills and rocks to be there sooner. It was all thunderous confusion and wild din. The press of bodies rushed past Dagentyr and blurred into all the colors of the rainbow, and goldshine, and the loud, violent rush of a thousand tongues speaking a strange, unintelligible language.

He was in no hurry to leave his place. Amid the joyful hundreds he felt lonelier than he ever had in his life. He moved to where he could see Bolgios, glad of a familiar face, any familiar face. Bolgios had been seeking him out, too. When their eyes met, they just looked at each other and turned away after a time, ashamed of their need.

"What place is this?" Bolgios asked despondently.

Dagentyr shook his head and leaned back on the ship. "I do not know." Astekar stood watching them from the rail above. He overheard and answered the question.

"This is home."

Dagentyr breathed deeply of the foreign air and thought, He's right, now this is home. He wanted to fall to his knees and deal a death blow to the earth itself.

"Look at the strange new things, warrior. See how much gold the rich wear, more than any of the chieftains of your land has ever worn. Even lesser people wear rings of gold in their ears, on their fingers."

He nodded grudgingly.

Sobbing and wailing, an old woman helped along by a younger one at her arm made her way to the water's edge and hurled curses at the sea. The corpses under the wet sail cloth stirred in his memory, and he was sorry for the woman who would never again see whomever it was that had meant so much to her. The taunting wavelets lapped at the hem of her robe and ran away. The young girl buried her head on the woman's shoulder and covered her face with her mantle. He was reminded of his grandmother and Kerkina.

Trying to overcome his sadness, he pulled himself up on the shored boat and sat on the rail for a

better view. Bolgios was more sullen and sat down
in the sand to pick at bits of seaweed and broken
shell. The old woman wailed again.

The beach was a field growing people. All the
space not taken up by the ships was filled with
bodies moving in joyful aimlessness. Ignorant of
his status as slave, a young girl with dark hair
trotted from the throng to Bolgios. She gave him
water in a clay cup. He took it, drank, and smiled at
her. He was much broader in the chest and back
since working as a rower. Lightened by the sun, his
hair fell to his shoulders, which were tanned almost
as deeply as Dagentyr's, in spite of his fairness. The
girl ogled his blond hair for a moment, touched it,
and was gone, whisked away in a frenzy of maternal
scolding. Bolgios stood looking after her, but the
mill and confusion made it useless. He hauled
himself up next to Dagentyr.

"This new place may not be so bad. At least the
people seem friendly, and there is the means to ease
loneliness."

"You're a simpleton. You may not live long
enough to get lonely."

Bolgios shrugged. Not such a long time ago,
Dagentyr's statement would have frightened him.
His eyes would have grown big, and he would have
gone silent for a long time, asking later for reassurance. Now it had no effect on him. Thick arms and
work had transformed him. A lucky and inconsequential spear cast had improved his self-esteem.
He had played at sailor and warrior, and the game
had made him brave.

"I am going to live long enough to do what is
expected of me and enjoy the benefits of it."

Dagentyr, in a rush of anger, grabbed Bolgios by
the front of his tunic. "You're letting the
waterman's words sway you. That is foolish. If you
let this place capture you, I'll have nothing to do

with you. Then you can stay or escape, but you'll do it on your own. Don't count living as a certainty. I've seen what a hero you are in battle."

Bolgios was briefly flustered. "The past is gone and the future is glorious, as the wise men say."

"You and the wise men are simpletons. Glory must have the means to move itself along." He let go and Bolgios scooted away.

Having had enough of the praise, Astekar shouted to the guards for the slaves to be tied; an escape would be easy in the crowd. Dagentyr put his hands out, and they were bound.

A new excitement came to the proceedings. Along the road, voices rose in a swelling roar that reached those on the beach, and when they saw, they joined in. Down the road, a procession was making its way to the ships. Bystanders bowed respectfully to the train and resumed their cheering. There were warriors in the lead with spears and huge shields, and behind that a two-wheeled chariot pulled by two squat but beautifully groomed horses. Priests, ministers, and nobles followed behind. A helmeted man drove the chariot. His arms were muscled, and his tunic was of spotless white. The crest of his helmet was white, too. Busy at the reins, he carried no spear, just a sword swaying at his side. He was an imposing figure, but the man at his side in the chariot commanded even more respect.

His clean, older face was lined in a dignified, kindly manner. The forehead was high, and the hair behind it grey, long, and gathered into a club tied in place with gold ribbon. His robe was not that of a young man or warrior, but a long, full gown in white, cinched at the waist by a broad blue sash. His fingers and wrists were ringed in gold. A long dagger hung from the sash. Dagentyr knew its pommel would be of gold. When the chariot

stopped and he stepped out, Dagentyr noticed that
his shoes were of soft blue leather, turned up and
pointed at the toes.

The driver of the chariot handed the reins to a
guard and dismounted behind the rider. As they
passed, the people made a broad, clear path to the
ship where Parush stood. He remained in his lofty
position at the prow as long as he dared without
showing disrespect for his father the king, and his
brother, first prince of Trusya, then swung himself
down in front of them.

"It is a joy to see a son return home in glory,"
said the old man.

Parush bowed, and they clasped each other in an
embrace. "Father."

"Thank the gods you are returned safe to us.
Your mother has done nothing but worry since you
left. She never let me forget that you were most
likely in peril the whole time, but you look healthy
and strong and are probably more a man than when
you said good-bye to us. She waits to see you and
bade me tell you that she is thankful that you have
come back."

"I will see Mother as soon as we arrive at the
palace."

"It will make her happy."

"I have thought about both of you on the journey." He embraced the helmeted figure in white.
"You look well, brother Hektu." The air was instantly chill.

"And you, brother Parush, look as well as always."

The well of conversation went dry. Parush
turned again to his father.

"I see that we have arrived before the
Ahhiyawa."

The king turned grave. "They are late this year,
gods be praised. The coast has been relatively safe. I
have bought men of Lycia for aid if there should be

fighting. We will be ready for them this time, if they come. Do you have news of them?"

"Vague rumors of ships leaving Knossus, nothing more. Idomnus readies a fleet for action, it is said. We saw but one Ahhiyawan ship on the sea, and I took it and burned it."

The old man grinned, broke into laughter, and grabbed his son's shoulders. "My son has grown and now murders the Ahhiyawan swine on the open sea! I knew this voyage would be good for him. What about this lad, Hektu? Has he grown and changed?"

"Aye, my father, he has. He has outgrown his aversion to fighting the Ahhiyawa, at least. Gods be praised that there was only one ship, or he might have returned the same man as when he left."

"Brother," said Parush. "Does jealousy prick at you for the things that I have seen and done beyond the Pillars and for this welcome I have received?"

"What lies beyond the Pillars does not concern me. The kingdom does. I am content with that. As for your welcome, all returning heroes deserve glorious welcomes. They cause the heart to grow bold and courageous when the time comes for battle. I am glad my brother returns in time to fight with us."

Parush's face was flushed. The king whispered discreetly.

"You are letting your tongues run away with you. The people should not see such things. Let us return to the palace." Then in a loud voice, "Parush! Ride with us in the chariot! Come, Hektu. The people should see my son's triumphant return to the citadel."

Hektu bowed deferentially, and all three mounted the chariot. Hektu snapped the reins. The guards lined up, the people cheered loudly as Parush waved, and the party rolled off on the winding road, the crowd following as though poured from a bottle. Only those with work still to do lingered on the beach, and all became calm.

Astekar had guards collect the slaves from all the ships.

"Quickly, march them to the city behind the king's chariot. The people should see what spoils the prince has brought back with him. We'll have the dock slaves unload the cargo and carry it up later. Till then keep watchmen posted."

They were prodded across the sand to where the ground firmed up and the road started its way to the citadel. Interested people walked beside them and talked among themselves of the captives. Dagentyr was aware of his height. He was taller than most of the men of this foreign land. Nearly all the slaves were taller.

Ruki was indignant. For the first time in months he was back with the other slaves, tied and helpless. If he was above staying with them during the journey and was considered valuable, why when appearances were most important was he reduced to tripping along with the rest? His hands ached for his comforting lyre.

The path worked its way over the hills that faced the sea, and straightened out across a narrow plain marked by scattered clusters of mud and stone huts, cultivated fields, and vineyards. Herds and flocks roamed the unfarmed pastures.

The fields had been left unattended, for everyone had gone to see the prince enter the citadel. Along the road, the tiny river flowed sleepily in its bed, lined by trees and bushes. Those who had been fetching water stopped to watch the king and princes go by and gawk at the band of ragged slaves.

Heat stirred the air, rippling Dagentyr's view of his new surroundings, and as he looked down the length of the road, he saw that the houses became larger and more numerous. Then, on a low hill, he noticed the citadel.

The walls were not as high as three trees on top of one another but were certainly as high as one. Massive and stark, made of stone, they rose out of the plain and the cluster of dwellings that cowered in their shadow. They were breathtaking, huge, made of uneven stone blocks placed together and fitted perfectly. They slanted outward at the base and were topped by battlements of squared mud bricks. Gleaming in the sunlight, the palace in the inner citadel looked even loftier. Dagentyr had trouble believing that it was constructed by anyone other than gods. His mouth dropped open as it had when he had first seen the ocean.

The road continued to follow the river across the plain, and the people continued to watch and cheer, yet he sensed constant vigilance and caution in the air. The animals roamed close to the fortifications. The herdsmen kept careful watch so that none would stray. It was a city ready for siege, ready to go behind the walls at a moment's notice.

Increasing in apparent height, the walls dwarfed the men beneath them. In the shade of the stone walls peddlers and craftsmen had set out their wares and pitched awnings. Everything was for sale, vegetables, grain, pottery, but all was forgotten when the chariot passed. Men and women left their wares and ran to catch a glimpse of the prince and see what changes the journey had wrought in him.

Farther out from the walls, the hide tents of the hired Lycians sat nestled around the black piles of ash that marked the lighting and relighting of many campfires. The return of the prince elicited little reaction in the camp, as did the slaves that walked behind in the dust of the chariot. The men glanced casually in their direction and returned to their work.

Eventually the road and river crossed. They traversed a stone bridge and climbed the other bank for their final approach to the city. The thin, dusty line of dirt and people led up to the huge gates, standing open, guarded on one side by a high tower.

The chariot rolled up to the gates. Curious and eager heads peered from the tops of the lofty walls. A crowd around the gate gave a final cheer, and the king and princes rolled in on their way to the palace. The people lingered long enough to watch the slaves straggle in behind. Dagentyr felt the cool shadow of the lintel stone cross his face as they passed under it. The guards at the gate let their spears relax from the salute when the chariot had passed and worked at keeping the curious crowd in order and away from the slaves.

The horses snorted as they were reined in, and the chariot stopped. The king dismounted first, the princes after him. Each of them raised his hands to the people, accepting the last trickles of praise, and then they were gone, accompanied by guards up a footpath to the palace sitting on the peak of the hill, above the other buildings. Its stone walls were high for a dwelling, and its portico was held up by two great pillars painted brightly in reds and blues.

Once again the slaves were separated. The women were taken away, Dagentyr did not see where, and the men were lined up against the inside of the stone guard tower and told to sit.

Ruki plopped down, perspiring from the exhaustion and heat of the walk, and from anger. He loosened the sash of his tunic and found that he was sitting next to Dagentyr.

"Time changes everything, warrior," he said bitingly.

Dagentyr had not heard the voice for so long, for they had not spoken at all during the voyage. It was like a ghost of the past speaking in a dream.

"That is true. It even seems to change the grati-

tude in men's hearts. How long have you waited to
say those words to me?"

"I hadn't wanted to until now. I owe all my
sadness and all my troubles to you."

"Nonsense. I could have killed you at two different times. I didn't; I spared you. Aren't you better
off now? Just look at yourself." He gave Ruki's
green tunic a derisive tug. "Don't you enjoy what
you are?"

Ruki lowered his head. "Sometimes I do, and it
makes me sick. I have not yet performed for many
men, so life has been bearable, but I fear that soon
it will be like the feast in your village. Then I think
that it would have been better if you had killed
me."

Dagentyr shrugged. "And do you think that I
would be here without you? Why do you complain?
What would you be at home, even in your own
village?"

"Do you hate me, warrior?"

"I have no special feeling for you either way. You
do not concern me anymore."

Ruki had no retort ready. A one-sided hate
seemed an unprofitable thing, but it was a hate he
had worked on, nurtured. In truth he hated the
world, but that was futile, so his animosity was
directed toward the warrior. The two men sat in
silence.

Soon, Astekar approached with Tuwasis.

"This one goes to the palace slave quarters," he
said, pointing to Ruki. "Take the others to the
Lycian camp. Tell their leader that they are in his
charge. I am told his name is Sarpedon. We have
nowhere else to put them. Tell him they will be
equipped from the royal armory. They can fight, or
most of them can, and he should have no real
trouble with them. Remind him that they still
belong to us."

Tuwasis was unhappy with his luck, being a herdboy to slaves while the other voyagers enjoyed glory, and were already pressing wine cups to their lips. He wiped his dry mouth with the back of his hand and ordered the slaves to their feet.

Out again through the gates they went, and along the circuit of the walls to the town of tents and windbreaks they had passed earlier. Now the men seemed more interested in them. They stopped their activities and came for a closer look.

"Gaping fools," Tuwasis muttered and then said, "I am here seeking Sarpedon, leader of the Lycians."

A man ducked into a tent nearby and came out with a tall, sinewy man with a long, curling beard and straight, dark hair. His nose was aquiline and noble, his dark eyes intense. He wore only a belted kilt, sandals, and a sword. He brushed a fly from his neck with a grace that gave dignity to even so trivial a gesture. The men gathered around him as he stood in front of Tuwasis.

"I am Sarpedon of Lycia. What is wanted of me?" The voice was a rich and resonant bass.

"These men are to be given over to you for now. They are warriors newly brought in from the lands beyond the Pillars by Prince Parush."

Sarpedon was unimpressed by the mention of the prince's voyage. The crowd murmured surprise and curiosity and scrutinized the slaves more closely.

"It seems I'm cursed to command every foreign straggler as well as my own men. And what of the Thracians if they come? Will I be blessed with them, too?"

Tuwasis shrugged. The self-importance he felt from the joyous return was of no use here. "Most can fight. The king will arm them, you need not worry about that. They are palace property. Do with them as you see fit for now. Watch this one." He gave Dagentyr a jab with his finger. "He's treacherous. I'd have him beaten to break his spirit if I were you."

"Would you? What good is a warrior who has no spirit?"

Tuwasis turned to ice. "Naturally it is up to you, my lord. You know best." He bowed with minimal respect and withdrew, taking the other guards with him.

"Why do the gods make it so hard to get along with one's allies?" Sarpedon shook his head, amused.

"He's one of the followers of Prince Parush, no doubt. Just off the boat and cocky as a stud bull," said one of the men.

"Like the prince himself," said another.

"They're not a bad-looking lot. Some of them even seem fierce. Big, aren't they?" Sarpedon walked up to Dagentyr and was tall enough to look him directly in the eye. "Cut their bonds. As long as they're here we should set them to doing something useful."

A black-haired youth stepped forward.

"Should we not see how they fight, these men who are sent to us? I've never even seen a man from beyond the Pillars; I want to fight one."

"Yes, so do I," said another man.

"It's a boring day, my king. Since there are no Ahhiyawa to fight yet, let's sharpen our skills on these."

Sarpedon smoothed his moustache. "My curiosity is as strong as any. The days are filled with nothing but polishing weapons and drinking. We should not grow slothful. Glaucus, fetch my weapons. I'll try one of these men myself. Shout to our men on the ramparts so they can watch from their posts. Who else is ready to try one of the newcomers?"

"I, King," called Droskios, the dark-haired one.

"And me," said another.

"So be it."

"My king." Glaucus trotted back carrying the king's spear and armor. "You, as our leader and champion, should fight the best of the newcomers. Let them choose their man."

He nodded. "A fair idea. All right, barbarians, who shall you pick to fight me? Choose the best. Do they understand nothing, these oafs?"

"I think they want us to pick someone to fight this man," whispered Blue-eyes.

"He's right," said Dagentyr. "Who shall it be?"

"I say you, Dagentyr." The man with the droopy moustache spoke. "You defeated the waterman. You should fight him."

"Why not you?"

"This man is a hand taller than myself. You have stayed strong. We have wasted away and are not fit to fight. Your chances would be better."

"Fight him, Dagentyr." Bolgios practically begged.

"Go on, warrior," said another slave.

"You are the one we want."

"Fight him," said Droopy-whiskers.

Dagentyr felt a surge of apprehension. Tuwasis had been overconfident, slow. This man was not. He would be quick, sly. False confidence would not take hold of him. He was a man who knew what he could do, or he would not be a leader of men.

But would his own people want him to fight if he were not good also? The potential to lead had been offered. To refuse was not only cowardice, but a shunning of all his past hopes. Great opportunity, Astekar had told him. He stepped forward and said, "I will fight. Dagentyr is my name, son of Ashak."

"He's the one, my king!" blurted out Droskios. "The treacherous one."

Sarpedon smiled, nodded, and searched the eyes of his opponent. "I think this man is worthy. He has the look, the bearing, the physique. Bring armor and weapons for him."

Someone was off quickly. Meanwhile, Sarpedon spread his arms and his herald buckled on his layered, crayfishlike corselet and then his greaves. His helmet was of leather studded with bronze knobs, and two bronze horns protruded from the forehead. The herald smoothed its plume. His great bullhide shield was given to him and its supporting shoulder strap adjusted to ease the weight.

Panting, a man ran up to Dagentyr and gave him a corselet of leather and a plain leather helmet with a short, bristly horsehair crest. A nearby warrior donated his shield and sword. His arm and shoulder immediately felt the uncomfortable strain of the heavy shield. At home, in the forest, shields were round and much lighter, but this reached from his neck to nearly his ankles. Because he had no greaves, its metal rim knocked bruises on his shins. The men cleared an area and formed a ring around it. Everyone pushed and elbowed his way in as close as he could to see the contest.

Dagentyr cursed under his breath. The helmet was too small and pressed the blood from his head. The shield was very heavy.

In battle gear, Sarpedon became fierce. The sharp nose protruded from his face like the horns of the helmet. His beard flowed down, and his teeth showed white and canine against its darkness. He seemed to carry his shield with ease. Glaucus offered the king his spear.

"No. Spears are unsure weapons. A misguided cast can mean death where none is intended. We'll use swords. Give us room. Back everybody!"

"My king! Are we sure that the barbarian knows that it is a mock battle, and not to the death?"

"Yes, Droskios. I think he knows. Come!"

The two approached the center of the ring. Dagentyr felt clumsy under the weight of the shield.

It pulled at his arm and shoulder like lead. He would have preferred not to use it, but Sarpedon would be too well protected to defeat, and he himself too open and vulnerable. All he could see of his adversary was the shield, and behind it a horned, helmeted head. To the side of the shield, he saw a tensed wrist holding a sword. He began to circle and immediately noticed the heat.

Sarpedon shuffled to counter him and then rushed in. Dagentyr braced himself behind the bullhide and lifted the shield. The blow shook the shield's taut skin and he gritted his teeth. Pushing his shield up against Sarpedon's, he raised the sword and brought it across in a sideways stroke. It hit the metal rim of Sarpedon's shield and chipped it.

Sarpedon rammed again with the shield, making Dagentyr stumble back under the weight of his own. The king's subjects cried out, "Well done!"

Dagentyr recovered his balance enough to avoid falling, but the Lycian pressed his advantage and rushed again, knocking him to one knee. It took inhuman effort, but he lifted his shield above his head for protection against the blows that thundered on his shield. He retreated to the edge of the ring and felt the rough jabs and punches of the Lycians as they taunted him.

"Go back in," called the slaves.

Sarpedon waited for him.

He adjusted his grip on the shield, lifted it off the ground, and went back in. His shoulder ached already, and he had given only one blow. Dagentyr knew skill would not carry him; he would need luck. Quick, he thought, take him off guard. He rushed, stopped, rushed again and pushed the bottom of his shield out.

Sarpedon was taken by surprise. He lifted the shield up, expecting blows, but none came and the bottom of Dagentyr's shield jammed him in the

shins. It backed him up and caused pain through
the greaves.

Dagentyr swung the sword, hoping to find something exposed and yet holding back in order not to
kill or cripple. Sarpedon blocked every cut, grimac-
ing with effort.

The air was full of flying dust kicked up by their
struggle. A thin, chalky film clung to Dagentyr's
wet skin. He caught glimpses of teeth and bestial,
flashing eyes, heard the Lycian guards shouting
down from their positions. A sudden stinging in his
forearm told him the king's blade had cut flesh.

"Fight harder!" screamed Bolgios.

The slaves jumped up and down and screamed
old tribal war cries. The Lycian men, all smiles,
shouted viciously. Dagentyr was grateful that he
could not understand them.

The sun on the walls was dazzling. The sound of
crashing metal echoed back to them from the stone.
Dagentyr's arms were fire, and sweat stung his eyes.
He ducked behind the shield and a portion of his
plume was shaved away by Sarpedon's blade.

The Lycian was making an all-out effort, perhaps
a final one. Blows were coming fast against
Dagentyr's shield. His shield arm ached for relief
from the strain. With what he had left, he threw
himself at Sarpedon, pushing with all his strength.
His sword arm came around. The blade found the
corselet and slid up, cutting a gash under
Sarpedon's armpit. The king yelled and gave way.

Dagentyr gave a powerful downward blow. The
sword bit into the shield and its rivets tore through
the tang that held it to the hilt. The blade stayed
lodged in Sarpedon's shield, and Dagentyr was left
holding nothing but a useless handle.

At their places on the wall the sentries raised a
great whoop. The slaves bit their lips and became
quiet.

Bolgios cried, "Be wary."

Dagentyr threw down the handle and grabbed his shield with both hands. Sarpedon knew he was in command again but did not let the barbarian's misfortune stir him to foolhardiness. An unarmed man was still capable of much.

Dagentyr kept the shield directly in front of him. There was nothing he could do now except edge around the circle as the king took his time to stab and cut at any part he was forced to expose. Heat and noise were everywhere, and sweat made rivulets in the layer of dust on his body. Sarpedon's bobbing plume moved in front of him like an attacking bird. He fought continuously for balance. Forearms and wrists felt the shock and ached worse than before. A plan came to him, but in order for it to work, the king would have to drop his guard.

To conserve strength in his shield arm Sarpedon took some of the weight on the shoulder strap, held the shield to the side, and in doing so, left himself uncovered. Dagentyr thanked his gods; this was it. He jammed the bottom of his own shield into the ground, lifted his body into the air, and with the shield as support, vaulted out, kicking both feet into the inside of Sarpedon's shield. The force threw Sarpedon's shield arm back with its burden of hide and bronze. The king felt his shoulder strain in the socket as the immense weight wrenched him backward to the dirt. Lycians and slaves alike sucked in their breath.

Dagentyr regained his balance and backed off. In his hurry, the shield barked his shins, and his exhausted knees buckled. He rolled into the dust and could not prevent the great shield from falling on top of him.

"Get up, Dagentyr," the slaves' hoarse voices implored.

He tried to lift it, hopeless. Lycian warriors started to move in to aid their fallen leader.

"Back away!" Sarpedon yelled.

The sentries leaned over the battlements in disbelief. All became quiet except the onlookers in the rear ranks who could not see what had happened. They voiced their curiosity and asked who had won.

Sarpedon, on his back, struggled to release himself from the shield's shoulder strap. He rolled, and fidgeted with his good hand, trying at the same time to keep the sword in his grip. Trapped under his shield like a misshapen turtle, Dagentyr flailed his arms and legs.

Sarpedon swore disgustedly and sawed at the strap with his sword. Blood from his cut turned to mud on his corselet. When the strap finally gave, he got up and kicked the shield. His shoulder was agony, and his arm drooped limply at his side. Then he saw Dagentyr pinned helpless beneath the shield and laughed. Not in many years had someone gotten the best of him. He knew that if Dagentyr had not fallen under his own shield, the barbarian's foot would have been on his throat and Sarpedon of Lycia would have known defeat, defeat under the walls of Trusya and before the eyes of all his men. Honor demanded that such a brave man not be shamed.

"Well done. Admirable, you savage pig." He laughed again and put his sword back in its sheath. "Glaucus, come and help me. There will be no one vanquished today. Lift the shield off the barbarian."

Dagentyr got to his feet with Glaucus's aid. "You fought well, warrior. You have my respect. We welcome you to our ranks, you others, too. But whose sword was lost here?"

"Mine, King," said its owner.

"I'll make up your loss with arms of my own." The warrior bowed. The king moved stiffly to

Dagentyr and held out his hand. "Welcome, warrior. Pandarus, see that these men are given a place to sleep, and food and wine if they desire it."

Dagentyr raised his hand also, and they clasped forearms, then Sarpedon turned, put his hand to his bleeding armpit, and Glaucus helped him away to his tent. The other men ambled away grumbling. Self-consciously, the guards went back to their pacing of the walls.

Suddenly the slaves were around Dagentyr, clasping his hands, patting his back, shouting their congratulations. They practically carried him away. Bolgios ran up with a cup of water from somewhere, and he took it in great, thirsty gulps, running his tongue over his caked, dry lips.

Blue-eyes came to him and took his hand. "My name is Callias, and you are the best among us."

"And I am Tingwahr," said the man with the droopy moustache. Then he smiled and offered his hand.

The slaves beamed at him, and he knew that from now on, he would be the one they would turn to for leadership, look to in battle when it came. He poured the rest of the water over his head and let the praise ring in his ears like sweet pipe music. He was a chieftain.

Chapter 18

Twilight had become Dagentyr's favorite time of day. After the heat of the afternoon when the smelly hide tents became unbearable and the flies swarmed over the camp in thousands and the busy traffic around the city fouled the air with dust and animal odors, it was peaceful and relaxing to stand guard on the walls, with the sun low and harmless in the sky. The people had gone home for the evening meal; fresh breezes blew in from the sea. The world was covered with soft, dusty light. Stone and brick turned to gold. Shadows from the walls fell over the camp and cooled it.

From his spot on the ramparts he had a breathtaking view. The mountains rose up in the east, behind him, and were growing dark. Before him the plain spread out, and the two green rivers crept along, meeting to flow off to the sea at Kiastu, the bustling port town where he had landed months ago. Beyond that, the plain's smoothness led to the broad sea, purple now as the sun prepared to make its plunge.

The passing of time had seen him, and all of them, go from nameless newcomers to men, men

who were part of the whole, accepted, worthy of
positions of trust like sentry duty. He took special
pride in that, for he knew that if he had lost his duel
with Sarpedon, they would be shining other men's
armor and fetching wood for the fires. He had
taught Bolgios the basics of fighting. Eager to
please, the boy learned quickly but was still no
warrior. The Lycians didn't seem to mind that,
though. He was one of the fierce northerners.
Dagentyr's fight had given them all a reputation, so
much so that even now when they practiced at
arms, the Lycians avoided them and fought with
their own.

It had been a good time in its way, but there had
been no chance of escape. Trusting that his time
would come, he waited and made the best of it. He
kept himself strong and he worked at learning the
new tongue. Even that was not as hard as he had
expected.

He looked around to see that no one was watching except the man on guard with him and then
took the shield off his shoulder and set it against the
parapet. The spear he set at rest too and adjusted
his cloak. Nights were growing cool. Summer
would soon be gone, and the city would relax,
knowing that the Ahhiyawa had missed a year and
would not come again till spring. The Lycians
grumbled at being summoned for nothing and
spoke constantly of going home.

"Ah, brr. I hope the night guard arrives soon. I'm
so hungry you could hear my stomach complain in
the land of the Hatti." His companion, a scruffy
man with a gap where his front teeth should have
been, shambled up beside him and pushed his
helmet far back on his head. "They should be along
soon, and then we can get off the wall."

Dagentyr nodded. "I like it on the walls this time
of day."

The man shrugged, and they relaxed at their

posts until the rattle of armor brought their attention to their replacements preparing to mount the wall from the path below.

"Good, they're here. Not too soon for me, that's for sure. I—" He halted abruptly and looked off in the direction of the palace. "Wait. It's her. Wait a moment longer at your post. Let the others come." He adjusted the helmet to its proper position and took up his arms. Confused, Dagentyr did the same. "Look there on the wall. Do you see? We're in for a treat, I'll tell you that."

Dagentyr peered down the length of the wall in the failing light. A cluster of people moved along the rampart at a leisurely pace. Two were armed men and the others women.

"What is this about? I thought you were hungry. Who is that on the walls?"

"Shh. Calmly. It is the Lady Helani. Do you not know of her? It is she that Parush stole from her husband and was the cause, or part of it, of the trouble. She is one of the bringers of the Ahhiyawan curse. She is very beautiful, some say the most beautiful woman in all the world. I confess I've not seen them all but, believe me, she's beautiful enough. What a woman, hair as black and glossy as a raven's ass. Stay a while and you will see her. They will pass and go around the entire city."

Dagentyr understood the gist of his speech. "Why would a woman walk the ramparts?"

The guard laughed and spoke behind his shield. "This is one of the only places and times she is safe from the people. She's hated like plague. That's why the men guard her; all the time she is guarded. She takes her evening walks here on the walls, away from the populace. That a beautiful woman should be the cause of such trouble." He sighed and shook his head. "If not for her and the Ahhiyawa I would be home on my own lands and so would we all, even you."

"This is the woman I have heard about?"

"Quiet. She comes close enough to hear soon. Pull yourself up and be discreet as she passes. Parush is jealous, I have heard. If you look at her too much, the guards will tell the prince. There will be bad feeling, and you are still a slave. Be careful."

The group came closer. Dagentyr ventured a cautious glance over the top of his shield. Outside the city gates he had seen women coming and going in simple dress, drab woolens. The nearing women glittered with gold and rich colors. Now they stopped and a woman walked to the wall's edge and pointed out something to the others. Light, falsetto laughter followed, and the group continued. The guards passed and stopped again as the women lingered to watch the sunset turn the mountains purple. The toothless one cleared his throat nervously. Dagentyr tried to stare straight ahead but could not. Curiosity was too strong.

There were several women on the wall very close to him; he could not tell which one was Helani. Then, a woman detached herself from the others and neared Dagentyr's companion. The man dipped his head and brought his spear across his chest.

Dagentyr felt his pulse quicken. She spoke to Toothless in a shadowed voice and he stammered something in return. He was riveted to his spot on the wall. She came closer until she stood in front of him. The air had the hint of an exotic, musky fragrance. She let the shawl that covered her head fall to her shoulders. He stared, then turned his whole body away in haste, remembering Toothless's words. Her watery laugh caught his ears and he heard her say, "Do not be so shy, warrior. Let me look at you. I am tired of everyone treating me as though I had the evil eye. Look at me if you like. I do not believe that I have seen you before. Come now. Please." Her voice was liquid.

Dagentyr faced her and let his eyes roam. Her eyes caught his, grabbed them. Stunningly dark and large, they were outlined in black and stood out against her pale skin. Her cheeks were high, smooth, and led to a delicate mouth with gently rounded lips. The face was set in a shaded grove of jet-black hair. Elaborate sets of ringlets, curls, and tails sat on the back of her head and fell down the sides of her face, all dressed and held by gold bands. A golden diadem ringed her head and its pendants fell against her white brow and nestled in the long ebony tresses. Her neck was adorned with frail golden wires. The gown she wore was long but bared her willowy arms and her breasts. Rich blues and purples alternated in the flounced, pleated skirt. Her waist was pinched with a scarlet and gold girdle, and a long embroidered apron of blue fell against the rich drapes of material. The golden bracelets at her wrists seemed bulky and out of place on her slender limbs.

With an embarrassed mumble, he lowered his head and crossed his spear as he had seen Toothless do.

She giggled; her handmaidens giggled in their turn. With her mirth, her breasts moved softly, and as his head dipped, he saw the nipples, large, and rosy with cosmetic. Toying with her shawl, she let its tasseled ends dance playfully over the pink circles. Perspiration formed under his helmet, and his legs tingled and were numb.

Instantly, the laugh was gone, and she was as serene as before. Her hands were still, the breasts concealed by the shawl. He dared not raise his head to note again the darkness of her eyes.

She raised a finger to point at a lock of his hair sticking from under his helmet. "I would have remembered a man with lighter hair like some of my own people, and certainly one so tall. Mehiya, come see, his eyes are green." A small woman ventured up, nodded frivolous agreement, and stepped back to her place.

"He is from the north lands beyond the Pillars, my lady," volunteered Toothless, "and does not understand the language well. Forgive his awkwardness."

"Already forgiven. Once he has been in Trusya as long as I, he'll learn the tongue." Dagentyr heard sadness in her voice, or was it sarcasm? "Beyond the Pillars? Then is this the man we have heard all the stories about? You defeated Sarpedon, didn't you?"

"No, my lady, he didn't. It was a draw." Toothless hurried to defend his king's honor.

She laughed again. "What is his name? I know the names of many of the men who guard the walls. You are Othroos, aren't you?"

"Yes . . . Yes, my lady." He was so pleased at her knowledge of his name that he lost his composure and could only repeat his salute clumsily. "Dagentyr is his name, my lady. Takes a while to get used to saying it."

"Dahguinteer," she said.

"Yes, my lady. You've got the knack right away. I— Pardon, my lady. I talk too much." He cleared his throat and took a step backward.

At the sound of his name, Dagentyr looked up again. She picked up the shawl and draped it concealingly over her head.

"A strange name but right for a man from a strange, exciting place." She smiled at him. Teeth like boar ivory showed behind the round lips, but they were not perfectly straight. He rebuked himself immediately for noticing so trivial a thing in such a woman. The bodyguard tapped impatiently on his shield. "Yes, Diamos?"

"It's time that we be on again, my lady. The prince doesn't like you to be out after dark, as you know. We should hurry if we are to make a complete circle of the walls."

"Very well. Truly it's too much, as if I were a child to be put to bed as it grows dark. May the gods bless my husband, so concerned is he for my well-being. Come, Mehiya, Niokethe, let's walk. Perhaps you could sing a lullaby for me, Diamos. Later on, of course."

The ladies giggled and walked by Dagentyr, taking peeks at him from behind their shawls. They walked less leisurely than before and soon were far off down the wall. The Lycian camp grew quiet and resentful as she passed. When she was gone, they continued their activity as before.

"Ohha, what did I tell you!" said Toothless. He stuck his tongue obscenely through the gap in his teeth and moistened his lips. "It's enough to make a man lose any thought to his appetite. She knew my name. Did you hear her say it?"

"Yes, I heard it."

"You'll tell the others, won't you? You'll back me up?"

"Yes."

"Ah, there's a friend. Here's the men come to replace us. Let's go and eat. It's hard to hate her. I don't care what the others say. It's a sad situation. She remembered my name," he said to their replacements.

Dagentyr tried to get another look at her before they climbed down, but it was growing too dark and they were too far away. He took his helmet off with relief. Its inside was wet with sweat. He understood how Othroos would look forward to having her say his name. Gods, put me on the walls at dusk for the rest of my life, he thought. "Dahguinteer," he heard her say. "Dahguinteer."

Chapter 19

Dagentyr and Bolgios carried their great shields across their backs, and their spears rested carelessly on their shoulders as they walked. The swords at their sides swung in rhythm to their steps, and it pleased them to feel the weight of the sharp bronze. Dagentyr took big steps.

It was the beginning of an autumn evening, mild and clear. The last light of sunset made the isle of Imbrios sparkle like an emerald in the blue sea.

For days it had turned colder in keeping with the season, and wind had stirred whitecaps on the ocean and waved the tall grasses in the marshes north of the city. The hordes of mosquitoes had abated. Then the weather had changed. The wind died, and the world returned to a freak summer. Trusya was carefree and rejuvenated, and on top of that, tonight there would be feasting.

The plain and the city were pale in the clear air. Guard duty at the port was over, and they walked the road back to the citadel from Kiastu. They passed quickly by the slow carts and lazy evening travellers.

"If we're not quick we'll miss the first of the festivities," urged Bolgios.

"Be still. Nothing much will happen until dark. Surely the high chieftains won't go to the palace until then. There's plenty of time yet."

"But if they distribute the gold before we—"

"Bah, there won't be any gold for us. We're still slaves; don't forget that. There'll be little gold for any but the high men and leaders."

"But the king has said that there will be good food for all and many women, for the common men, too, like us."

He nodded. "That is true, and it is what you will have to be content with. King Priasham will win the Lycian favor with his gold and food and women, and convince them to stay through the year to guard against the Ahhiyawa. That is why the Thracian men have come as well. The king's gold lures men over great distances. He is afraid to have his city face the enemy alone. He wants to be safe and sure."

"But there has been no fighting, and now the ocean storms will prevent travel."

Dagentyr shrugged. "Even so, the king invites Sarpedon and his captains to a feast in the great hall of the palace and plies them with favors and gold, and we get food and women." He shrugged once more and pulled his beard. He had let it grow longer, and his moustache had a much more respectable droop.

"What do you think? Will Sarpedon stay?"

"We will see after tonight. He may; he is an honorable man. I hope he does. As long as our fate is linked with the Lycians we will be better off."

The camp was in high spirits. Anticipatory laughter filled the tent city, and the men milled about the fires, heaped higher than usual and already blazing beneath sides of beef and pig. Palace attendants and slaves had spread cloths and placed food and drink on them. Female voices mingled with the masculine roar of the place as

Sarpedon and his chiefs mounted their chariots to enter the citadel, and the first of the hired women arrived to serve.

"Dagentyr, you have arrived!" Tingwahr ran up to him and shoved a goblet into his hand. "We were worried that you would be late. Come and see. The camp is filled with food and already there are women around our fire. They have been sent from the palace and others bought in port. Aye, and some of them are comely."

"I'm glad to see you so happy. One would think that the feast was in *our* honor."

He laughed. "Does it matter? If the time for feasting comes, take it and make the most of it."

Bolgios shed his weapons quickly and made his way to the fire where the tribesmen sat tearing at roasted wild fowl. The men were glad. Callias sat with a painted woman on his knee, and he took advantage of her stylish, open-fronted bodice to cup her breasts with his big hands while she shammed protest, and the others ogled and joked rudely about their turn. Other women came later. The strangeness of the barbarians drew them. The bored, dockside whores were in search of any novelty.

Bolgios fretted and hovered near Callias's woman. He became angered and pushed the boy into the dirt playfully but with enough authority to say, let be.

Dagentyr sat down and concentrated on the wild fowl. When he was done, he tossed a picked leg bone into the fire and let his eyes swim in the bright colors of the women's clothing. His mind turned automatically to Helani on the wall, the brief glimpse of her eyes, her tantalizing words. The memory of her face, lovely and dark, made him think of another, red-haired, light-eyed, distant. Guilt wracked him, for the woman of Trusya made him think less of Kerkina, and less kindly. Helani's

dark features superimposed themselves on every
nearby woman's and stayed when he looked away,
like the afterimage of a bright lamp flame. A
burning log popped and sent a gay shower of sparks
leaping into the stars.

Tingwahr did a dance past the fire and sat down
on his rump. "Dagentyr, it's nights like this that
make me glad we are here. I want to piss on the rest
of the world."

"You are happy, then?"

"Yes, happy for now. And you? Are you a happy
man?"

"The pleasures of this place are hard to ignore,
but even if I gave in to them I would not be happy."

"Then don't be happy, be content. Surely that is
not quite as hard to be. Look at this place, the food,
the . . . Ah." He creased his face up to look wise. "I
know. You pine for the Helani woman. How many
times did you tell us the story of her walk on the
wall. I can see your problem. Woman-sad, that's
what you are. But there's no reason for it. Take a
look at these the king has sent. We can have our fill
tonight, all of us, but you should have the first
pick."

Men were singing songs of Lycia at a nearby fire.
A slave came among them and placed a jug of wine
before the blaze. In and out between the tents, a
band of musicians pranced, playing pipes, lyres,
and sistra. A crowd of drunken men followed
behind them, stomping brutishly, angry because
there were not enough women for all and they had
lost the draw for first. They circled Dagentyr's fire
and the music quickened. Tingwahr tugged him to
his feet and moved him to one of the women. The
other men moved off. None questioned his right to
choose first.

She was stocky, short, olive-complected. Her
dress was worn but more colorful than the rest,
yellow and red and white, studded with tiny bronze

flowers. Gold tassels gleamed at her ears. The clothing was not plain enough for the slave girls of the palace. She was of the port and made a living at this trade. She saw Dagentyr and smiled. Her hands were feather-light as she motioned to the musicians and spoke.

"Slow."

They stopped the riotous play and began again, softly and sensuously. The woman moved away from them and removed her spangled vest completely. Naked above and jumbled rainbow below, she turned with the music. Her ample flesh rippled with the sistra's shiver, and she was a serpent.

The barbarian men stopped everything to watch her. Drunken Lycians stopped and sat down where they were. Her arms swirled, quivered, caressed, teased. Along the ground, her feet skipped silently, and she *was* the music. Faster she twirled, till the spinning skirt fanned the flames sideways. It was in her way; she raised it. Lycians hummed and commented. Bolgios scrambled closer to peek under its folds. She closed her eyes and relaxed her neck. Her head rolled, disconnected. Dancing for Dagentyr, she stepped close to him and continued her spin. Against the red blaze, her silhouetted legs were black. The joining of her thighs was black and mysterious. She stopped. The music ceased. The skirt fell straight with a clinking of the bronze flowers.

"Ah," the Lycians cheered.

"Who needs a Helani when there is a woman like this, Dagentyr?" said Tingwahr.

Dagentyr snorted. He resented the mentioning of her name in the same breath with the whore. The woman came willingly to his lap. She rested a cool, wet forehead on his shoulder and raked her fingers through his hair. The nearness of a woman fired him. He noticed the heat of the flames more acutely.

She waved her hand at the musicians, and they went away like blown leaves, the warriors behind them hot with waiting. But there was one who stayed behind in the firelight, and Dagentyr recognized Astekar by his casually confident stance.

He folded his arms across his chest and walked between the revelers to Dagentyr. His robes were long now, rich, and he sported opulent jewelry. "And are you Trusian yet, warrior?"

The men became quiet.

"It has been a long time since we have seen each other," Dagentyr commented.

"I was giving you time."

"You came to the camp just to see me?"

"Of course not. I am in charge of the festivities. I like to see that they are going well. I like to know the details, if the warriors are enjoying my work." He made a questioning face. "Well?"

"You do many things well. This is more enjoyable than most of them."

"I thought you would like it. You will like it more and more, but much depends on you."

"You still think you can make me into whatever you want, don't you?"

"I'm positive. Already you have given in to some of the lures. You have eaten the food of this feast, taken wine, haven't you? So then, you've taken the first steps. You may give in yet again this night." He raised an arm and indicated the dancing woman.

"You aren't the only one to tell me that much depends on me." Dagentyr's voice became menacing. He stepped closer, and in the distorting glare of the fire, the difference in their heights was truly astonishing. It was not lost on Astekar. Though he did not back up, would not, the mirth left his face, and caution took its place. "The lures. You think I'm caught? What of the fish who takes the hook and then struggles free? He's better off, isn't he, because he's learned of treachery and stolen the bait as well. Such fish smile at the fisherman, trader. I'm smiling at you now, and I will smile when you die. I'll take this woman tonight so you'll think I've swallowed the hook."

Astekar's hand was inching slowly to his dagger. To have Dagentyr so close and armed was discomforting.

Dagentyr reached out and snatched hold of Astekar's wrist. The trader tried to pull away and could not. Slowly, and without protest from Astekar, he pulled a golden ring from the trader's finger.

"You are right about the lures being enticing, though." He let go of the hand and put the ring on his own finger.

"You're more lost than you think," Astekar said as he backed away. The shadows hid his expression, and he turned from them and walked away.

Callias's woman broke the quiet. She giggled, then pulled him toward one of the tents. He bellowed a good night and flung the dregs of his wine into the dust. The men cheered.

Dagentyr felt the dancing girl's eyelashes flutter near his ear as she kissed his neck. He took her face between both hands and placed his lips feverishly against hers. She was not Helani; she was not Kerkina. No matter. Bunching the tail of his tunic in her hands, she pulled him away to the bushes bordering the camp.

The woman was sleeping soundly when he went to fetch his cape to throw over her. Dry leaves rustled in the faint breeze and accompanied her shivering as the music had accompanied her dance. Camp was quiet. Sated, drunk, tired, the men and women slept among the empty wine jars and greasy cloths covered with bones. No one saw him fetch the cloak and return to the brush. The woman sighed, clutching the cape and rolling away from him. He wished that he was asleep like the rest, or

drunk. The woman was spent, and he was bored
and lonely. Fallen grasses cushioned his head as he
lay back to look at the night sky.

Was this a good time to escape? Funny that his
thoughts would turn to that now when all the other
men of his land were content, stuffed with the new
wonders of the place called Trusya. He admitted to
himself that it was much easier to forget about
escape, lie still and feel the breeze.

The noise of the fire covered her footfalls so he
could not hear them. "Dahguinteer?"

He sat up and parted the bushes. His stomach
contracted in shock and surprise.

"Dahguinteer, are you here?"

A woman was sneaking through the camp, picking her way over sleepers and clinging close to the
shadows and the concealment of the tents. She
didn't speak loudly, just loud enough to be heard by
anyone who was still awake. The cover of a lean-to
close by attracted her, and she skittered across to it,
pulling her scarf close to her face.

He stayed where he was and watched her skirt
the campfire, taking random glances at the various
men asleep around it.

"Dahguinteer?"

By Teshub! He swore by the new-learned Trusian
god. It was Helani calling his name and looking for
him. What sort of omen was this and what should
he do? He checked the woman. She was still deep in
sleep.

"Dahguinteer. Dahguinteer?"

His ears burned. Quietly, he left the bushes
behind. He wanted nothing more to do with the
woman sleeping there and did not want Helani to
know of her.

"Dahguin—"

"I am here."

She stopped. "Shh. Come here to the shadows."

How strange. Her voice was not as he remembered and her manner changed. He did as she asked

and she backed away next to a dark tent. The dumbfoundedness he experienced on the ramparts returned, and she had to command again before he stepped up close to her. It was not close enough to satisfy. She grabbed his tunic and pulled him against her, speaking in his ear. "We must not be seen." The shawl fell to her shoulders. It was the serving girl, Mehiya. It took him aback. Instantly, disappointment stabbed him, but then why was the lady's serving girl seeking him?

"I thought you were Hel—, the Lady Helani."

"Don't be silly. A queen does not skulk around in the shadows of a common soldiers' camp." She smiled a derisive little smile. "She has others skulk in her place. Now listen to me. My lady desires to see you. Does that surprise you? It does, I can see. If you come with me, I will show you the way. You must cover yourself. No one must see."

"Why does she want to see me?" he asked, suspicious.

"What does it matter? Do you wish to come or will you stand here and stammer idiotically like you did when you met her? I'm wasting time. The night is perfect, the time short. The men are all drunk. The great lords are all still in the hall but the women have retired to their chambers. Prince Parush will be too drunk to walk or see. It is a night when no one will notice us. They do not come often." Fighting the hesitation was hard. He did not know what to say, but inside, his heart said go. "If you have not the stomach for it, I—"

A coarse grunt signaled someone's entrance to the hearth circle. A Lycian man walked by, holding his belly. Mehiya threw herself into Dagentyr's arms, and he pulled her deeper into the shadows. The Lycian hiccoughed and continued on, groaning.

"We must hurry," she said, wrapping the shawl tight about her face. "I'll say it again. If you have not the stomach for it, tell me and make my task easier. If you are a true man, grab your cloak and follow me. Keep quiet."

Her words had a memorized quality, like a song that had been sung over and over. He had heard women's tricks to appeal to men before; Gertera was good at them. Suddenly, he did not like her.

"I will come."

"I knew you would. You northerners are real men, so I have heard. Now get your cloak and cover your head."

Not wanting to wake the woman in the bushes to claim his cloak, he took Bolgios's, which lay unused at his side. His own would be gone tomorrow. The woman would take it as her due.

Mehiya led the way to the walls. There was a light flickering near the western shore. A light. He paused and the blood leapt forward in his veins. The watchtower on the point was signaling.

"Look. The light is lit in the tower." He tugged her shawl to stop her. "There must be ships coming."

"Can't you be quiet? Why do you mumble about ships? Why should anyone sail in at night?" She walked on. The lesser gate to the northwest of the city was ahead.

Horses' hooves and the wooden rumble of chariot wheels stopped him short before he could catch up with her. A voice shot out of the blackness.

"The Ahhiyawa!"

Not now, he thought.

The charioteer stopped at the edge of the camp and screamed, "Up and to the citadel! The Ahhiyawa have landed. They are in Kiastu!" Wild-eyed and unarmed, the chariot driver turned the team back toward the road and galloped for the main gate. Sentries atop the walls picked up his warning and ran to sound the alarm. "Alert the palace," called one just above them.

The camp stirred. Drunk and sleepy but quick-

ened by the shouted words, the warriors got up
quizzically. The cry spread through the tents and a
woman somewhere screamed in dismay.

Dagentyr stood rooted, watching the encampment come alive. Callias got up and peered out of
the tent questioningly. Bolgios and Tingwahr wandered around in puzzlement. The woman stumbled
out through the bushes and asked what was wrong.

"Mehiya, we—" He turned, but she was gone.
There was a brief wave of colored skirt as her bare
feet carried her through the gate and behind the
walls.

"Dagentyr," yelled Bolgios, "what is the matter?"

There was no time for talk. It was not far from
Kiastu to Trusya. The messenger had made the trip
quickly by chariot. It was possible that Ahhiyawan
warriors were close behind.

"Get everyone up! Take your weapons. Get ready
to take everything into the citadel. The Ahhiyawa
have landed. Hurry!"

There were faces everywhere and bustling panic,
sleepy faces, resolute faces of warriors hurriedly
buckling on armor and tripping into their greaves,
the frightened faces of the first townspeople and
outskirt dwellers hastening down the road or into
the camp for no other purpose than to be near men
who had the comfort of weapons.

Everyone was shouting. In the blink of an eye,
camp was being hastily broken and people made a
living stream to the gates.

Dagentyr darted back to the campfire and
grabbed his weapons, keeping an eye out for all his
men. They were all there, gathering what they
could.

There were Sarpedon and Priasham and the
other captains, interrupted at the feast with wine
still on their lips, standing on the wall above the
northwest gate.

Still the people came, in terrified groups, holding children and desperately salvaged bundles of possessions. It was difficult to hear anyone distinctly above the clamor. The Lycians were grouping under the lesser captains and working to clear the camp of people.

"Dagentyr!" In the confusion, Sarpedon had seen Dagentyr and recognized him readily. He fumed and gave his orders from the wall. "Take your men to the road to delay the Ahhiyawa if they are coming. We must have more time to get the people inside. Take others with you, anyone you can. All of you! Go to the road. Hold them off."

It was quiet. People trickled in from Kiastu and the farm lands. The western horizon was lit up as the huts and ships of Kiastu fell to the Ahhiyawan torches.

They stood shoulder to shoulder, shields together, waiting, adjusting armor straps and peering toward the burning village, expecting screaming, bronze-carrying men to plunge at them from the night. Bolgios shivered even though it was not overly cold. They waited until the last stragglers from the countryside went by. An old man and his wife thought they were a band of marauders and screamed for mercy until a Lycian spoke to them kindly and convinced them they were friends. No Ahhiyawans came.

"They must be content to sack the port and wait until day to meet us," said Dagentyr.

The voice of panic had died down, and they were alone. It was agreed that it was time to go back. Closed and barred, the northwest gate was secure and tight as a dried skin. They went around and entered through the main gate. After they were inside, the wooden doors were swung laboriously into place, and the huge crossbars were knocked into their fittings.

Dagentyr sighed with relief and mounted the

rampart next to the gate tower. Others were there besides warriors, hugging relatives or friends and watching their homes incinerate. Flames neared the city as the Ahhiyawa worked systematically and steadily, burning and pillaging as they came closer. Fire crept up the plain like a lethargic, scorching wave.

The breeze switched directions and blew south, bringing with it sporadic screams of rage and death. Not everyone had made it to the citadel. He counted his men again. All were there. Sarpedon's voice dug into the quiet as he came along the walls asking for news of his party on the road. Dagentyr detached himself from the gaping herd and spoke to him.

"Lord Sarpedon, it is I, Dagentyr. The party has returned and the gates were closed behind us. All returned."

"The Ahhiyawa?"

"There were none to fight."

The king was very close to him, but the night made his face a blur. "Tomorrow perhaps."

Bolgios was calm and did not start when Dagentyr came up behind him and put his hand on his shoulder as he gazed over the burning plain.

"It seems as though Sarpedon has had his mind made up for him. There will be no escape from this place until the Ahhiyawa leave or are driven away. I thought of escape tonight, but—"

But what, he thought. But the lures were too strong? He felt ashamed, defeated, and wondered if Astekar knew that the strongest lure of all was the dark woman named Helani. The faint bellow of a bull drifted over the walls from out beyond the vineyards, followed by the sharp, savage cry of a man.

Chapter 20

The day was bleak. The mountains were swathed in the overcast. Like leaden slag, the clouds boiled up, threatening rain. Helmet plumes swirled everywhere, tossed by the cold wind. Guards on the walls stood with their feet far apart, shields held edgewise to the gusts. The wooden gates stood blank like clean wax tablets with no writing, indicating neither death nor life, victory nor defeat.

The warriors stood crowded in a mass in the space before the gate, all weapons polished, held tightly. Shields bumped against each other as men swayed their weight from foot to foot, nervously.

Dagentyr was near the back of the group, standing among the lighter-armed footmen. Princes and chiefs rode in the fore, girt in their bronze corselets and shining greaves, helmets of metal or leather covered with boar's teeth upon their heads. He recognized the dark and handsome Prince Awunash and a few of the others, their chariots lined single file, waiting their turn to exit the city. Parush was in his chariot. So was Sarpedon, with his hands grasping the rail, looking back at his men, showing them strength. The air was fogged with frozen breath and the strong smell of the horses. It was like being in a well of watery moon-milk.

Outside, the taunting and jeers of the Ahhiyawa came and went with the flow of the air. Weeks had seen no fighting. The portents were always seen as unfavorable by the Trusian priests. They stayed in the fortress. The Ahhiyawa were content to raid the coast and stay by their ships, enjoying their spoils. During that time, they had built fortifications and walls between the ships and the city. At dawn, they had marched up the plain in hundreds, like lean wolves, and called for battle.

Bolgios stood holding his bow. Dagentyr had picked the weapon for him for his first battle. Bowmen hung back out of the heavy fighting, and it would be safer for a young lad there where the excitement of first battle would not drive him to foolish bravery. His spear cast at the Ahhiyawan ship months before had not been all luck. He had a good eye and transferred his aim to the bow; he had the brawn now for a powerful pull.

Dagentyr took Bolgios aside. "Stay back with the other archers. Be valorous but not reckless, and gauge your shots well. If you are hurt, go behind the lines. May Tyr, the god of war and cunning, go with you." They clasped arms.

He gave his men a final looking-over. Straight, tall, and fierce they stood, not armed as splendidly as the rest but just as imposing with their greater height and hardened expressions. "Tyr be with you," he said to them, and they nodded. Thoughts of killing quickened their breathing.

The horses snorted in impatience and stamped at the ground. Each man looked to the walls where the king, queen, and Hektu were performing the ritual. High above the warriors, a seer killed a goat and studied its entrails. When the signs were announced fair for victory, Hektu raised his spear, gave a shout, then loped down the steps to his waiting chariot. "Men!" called the king. "At last the omens are good. May the gods go out on the field with you to make war on the Ahhiyawa, and may glory be our reward!"

The queen added her blessing and made sacrifice to the gods.

An impatient Hektu thumped his spear loudly on his shield. His driver fought to control the agitated beasts.

"Open the gates, the quicker to gain glory. Men of Trusya, the god of war kills with us today!"

A roar went up from the Trusian throats and the gates were opened. The wind blew full in their faces. Chariot followed chariot out at a gallop and the ground vibrated with the pounding of hooves. The footmen lurched forward like a slow-moving animal and poured out the gate through the chariots' cloud, howling oaths and war cries. The downhill run to the plain gave them speed. They ran uncontrolled to the Ahhiyawan line that stood like a wall of living stone, waiting for them.

Dagentyr and his men cried the tribal war calls in their own language. The wind forced their words back into their mouths and blew their hair out straight behind them. Bolgios made feeble groans between heaving gasps of excitement and fear.

When the Trusian chariots neared the line, the first arrows began to fly. Their paths were silent in the noise of the wind and streaked to earth like things in a delirious man's nightmare. Ahhiyawan chariots left the line quickly to meet the threat, and the real noise of war, the clank and thud of bronze on metal and leather and bone leapt up from the plain.

Dagentyr followed Sarpedon, keeping the tall figure in sight, watching the horsehair plume as it rocked with the motion of the car, then the chariots outdistanced them and were hidden in the clouds of dust.

Behind the melee of horses and wheels, the footmen advanced. Slingers, archers, and lightly armed spearmen threw and retired out of range. Dagentyr had never seen fighting like this. There were so many men. The ground rumbled with the noise of the chariots. There was no forest to run to, to blend in with. He made a quick run to the front of the line, and hurled his first spear into the Ahhiyawans. It flew over the first rank of shields and landed somewhere in the thick of the men. He couldn't see if it had done its work or not.

Back and forth the lines of men undulated, gaining, then losing ground. Sometimes they would meet, break up, blend. Men fell silently in the agonizing scream of the wind.

The Trusian line broke. From nowhere an Ahhiyawan chariot rumbled through the men. People tumbled and scrambled to get out of its way, and Dagentyr saw that he was the intended target. He started to run from its path but knew it would be useless. He set his feet and threw his second spear full into the chest of one of the horses. The beast reared up, snorted blood from its nostrils, and fell dead in its traces, tripping its neighbor who went down headfirst with a frenzied squeal. The car halted with a jerk. Over the front rail went the driver and fell on the dead horse in a tangle of reins. Cursing, the remaining warrior grasped his spears, stumbled out of the wreck, and came for him. Ten paces away the man let fly the first spear.

Dagentyr ducked behind his shield and the point was deflected up into the grey sky. It fell butt-first in the dirt behind him. There was fire and anger in his bowels now. He pulled his sword and rushed in. The Ahhiyawan had no time for a second cast and stabbed out with the spear in quick, lightning thrusts.

He butted himself in and cut the spear below the shank. In a fever, he slashed into the man's face, cutting through nose and eyes. The shield was dropped; the man fell screaming, clutching. Dagentyr drove his sword between the corselet plates. The Ahhiyawan tensed, the sinews in his neck stuck out, and then he was quiet.

Turning away from the man, he saw Tingwahr cutting the unconscious driver's throat and taking his helmet.

"Come over here!" said Dagentyr. "Give me help!" Callias leapt forward, and he and Tingwahr and Cingetos helped him pull the body away. The greaves were slick with the dead man's sweat, and he worked tensely to unbuckle them. They ripped away what armor they could before Ahhiyawan attackers came to fight them for the corpse. Another chariot was approaching, and its rider's spear was poised to strike. "Let be!" Dagentyr shouted, and they fell back. A wall of Ahhiyawan shields encircled the body.

With a grunt, the galloping spearman let his bolt fly. It caught Callias in the back. He wore no armor. The blow knocked the wind from him and a jagged point stuck out from his breast bone. He was thrown headlong. His shield fell. The chariot veered away.

Dagentyr was aghast. "Tingwahr, Cingetos! Take him." They grasped him by the elbows and dragged him. His toes left ruts in the dirt like miniature chariot tracks. When they laid him down behind the lines, their hands were red. Keen pangs of regret made Dagentyr want to cry. A comrade lost here, far away, with no women to mourn or priests to give tribal rites, brought sorrow tenfold. The Trusian men at arms took little notice.

He tore the spear free in anger. Bolgios ran up from somewhere and stopped short, staring at the closeness of death. Tears filled his eyes. He wiped them away with the back of his dirty hand.

Dagentyr's sense of loss was acute. "This is my fault. I am leader of my men. I am responsible."

"No," said Tingwahr. "There was nothing to be done. He died as a man should, any who dared to call himself a warrior."

The band of barbarians looked into each others' eyes and took up their weapons. Callias would be safe here; he had no armor to steal. He was not important enough that glory would be gained in mutilating his corpse. Dagentyr held the reddened spear and shook it at the Ahhiyawans.

"Shit-brains, eaters of filth!"

Tingwahr set the driver's helmet on his head. The severed and blood-stained chinstrap dangled at his jowls. Again, they raised fierce words to the war god, to fire their hearts with bravery, frighten their enemies, and drive the memory of death away.

The river plain was a wind-beaten, dusty slaughtering place. Joints became stiff with toil and the chilling bite of rushing air on tired muscles, and now, even the wind could not blow the plain free of dust, and horse odor, the smell of blood and burst entrails. When Dagentyr or the others came upon wounded Ahhiyawans, they thought of Callias, and killed.

Sarpedon raced past in his chariot, bound for another part of the field. He called encouragement to his men. Dagentyr did the same, and they threw themselves into the Ahhiyawans. He picked out a man whose shield was all black and lustrous, and called, hoping that he would be understood.

"You, Blackshield! Come out alone to me. Coward! I'll spit you like a kid goat over a fire!"

The man heard and understood, some at least. He left the ranks and stood in the open.

Dagentyr advanced and threw, and the meeting was over quickly. The black shield was beautiful but poorly made. As the man ducked behind it, the spear that had felled Callias tore its way through and pierced his side. Leaving his weapons behind, he pulled the spear free and crawled back to the cover of his friends.

A man stepped forward and raised a stone to hurl at Dagentyr, but Bolgios's arrow hit him in the belly. He squealed and fell in a grotesque sprawl;

then Dagentyr was buried in a hail of arrows and rocks that drove him off.

"Dagentyr, look! The Trusians are falling back. We will be cut off if we don't move away," said Cingetos. An arrow struck the soft earth between them.

His heart rolled over. The Trusians were steadily being beaten back up the plain to the city. Many had already taken to the chariots and driven through the scattering footmen.

"Back with the others!"

The Ahhiyawans were on top of them all the way, advancing with a metallic clanking and ugly, unified voice.

Little by little, Dagentyr's band caught up with the Trusian men. Sarpedon was on foot, storming in front of the Lycians like a lion.

"Stand here with me and fight! Don't run like these Trusian women. Look at them, not fit for war or manhood. Stand and fight! If the gods give glory to anyone in this battle, let it be us!" In the middle of the rout the Lycians turned and reformed. The Ahhiyawa were following the retreat like dogs on a blood scent. Dagentyr told his men to stand fast, and Sarpedon spied them.

"Even the barbarians stand truer than they do. Cowards!"

Two chariots were thundering up the hill, one Trusian, the other Ahhiyawan. There was a cry as a spear dropped the Trusian driver, and the chariot, uncontrolled, strayed into a vineyard and tumbled over, spilling its warrior onto the ground.

"Who is that man in trouble?" asked Dagentyr.

"By his armor, I believe it is Prince Awunash," Sarpedon responded.

The pursuing chariot reined up sharply in a cloud that hid the action from them for a moment.

Dagentyr jumped forward and ran toward the car. He would show them bravery; under Sarpedon's eyes he would show them what he could do that the Trusians would not. Cowards got nothing. Brave men reaped benefits and won honor. His men saw him go, and after their hesitation of surprise, whooped wildly and followed him as fast as they could go.

Time was short. He pushed himself to the limit, and his thighs ached from running with such weight. The Ahhiyawan hefted up a great stone to send it crashing down on Awunash. Dagentyr cursed to himself that he was too late and would have to fight the Ahhiyawan not for glory, but to survive. Someone behind him saw that time was needed. A well-cast spear landed at the Ahhiyawan's feet, drawing his attention. He let the stone fall to the dirt as he saw Dagentyr running down on him.

The warrior shouted an order. Slashing wildly, the Ahhiyawan's driver cut the horses of Awunash free and raised another cloud as the chariot rolled away with the horses in tow. The warrior was alone in a whirl of dust. Dagentyr straddled the prince and held his shield over him.

"Come on and die, Ahhiyawan," he shouted.

The man drew sword. He was immense. He towered over Dagentyr, who was reminded of Vorgus. The comparison churned Dagentyr's hate. He stood his ground as the Ahhiyawan charged again and again, trying to dislodge him and reach the prone and unconscious prince. Dagentyr shouted to give himself strength, and none of the Ahhiyawan's strokes found Awunash.

The warrior saw the others coming and stood back hesitantly. One of Bolgios's arrows drove into his shield. Dagentyr grabbed the prince's wrist and dragged him away during the pause. Thinking better of the fight, the big man backed away. His chariot drove near in a rush. He stepped in and was gone.

"Pick him up." Dagentyr could see that the prince's hip was smashed and bloody. The tunic round it was shredded. Awunash moaned and regained consciousness briefly as they carried him. They grunted under the weight of his bronze armor. Dagentyr and Tingwahr covered the rear, and the carriers slung their shields to protect their backs.

Sarpedon ordered his men down to give them support and sent his own chariot to take the prince to the city. "Bravely done," he said to Dagentyr. "You're worth a hundred weak-livered Trusians."

Hektu drove up in a flurry of impatience.

"Why do you wait here? You'll be cut off, stranded. Retreat with the others. What's the delay?"

"Run away with your children whose feet point backward and know no direction but shameful retreat, Mighty Hektu, prince, first of the warriors of Trusya. If not for us your brave Awunash would be dog meat now. I've heard you say in council how disgraceful it is to bring in your allies; Trusya can fight on her own." Sarpedon shook the point of his spear at Hektu. "If the gods hadn't made us honorable and the fight were not already upon us, I'd pull my men out and enjoy watching Trusya burn. Dagentyr here and his northerners saved Prince Awunash, and we stay to hold the field while Trusya runs away. You sicken me, Hektu."

Ahhiyawan rocks and projectiles took to the air again. What had once been the Trusian part of the plain was now the front line of fighting. Hektu drove off red-faced, teeth gritted.

Dagentyr had listened to Sarpedon's speech, pleased. They would know his name, his deeds. He had been used to shame the crown prince of Trusya.

The fighting went on. Hektu rallied his men. Overhead, the sun fought to shine while the wind blew at it like a demon at a lamp flame. A worried man in a bloody tunic found Dagentyr and pulled him out of the fighting.

"You are Dagentyr, the northern warrior?"

"Yes."

"Come with me. I speak for Prince Awunash."

He followed, reluctant to leave his men. The prince was far behind the battle, near the city walls, still in the bed of Sarpedon's chariot. His wound had been roughly covered with a cloak.

"Why does he stay here on the field?" asked Dagentyr.

Sarpedon's driver shrugged. "I tried to take him into the city. He would not go until he saw you, the man who saved him."

"Speak quickly," said the messenger, "for he is weak and succumbing to chills. The faster you end the talk, the faster he can be cared for."

Dagentyr went to the prince and knelt down.

"Lord Awunash, it pleases me to see you alive."

The prince opened his eyes and turned his head to see.

"You are Dagentyr. I would not be alive without your help. I owe you a great debt, but I would ask a further favor of you though I know it is too much."

"Ask."

"You see my armor there by the wheel? Put it on. The men might be disheartened to see me fall. I am not so famous as Hektu, but the men know and like me, especially my own warriors. If they could see me wounded and returned so quickly to the fight, they would gain courage. The Ahhiyawa are strong in number and spirit—" A pain shot through him and he winced. "If you wear my armor, fight in my place, they may think that you are me. Please."

"But you have no beard."

"They will not notice."

He was touched by the prince's bravery, his loyalty to his people. "I'll do it."

"Good," said the worried messenger. "I'll help you into the prince's armor while he is driven to the city. We will wait here for the driver to come back to take you into battle. Give me your own armor."

It was a longer wait than he wanted. He spent the

time relishing the feel of the prince's fine arms and congratulating himself on his good fortune. This would be something, an adventure.

The armor was too small, as most of the Trusian stuff was, but not by much. The corselet was bronze, heavier than he cared to wear. The helmet was covered with plates of bronze, with long guards for cheeks and neck. It was plumed in white horsehair. Padding in the embossed greaves prevented the metal from chafing the skin. The shield was the favorite of any he had seen, round on top, concave below, lighter than his. A worked and polished silver boss covered its center.

He felt himself shamed, standing idle while the battle continued, but soon the chariot came back. To frighten the Ahhiyawa more at the sight of him, the messenger smeared blood on his tunic. Dagentyr climbed into the car, grabbing the railing clumsily, and they were off.

Passing the ranks of spear throwers and archers, he let out a nondescript yell as he thought Awunash might have, a mumbling cry lest they hear his accent and know him to be a fraud. He kept the shield high to hide his chin. Men cheered as the horses and car whipped past. Faltering groups, straggling their way to the city, were amazed and gained new enthusiasm to turn and face the fight. Here was Awunash, supposedly badly hurt, yet returned by the gods, whole, and mad with lust for killing.

They rode into the thick fighting and dashed forward and back in front of the Ahhiyawa, who shrank back at the sight of a near-dead man raging in their midst. He felt the power he held over them, the shock and fear he inspired clad in his bloody, spectral guise.

The chariot slowed to make a turn. Relative stability came to the car, and he threw his spear. An unlucky man took the point in the chest and slumped back on the shields of the men behind him. Death rode on his side now, and invulnerability.

A stone struck one of the horses' rumps and nicked the skin to the blood. The driver could not keep the team from shying, and they ran from the fight. The animals were lathered and tired, the best indication that the battle had worn on long. In their path a wounded Ahhiyawan was being helped to his feet by a companion. They drove at them and ran them under the horses' hooves and racing wheels. Dagentyr ordered a stop and leapt from the chariot, thrusting his sword through the one man still alive. He was hoarse from yelling and sucking in the harsh air.

"Prince Awunash!" A ragged, retreating warrior ran to them and spoke. "The men retreat again in spite of your example. The Ahhiyawa press hard on all sides. The men of Lycia have left the field altogether, for Sarpedon has fallen hurt. Hektu and his men fight to give the others time to reach the gates." The fellow gaped dully at the wisps of light hair and beard.

"Very well," said Dagentyr before the man could speak again and work out the strange appearance. The driver snapped the reins and they rode off, leaving the confused man standing by himself.

Hektu raised an inquisitive eyebrow when they approached.

"Prince Awunash," he said, "I'm glad to see . . . There were rumors." Worry was evident on his face as he recognized Dagentyr. "Why have you taken Awunash's place? Where is he, hurt, dead?"

Dagentyr put up his hand. "Alive the last time I saw him, and safe in the city."

"The prince is hurt but not dead," confirmed the driver.

Seeming resentful, Hektu instructed his driver to head for the city. He called to his men, and they followed him up the hill. The Ahhiyawa were tired, and content to let the Trusians escape. Their war cries and threats followed them through the gates. The more adventurous raiders played their antics close under the ramparts, in range of the archers who cursed in frustration as their arrows were dodged or caught on bullhide. Ahhiyawan chieftains drove their chariots around the walls and scoffed, leisurely stripping bodies that they came to. Inside, the city walls reverberated with the cries of wounded, weary men, the frantic snorting of spent horses, the noisy questioning of townspeople.

Dagentyr took off the helmet and fine armor and laid them in the chariot bed. Around him, men stared in surprise to see the ghostly Awunash undergo metamorphosis. There was a joyous shout, and he recognized his men standing far back in the crowd. Thinking him dead, they had retreated in dismay, and his change into himself gladdened them as much as his impersonation had pleased the Trusians. To his surprise, other warriors near him cheered, too.

He dismounted the chariot and went to his people. His weak legs made him aware of his fatigue. Bones seemed to turn to water in his knees. With the battle done, he remembered that he had just finished his first chariot ride. The ground wobbled and rolled under his feet. His skin smelled of spattered horse sweat. Blood matted his tunic. He became aware of the cold, and he was famished.

Hektu eyed him with hatred and flung down his helmet in disgust.

As a planter takes pride in his work, even though they had given up the field, he mused that his furrow was well plowed. Then, he gave himself up to sadness and shivering. He thought of Callias, dead, and of his warm cape, wrapped snugly around some whore's shoulders.

Chapter 21

With the patience and determination of a burrowing rat, Ruki shouldered his way into the crowd to where he could see better. Lamps in the hall burned low and slaves passed inconspicuously through the painted pillars to refill them. The fire in the central hearth still burned brightly, mellowing the brilliant hues of the marine murals on the walls and the inlaid floor.

Eight days of fighting had come to nothing. The feast had not been merry. Men sat around the fire or stood as their rank dictated. Most of the women had retired to their quarters, leaving the men to counsel and drink. Helani and some of her serving women hung on. Sarpedon sat leaning on his crutch, nodding at what was being said. His bandaged thigh rested on a cushion. Luck had saved him; none of the major arteries had been cut. In his weakened condition he was getting drunk easily.

Antior, one of the elders, was speaking to the assembly.

"I don't say any of this to Hektu's discredit. He is a great war leader and the warriors of Trusya are brave. I have faith in their ability; but it's clear from today's outcome that the gods desire some solution other than war. Why else would the sky split open and rain in such torrents that battle was impossible, and just as the gates were being opened?" He paused for the muttered reaction of agreement. "And what other possible solution is there but to give the woman back and have done with it?" Thunder in the background seemed to lend the truth of the gods to his speech.

"My lord Antior is bold to speak of it in front of the lady. Perhaps he forgets the rules of courtesy he was brought up with," interjected Hektu.

Ruki smiled in glee. He had grown used to, had learned to love the inner life of the palace. Controversy was its lifeblood, and intrigue made the blood flow. He was learning to use his eyes, his brain.

"The time for cordial pleasantries has passed," Antior went on. "The vultures feast on Trusian sons even as we feast tonight. I realize that Parush's marriage is a family matter and touches Prince Hektu to the heart, but it matters little in comparison." He was an eloquent man, robed in the long gowns of the more aged, wavy grey hair swept back over his ears. "It is time for the Lady Helani to go." Helani lowered her head and stared demurely at the floor. "Give her back to the Ahhiyawa. Let Mensalakus cart her back to Spartusha and give them a good excuse to leave, an excuse that still leaves their honor fulfilled. They too must be growing tired of the fighting."

"Antior is very free at giving away a woman that is not his." Parush rose to his feet.

"No freer than Prince Parush is at taking a woman that is not his." The prince turned red with rage, but Antior did not stop. "It's time to rectify a wrong. We've defended you and this woman long enough. Our honor and loyalty are not in doubt, but the time wears on, and the dead men pile up. It's our common sense that's in doubt now. If we give the woman back and they continue to fight, they do so at the risk of angering the gods."

Hektu interrupted him. "The woman is a curtain to their real purposes, the trade routes. Ahhiyawan power is what is at stake here, not right or wrong." Helani gaped at his remark.

"Aye." Parush jumped in behind his brother's lead. "Does Antior expect the Lady Helani to put herself in such danger? What kind of reception will she receive at Mensalakus's hands?"

"Men suffer the effects of their deeds. Women should do no less. She came willingly, didn't she? Part of the responsibility is hers. Let her face her fate as the men lying dead on the plain faced theirs."

"Not all men of Trusya are as faint-hearted at the prospect of battle as Antior," said Hektu. "If the battlefield is the only place this can be decided, so be it."

"If Hektu calls me coward, he forgets himself! I am an old man, yes, but I did not get to be old by being cowardly. Many men in this room will vouch for that, your father among them. I did not live to be grey by being stupid. Glory is good, but even the gods laugh at bravery when it masks foolishness. You young men fight for glory and leave us to think on the effects. Has Hektu forgotten the outcome of his battles so far?"

"Old woman!" shouted Hektu.

"Gentlemen!" Priasham stood and raised his voice as loud as he could. "I'll not have the council chamber degenerate into such bickering. Infighting will accomplish nothing, and we have much to lose. We all know of Antior's bravery and wisdom, and of Hektu's valor and ability to lead men. No one's honor is in question here. Let us hear from others of our ranks."

"I'll not keep my views secret," said Sarpedon, shifting himself to sit more upright, adjusting the cushion beneath the tender wound. "I hold with Antior. The woman's good for nothing but trouble.

There's not a man in my camp who feels differently." Dagentyr cast his eyes to the floor. "Prince Hektu knows already what I think of him; I need not place caution in my words.

"We came because of you, Priasham, because you asked us honorably, because our people have been friends, yes, and because you offered gold. For the sake of this woman we're expected to stand alone while the Ahhiyawa cut us to pieces. We have fought well for you, and what's the reward? I'm speared through the leg, and my men fight and die without me. I say give her back and see what comes of it. What is there to lose?"

Glaucus stood at Sarpedon's right as his secondin-command and spoke agreement in the buzz of conversation that followed. By reason of his valor in battle and his recent saving of Awunash, Dagentyr stood at the king's left, aware that some of the leaders watched him with suspicion, dislike. He felt lost and useless. The heated emotions made the Trusians speak hurriedly, and he could not follow. Still he sensed what was going on, knew who was on what side. They both knew that Sarpedon wanted to say more, but he was weak and pained. Dagentyr handed him his cup.

"Sarpedon's words have a bitter cast to them," said Parush. "Why should we heed the words of foreigners who are here only for our gold?"

"Because you need us, you silly pup!" Brusque and burly Rhesos of Thrace stood up. His accent was thick and barbarous, his upper arms tattooed in vivid blue swirls. "Sarpedon speaks words of wisdom, as does Antior. If we had not been here, the Ahhiyawa would be drinking in this hall now, using your corpses for footstools." He sat down and called for more wine.

"There you have it, men of Trusya. Our allies have as much as said that they do not care for the fight, or for us. I have always said that this was a

matter to settle ourselves." Hektu got up and made
a show of pacing round the hearth as he spoke.
"What could be more useless to us than men who
don't care?"

Sarpedon curled his lip and started to speak, but
Glaucus put a firm hand on his shoulder to subdue
him.

"Enough of this," said Antior. "I personally
thank the gods for our brave and loyal allies, but the
question has been put forth. Let's answer it. Do we
give the woman back or not?"

There was silence. Hektu stopped his pacing and
went back to his seat next to the king. Priasham
took a deep breath.

"I am king of this land, with power to decide one
way or the other, but Parush is my son; it is not
right for me to make a decision that is his, that
concerns his own wife, who I confess has won my
heart and who I think of as a daughter. Parush,
what do you say? Will you give her back to
Mensalakus?"

"Idiocy," muttered Sarpedon.

"No, I will not." The omnipresent Astekar stood
behind him and leaned down to speak in his ear.
The room broke into shouts of agreement and
resentment. When he spoke again, he had to raise
his voice to be heard. "However! I will give back
the possessions that came from Spartusha with her
and, besides, will donate fine wealth of my own as
compensation. I propose this to Mensalakus, but I
will never give up the woman."

"What folly!" Antior said.

Dagentyr looked at Helani. Priasham's good
words and Parush's resolve gave her the courage to
raise her head up again and glare at the hostile men
around her with thinly disguised defiance. "I am
proud to be the wife of such a noble man and
belong to such a great house as that of Priasham,"
she said.

When Dagentyr had come into the chamber earlier, he had not expected to see her there. He was off his guard, but when it had become apparent that there would be no direct contact between them, he had used the time to study her, to accustom himself to the effects of her beauty. There was nothing between her and Parush, that much he guessed in spite of what she had just spoken. When she returned the prince's touch, her hand was wax and her eyes became glazed jet. She was a woman working hard against hate.

She had seen him looking at her and smiled. When she caught him staring, he looked for some excuse to turn his gaze away. She knew no such embarrassment and looked into his eyes directly, deeply, then some movement nearby would distract her and she would return to the feasting, blinking her shadowed eyes with deliberate slowness, eating each delicate morsel as though she were making love to it.

Ruki had watched Dagentyr throughout the evening. Parush was always on the lookout for infidelity from Helani and might reward information about men who cast envious eyes upon her. So he watched and sang his songs for the banquet, and watched more.

Dagentyr was so wrapped up in Helani that he didn't notice the little man much during the night, only when he sang and became the center of attention. He was in the front row of men now, clutching his lyre and smiling queerly at Dagentyr, if what his twisted features did could ever be called smiling.

"Quiet, quiet." The room grew silent at Priasham's plea. "So be it. Tomorrow a herald shall give our offer to Mensalakus and the Ahhiyawa. Please the gods, they will accept."

"Please the gods, it should snow in summer." Antior spoke. "This is nothing more than bribery.

The pirates will accept your offer. They will take
your wealth but they will stay, to take ours."

As if he hadn't heard, Priasham continued.

"I will also empower the herald to propose a
truce so that men of both sides can bury the dead. I
doubt that the Ahhiyawa will say no to that."

Antior clenched his fists in frustration. "May I
take leave now, my king? It grows late, and my tired
voice seems to beat uselessly against the rafters."
The king nodded his permission. "The others will
need their sleep as well if the fighting is to go on."
He bowed, shoved his hands into the long sleeves of
his robe, and walked from the chamber. The room
sighed to see the main opponent quit. Priasham
called an end to the feast.

Glaucus and Dagentyr helped Sarpedon to his
feet and handed him the crutch. The bandage was
bloody again. Sarpedon blanched at the pain that
standing caused him. They said brief good nights
and withdrew. There was a dull clap of thunder as
they left, and they heard the rain start again and
beat against the palace roof.

"Dahguinteer?"

It was after they had taken the king to his
quarters. Glaucus took charge of Sarpedon, and
Dagentyr wandered back to his own tent, out
through the palace enclosure and the streets
crowded with the hovels of the people, slick with
the icy downpour. He was about to enter, ready for
sleep, but the silvery, familiar pronunciation of his
name prevented him.

The rain had driven everyone to shelter, everyone but the robed and hooded figure standing in the
relative dryness next to the outer walls. He knew it
was Mehiya, and he knew already, had known since
his first summons from her, that if it came a second
time, there would be no hesitation.

He made his way to her, splashing through the

puddles. It was easier than it would have been on
the night the Ahhiyawa came. The wall sentries
were too concerned with keeping warm to notice
them and the ice-cold rain left the streets bare.
Mehiya knew the rounds of the palace guards well;
they encountered no one, and soon they were in the
palace. Their feet left prints on the dry stone floors
and steps as they climbed up to the second level.
The hallway was dark. Mehiya carried no lamp. It
was odd to feel his skin tingle as it did before battle
and for no other reason than sneaking through an
unlit hallway to a waiting woman.

Midway down the narrow corridor, she knocked
twice on a broad wooden door. A bolt was lifted
and the door swung open, letting dim orange light
stab out at them. They slipped in. Mehiya and the
serving girl who had unlocked the door left as
quietly as if they had never been there at all. He
refitted the bolt.

The room was cool and open to the storm.
Braziers around the bed radiated globes of warmth
and light. The bed itself was large and covered with
a spread of sewn furs. Through his sopping shoes
the chill of the floor crept into his toes. A breath of
sweet burning incense flavored the fresh night air,
and he heard a dreamy sigh of pleasure or melancholy from the balcony, its doors thrown open. He
went to the center of the room, feeling foolish for
moving on tiptoe. A clap of thunder startled him. It
sobered him into bravery, and he looked around
the doors to the balcony.

She stood wrapped in a white bedcloth, and the
black hair fell against it like an indelible stain. Her
eyes were closed, and she arched her neck ecstati-
cally, letting the blowing drops land against her
face. The wind beat the cloth around her legs and
showed them through clean, sculptured folds, like
stone. He flushed in spite of the cold.

With no surprise at his being there, she shook her

hair and turned to him. Minuscule drops hung on
her eyelashes and she blinked them free. She
walked to him like the strange beast on shipboard
had, silently, intently, and he felt the sudden touch
of her fingers on his hand. It started as he had
imagined it hundreds of times, with the simple
saying of his name.

"Dahguinteer."

A myriad questions raced through his mind—
why me? why no guards? what of Parush?—but he
felt they would cripple him once asked and reduce
the night to reality.

It was an effort to pry his fingers loose from the
wooden door and brush the damp hair back from
her face. His rough knuckles rubbed her cheek, and
she sighed again and grabbed his hand in both of
hers. The odor of incense seemed to emanate from
her. She tugged his tunic down over his shoulders
to his waist. When she ran her hands over him, her
skin went to gooseflesh, and he knew it was not
from cold alone. As for himself, every nerve was
fire, and there was pressure in his head, behind his
eyes. Her lips brushed against his, not in a kiss, but
more in a promise of one to come. She walked to
the bed and, midway, let the robe fall to the floor. A
pulsing ache moved down his legs, making them
unsteady.

What a fool Parush was, he thought as he took
her in his arms and they slid beneath the thick fur
coverlet. What a stupid fool not to be here in his
place even if it took four strong men to hold her and
shield him from the bites and screams of her hate.
He suddenly felt very sorry for Parush, but then,
fools deserved their fate.

The dismal splattering of water pouring from the
eaves onto the tile of the courtyard was the only
thing that kept Ruki company. He chuckled in
admiration at the system that had left no guards on

the woman's wing of the palace when the man and woman had sneaked in, and now that they were safe inside, had the men at their usual posts, alert for intruders. Rumors were numerous among the household slaves about Helani's personal guards accepting certain favors in return for their inconspicuous absence when it was needed. The reason he's never caught her is because he doesn't try or because he doesn't want to, Ruki thought. Her deception is as plain as the sun in the sky.

A freak gust sent the cascade spraying into his face, and he huddled deeper in his shadow. He thought longingly of his bed, tucked away in the corner of the slaves' quarters, and his fellow slaves asleep and warm under their blankets. He sneezed with no worry that it would give him away; the storm covered every sound. An opportunity had been given to him to use his eyes and ears effectively, for revenge. If there was one thing that he had learned, it was that such chances were not to be squandered.

The light from her room leaked out onto the balcony and just barely made her visible, standing in her bedclothes, the perfect vision of a sacrifice to the storm god. He sat down cross-legged and double-folded his cloak to separate his back from the cold stone wall. The corner of the courtyard where he lurked was steeped in darkness. As he watched, he became aware of another figure moving in her chambers, peeking out from behind the doors, a figure to which she moved. That would be you, wouldn't it, warrior? he thought. I followed you as soon as you left the feast, and you didn't even know. Mehiya thinks that she is the only one in the whole palace who is wily, and clever at matters of intrigue.

She disappeared inside and was gone from view. He chuckled again in amazement. How he wished to be some villainous night bird with black wings,

to fly to her balcony to see for himself the wild
thrashings and outcries the prince babbled about in
his drunken stupors.

"This is the beginning of your undoing, warrior,"
he said to the empty balcony and drew his shaking
legs up under the cloak.

The more he watched and formed the chamber's
happenings in his thoughts, the more he became
aware of a sick feeling, an emptiness like hunger.
Tears came, and the realization that more than at
any other time in his life, he wanted a woman. All
the women slaves laughed at him, even the kitchen
sluts. Sometimes they would play at affection to
torment him. One had even lifted her skirt to him
and then thrown a bowl of table scraps over his
head so that he smelled of wild onions and sour
milk. How could there be any approaches made?
What could wake any tenderness toward such a
silly, shriveled man?

"I'll keep this vigil, warrior, in spite of the chill
and ague it may bring, and I'll see you dead for it."

He had a desire to rush to the prince and shout of
Helani's infidelity with Dagentyr. No. I'll wait. The
prince might be angry with me. I'll wait until the
time is right. Besides, the warrior's defeat will be
worse if he has time to think that he has won. I'll let
him enjoy for a while longer.

It was still dark when the man and the servant
girl left the women's wing. He had dozed fitfully
and was lucky to see them escaping. The light from
Helani's chamber was gone. Everything was dark.
He was not sure what to do now that the evening's
mission was over. Following Dagentyr to his tent
would serve no end. He stood in the cold for a
moment, noticing that the rain had stopped. Limp-
ing on stiff joints, he discarded for the time being
the job of intrigue and hobbled his way quietly to
his waiting bed.

Chapter 22

One hand clutched the bronze earring while the other gently fingered the new one of gold stuck through his lobe. It pulled down with a weight that made him constantly aware of it. His imagination gave the yellow metal an extra warmth that the bronze did not have. Here was prestige, although in time the green stain would disappear forever. With a flick of the wrist, he sent the old earring spinning through the snowflakes into the struggling fire. Success had its sorrows. Helani had given him the gold as a love gift on a firelit evening as the wind huffed through chinks in the doors. He had kept the old one with him for a while, but now it was time to have done with it. The men were surprised to see the gold. He made up a story about stealing it from a dead man in a skirmish, and they believed him.

The long days were cold and calm, impressive in their calmness. Bad weather had put an end to the long skirmishing and hunting forays into the nearby mountains. Food was becoming scarce. Deep mud made the chariots founder, and the sting of winter took the fight from any man. It was a time of sitting safe around fires, feasting, telling tales,

drinking wine, for Trusian and Ahhiyawan alike.
Enemy fires speckled the nights like stars banished
to earth, and in spite of the weather, the men were
glad, for spring might bring the time to die. So
Dagentyr sat, bored but content, in front of his tent
in the midst of the Lycian camp. The dreary
collection of windbreaks and lean-tos clung to the
frigid earth beneath the western rampart like a
frozen barnacle. Snowflakes died all around as soon
as they touched ground.

Sarpedon hobbled in and out between the tents,
helped by his heralds, taking his daily exercise,
seeing his men, for after many days he was again
able to walk. He fussed at the two youths, embarrassed that he needed them at all. If it had been
anyone but Sarpedon, the sight would have been
comical. His legs, thinner from disuse, protruded
down from the bulk of his body, which was
wrapped entirely in a thick fur cloak. Dagentyr
raised his hand in greeting and Sarpedon saw him.
Something seemed to enter the king's mind. Whatever it was, he appeared to think better of it, then,
setting his jaw, changed his mind and bellowed to
be helped to where Dagentyr was sitting. His long
walking stick probed the ground like the feeler of a
huge wooden insect. He was animated, and his eyes
glimmered with drink, for he drank much wine to
take away the pain of the wound.

"Greetings, Sarpedon," said Dagentyr.

"To you also. I wish to speak to Dagentyr alone,"
he said, and eased himself to the ground with
difficulty. His manner was preoccupied and troubled. "All right, you fidgeting ninnies, I'm sitting
now. You're no longer needed. Off with you!" He
arranged himself so that his rump was nestled in
the fur and not on the damp earth and pulled the
cape over his head. The heralds moved off warily,
beyond reach of the walking stick.

"Bolgios, Bolgios! More wood for the fire. The
king visits us." Dagentyr's call went unanswered.

"Never around when he's needed lately. Too important to fetch wood. He killed his first man close in not long ago. It's gone to his head."

Sarpedon waved Bolgios's absence off with his hand and scooted closer to the fire.

"Dagentyr, you are a stranger here. You are a man away from his land, his home. You have family, yes?" The king gave him no time to answer. "Then you are the man to talk to because you will understand me. I speak to you also because I think we are alike, and because I have respect for you. No man has beaten me in combat in many years, many, else I would not be king." He brushed a rogue flake from the hawklike nose. "You are a brave warrior. I can depend on you.

"My heart is heavy with winter. I am strong, but when the good things of the earth roll themselves up and hide till spring, I shrink inside like a child." He brought his hand up in front of his face and slowly made a fist. "The cursed cold makes my leg ache and throb, and there isn't the fighting to keep my mind off loneliness. I have a family in Lycia, a woman and a new babe, a son I held only once." The fist tightened, was shoved under the fur. "I have a warm hall and men who call me king and respect me, not like these good-for-nothing Trusians. When the king is away his nobles and neighbors plot to cross the borders and take . . . take." He had spoken to the fire but turned now. "It is sad that a man trades his happiness for gold." The word "gold" stood apart. "If I had the decision to make over again, I would be home now, laughing at the wind, with a slave girl rubbing warm oil into my skin."

"I know the feeling that my lord Sarpedon speaks of. It was not my choice to come here. I am here because I was unable to see men as they are. Perhaps the glint of gold took away your sight." The gleam at his ear felt suddenly conspicuous. "I imagine the gods can steal vision from whomever they choose."

"Do you think often of your home?"

Dagentyr folded his arms around his knees. "As often as I can." He snickered cynically. Was that a lie? he wondered.

"Tell me of this home of yours, and then maybe it will loosen my tongue to tell you of mine, and we will both feel better on this disgusting day." He looked around and spit. The snow whitened Sarpedon's shoulders and head. "Is it very different from here?"

He thought back. Helani had asked him the same question just days ago. He had told her in detail, leaving out Gertera, Kerkina, working to form the words clearly while she played distractedly with the curls of hair falling on his forehead. He made it sound better than it was, but it was good to talk of it to someone who did not know, who listened. Talk was something she usually never bothered with under the bedclothes. Images of a hungry jackal devouring prey popped into his head. He had thanked the gods for the interlude of conversation.

"There are stories that the men of the north eat their dead," she had said.

"No, that is only a story."

"Ooh." He read disappointment in her manner. "And is it a land of giants?"

"No, but there are ghosts in the woods, and demons, and wolves." Then he added, "There is one giant."

"And will you be a hero, a killer of giants?"

"Yes. It is foretold that I will be. I must."

"Dahguinteer, my giant-killer!" She fell into hysterical giggling, and he put his hand across her mouth to quiet her. "But it does sound like such a dark place, dark and chilling, the forests full of mist and fear. I'm frightened by it all. Look, it makes me shiver. Hold me, very tight. There, now I'm not afraid anymore. You can tell me more; I want to know more." Her eyes sparkled when he touched her and when he spoke of Fottengra. When he had finished telling her all he knew, she whispered into his ear. "I want to see it. I want to feel the darkness, the cold air of the forests. Take me with you. Will you let me run away with you?"

"And how am I to run away?" he asked, avoiding the question. "The Ahhiyawa . . . I am not even sure I know where home is anymore."

"Then run with me to Aigypta. We must run to catch the excitement, to find the spark. We must hunt it like my husband hunts lions."

"Am I not enough spark for you?"

She tapped him on the nose like a mischievous dog. "No man can retain his heat forever. A fire that burns in the same place for too long dies. It feeds on itself, then dies, burns out. We must run, and wherever we go, we'll live new fire, and when the places we see are burned out, we'll move on and leave behind only the ashes." She spoke in a rising voice, and her eyes blinked rapidly in excitement. She stared off into space as she spoke, as if she could see the places unfolding upon the walls like magical murals. Then she sat up in the bed and leaned over him. The ends of her hair dangled in front of his eyes. "Run with me, Dahguinteer." She said it like a prophetic pronouncement, an incantation.

Because she could reach down inside him and pull it from him, he told her, "I will run with you, and when we leave this slavery behind, I'll carry you off in my arms and we'll go home to the north, to the forests."

She leaned down and kissed him. "Say the words yet again, Dahguinteer, so that neither one of us will forget them, so that they will be like a spell, so they can do nothing but come true."

He said the words again and felt small, lonely, uneasy at her choice of phrases. He was cold despite the thick fur of the coverlet and pulled her to him for warmth and to keep her from speaking more.

"Dagentyr, stop staring into the fire like an idiot. I asked you about your home."

"I am sorry, Lord Sarpedon." He came to himself. "It is not so grand a place as this, but dark and forested and secret. There is no place to hide here except this pile of rocks. You have had to make your own hiding places. The gods have given us ours. From the sacred grove you can look over the hills and see nothing but trees and the fog rising up to the sky. There is no roar of ocean, just the sound of slow rivers over rocks. I think the men are the same. There are those to be respected, and those others."

Sarpedon cleared his throat. "Have you any wine?"

"Yes, but it is cold."

"No matter."

He rose and brought it from the tent.

"And do you have a woman there, a wife in this dark, green place of yours?" the king asked.

"No, no wife," he lied. "But there is a woman. We have known each other since we were children, and our fathers knew each other. Our mothers washed clothes together at the river. Bolgios!" When there was no answer, he brought wood himself. The replenished fire sent up a column of shimmering heat where the snow had no dominion.

Sarpedon drank quickly and offered halfhearted grunts and nods of approval at his description of Fottengra. Dagentyr guessed that he was not truly interested and was only waiting for his own turn to speak and unburden himself. He stopped short.

"It pains me to speak more of it. I am here now after all, and home is as far away as anything can be. Tell me of Lycia."

Sarpedon made himself comfortable for the telling of a long story. Dagentyr was amused and saddened at the same time.

In the middle of his tale the king stopped abruptly.

"Enough. I'm wasting words. That is something I am not used to. There is a reason for my visit, beyond this talk. I see that there is gold at your ear. I had not noticed it before."

"Yes. I took it from a corpse during battle."

"But there has been no fighting for a long time. Why have you waited so long to wear it?" His eyes became slits.

Dagentyr felt himself under scrutiny. How shrewd was Sarpedon? His mind raced for answers.

"It is hard to break with the past."

Sarpedon was not satisfied. "It is a kingly ring, Dagentyr. The work is rich and intricate. Common warriors do not wear such things. You are absent from the camp often, mostly at night, aren't you?"

He had no answer ready and kept quiet. The king's words froze on the air and hung like a veil between them.

Sarpedon sat pensively for a long time.

"You are a good man, Dagentyr. I may be a fool to tell you what I am going to; no one can truly know another's heart. When I was a younger man, I would walk from tent to tent when there was fighting to be done and speak to my men to find out their minds. I have no need here. I know that my warriors long for home, and the winter makes the longing worse. I have made a bargain with Priasham. I'll not break my word. I said I would stay to fight the Ahhiyawa, but if they go, then we will be free to take our gold and leave. So it has become my task to make the Ahhiyawa go."

"Isn't that what we are trying to do?"

"Yes, but I am speaking of ways other than war. Already there are many orphans in Lycia. With the coming of spring I wish to lead my men home. I think there is a way it can be done without losing honor." He looked around to see that no one listened in. "I take no credit for thinking of the plan; it is Antior's. You heard the way he talked at the council. He spoke wisely. I have also spoken to

Awunash about it. We have had much time to discuss it as we sat over our wounds with wine cups in our hands. It was not hard to get his aid. The king ignores him, too wrapped up in Hektu's deeds to notice those of any other. We know that Helani will not go back to Mensalakus of her own free will, and Parush will not give her back, but what care the Ahhiyawa how she is returned? We must provide them with the opportunity . . . No, let me be truthful. We must turn her over to them ourselves. It is in our hands. It's a thing that goes against my feelings, but my people come first. I'm ashamed of nothing that is best for them."

Dagentyr was shocked. "What does this have to do with me?" He feared the answer.

Sarpedon shivered and wiped the wine from his lips.

"It was thought that you knew the Lady Helani better perhaps than most others right now. Such a man might know things that would help, and he might be able to provide a needed chance to . . . to capture the woman unaware."

"And?" He fought to keep an uncaring facade.

"Listen, Dagentyr. I do not call you liar, but I can show you several men, here in this very camp, who sport gold where they did not use to, gold not earned in battle. How do you think Diamos of her guard rose to where he is now? Through bravery? Bah. Rumor can run through a camp of bored men as easily as through a pack of kitchen slaves. Helani is always a cause for gossip."

"What are you saying?" He tried to hide his growing fear and anger.

"I'm saying that you are the man we need. I say also that I care not who Helani beds with. She has the soul of Ishtar. There are few men in the citadel who have not rolled with her a time or two. Parush is under a spell and cannot see."

"You will tell me next that I too am under a spell."

"Then I am right?"

"I have admitted to nothing. I have no wish to see my head on a pole. Parush may be under the sway of magic, but he has power. I am a slave." The gold ring turned to fire.

"All right! If my insinuations are false, may the gods punish me accordingly, but hear me out." He returned to a whisper. "I am a man you can trust. I think highly of you, as does Awunash. Do you show us so little honor in return that you declare us to be untrustworthy?"

"I am sorry. You are the most honorable of the men I have met here. You do not deserve my mistrust."

Sarpedon held his hands out to the fire. The brief fall of snow was ceasing.

"I will not force you to take part in something that goes against your heart. Think over what it is you most desire: the woman, or dispersal of the Ahhiyawa."

"I am a slave, Lord Sarpedon. My lot stays the same whether there is war or not. I cannot march away with you when you pack the tents and go."

"I will see that you do. I promise you that."

It was as if a thunderbolt had struck his senses. "You would do that? What of my men?"

"Them, too. I will see that you go with us if I have to buy you all myself, and I will help you find a ship that is journeying toward your home. The end of war will mean a homecoming for all of us."

For a moment he could see Fottengra as clearly as if he were there. The remembrance of Helani's fingers on his skin worked to blot it out.

"I think that I—"

"No! I can hear what your words will be even before you say them. Do not tell me that you love the woman." He lashed out at the fire with his walking stick. "Do not say such a thing to me. If you say it out loud you may begin to believe it. Do not convince yourself that she cares for you. Our

plan will take time to form. Take your time, too.
Think on what I have said and consider what your
choices are. Let the end of winter bring your
answer, before more men die. Now, help me up."
Dagentyr lifted him to his feet and steadied him as
he got a good grip on the stick. The snow on his
shoulders spilled off as he stood. "This before I go.
We will do this thing whether you join us or not.
Keep our secret. If your heart runs away with your
mouth, I promise you death."

"I am trustworthy too, my lord."

"Do not be indignant. It's just that we are playing
a game more dangerous even than war. Take my
hand as a symbol that we trust each other. Good.
Where are you, you lazy dolts! Help me here!" The
heralds scrambled to escort him.

Dagentyr put his fists to his head in frustration.
The gods gave men choices to torment them. What
is the mighty north-warrior supposed to do now?
he thought. The chieftain had been offered a chance
to free himself and his people. He sat down again
by the fire and shivered for the first time since
awakening.

Nightfall brought more problems. Mehiya came
as she always did but spoke urgently, saying there
was no time to waste. It was enough of a habit to
him that he followed her quickly, as he was told to.
Helani waited for him in her chamber, dressed as
for a journey in the robes of a common woman.
Her head was scarved in dirty rags. When she
kissed him, her excitement made the embrace brief
and routine.

"Dahguinteer, we have to be off quickly. I am so
excited my hands are shaking. Look. I have never
dressed like this before. The wool is coarse and
scratchy, but it is different. I like it."

"Why is there any hurry?" he asked in confusion.
"For what reason do you wear peasant rags?"

"Shh." She drew her hand softly across his lips.
"There is no time to talk or explain. Here, put this

on." She handed him a smelly bundle of cloth, and he unfolded it.

"But this is the robe of a woman. I cannot wear this. What does this mean?"

"Oh please, for me, put it on. It's the only disguise that will get us out through the gate."

"Through the gate now? Explain this to me."

"Dahguinteer! I have been trapped here too long. The streets are clogged with people. Can't you feel the ramparts falling in on us?" She wore no cosmetic, but her cheeks were colored with her agitation. "We must get out to the fresh air, to the sea!" She clasped the front of his tunic in her fists. He held her wrists, truly concerned for her mind.

"Are you mad? How do we get through the gates, even dressed in these? The gates are not open, and the guards will let no one through."

"Yes! Yes they will. Tonight the gates will be open at intervals all through the night. The city runs low on water." She spoke so fast that her words ran together. "Tonight they send the women out to the river under armed escort to replenish the supply. There are many cisterns to be filled, and it will take all night. In the darkness they hope the Ahhiyawa will not see. It's perfect for us! Do you know how I prayed for something like this, for something different? We will sneak out with them and then slip away. Dahguinteer, have you ever seen the ocean at night?"

"Yes, I have when—"

"But you have not seen it with me. It's so stark and cold. It cleanses. We will run into it and be rejuvenated and purified. You will come with me."

He could not believe what he heard.

"Have you thought about what you are saying? You expect me to sneak out as a woman and go with you to the sea?" He let the distasteful robe slip to the floor. "I'll not do it. What if we're discovered? It's a long walk to the ocean, and the Ahhiyawa are bound to have scouts posted. Are you so anxious

for adventure that you would risk capture by them?
Is that what you had in mind? What if we can't get
back into the citadel, if they decide not to work till
dawn? Do we go begging at the gates to be let in like
lost children? It's dangerous; it's stupid."

"It's exciting. If danger has to be the maker of
excitement, then let it be so. I don't care. I need to
be alive and feel something in my veins besides
lethargy. If there were no danger, I would not do it.
We waste so much time standing here!"

"No. I will not do it. You can't really mean any of
this."

She stopped her clutching. "You have said no to
me?" He said nothing.   "Of course you will go; I
have asked you to. You love me, don't you? Tell me
that you do. Whisper it in my ear and kiss me and
let us go share this night."

Doubt kept him from speaking. She had never
asked him to say that he loved her. He had never
expected her to ask, for she did not seem the kind
that needed to hear it. Actions were what she
believed in. He had almost admitted it to Sarpedon, but his tongue made no move to say it now. It
was as if telling her would chain his soul to her
whim. You may begin to believe it, Sarpedon had
said.

"You will not even say this to me, whose caress is
freely given, whose—"

His will gave way.

"Yes, I do love you, but I will not go. You must
not go, either."

"Run with me, Dahguinteer."

"No."

She took a step back, and her sandals scuffed the
floor. Her voice was as harsh as the sound of leather
on stone. "Do you have any inkling of what Parush
would do to you if he even thought that you had
made advances to me, if I went weeping to him that
you had compromised my honor with lewd sugges-
tions, or worse?"

His heart went chill.

"You would tell him that?"

"No, no, of course not, sweet warrior." She turned her black eyes away, took one long breath, and expelled it in a hiss. "Why do you make me say such things? I want you with me." The smell of sweat clung to the wrappings on her head. She pressed herself against him. "I must go, with or without you. Who will be there to protect me if you stay behind? I can make the walk quickly. I am not frail; you know that." She stooped and picked up the robe. "Please. Put this on and go with me."

He paused and slipped the hateful thing on over his head.

"Pull this scarf close around your face so no one will see," she said. "It will be dark. They'll quench the gate torches so the Ahhiyawa cannot see us leave. Mehiya has found water jars for us to carry. No one will think twice about us. It's time. Wait." She giggled at her own cleverness. "Perhaps if you stooped over as if you were old, you would be more convincing." Swallowing his humiliation, he stooped, and she placed a water jug in his hands. "When we go, carry it on your shoulder as the other women do."

"Other women," he grumbled, and felt uneasily to make sure that his dagger was strapped to his side. With the feel of women's clothing against his skin, he was not sure that he had meant his hasty declaration of love.

Mehiya handed Helani a shawl and a jar, and they left. Dagentyr shuffled like an old woman, and she twittered like a child playing hide-and-seek, all the way to the gate.

The women were gathered at the postern, surrounded by guards. The wait was long, much too long for Dagentyr. He bent even lower, held the jar up by his face, and held his breath. Embarrassment made his ears burn, and raw fear tickled his stomach, fear more dreadful than that of dying in battle.

That was as it should be; if he were found out, in women's clothes, sneaking out with the wife of the prince, Dagentyr the warrior would die shamefully. What kind of woman was she? he wondered. He felt her next to him, quivering with the tenseness of the moment, and he knew that she was enjoying all of it.

In complete stillness the torches were snuffed, and a whispered order sent the gates swinging open. Like a beetle, the group skittered down the hill to the riverbank. All the way the men shushed the women and tried to keep their own armor from rattling. A big, lumbering woman stepped on his foot, and he checked himself just before blurting out an oath. The freezing air gave him no chance to sweat. His fingers were cold on the jar.

They reached the river quickly and began to fill the jars. Dagentyr and Helani moved to the end of the line of women on the bank, apart from the rest. The tamarisk bushes showed up as blobs of nothingness against the dimly moonlit plain. There was a large one nearby. The guards peered around nervously, trying to dart their eyes everywhere at once. A night bird called out from the reeds on the far bank. The men turned to the sound, and Dagentyr and Helani slipped behind the bush and pressed themselves to the ground until they heard the crunch of footsteps and chink of bronze that meant the party was on its way back to the citadel. Dagentyr felt the unpleasant thump of his heart against the dirt and was glad when they got up and started to the sea.

The river was shallow. Flood season would come later. He gritted his teeth against the dull, painful ache of the cold water as he carried her across its stream.

"We've done it, Dahguinteer! We've done it, we've done it!"

"Be quiet. We're still in earshot of the city."

Reeds snapped loudly as they moved through

them, but finally they broke clear and could walk quickly. The soaked bottom of his garment dragged and turned muddy and stiff.

"There's a little bay to the south, and a beach," she said. "It's farther but we must get there." The escape was already made, the thing done. She was like a dog with no rope to hold it. Words would have no effect on her.

By the time they reached the bay, he had walked off the pain of the cold, but his chest hurt. He wrapped the dirty scarf over his mouth.

"It's foolish to be here. The spirits of cold get sucked up in a man's breath and give him the lung fever. You can die from it."

"Don't be ridiculous."

She went to the beach. He scanned the area. A small cluster of huts stood near the edge of the sand.

"Helani!" he rasped. "Why did you come here? There is a village. We're sure to be seen."

"No. All the people are in the citadel, and the Ahhiyawa have laid all the coastal towns to waste. There is no one here. There was once, but not now. Come." A second look revealed that the huts' roofs were fallen in. Probably when fire gutted them, he thought.

He took the hand she offered and went to the water. Small waves rolled in calmly. Their white edges seemed luminescent in the dark. Winter storms had thrown seaweed and debris on the beach. It was littered and ugly. The air smelled of dead sea life.

She let go of his hand and wriggled out of her clothes. The black hair, unadorned, was set free of the wrappings. When she was naked, she looked at him like a young girl caught bathing, then ran with a squeal across the wet sand and into the sea amid a shower of kicked spray. Her white body seemed to fall into a well of blackness as the water enveloped her. He heard the squeal more in his bowels than his ears and spun around to see if it had alerted anyone hiding nearby.

She began to swim when the water was deep enough. He wished her back onshore and wished also that he had never come with her. Feeling exposed in a standing position, he knelt. The sound of the water put him on edge. It would cover the sound of approaching footsteps. Helani's arms showed pale in the black water for a moment. He worked to keep his eye on her and yet be on watch, for what he did not know, and then he heard a sound.

A look down the beach made his pulse race. There was movement! A swaying of black on black caught his eye, then came the sound of a cough and the click of armor. He froze. Straining his eyes, he picked up moonlight on the white dappling of a shield. While fumbling for the dagger, he crawled to the water's edge. Helani still swam but at least she was heading in. He risked coming to a standing position and waved his arms at her to hurry. She saw him, and he rushed back to fetch her clothing. The white dappling moved back and forth. Its owner was on the move and walking nearer.

Night had played tricks on his eyes. She was not out as far as he thought. Before he could signal her to be quiet, she burst from the water breathlessly and ran to where he stood.

"Dahguinteer, I am alive again." She sought to kiss him and pull him down prone on the sand. Her skin dripped seawater and rose to tight gooseflesh all over. A flick of her head sent the wet hair out of her face and down her back. Her hand was ice, her breathing rapid and short. "Now, Dahguinteer. I'm ready now." He shoved his hand over her mouth.

"There are Ahhiyawa on the beach. Say nothing." He held her close and spoke in a desperate hush. Shoving the robe into her hands, he grabbed her by the wrist and headed away from the water. Running footsteps followed them, and they heard a single word barked out. He had thought the man to be farther away but was wrong.

"He said to stop," Helani whispered back to him. They obeyed the command. "Why are they here?"

"Quiet. They're probably out to see if anything in this hamlet was overlooked. The winter is hard for the Ahhiyawa, too. This man may be an advance scout. If we're lucky the others are far enough behind."

Dagentyr shoved the blade up into his sleeve and assumed his old woman's stoop with his back to the approaching warrior. The man came up to them with his spear ready to throw. When he saw the naked Helani clutching her bundled clothing in fear, he lowered it.

"What is this?" he said. "A young girl and a hag out for a night swim? Such a pretty girl, too. What a prize I've won. And I thought this trip would be useless. You're mine now, girl. You! old woman. Bring her here."

Dagentyr took her wrist and, keeping low, shuffled arthritically toward him. The Ahhiyawan let the spearpoint sink to the sand. Dagentyr leapt out. The dagger came out of the sleeve, and the man had no time to scream as it was plunged through his neck. He fell with a clatter, and Dagentyr fell over him. As he got up he heard Helani behind him.

"Is he dead?"

"Come, we must go. Move now, Helani, now!"

"You killed that man for me." Her eyes were wide, and her mouth hung open, in wonder, he realized suddenly.

"What?"

"You have killed a man for my sake." She shivered violently. "He is dead, isn't he?"

"Yes."

"I must touch him."

"No. Get dressed now. We must run."

"Please let me touch him. I can see battle from the walls, but I have not known it." The corners of her mouth turned up in a smile. He had the urge to slap her but did not. It might be a thing that she would remember bitterly later on, and men died for striking queens. He grabbed her arm and pulled her off toward the city. When he glanced at her, she was looking back over her shoulder at the indistinct lump on the ground, with the same bewitched look on her face.

They said nothing on the journey back. All breath was needed to move quickly. In sight of the river they slowed and went more cautiously. She waded the river herself, holding her skirt above the water. Wet clothing might look suspicious on their return. He sheathed his dagger, imitated her, and felt more than foolish.

The jars were where they had left them. The gate lights were still out. Waiting for the next party, they caught their breath, and when the women came to the bank again, moved out quietly to fill their jugs with the rest.

The climb up the hill was more difficult than he would have imagined. It was hard to balance the heavy jar on his shoulder and try to keep his face covered with the scarf. Halfway to the gate, he lost track of Helani but was too tired to care. He wanted to forget her. Once inside the walls, he set his jar down as if to rest and simply walked away from it to the darkest place he could find, a narrow alley between two houses. Even there, homeless ones had spread awnings and built their fires. He heard snoring and moved silently, leaving the clothes in a heap. Praying thanks to the first god that came to his head, he found his tent. There was wine, and he drank deeply.

"What kind of woman?" he mumbled as he flopped into his bedding.

Bolgios awakened and rubbed his eyes.

"What did you say, Dagentyr?"

He kept silence.

Chapter 23

The morning was not so different, only clearer than normal, and colder, cold enough to freeze the ground solid. Fighting would be possible. Rivulets of ice cascaded in silent stillness down the masonry of the ramparts, and as Dagentyr pushed the tent flap aside, tiny icicles broke away in a brittle shower of tinkling crystal. Tent tops were covered with layers of snow. Men grumbled as they left the tents and the disturbing of the flaps sent cold white falling on their bare necks.

Camp woke listlessly, sad to break the comfortable hibernation of the night. Men scrounged here and there for dry firewood and food.

It was the urgency inside him that made the day seem different. His stomach felt like he had eaten a bad melon. Despite the cold, he knew that spring was coming, spring that would mean a decision. That was the cause of his worry, more so than the possibility of combat.

Stretching impatiently, munching on a half-eaten barley cake and a hunk of cold meat, he called for Bolgios. The boy's pallet had been empty. If there was to be war this day, it would be wise to practice

at arms, warm the muscles, accustom the hand to
the grip of the bronze. They had been idle a long
time, and he did not want Bolgios to become
self-important and forget to practice his skills. If a
warrior let himself get dull, he was soon finished.

Tingwahr squatted nearby, uselessly prodding
the ashes of a dead campfire. The ends of his
moustache fell like dirty icicles.

"Bolgios isn't here, Dagentyr. I told him last
night to remember to fetch wood for the fire and see
that it was burning well before he slept, and here it
is as dead and cold as a goblin's touch." He stood
up and blew his breath through puckered lips,
sending out a thick, deliberate fog. "I'll find more
myself and start the thing over again. I'd hate to
fight today and die having missed my last chance to
sit in front of a warm fire." With a sweep of his
arm, he sent his cape swinging back to cover his
shoulder and went for the wood.

"I'll make myself useful and go with you," said
Dagentyr, glad to be able to put the nervous energy
to some work. "You did not see Bolgios this day, or
last night?" he asked as they plopped the wood into
the firepit and Tingwahr went to fetch a live ember
from another.

"No. He is never underfoot anymore. In truth it's
hard to find him about, especially at night. With no
fighting I suppose he's had time to discover other
pastimes." Tingwahr stamped the earth. "It's cold
enough to freeze the ground. Will there be war
today?"

Dagentyr watched the new fire leap on the fresh
wood and smoke heavily until the flames took hold.

"What was that you said?"

"I asked if there would be fighting today?"

"No . . ." At night. Being absent at night was
something he understood, something they had in
common. He felt a ripple as though the melon had
churned over inside him. Who were the other

pastimes? "Where is that boy? We, he more than I, should be practicing at arms!"

Tingwahr went to him and put a hand on his shoulder.

"You seem worried for him. Why fear? He's not the only man who spends his nights in the whores' part of the city. Why, you yourself—"

"Do not speak of that."

"I'm sorry." He cleared his throat, perplexed. "But after all, he's young and has killed men in battle. He doesn't need the benefit of your worry."

"The fact that Cingetos has killed men does not save him from your concern." Tingwahr nodded. He and Cingetos had become bedmates. In battle, their companionship made them fight closer together, and more fiercely. "Perhaps you are right. I am not myself lately. I do not sleep, and when I do, I dream strange, fitful dreams."

"You sound as if your turns in the whore's quarter have done you no good. I— Oh."

Dagentyr stared straight up at the perfectly clear sky and changed the subject. "I think men will die today. Will you have a match with me, to get us ready?"

"I'd rather get ready with a jug of wine and a woman, but as you say. I'll get my weapons."

Dagentyr rubbed his hands together and blew hot breath into them. With a shake of his head and a quick look at the walls, he turned on his heel and ducked back into the tent. Bolgios's empty bedding stared him in the face.

"Dagentyr?"

When he looked out, he saw Cingetos lumbering up to him, armed, and chewing furiously at a hastily procured morsel.

"What is it?"

His words were muddled, spoken through the food. "It's Bolgios. I am supposed to be on the walls this day, and he should be with me. We both lost the draw yesterday. I can't find him anywhere. The leader of the guard will be angry. Do you know where he is?"

"No, but I will try to find him for you. Go now."

Cingetos thanked him and went to the rampart steps where the morning guard was gathering. Tingwahr poked his head out of his tent. "One moment and I will be ready."

Dagentyr acknowledged him with a wave of the hand. It was not like Bolgios to miss any kind of duty, so proud was he of his new-won status as warrior. The day seemed colder still. When he heard someone call his name again, he thought it was Cingetos coming back, but he found instead two Trusians in front of him, Parush's men. They looked at him blandly, and one of them spoke. His cloak was finer than most, bordered in blue. He was evidently a leader of the guard.

"You are Dagentyr, are you not? But then I know you are; I recognize you. The whole town has heard tell of you now that you have boosted your name through your . . . deeds." The other guard suppressed an arrogant snicker and twisted the butt of his spear into the hard dirt. "We come from Prince Parush."

"I know. I recognized your manner."

The guard frowned and his companion squeezed his spear harder. "We're not here to trade talk with you, barbarian, but to escort you to the prince as he has instructed us. He wishes to see you." Tingwahr backed out of his tent, carrying his weapons. He saw the two guards and came to Dagentyr's side with a questioning look. The men became wary. The spokesman pulled the tip of his beard into a point. "Well? We have told you. The prince wishes to see you, now." Dagentyr made no move to reply. "Without any further delay." The last words were spoken harshly, with biting emphasis.

"What goes on here?" asked Tingwahr and made a move to hand Dagentyr his sword.

"You won't need that," said the guard, quickly pointing to the sword. "You know that weapons are not permitted in the palace." The other man raised the spear off the ground and leveled its point at them.

"It seems as if they want me to go to the palace to see Parush."

"You *will* go to the palace to see him." The spear carrier spoke up for the first time.

Tingwahr, who appreciated being threatened as little as Dagentyr did, pursed his lips in anger. "What is this? Why do you threaten? Cingetos!"

Cingetos had been watching from the steps and started over. Koricus and Varnac woke and came from the tents scratching their beards. They roused all the others. The spokesman saw them and became nervous as the odds worsened.

"Listen to me. There is no need for any trouble here."

"Why should there be any trouble?" said Dagentyr, and inside he knew there was something wrong. Bad things had happened or soon would.

The guard shuffled his feet.

"The prince is waiting. I can call out the entire palace guard if I need to, warrior. The Lycians will make no move to help you." Still, Dagentyr waited. With the mention of the palace guard, the spear carrier breathed easier and regained his haughtiness. "This affair concerns you not so much as a friend of yours. The prince wishes to see you about him."

Dagentyr felt his stomach shrink. His imagination formed ugly things. He was found out. He became fearful again of dishonorable death, as he had during the ocean storm and the night on the beach with Helani, and with the fear came shame.

But who was the friend? Answering that question drew up even worse fears.

Cingetos was close and Dagentyr put up a hand to keep him where he was. "It's all right. Back to your post. I am going, Tingwahr. Tell the men that everything is well. I will be back if there is battle. Let Glaucus know where I have gone so he can tell Sarpedon in the event I am missed." He felt it a good thing to use important names and knew that with Sarpedon's new interest in him, he was not using them vainly. He made sure the escorts heard every word.

Tingwahr held his elbow. "Dagentyr, this looks like a bad thing. Stay. We can fight these two."

"Then what?" Reluctantly Tingwahr released him. "Do as I have told you." The Trusians smiled grimly, glad that their task was growing easier, gladder still that major trouble had been avoided. Cingetos and Tingwahr continued to stare at them with murderous eyes as they let Dagentyr take the lead and walked off behind him in the direction of the palace enclosure.

They did not wait long in the antechamber that led to the prince's rooms, just long enough for the pompous guard to tell his mission to the slave at the door. The old slave withdrew inside and Dagentyr listened to his weak, rasping voice as he announced their presence, then the doors were thrown open and they were ushered in.

His breath caught in his throat. Helani was there, sitting on a cushion placed on a stone ledge that ran down one side of the room. She kept her gaze away from him and wore an expression of calm that was betrayed only by the way her fingers ran over the material of her skirt and played with its glittering, golden trappings. Astekar stood far back in a corner of the sumptuously appointed room whose frescoes were gaudier than those of the main hall itself. He looked apprehensive and tired.

There was a wooden table in the center of the room, draped with a clean white cloth, and on it, the prince sprawled naked, belly-down, with his arms over its sides, while an awesomely muscled man massaged him with heated and perfumed oil. Sitting on a short stool near the table was Ruki. In his spasmed features, Dagentyr could read triumph tempered with disappointment.

"We have come back with the man as you commanded," said the guard. Parush groaned as the man worked, and raised his head just high enough to see them.

"Yes, I see that you have. Good. You may go now and wait outside until I call you." He let his head droop again in relaxation. There was a puff of cold draft as the door was opened, then closed. "I won't ask you to sit, a slave does not sit in the presence of his owner, and I'll say what I have to say to you from here. I don't want to trouble myself with you any more than I need to." The flesh moved like water beneath the fingers of the muscled man. "That"—he raised an arm in a halfhearted indication—"is the Lady Helani. You may or may not have seen her before." Dagentyr bowed his head to her, seeking to read what had transpired in her eyes. "The man on the stool is my slave, my musician, my buffoon. I believe you are familiar with each other. Lately, he has been other things to me, as well. He has been a watcher, a guardian, a singer of songs. He has sung like a magic bird and has brought to me the most fantastic tales of love . . . of passion. I cannot fully comprehend where he gets it all from. His songs say, Parush beware, it is not easy to be the husband of this, a beautiful woman. There are men who would try to make a mockery of your marriage to her. Evil men, contemptuous of civilized ways, foreigners who might be more easily tantalized than most. Guard your woman well against them, for she is a prize."

He angled his head to her and smiled, then relaxed again as the man went to work on his shoulders.

"So I did this, warrior. Last night I had her watched and guarded by my own men as well as by her personal guard. So secret was I that even she did not know of her protection." Helani blinked nervously. "She thanks me for it, don't you, Helani, loved one?"

She came back to herself and answered sheepishly.

"Of course, husband. No wife has a man who cares for her more. I was surprised, yes, and truly grateful that he was caught through your devices, this villainous sneak who would have shamed our joining." Her recitation done, she folded her hands in her lap and scowled at Dagentyr. "These barbarians are a shameless, bestial people." She allowed a tear to form in the corner of her eye.

"Yes, of course they are. On the recommendation of my songbird, we lay in wait for those lecherous men and last night we caught one. Caught him in the women's quarters actually opening my lady's door. That's shameful, isn't it, warrior? How could we have suspected that he would have gotten past the sentries? We never suspected such cleverness, did we, Helani? Did we!" The prince's voice was the growl of an animal.

Helani started in fear. "No, my husband. It's frightful." She let the tear fall down her cheek and brushed it away with a trembling fingertip.

"Startling, I agree." Parush's neck was tense, his face red.

Dagentyr stood on the cold floor, and the room was chilled with more than winter. He wished that the conversation was over, its point made, its lesson learned. He dreaded where he thought the words would lead next. If the prince had found out, he was dead.

Parush spoke, warm and comfortable with his

hot oil and simmering braziers to warm him. As Dagentyr watched, he raised a golden goblet of wine from a stand and drank. "But we caught him and shame was averted. Caught him in the hallway, tall, and blond as a new field of emmer."

At that moment, Dagentyr's fears for himself vanished into nothingness, and he became sick. He knew of only one person who fitted Parush's picture. The room reeled in front of his eyes. He clenched his hands into fists and bit hard at his lip till he feared his teeth would pierce the flesh. "He's a northman, warrior," said the prince. "One of yours, I believe. You are the self-styled leader of those people, aren't you? He is, therefore, your responsibility. Not so hard there, oaf, gently. Ruki thinks that perhaps more of your kind might have been skulking around palace places at night." He lifted his chin to stare directly into Dagentyr's eyes. "You are here because I wish to tell you to keep control of your men. They are your charges and my slaves. Blame could as easily be laid on you, so some would say."

"What of the man?" Dagentyr forced himself to speak and break control of the numbness that held his brain. "Bolgios is his name. What of him? Where is he?"

Parush raised himself to his elbows. The man pounded the small of his back. "Ahh. The gods have struck their justice satisfactorily. He had to be punished. I let the Lady Helani choose the fate herself. Tell him, tell him yourself what you picked out for the man."

She cringed under Dagentyr's glance but went on despite her dread, resuming the mask. He saw the odd glimmer come into her eyes, the ethereal vacuousness she had worn when he had stabbed the Ahhiyawan on the beach. Growing more and more aware that she herself was far removed from danger and reprisal, her story was poisoned with a certain morbid delight. "Had he entered," she said, "he would not have been fit to look upon me or touch me with his coarse hands. I have had it ordered that the eye that meant to shame me be struck out, and the hand that meant to violate me be cut off." She looked at Dagentyr almost challengingly.

"And you have had your chief serving girl beaten for not seeing his approach, haven't you?" cooed Parush.

"Yes."

Dagentyr knew it to be true. He imagined the fiery and perhaps bleeding welts on Mehiya's back and realized that Helani had beaten her not for failing to see Bolgios's approach, but for failing to see him in safely. He felt pity for her, though he did not especially like her. She was merely a toy, something for Helani to use, as were many others, he suddenly realized. A swelling lump in his throat prevented him from swallowing, and he noticed his vision constricting with rage and hatred. His head was near to bursting. As he moved his lips to speak, he fought not to slip uncontrollably into the language of the tribes.

"And was this thing done?" he asked falteringly.

"Yes, warrior. It's all been carried out. He will be put back in your care to do with, well, whatever you please. I doubt he will be good for much." Parush was close to exultant laughter.

Dagentyr looked at each of the people in the room. Helani sat placidly again now that her story was done, and he wished that thoughts had the power to kill. Astekar stroked his chin in what Dagentyr thought was actual dismay and did not look him in the eye but lowered his head and stared at the flooring. Dagentyr understood. Astekar knew that it was settled now. The warrior would never succumb to Trusya's comforts, would never do anything but hate Trusians. The investment was lost. In the middle of the prince's wretched victory, Astekar had suffered defeat.

Ruki began to pluck a simple melody, working hard to force the corners of his lips up and hold them there so Dagentyr could not possibly mistake his expression for anything but delight. His eyes said, Next time my catch will be bigger. The muscled man worked on absently, oblivious to everything. The smell of the oil soured in Dagentyr's nostrils.

"Well." Parush relaxed on the table, set the goblet back on its stand while the supple fingers kneaded the sinews of his neck. "You may go, Helani. Guards!" The doors opened instantly and one of the men entered. "Escort the lady back to her chamber and watch her well while she waits for me." He directed the last words to her and waved for the massage to stop long enough to raise himself and point a finger at her. "While she waits for my return and then my every pleasure . . . every pleasure," he repeated, "lovingly, uncomplainingly, like the high-born woman that she is." He spoke with the hardness of granite.

She rose and her skirt rustled to the floor like a death rattle. She dipped in obeisance and retired with the man. Dagentyr watched her go and knew that she silently uttered every awful curse that she could think of. The doors closed again.

"Stay awhile, warrior," said Parush as the massage resumed. "I have other things to say to you that Helani need not hear. I think what Ruki tells me is true. He led me to believe that we would find someone other than we did. I am not a blind man, except when I choose to be, and I have preferred to be sightless for a long time now. It takes away the sting, but I know what kind of woman she is. I know better than anyone else, and I know how she uses men and discards them because I was one of the first ones thrown on the midden. Because I have overcome my own stupidity, I don't have any particular sympathy for yours—yes, yours. I do not doubt what Ruki says is true, but I am faintly glad that you were not the one trapped."

He waved the servant off, and the fellow bowed and left by a side door. Gathering the cloth about him, he raised himself to sit on the edge of the table. He rolled his shoulders in their sockets and sighed. Astekar reached into a chest and pulled from it a thick woolen tunic of white edged in Sidonese purple. He walked up and helped to slip it over the prince's head. "Listen well, warrior. There will be no more blindness. It bores me now and saps my manhood. I will not be outdone by my brother. I will not be outdone by Helani, and I will not be outdone by you! I'm going to start giving the bitch what she deserves and start taking what I deserve. There will be no room or time for anyone else but me! I feel lenient. That is why you are still alive. You and I will never speak of this again, hopefully will never see each other again, and you will certainly never see her again." Astekar slipped a golden arm band over Parush's wrist. "That is all."

It was a while before the shock left Dagentyr and he could move or speak. "And Bolgios?"

"I have said he will be returned to you. Go now. You'll need no escort. I'm sure you know your way around the palace." He hopped from the table and knitted his brows together in a frown. "If you should try to see her again, I'll kill you personally and relish it."

Dagentyr thought of Helani's imaginative punishment and the sick pride she had taken in it. He had been foolish. Hot tears of rage and, worse, of shame blinded him even as her beauty had fogged his senses. He wished for a weapon to plunge into anyone nearby—the skinny worm who had revenged himself in this way, the callous prince, the embarrassed trader, the spider who had just crawled back to her quarters. He brushed the tears away with clenched, shaking hands.

"I will not try to see her again, Parush. You need not fear that. Save your fear for other things. Save it for me."

He stood riveted eye to eye with Dagentyr.

"Get out. Guard!"

The man entered as Dagentyr turned and stumbled his way into the antechamber.

"Find Diamos, the head of Helani's bodyguard," he heard Parush say.

"You wish me to bring him here to you?"

"No, idiot, I wish him dead!"

The door closed again, and he was alone in the anteroom with the old slave. He stepped back into the cold but felt nothing. From the ramparts, the signal trumpets were calling the men to arm themselves. The Ahhiyawa were moving up the plain ready to take advantage of the hard ground.

The battle was a thinly strung series of smells and sights punctuated by men he slew, whose eyes he saw briefly as they fell. He killed, and knew with savage gratification that he killed, but his feelings ranged no further than that. He hacked and cut and wielded the spear, possessed by the anger in him. Instinct took control. The rough bronze was a mad thing doing its blood-hungry will through him. He was its servant.

Even his own men shied away from him, fought next to him but apart, not sure who he really was, seeing the rage. He had said nothing to them on his return from the palace. He answered no one but went straight for his weapons in a way that put fear in them that he was drugged or enchanted.

When the skirmish was done and the men were slumping home, he put his sword away in its sheath, hoping that he would return to himself, free

of its sway. He remembered the stinging cold in his
nostrils and chest, the numbing ache of worn
muscles and frozen fingers, red and raw with winter
and blood. He thought vaguely that he had fought
well, but like a broken necklace whose beads have
scattered on the floor, the memories and events had
no connection or continuity and were merely a
collection of happenings. He could not even remember having seen Parush in his chariot but
realized that he must have been there. Purged by
the fight, his thoughts began to clear. Tingwahr
became brave enough to approach him then.

"Dagentyr, is it you? Are you with us again? The
others are worried about you. The way we saw you
fight, we were not sure. They were on edge that
Bolgios didn't come with us."

Dagentyr shook his head to dispel the deafening
clatter of chariot wheels on frozen earth that stayed
in his ears. His drooped head looked at his feet
moving up the path. Outside the gate he stopped.
The line of retreating men and weary horses continued past. He looked at Tingwahr.

"Bolgios will never fight with us again. His
meetings have been with the Lady Helani, and
Parush has found him out. Helani has had him
maimed, one eye, one hand, gone . . . and I could
do nothing!" His body shivered with a chill. A sea
wind was blowing up.

Tingwahr's eyes widened. "What? Is this true or
does some madness left over from battle make you
say this?"

"It has happened. That is why I was called to the
palace. I don't think she cared, not really, nor even
if I had stood in his place. Her punishment then
might have been even more elaborately devised."

"What is this you're saying?"

He shook his head again. "Nothing."

"Then Bolgios is truly maimed?"

"Yes."

They turned and passed into the city. His men were close behind him, talking in hushed whispers, concern wrinkling their foreheads. Tingwahr became quiet, an unbelieving look set on his face. He signed against evil and uttered a death curse. Moving on alone, Dagentyr was aware that Tingwahr had dropped back to tell the others. There were half-shouted exclamations of disbelief, muttered oaths, questions. All had fallen silent by the time they reached camp.

Bolgios was there in the tent, roughly thrown on his bedding, uncovered, shivering and convulsed with cold. His tunic was torn and spattered with crusty blood. His arms were clutched over his chest. The end of one was blunt, wrapped with a soaking rag. Dagentyr saw it was the right hand.

"They didn't even leave him his sword hand," he said to Tingwahr and knelt down. A length of cloth had been wound round his head to cover the missing eye; it was thick with clotting blood. The cheek bone beneath the socket showed bruises and swelling. Bolgios rocked his head back and forth on the bed and whimpered at Dagentyr's touch. The maimed arm rose like a club to push him off.

"No, Bolgios. It's Dagentyr. There are none here who will hurt you. No one but friends, your people. We are going to protect you. No further harm will come to you."

Bolgios's dry lips parted. As he turned to speak, Dagentyr put his hand to the boy's head as gently as he could and cursed. He was hot.

"Dag . . ." He moistened his lips with a thick tongue. Dagentyr called for wine. Tingwahr relayed his call, and one of the men who stood in a half-moon round the tent opening went for it. "Dagentyr. I did not fight today and am ashamed. Mehiya heard the footsteps and left me in the hall alone. There was no chance to run. I, I can't even see you!" He struggled to open the good eye and failed. "I never told you about her. You would have called me stupid. It never seemed dangerous, and she told me she would always protect me."

"Hush. Think of sleep and good things. Think of sleep after a good, hard fight, after good food and a fierce roll with a captured woman." Dagentyr took the wine when it came, poured it on the bottom of his tunic, and sponged Bolgios's lips. He sucked the cloth dry and some was poured into a cup for him to drink outright. The groan he let out when his head was raised to drink split Dagentyr's heart. He wiped his dripping nose with his fist, and the dim firelight outside blurred and dazzled in his tears. Tingwahr was grim-faced, but his hands shook.

"Listen, Bolgios," said Dagentyr. "There will be an avenging. Rest now and we will do it. Fetch the Lycian camp surgeon," he said to Tingwahr. Bolgios had gone unconscious.

The camp surgeon was an impressive man built like a regular warrior, but lame. He purified the stump with fire and anointed the wounds with salve, putting fresh bandages to them. He was mixing a potion in a small bowl and Dagentyr spoke to him.

"What is his fate?"

"I do not tell fortunes." His answer was short but not cruel or sarcastic. "The wounds are bad, not good clean ones, and there is fever. He could live, gods willing, or he could die. This is a draught of poppy for sleep and relief of pain. Give him wine if he asks for it." Dagentyr stared at him, expecting more. "There is nothing else to be done. Pray to your gods if you wish." He turned to administer the drug.

Nothing to be done, he thought. We'll see.

The surgeon shook his head as he went away with his assistant. Dagentyr peeked back in the tent. Bolgios seemed to sleep. The drug was quick. The new bandages showed red already.

Bolgios's bow lay on the ground next to him. When the Trusians had left him in the tent, they had knocked the quiver about, and the arrows were scattered haphazardly. Their points gleamed mockingly. Tingwahr called Dagentyr's name just outside. The men were gathered with him.

"We have talked, Dagentyr. We are all agreed. There must be vengeance for this." They muttered solemnly. The firelight behind them shot their shadows across him.

"Then we agree. You must trust me. I know what can be done."

"That swine, Parush, must not live through another battle. It must be seen to."

"There must be another reckoning first, and that is something I must see to."

Tingwahr was angered. "I do not understand you."

"I'm telling you there's another thing to do first. Would you kill Parush and jeopardize a chance to leave this place and return to your homes if I could settle the matter another way?" That had the effect he wanted it to. They stopped chattering and darted their eyes at him questioningly, in wonder. "It is something I cannot tell you and neither must you mention to anyone else that something is afoot. I'll have your oaths as warriors." They nodded and clasped their hands to the hilts of their weapons. "Trust me. Cingetos and Koricus, stay with Bolgios and make him comfortable. Do what you can." He smoothed and straightened his tunic. "Tingwahr, fetch Glaucus and tell him that I must see Sarpedon tonight, now. Tell him I want armed men to go with me. I'm not popular at the palace. I'll explain that to you later."

How glad Sarpedon would be to see him, early, before spring. With what help he could give, he swore to see the bitch turned over, for he was sure that it was what she wanted least, a return to mortality with no more men offered up for sacrifice on her soft, fleshy altar. How devastated Parush would be to lose her. The sooner he saw Sarpedon and the plot was forged, the better. It was one sure step in many months of stupidity. As much as was possible, he felt relieved. Then a fresh thought came to him. Ruki also had to be punished.

Chapter 24

Sarpedon received him expectantly, called for hot wine to be brought in, and then dismissed the servants and guards. His quarters in the palace were not large, but comfortable and heated well with many braziers that made the walls seem to glow with dim warmth. Glaucus himself had escorted him to the palace with two other armed men. The palace guards had looked sideways at him as if they recognized him, but because he was in Glaucus's company, let him pass. The two men stood on guard outside the door. Glaucus pulled the king's chair closer to one of the braziers, then he went to the little window to watch there. When a servant returned with the wine, he lit the lamps before he left, and the room became brighter. Its walls were plain plaster. The bed loomed large in the center of the floor.

Sarpedon eased himself into the chair, grimaced at an ache in his stiff leg, and motioned for Dagentyr to sit as well. A cushion was nearby. Dagentyr pulled it to him and sat. The king lifted the wine cup to his lips before speaking, and his voice seemed richer in the sleepy surroundings, and touched with sadness.

"I am glad that you have come. I knew you would, but how much better it would have been if you had come without such sorrowful prompting. We have heard of Bolgios. People talk of nothing else. Parush struts around like the king of the roost."

"Like a boy who has suddenly been told that he is a man, like a jackal that is proud of evil deeds done at night."

Sarpedon nodded. "I am sorry about your friend. It is no fit fate for a man."

"You have been right all along. I was a fool not to have seen it. I have come to give you my help."

Sarpedon pointed to Glaucus at the window, his hand working nervously round his sword hilt. "As you can see, this is a dangerous business. Even a king is not safe from eavesdropping in this place. The Trusians are notorious for intrigue. There will be bad consequences for us, all of us, if any of this is found out. So then, knowing this, you're totally committed?"

Dagentyr nodded.

Sarpedon rested his elbows on the arms of the chair and held the cup between his hands. He swirled the wine and studied the changes in the rising steam. He was dressed in a long woolen robe of some dark color. In the dimness of the room, Dagentyr thought it to be blue or purple.

"I am sorry you were brought to the plan in this way."

Dagentyr shrugged. "It's a matter of vengeance now, of honor. She must pay. It will be easy enough to make Parush pay, that I can see to alone, but her case is different. It will be a joy to see the look in his eyes when he knows she is lost." He drank deeply of the wine and fought the lump that was rising in his throat again. The steamy vapors played in his nose.

"Your revenge on Parush is your own business, but it must wait or it could endanger our plans. The woman is a curse. Lakowon the seer has said so, and the other priests agree. She is the cause of this. The displeasure of the gods must be averted. It will be if the woman leaves. I know it!"

Dagentyr agreed. "It will be the best thing that can be done, for everyone. It's not going to be easy. Parush has changed. Helani will be almost impossible to get to. Her bodyguard is abolished, and the prince's men watch her. It is a different situation than before."

"Do you have anything to suggest?"

He thought. Of course the familiar and lenient guards would be gone, and the prince's men would be hawk-eyed. But he knew that Helani was not the kind of woman who could be cooped for long, in spite of the difficulties. Also, he trusted in Mehiya's shrewdness.

"I think," said Dagentyr, trying not to sound presumptuous, "that there is a way."

Sarpedon turned to Glaucus, then back again. He drained the cup at one pull. "But how are we to get her? That is our problem."

The flicker of an idea woke in him, a remembrance of a time and place that would have been perfect.

"We could take her, perhaps, outside the walls."

Glaucus stirred at his place and listened more intently.

The king was amazed. "How is that possible? It would be good, but how can we?" He put the cup down excitedly.

Dagentyr hesitated before plunging on. He followed Sarpedon's example and drank his fill from the cup, then told the story of his jaunt beyond the gates in woman's costume. When he was done, Sarpedon sat flabbergasted for a moment. The only sound was Glaucus clicking his tongue in astonishment. The king shook his head in disappointment at such a missed opportunity.

"It will only be a matter of time before she will try something like this again," Dagentyr said.

"But the danger is far greater now," interjected Glaucus.

"It will not matter. The danger will make it all the more attractive. It will draw and excite her like nectar draws bees."

"Is there anything we can do to push this meeting along?" said Sarpedon.

"I think not. She will suspect. Helani must send Mehiya to me without suspicion. Then I can encourage her to venture out again. Better yet, I'll tell her that I am going to run away with her. Away from here, back to my land. What better time for us to go?"

"Isn't that farfetched?"

"No, Lord Sarpedon, she has asked it of me. Do you trust me on this?"

He shifted his weight. "Yes."

"Now that Parush knows of you two, will she send for you again?" Glaucus added a negative note.

"I do not know," he was forced to admit. "I believe she will." He wished there was more wine in the cup; he felt in need of it.

Sarpedon scratched his chin. "Then must we wait until the city fills the cisterns again?"

"No. There could be another way. We need wait only till the next dark of the moon."

"Explain."

"You can see to it that all the wall guards above camp are my men. It will be her turn this time, to dress as a man. We will mount the walls as if to relieve the sentries, then we could escape over the ramparts if rope was handy. I could take her then, bind her, and carry her close to the Ahhiyawan camp. They would find her in the morning."

"It is good. Then there is nothing to do but wait and hope that she sends for you soon. I will tell

Antior and Awunash of what you have said, and I will wait to hear from you. Go now. If asked by the guards, tell them that you came here to complain of Bolgios's treatment, then let it be known that I offered to do nothing. That will be a good tale to kill suspicion." He stood up a little stiffly and called for his cup to be replenished. "Drink, Dagentyr, for the help that we can give each other, for our cause."

"For home." He held up the goblet and gripped his hand more tightly around it.

"Both our homes."

Glaucus nodded.

They drank and sealed their resolve.

When he returned to camp, he was aware of elation. He told the men of his plan so they would know what sort of vengeance they were taking and swore them again to secrecy.

The dark of the moon approached, and yet Mehiya had not come. With each waning day, Bolgios gave more cause for worry. His wounds would not heal. He seemed to be unable to gain strength and often was not himself. His fever was stubborn and the demons in him strong.

Dagentyr and his men were edgy, knowing that the summons from Helani was overdue. Winter was still on the land but did not rest heavy. It was becoming milder, unusually so. The trumpets summoned the men from the tents. They gathered in their accustomed place before the gate. Hektu mounted the wall and shouted to the people.

"It is a day out of place. Spring in the midst of winter. A good omen! Today we will fight. We will finish the Ahhiyawa on this day that has been made for us. I will not return to the citadel until they are gone or until I fall. Better the people of the city should refuse us entrance, and we should die at the very gates, than retreat through them again. I say that this will be it!"

The warriors gave a single, tense cheer.

Sarpedon was in high spirits. The leg was well enough for him to ride again. The sun was glinting off his polished leather and bronze. The horns of his helmet made him look like a sleek bull looking for trouble. He was carefree, back with his men before battle, where a king should be.

The gates opened, and the men swarmed out like locusts. Sunlight glittered like a shower of hot sparks on the charging men. Chariots plowed ahead of the footmen, and the hooves battered the turf. War cries drove the ravens from the field, and they retreated to safety to wait.

Their number was already decreased by two, and Dagentyr told the men to take care. They kept a close eye on each other and went shouting and slashing as a tight unit.

To their surprise, the Ahhiyawa wavered and broke. With the Trusians pressing hard and the river at their backs, they gave way and fled. Archers and slingers followed close behind them, keeping the fleeing men under falling rocks and arrows. If Bolgios were here, his bow would be cutting down many as they ran, Dagentyr thought. Wounded men tried pathetically to rid themselves of their armor and crawl to the riverbank to die in peace before the Trusians reached them. Dagentyr and his men caught many and slew them.

Sarpedon and the other leaders kept up the pressure, urging the men to leave the spoils for later and keep pushing the Ahhiyawa back to the shore.

In the car of his chariot, Sarpedon smiled through the dust and sweat. "Come on! Pick up the march. We'll be the first there, the first to see the Ahhiyawa drown when we push them into the sea!"

They cheered him.

Behind, the horns of Trusya blared, rejoicing in the advancing army, and the men were strengthened by it. They were eager for the battle to resume.

Dagentyr walked boldly at the head of his group. His heart was glad to be out of the city, walking unimpeded over the land on a fine day, closing steadily on the beach where the black ships were shored up, ripe to be burned. So sure and cocky were some that they lit torches as they went and waved them bravely over their heads. The flames sputtered and left streaky black lines of smoke on the air. They gave off an unpleasant, sooty odor, masking the smell of death.

On the fringes of Kiastu, or what remained of it, the Ahhiyawa turned to fight. The battle was feverish. At their rear stood the earthworks and low rock wall, torn from the humble stones of Kiastu. They had dug a ditch in front of it and lined it with spikes, honed roof beams from houses, broken spears. Behind the wall, the masts of the ships stuck up plainly.

As darkness and exhaustion fell over the plain, the Trusians were driven back far enough to allow the chariots to retreat through the gap in the wall. Rough gates of timber were closed behind them. The footmen scrambled back over their stone barriers. The first star blinked on in its place and, in the distance, the city torches answered. The Trusians pulled farther back on the plain, out of easy striking distance from the wall.

Sarpedon galloped up to his men.

"We stay on the plain tonight! Hektu meant his boast. They are sending food from the city. Send some men back across the plain with torches. We don't want the spoils picked clean and none for ourselves." He was full of vitality and exuberance. Hopping from the car, he removed his helmet and spoke to Dagentyr. There was a line across his brow where the helmet had kept the dirt from his skin. "It was a good fight. If the gods are kind tomorrow, we will not need the plan!" He gave Dagentyr a slap on the shoulder and remounted.

"I hope you are right."

"Dagentyr," said Glaucus. "Your men fought well today. Pick another, and the two of you go for spoils first. Send the others out in their turn. You deserve your share."

He chose Tingwahr.

The torches were poor, giving off little more than a small lamp's glow. There were many on the field, bobbing like bluish fireflies over the corpses. Many of the men they came to were already stripped of valuables. The cry of horses came from out of the dark as someone came across a stray team wandering among the grasses. The river rushed away, filling the air with its babbling and smell. They gathered up what they could, jewelry, weapons, wrapped them in their cloaks, and went by the river to pause and splash the dirt away from their faces.

The water was sweet and cold. Tingwahr knelt by the flow, submerged his head completely then drew it back, sputtering and blowing. As he sat on the grass, he tried on an amulet of silver and, deciding that he liked it, kept it on. Dagentyr put his bundle of booty on the bank and let his feet hang into the stream.

"Will victory in tomorrow's battle truly mean that we will sail for home?" asked Tingwahr.

"I trust Sarpedon's word. He has said that he will free us."

"And what if there is no victory?"

"Then we have the plan."

"Will it work? Tell me your heart, not what you think. I'm asking as a friend, as your good friend, for I do not get any sense of coming glory. It is something that a warrior is supposed to feel beforehand. It is what the gods give to him to make him brave."

Dagentyr was uncertain himself now about the plan. Death had come to the plain again, and Mehiya had not visited. There had been little word of Helani. The rumors said that Parush kept her locked in her rooms. Her walks on the wall had ceased. He knew now that they had underestimated the prince.

"I had hoped," he said, "that the plot might have worked already. My heart longs greatly for home."

Tingwahr rubbed his sore ankles. "I hope that there are some of us alive to go back."

They exchanged glances. The night crept into Dagentyr's memory and changed the flowing water into the river below Fottengra. He was sure that there was something waiting for him there. He refused to believe that life would end here with an Ahhiyawan spear thrust. It must not! Smoldering emotions pent up for nearly a year burst out. He slapped the water with his open hands and listened to the shower of drops land like rain on the surface.

"If there is defeat tomorrow and the woman does not come to me soon, we will find another way. Each day I spend here is like a drop of blood leaking from my veins. It is not right!"

"There was a time not long ago when you might not have felt that way."

Dagentyr dipped a hand into the water and rubbed the back of his neck. "I have always wanted to go back. The bitch didn't change that desire, just obscured it. Bolgios was the one who wanted to stay, and now . . . Do you want to go home, Tingwahr?"

He answered carefully, choosing his words.

"You are our chieftain, but none of us are from Fottengra. Our homes are elsewhere. I will stay by you now, the others will too, but when we go back, will you hold us, or let us go our ways?"

"Each man must go where his place is. I'll prevent no man from going where he wishes. I never would have."

"I am sorry I spoke of it."

"Do not be. There is no reason why you should

cherish your home any less than I do mine."
Tingwahr smiled. "Tell the others this. They should
not have to worry over it."

An object was floating downstream. Snagging
and tangling in the rushes, it turned and moved
toward them in the dark. Dagentyr leaned as far as
he could over the water and held the torch out at it.
It was a man. Handing the light to Tingwahr, he
waded in and pulled the body to the bank.

"Does he wear gold, Dagentyr?"

He moved the torch up and down the prone
figure. "No."

The man wore no armor. He was Ahhiyawan. His
skull had been caved in by a blow, but the water
had washed away the blood. The wound showed
pink and lifeless grey where the bone had been
pushed into the brains. His mouth was open like a
yawn and was filled with water. The tunic he wore
was not holed or stained, just wet. It was the color
of ripe emmer or cheese. The neck and hem were
edged in crude stitchery of light blue. Dagentyr
examined his own garment, dirty, worn, frayed. He
stripped the man and took the cream-colored tunic
for his own, wet as it was. Perhaps a new tunic
would be symbolic, magical, signifying a fresh start
that would carry over into the rest of his life. A
fresh start was due him, a fresh start for home.

At dawn the Ahhiyawa attacked from behind the
wall, hoping for surprise. The sky was pale, the wall
black. The horses' hooves thundered out.

"They're coming," said Dagentyr.

Long before dawn, Sarpedon and Hektu had put
the men at the alert. They rose up on command and
moved forward. In the first light the horses were
huge and the men behind them dark monsters,
grunting, and snapping reins. Dagentyr and his
men fought savagely, with the knowledge that if the
Ahhiyawa were driven into the ocean, they could
leave, venture south with Sarpedon and take ship

for home. The new tunic was darkened with sweat.
His shield bristled where the arrows had grown like
sprouting weeds. Ravens fought for their place on
the field and left only when men or horses were
nearly on top of them.

Something gave in the Ahhiyawan center. There
was consternation and a scuffle to help someone
behind the lines. They wavered.

Sarpedon and Hektu called to the men to move
on again.

Dagentyr wanted to fly and strike instantly.
"This means home!" he cried, and the words put
new life into his legs and arms. The air was sucked
into his lungs with deep, churning regularity. The
other tribesmen sensed it too, and they rushed up
with him.

There was no attempt to hold before the wall.
The Ahhiyawa fled. Many of their chariots had
been abandoned. Drivers and riders ran through
the spiked ditch, for the hurry to get through the
gate had clogged it with a backwater of men. The
Trusians followed them in.

Dagentyr shouted, "Don't be too eager! Careful!
Use your shields!" They hesitated, but the rush of
men behind them propelled them on, and they
were down among the spikes before they knew it.
He put his shield up over his head. A rock glanced
off, and the point of an arrow appeared, jabbing
through the hide. Cingetos stumbled and fell.

Sarpedon was there suddenly, and Glaucus. They
had left the chariots behind and advanced with the
rest.

"Scale it! Leave the gates to those milk-blooded
Trusians. Over!" cried the king.

Up close the wall was not as high as it had
seemed. In places, it was a breastwork no taller
than a man, only meant for checking the rush of
chariots. It was rough. There were many handholds
and crevices.

Dagentyr barely knew what he was about before he found himself reaching up, clinging to rock, and jamming his foot into a crack to push. He discarded his spear. Sarpedon was already to the top, kicking the stones of the wall down. The defenders must be fleeing farther away from the breastwork, Dagentyr found himself thinking, then he was up and standing on the wall. He drew sword.

Glaucus was pulling himself up behind him. An arrow sang past Dagentyr's shin and struck Glaucus in the shoulder. He clattered back to the base of the wall.

Sarpedon saw him fall and stopped.

Dagentyr felt the hesitation. "We need to go on, Sarpedon. Push forward!"

Their eyes met. They knew that crushing the Ahhiyawa was the best solution, drive them into the ocean like rats. They took courage from each other.

They could see the ships and the men scrambling between them, looking for some place to go. It was a marvelous sight. Bright sand gleamed in the sun and dazzled them. The beach was choked with ships, twice, three times what he had ever seen before. A band of Ahhiyawa approached them. He remembered nothing of them, only that they were cut down, and he walked over them to the ships. Hektu and the Trusians spilled through the gate.

There was fire to be had in plenty. Cooking fires still burned everywhere on the beach. Dagentyr reached down to one and grabbed a burning stick. Checking to see that his men were there to share the glory, he rushed to the nearest ship and cast it aboard. An old man rushed to stop him. His eyes were wild. He was unarmed.

"Stop it. No, stop!" he cried.

Dagentyr stabbed him through and searched for more fire.

The crackle of flames began to grow as the beached ship caught fire. As more Trusians poured over and through the wall, the beach became solid with men. The melee spread till the whole length of sand was crawling like a honey cake covered with ants.

In the middle of it, Sarpedon called his men to rally around him. Forming a crude line on the narrow strip of sand, they pushed forward. With desperation the Ahhiyawa held on. Their archers hid, and shot from the ships. Where men trampled over the fires, flaming and smoking debris was kicked like chaff. Slaves and unarmed men tried to fight the fires and save the ships that could be saved. The air grew thick, hazy, and the men coughed as they fought. Dagentyr's eyes ran and smarted. The charcoal stench clung to his clothes. His shoes filled with sand.

At the far end of the beach there was a disturbance. The shouts of many men came to them. Dagentyr did not know what was happening. The Ahhiyawa raised a paean, and it spread like fire in a dry forest. The Lycians fought to break through. Their push had lost its momentum, or had been stopped.

Like a thunderclap, the Ahhiyawan line parted before them and fresh, well-armed men burst through, scattering the Trusians.

Sarpedon called "Hold!" but it was useless. They were broken.

Men kicked a hail of grit into the air. Fighting to scrape sand from his eyes and mouth, Dagentyr ran. In the confusion and smoke he saw Sarpedon, off balance, falling, a spear stuck through his chest. He went from sight, and the ranks of men closed over him. A wail went up from the Lycians.

"Dagentyr, fall back with us, hurry!" Tingwahr called to him.

He was stunned. A hurled stone struck him in the back and staggered him. No! he thought. They had set the ships afire. As he ran, he glanced over his

shoulder to see his pursuit. Sarpedon's body was
being contested. The Lycians were dragging it back
by the foot, toward the wall, but new ranks of
Ahhiyawa were pushing forward. They gave up and
dashed for the wall.

Dagentyr heard Tingwahr's call again. He
reached his men, then the wall. The stones dripped
and melted in front of him. He blinked away tears,
not of hate or rage, but of sorrow, for himself. Then
there was nothing but running, and hoping that the
Ahhiyawa would not follow up the rout.

The city looked like a child's mud castle in the
distance. Jubilant, angry cries rose from the
Ahhiyawa behind them. He kept his eyes to the far
battlements and left his hopes lost in the sand of
the beach.

Chapter 25

There was weeping in the city, coming from some hovel somewhere on one of the paths to the palace. It was a sound that was at home in the night and in Trusya. The Lycian camp was tomb-silent. The men shuffled aimlessly about their fires. Sarpedon's death seemed to have taken everything from them. They were children.

Bolgios rolled to his side and moaned. With his remaining hand, he clutched his cloak and struggled slowly and weakly to pull it up over his shoulders. He was ashen, thin.

The camp surgeon leaned down to offer him broth, but he rolled away again and would not eat. The surgeon stood, shrugged.

Dagentyr cajoled. "Eat this, eat something. Strength is what you need. How are you to fight with us again if you will not work to regain your strength?" Bolgios murmured some unintelligible reply through clenched teeth.

The surgeon motioned Dagentyr outside. "I have no more time to stay with him. I'm very busy tonight. At any rate, I've seen enough."

Dagentyr's brow wrinkled in concern. The other men were waiting close by to hear news from him.

"You've seen enough already? But you did not stay with him long. Is he so much worse, then? Is it that plain to you?"

The man tried to seem unhurried, worked hard to smile, and put his hand to Dagentyr's arm. "I have watched his illness enough to know." He paused, then spoke slowly and softly. A smooth feel of kindness came through his words as it always did when he was truly concerned. "It's going to be very bad."

Dagentyr prevented him from going on. "Wait a moment." He looked at the others standing very still and stern but worried, their eyes questioning. He knew their insides were knotted, too. If the news was bad, they all had a right to hear it together. The surgeon's way of speaking would be gentler. They would benefit from the compassion of the Lycian's voice. He motioned them to join him.

"Now tell us," he said.

The surgeon looked at each face, fidgeted with his beard, and sighed. "It is the lockjaw, common enough after wounding. Often I have seen it, too often for my taste. I am sorry; I can give no reason why the gods do these things."

"What can you do?" Tingwahr asked.

"What I have done before now. There is nothing else."

Tingwahr's eyes searched the ground around the campfire. They could all see Bolgios's shadow on the inside of the tent thrashing in misery. Tingwahr spit into the flames.

Dagentyr would not let it go at that. "What more can you tell us?"

"What more is there to tell? It is the lockjaw." He was beginning to show impatience again.

"And will he be alive tomorrow?"

He nodded. "Yes, but I—" He looked more concerned than before, embarrassed. His lips closed tightly over his last word.

"But?" Dagentyr stepped closer.

The men looked straight at him. Their eyes had ceased their anxious wandering.

"There is no harm in telling, but I must tell you quickly and be off. Glaucus is waiting for a potion that will take away the discomfort of his wound. He is anxious to leave. Camp will be broken soon." He saw the shocked eyes. Dagentyr's head inclined in puzzlement. "I will not be here tomorrow to help Bolgios. We are going away, this night, we are going home. Glaucus commands it. You would have been told with the other men."

Dagentyr's throat tightened. The news came like lightning across a moonless night.

Tingwahr pushed forward. "We were promised, Dagentyr . . . remember?"

"Silence. I will find out more."

Tingwahr kicked the ground. Cingetos, who did not understand as well, asked him what had been said. Tingwahr told them all in the language of the tribes that the Lycians were going.

"Dagentyr," cried Cingetos. "That means we go, too. It is part of your plan." He was excited, clapping Tingwahr's shoulders with his big hands.

"Quiet." He turned to the surgeon. "Was Glaucus trying to keep this news from us?"

"Should he? No one has been told yet. I know because I had to judge if Glaucus could travel. Why do you expect some kind of deceit here, warrior?"

"Do we go then, Dagentyr?" asked Tingwahr.

"Is this it?" Cingetos's eyes were bright, anxious.

"Glaucus is fit for a journey, then." Dagentyr was suddenly aware of unease. "What of Bolgios? Will he stand a journey?"

"No, he will die." The Lycian seemed sure.

"And if he does not travel?"

Tingwahr shouted, "What are you saying, Dagentyr!"

The surgeon was just as sure again. "He will die, almost certainly."

"What is this 'almost' of yours?"

He shrugged his habitual shrug. "I have seen men survive it. Not many, not often. The gods can be cruel or kind; call it what you will."

"A journey will kill him?"

"It will. I must go." He nodded to Dagentyr, to the rest, and limped away in the dark.

"What is there to do? Do we go or not?"

"Quiet, Tingwahr. Glaucus is a good man. He heard the king give his promise to me. He will come, I know, and ask us to go with them, he will."

Tingwahr smiled with relief. Drusos let out a restrained whoop. They fell to babbling among themselves.

"Do we gather what is ours and make ready to leave?"

"No. We wait. There is what the Lycian has said to consider. Bolgios will die if we leave." What a shock it was just to say it and know that leaving might be a fact, not some hidden plot, not some dream. "What has happened to your concern?" Tingwahr started to speak. "No, say nothing, think. There is a choice to make—stay and see if Bolgios lives. Go, and kill him. I as chieftain, and you yourselves have called me this, could make this decision for all, but leaving is a hope we have held a long time." He was stricken with sadness. There had been so much agony in the choices he had made, agony for others. He did not want his own choices to hurt his people any more. "I will throw position away. You will make the decision for yourselves. I told Tingwahr last night that I would hold no one when the time came for each man to seek his own home. I did not think it would be like this, but I will not break the pledge that I gave him, or you. Go if you wish, no one will stop you. I do not think anyone will care anymore if we go or stay." He thought of Astekar, who knew the game was over.

Tingwahr was quiet. Dagentyr thought it was a silence he was forcing. His face was still agitated and unsure. "This could mean home," he said at last.

"Yes." He looked him in the eye. "It can mean home for all of you, all but one."

Tingwahr indicated all the others with open, pleading hands. "Do you not know how we feel at this news? At last—"

Dagentyr strode up to them. "I, not know! Who are you to say that? Who are you to put that in front of me!"

"It was not meant." Tingwahr put his palms up in apology. His face fell. He could talk no longer and went to the edge of the camp to stand alone.

The brusque Cingetos looked disconcerted and sheepish. He ambled away to stand next to Tingwahr. The men coughed, looked at Dagentyr with blank, chastised faces. There was a muffled moan from the tent.

A herald came through the camp, tent to tent, and called for the men to break camp and prepare to leave immediately. The Lycians set to work instantly, as if it had all been suspected. There was only mild surprise among them and exhausted relief. They were able to ready themselves quickly, most leaving the tents, taking only bare necessities and loot.

Tingwahr's back had stiffened at the herald's call. The others were anxious to know what to do. Dagentyr was still staring into the flames as Glaucus stepped into their camp circle.

"So, Dagentyr. We are leaving." He was drawn and his face creased now and then with pain. His arm hung in a hastily made sling, but he wore his armor and weapons. The dead king's heralds were beside him. "I know of the king's promise to you. He would not have forgotten and now I will remember for him. Tell your men to gather what they want and come. You have no marks that say you are slaves. No one will notice you, and the Trusians will not stop us." He grimaced. "They had better not attempt it. Tonight we leave, if we have to force our way out."

Dagentyr stood and bowed his head in solemn greeting. "Many thanks to Sarpedon and Glaucus, both honorable men."

"The Trusians will not see it so. My king gave his word to come and fight the Ahhiyawa. He fulfilled his promise, and I am not bound by a pledge not given out of my own mouth. While the king lived, but not now. It was a bad decision to come here, but we could not know. So, come."

"We are grateful. Those of my men who wish to go may leave with you."

"I am unsure what you mean." Pain was making him irritable.

"Bolgios will not survive a journey."

Glaucus seemed to pause a moment to place the name. He nodded. "I am sorry. You will stay here with him? There may be no better chance than this."

"He is one of my people."

"I do not argue. I only say take care in making your decision." A herald handed him his helmet. "Already it seems so late, and we still are not gone. Tell the men to hurry." The herald sped away shouting the commands. "I should be elsewhere. We leave by the lesser gate, tell those who wish to go. Come with us, Dagentyr." He held his arm out for Dagentyr to clasp.

"I must think," he said as he took it. The choice was gnawing at him, too. His head swam. There could be no harder decision.

Glaucus turned without comment and left to see to his men. When Dagentyr turned round to his people again, Tingwahr stood in front of him.

"I have been rebellious in the sight of my chieftain. I am too good a warrior for that. I do what Dagentyr tells me. May his decision carry for all, is this not right?" He implored the others.

"It is," said Cingetos. "It has been so since our arrival. There is nothing to change that now."

Tingwahr saw them all nod. "As it should be." He took Dagentyr by the arms. "Make our decision, and let your choice keep us from shame." There were tears on his cheeks. He could hold Dagentyr's gaze only briefly, then stepped away.

How many times must their eyes be on me only, he wondered in anguish.

"I must go, a short time only, to be alone. When I return, I will say." Still unable to look at them, he left the fire, the camp circle, the eyes and anxious hearts. He felt emptied of all wisdom and courage.

The stars were above and filled him with awe. The star-snake was there, looking the same as it always did, a ripped-away piece of home that dogged his life.

He set off along the walls and then up the stone steps to the crown of the citadel where the temple of the Trusian gods stood by itself, deep in its own shadows. The palace was near, and the lights burned in every window and portal as its occupants had been awakened by the alarming shouts from the Lycian sector. Perhaps Priasham was already on his way to plead with Glaucus. Dagentyr wondered if the king would go on his knees.

From one of the vendors that lived near the temple, he took a crude mud figure in a strange, conical hat, giving the man his golden finger ring in exchange. The offerings were awkward, crumbly, for the makers could not bring clay from outside the gates and modeled them from the poor dirt of the streets. The old man paid little attention to him and huddled near his temple wall. Dagentyr studied the strange figure and went in.

The priests eyed him curiously, not totally approving as he came in, so different was he in appearance. With wrinkled hands, one of them took his gift and placed it upon the altar stone. It sat there with all the others like it, with nothing to say. The fire in the hearth threw their shadows flickering hugely on the walls and made the room seem crowded.

The dim, airy shadow presences gave him no feeling of assurance. They were apparitions with no substance or heart. He beseeched the gods he knew, those of the home forest, and waited for a sign. Let it be like Irzag told me. Let the answer be as plain as it was then, he prayed.

When he opened his eyes, the airy ones were still there. There was no sign. His gods were far away and he was still empty. There were no answers here.

If I have only me, then it will have to do. When it was said that Bolgios would die certainly if he left, my heart rushed to say, stay. Things blurted out in haste are often true. Maybe that was my sign. We will stay.

He had hoped for some kind of relief or satisfaction once the decision had been firmly made, but there was none. He left the temple knowing that he had taken from his people their best chance for freedom. The choice, though right in his mind, left a heavy burden on his conscience as leader.

The encampment seemed to have grown quiet. Most of the Lycians were already gone, assembled at the lesser gate ready to start out on their long walk home. Their fires still burned, like memories.

Dagentyr took a deep breath, told himself that he was right in his conviction, and went to his camp circle.

The men were seated around the fire calmly. Drusos and Koricus were laughing at a story Cingetos had just told. They seemed relaxed.

Tingwahr saw him, stood, and brushed off his rump. "There you are, Dagentyr." He looked around him. "The Lycians have left much. Some of us have taken new tents. Each man may have his own if he wishes. Do you hear how quiet it is now, quiet like the forests used to be."

They smiled at him, and nodded their agreement.

"More loot for us now," said Cingetos.

Tingwahr came and escorted Dagentyr to the fire. "Sit down with us. We have found an abandoned jug of wine in one of the tents. It's heating in the embers now. When it's ready we'll all drink together!"

They cheered, for no other apparent reason than the wine, but Dagentyr knew better and felt a warmth grow in him as if steaming wine had already been poured down his throat. He looked at each man and grinned as they did. He had not made a decision to condemn them to servitude; they had made their own choice and here they were, confident that they had made the right one, as they were sure that their chieftain had chosen well.

Nothing else needed to be said.

Chapter 26

It was spring. Dagentyr stood on the walls watching the chariot make its rounds, back and forth, with its gruesome burden dragging behind it. The body danced with unnatural life as it hit rocks and obstructions in its way. The limbs flailed stiffly, for Hektu had been dead for several days. It was now hard to recognize the thing behind the wheels as a man. As he watched, the body flipped over to its other side and plowed up a trail of dust. He could not tell which was belly and which was back.

The chariot finished its loop just out of bow shot. Its driver gave a whoop, turned the animals sharply so the wheels skidded sideways over the ground, and reversed his run along the walls, pushing the beasts to all the speed they had. Each crack of the reins and victorious war shout brought moans of despair from the watchers on the walls. The whole city seemed to take in gulps of air and sob them out in sorrow and fear.

The king and queen stood off on the high tower of the main gate and shouted pleadingly at the charioteer, uselessly. The driver made obscene gestures and shook his fist, followed by his aura of dust and death. The queen sagged against the king's knees in weeping. Priasham put his hands to his face and wept, unable to help her up. His guards steadied him and one carried the queen away. Priasham leaned on the wall and beat the stones with his fists. He had to use the fingers of two hands to count the sons he had lost.

The mourning was great, and more people wailed to see the king and queen so greatly distressed. Parush stood apart with nothing given away in his demeanor while the lesser princes took the job of comforting. His mouth was set in a sneer, for the driver or the dead lump behind him Dagentyr could not tell.

The chariot came again, finished with the southward run, wheeling around to start the ugly business over again. When the horses wearied, the man would drive back to the Ahhiyawan camp, ready to start the spectacle once more when it suited him. No one had ventured out of the city to stop him. Priests had hailed the prince's death as a bad omen. It struck fear into the warriors, so the gates stayed shut fast and the driver went his way unmolested. Occasionally, an enraged archer, feeling that some gesture of defiance was necessary, would loose an arrow though he knew it to be too far.

The cockscomb of dust grew as the chariot neared once more. Behind it, the mangled corpse struck a rock with a loud and nauseating thud that turned the watchers away.

Hektu had gone well, and most of the city had seen him die, crowded as they were on the ramparts. It had been single combat. Dagentyr did not know the Ahhiyawan's name but had watched the fight. The people on the walls had shouted encouragement in a roar, and the Ahhiyawa cheered their champion from the field. Several times, archers on the walls thought that the Ahhiyawan was in bow shot, but all missed, their aim cramped by the fear of hitting Hektu.

Hektu had fallen dead, speared through the throat, no screams but those on the walls, and quick as summer lightning, the Ahhiyawan had attached the body to his chariot and galloped back to the ranks. Only Hektu's sword and shield were left. So stunned was the city that it did nothing, and the Ahhiyawan came to take them later.

The Ahhiyawan waved defiantly as he dashed past, and Dagentyr had an odd desire to wave back. He watched the wretched puppet cavort in its sea of dust and knew that he didn't care. Who had come to see Bolgios when he had died of lockjaw? Who had turned out at the late hour to mourn beside the grave when they had buried him next to the rampart?

The funeral night had been frigid, blustery. They had wrapped him in the best cloak they could find and put grave goods out for him, a dagger, a jug of wine. Dagentyr could not part with Bolgios's bow. He had reached up carefully to his ear, removed the golden earring, and nestled it in the dark earth. It gleamed there until he covered it. She hadn't even given him one of his own, he had thought. Dagentyr felt clean for being rid of it and was sick for having parted with his old one.

"Don't worry, Bolgios," he muttered. "They will all pay."

Helani made a brief appearance to grieve for Hektu as the Ahhiyawan turned the chariot back to the camp. With their sorrow at a peak, the crowd threw stones at her, and Parush had the guards whisk her away under their shields.

Dagentyr saw her fear and was momentarily pleased, but in his heart, he was despairing. It seemed to him for the first time that he might never reach home.

Unseasonal heat became a thing as miserable as the cold had been. The city was high with the smell of refuse and excrement and packed people. The mosquitoes came from the marshes and filled the nights.

Varnac fell in a skirmish, and Cingetos took a sword cut across the shoulder but did not die. The men were becoming despondent, disappointed that revenge had not been meted out. Dagentyr resolved that things must be made to happen.

On his return from a skirmish by the river, he came across a dead Trusian. An arrow stuck from his chest, and the press of the fighting had not broken it. The fletching was messy and askew, but it would do. He knelt over the man, drew his dagger, and cut out the shaft. Hiding it beneath his shield, he took it into the city. There, in his tent, he cleaned it of blood, honed the point, and repaired the clipped feathers. It was a straight shaft. Good, he thought. He was only allowing himself one shot. His aim would have to be inspired, assured. He told his men of the arrow and what he would do.

"We must be ready. Be prepared if I signal to you."

When battle came next, he took Bolgios's bow and quiver with him and gave solemn nods to his followers as they went out.

The heat was intense. The river had overflowed its banks, making parts of the plain a quagmire. Men wore little armor and were in no mood to fight for long.

Parush positioned his chariot in Hektu's old place at the head of the Trusians. It was rare bravery for him. He was blown up with his victories, few as they were. It was a good time, the right time.

The fighting was hot and savage. The heat boiled the emotions. When the battle reached its peak, they fought to be close to the prince. The hubbub and dust created a good screen. Parush left the chariot to go on foot and fight in the front. It was a dangerous place to be, but he did not seem to care.

"Now," said Dagentyr. The men shuffled forward with heavy feet, raising a dusty cloud. They held their shields high to block Dagentyr from sight. He let his own shield fall, nocked the Ahhiyawan arrow, and prayed for aim. He waited for the prince to turn; a backshot would be suspicious. His fingers left the string, and the arrow streaked silently in the din. The bow vibrated resonantly in his hand.

Parush stood shocked for a moment, then his eyes welled up with horror, and his hands reached to clasp the shaft where it lodged quivering in his groin. His knees buckled and he went falling backward. His helmet came undone when he fell, and rolled for a moment before coming to rest.

Dagentyr let the bow fall to the ground to be trampled by the battles to come. It was right to leave something of Bolgios on the field where he had fought. He picked up the shield, and without thinking any more of it, urged his men on to the fight. Each one wore a half-smile, as he did himself. They fought as though they had been refreshed with cool wine. Dagentyr pictured the driver of Parush's chariot riding swiftly back to the city with the news.

The fighting ended as it always did. Both groups wearied quickly and quit the field. Tingwahr spit on the ground and snickered. "There's a day's fighting well done."

The rest nodded amiably in spite of their tiredness. Dagentyr felt peaceful inside, freed of the burden of a heavy responsibility.

The news did not take long to spread through the city. Parush had fallen and bled to death on the way to the citadel. There was no great sorrow. Instead, the city seemed to breathe easier, and new hope was raised in the hovels and filthy streets. Surely it was apparent that the gods had struck him down in retribution. The streets were alive with the chatter, and no one did anything to repress it. It was hoped that the Ahhiyawa would feel that vengeance had been fulfilled. Perhaps they would go home satisfied. There was much cause for talk and discussion in the town. The torches burned late.

Now that the thing was done, Dagentyr felt emptied but thankful. He went roundabout through the town to hear the talk, up and down the narrow alleys between the houses and down the steps again to the gates. The lamps were all lit, the people awake. From the shadow of the tall tower, a beggarwoman hobbled to him on rickety legs, calling for food. The sentry on top peered over in the darkness and raised a hand in greeting. Dagentyr raised his. The guard went back to the outer side to stare at the plain.

Dagentyr moved on up the wall, toward camp. He stopped. The old woman followed him, still calling for a bit of food for the gods' sake but shuffling more quickly than an old woman should have been able to. He quickened his step for a while and turned. She was still there. He tingled with anticipation. Stepping close to the bottom of the wall, he waited. The old woman approached. In her eyes he saw something young, not in keeping with the dirty hands and wisps of grey hair that flowed at odd angles from under her shawl.

"Hello again, young warrior."

It was Mehiya, not the old Mehiya, though. She was changed. She was now the girl who did what she was told, exactly, uninspiredly, because she was told to do it. He could see she took no pleasure from it as she once had. The fox did not play in her eyes anymore. Her biting and quick wit had changed to mere surly insult. She was a tool now and not a conniver, not a gamester.

"Mehiya."

"Who else?" Her tone could strip trees of their bark.

"Did the wounds scar badly?"

She laughed, and it was truly the laugh of a bitter, old woman. "Yes, they scarred badly. It was all I could do, pleading as I did, bleeding, on my knees like a dog, to keep her from having me killed. And your scars?"

"Almost gone, almost. Helani sent you, of course."

"Yes. I've looked for you since nightfall. I saw you were not in camp. It is chance that I found you tonight."

"Is it?"

She looked at him stupidly. "I'm here for a purpose," she said.

"And so soon. I'm surprised. The prince is barely cold. Fate is cruel, isn't it?"

"No, not this time. Even at the palace the mourning for Parush is small. His death is a boon."

"It seems as though the Lady Helani's mourning was especially brief."

"I waste talk. Parush is dead. Helani is free. The guards no longer watch her. The king has a soft spot in his heart for her, and the queen is too desolate with grief to care. Helani's position is precarious, though. Antior is resuming his talk of returning her. I do not think that the king will do it. She is the only thing left of his son."

"She wishes to see me?"

"Yes. I will come to you later. It will be soon, I suspect, but things are tricky as they have always been. She wants you to know that she craves you still and begs you, do not let what has happened stand in the way."

"Her hunger must be great after so long."

Mehiya shrugged. "Scold me off."

He nodded. "Away, hag! I've nothing for you. Elsewhere!" The guard noticed them briefly and resumed his pacing. Mehiya walked away and blended into the shadows.

Dagentyr smiled to himself there in the dark. The day was too full of good fortune.

Chapter 27

Two women screeched excitedly at each other across a garbage heap. Their crow calls sounded loud on top of the unusual silence of the day.

Dagentyr's temples beat achingly against the confines of his helmet. Last night's wine had soured his stomach. His eyes felt scarlet. Mad insects seemed to buzz in his ears, and the harsh interruption scraped up his spine like a daggerpoint. Where, by the gods, were the Ahhiyawa? Morning was half gone and still they waited in camp for the pirates to approach. The past days' fighting had been so fierce and regular. What were they doing now, feasting, gaming, resting?

"Why don't we go out after them?" said Tingwahr. "We're probably playing their game. They want to unsettle us with waiting."

"The Trusians are wilting like grass in the summer. They've lost their stomach for the fight," said Dagentyr. "They've seen important men die, and no one wants to be the next. They say around the streets that the city's cursed now and that Hektu's and Parush's ghosts will watch the city burn. I wonder about it myself." He sat down on the

ground. If they had to wait, he would at least wait
comfortably. He would not stand all day and go out
leg-sore.

A fly crawled across his forehead. He flicked it
away. Around the garbage-strewn streets, they flew
in thousands and tormented the cramped hovel
dwellers. Orders had been given out from the
palace, and now filth was being dumped over the
walls. Outside, the pyramidic piles of refuse grew.
The Ahhiyawa had pressed hard. At night, men
were sent to harass the water crews. The water was
running out and turning bad. Tingwahr was troubled with stomach pain. Food went through him
quickly. He was gaunt and irritable.

Dagentyr slipped his helmet off and cursed his
foolishness at drinking so much, but he wanted
more wine now, as badly as he had wanted it last
night when it had smothered out the troubles.
Nothing was working out. No night excursions for
water meant no adventures with Helani. The constant fighting left no time for a meeting. Three
weeks had seen nothing of her and only momentary
sightings of Mehiya. He swilled his mouth with
tepid water from a nearby jug and spit it out.

Tingwahr sat too, clutched his hands to his
stomach and rocked back and forth in pain. "What
will I do?" he joked. "No time to shit in the middle
of a battle. I'll have to crouch behind the lines like a
dog and shout for cover. What a time for a man to
be killed."

Dagentyr reached out a comforting hand and
patted his arm. "Drink some wine. Maybe it will
take away the pain."

"What? Stumble onto the field like you stumbled
around here last night?" The jibe was good-
natured. Dagentyr put his hands to his head and
made a show of moaning.

A high cackle from the women pierced his ear-
drums. The smell of their meal made him want to
go behind a tent and vomit.

"It's all coming to a head," Dagentyr said seriously. "The water won't last. I may even be relieved to know it. It's definite, final."

"Death's a poor compromise. It won't bring us any closer to home."

He rubbed his palms over his face. "I'm too sensitive to the despair of the place. I'll vow this, though, if the Ahhiyawa give up and sail before winter, we'll sneak off and take our chances."

"And Helani?"

Another woman shuffled briskly toward the two crows, nearly knocking a garbage-hauling slave to the ground. She was shrill. Dagentyr's temper snapped.

"Quiet, you dimwit bitch!" He scowled menacingly at them and shook his spear. "Any more and I'll throw that stinking pot of slop over your heads!"

The woman blanched and hustled to kneel before him.

"Forgiveness, sir. I was excited, with the news, I mean. I just heard it." He expected her to leave, but she stayed, eager to tell her tale to anyone.

"Keep your women's prattle to yourself."

"No, sir, not prattle, strange news. I got it from a sentry."

Tingwahr said, "What is the news?"

"Down at the main gate, I heard a guard yell it. He said there was something odd far out on the plain by the Ahhiyawan beach."

"Well," said Dagentyr. "What is the something?"

"He didn't know. Only said that it was like a brilliant fire, or another sun rising up from the water."

"That is all you heard?" asked Tingwahr.

"Yes, that is all."

Dagentyr waved for her to be gone, and she backed away to the other women and began to talk fast, so that she would not be done out of telling the tale again.

Behind her the rumor had followed. It passed like the fire does from tree to tree. The streets soaked up rumor and poured out different rumor. The ailing city stirred.

"What do you suppose it is, Dagentyr?"

The news interested him, too. "I don't know."

Not waiting for the Ahhiyawa, the warriors of Trusya left the city, formed their lines on the plain, and walked toward the distant beach, eager to see the strange thing. When they were clear of the gates, they saw it, a ball of fire next to the shore, dazzling, brilliant, but unknown. The ranks halted and had to be coaxed to go on.

"What magic do the Ahhiyawa use now?" asked Dagentyr. "There is something wrong today, Tingwahr. I tell you there is. I can feel it like claws against my neck."

The lines were oddly silent as they moved. Dagentyr recalled dreams where warriors had met silently in his head. It was like that. Each man was hot with curiosity, and still they were silent. The fireball hung on the near horizon and shimmered.

There was work to take care of. Battle leaders sent men to collect the dead and take them to the city. The corpse details left quickly and were glad not to venture farther to the shore.

Dagentyr was sweaty with nerves, and his apprehension infected his people. "What is it, Dagentyr?" asked Cingetos.

"I'm not sure. It's many things. Where are the Ahhiyawa? What is the golden ball up ahead? Gods! There's something in the air."

The light shimmered, drew them to it insistently. Like a huge, gleaming eye, it winked and flickered. No one thought of anything else. They were coming close to the wall.

Dagentyr held his shield close in, and his thoughts turned to memories of strange forests. Hearing again the sounds of owls and the howling of the wolves in the night, he shivered in the heat.

Tingwahr said, "You look like there's a demon on your shoulder," and laid a hand on his arm. Dagentyr jumped at the touch.

"There's a strangeness in all this. None of it seems right. I'd expect ambush from the Ahhiyawa, but where are they?"

"And what of the gleam?" said young Drusos, infused with Dagentyr's fidgets.

"Look! The wall!" called a man.

The sight of the wall emboldened them all to speak in girlish twitters of surprise. Amazed talking began in the ranks.

The wall was deserted. They stopped short.

No campfire smoke rose from beyond the stones and the forest of masts was not there. The gleam was too bright to look at. They kept moving.

"By the gods!" A Trusian leader shouted. "Come this way. Change the angle from which you look upon it!"

Everyone rushed to obey, moving over the plain toward the wall gate. The ranks dissolved. They were an amazed rabble. The gleam separated, fragmented into a thousand smaller gleams.

Dagentyr felt that his heart had been cinched with a chain. The names of a hundred gods mingled in the air as they were called on in wonder and awe. Fragmenting further, the gleams shimmered like a desert mirage. The sunlight reflected off finger rings, golden bowls and bracelets, goblets, baubles, all stirring in the freshening sea breeze. Now they could see the light play on the rippling, spiky mane of treasure.

"No!" Dagentyr said the word before he could think to stop himself. Once again the smoke billowed up to him and Irzag's beak-nose poked out from the mists of shock and memory. "No!" He screamed it with his soul to drive it from his sight. He threw his spear at the thing and it clattered off the stones of the wall.

Showing above the gates was a massive head

hung with every Ahhiyawan ornament, a head whose golden mane had shown to the gate guard and to them only as a brilliant, rising sun, the head of a golden horse.

"Dagentyr?" Tingwahr said. "What is wrong?"

"I have been warned of this." He grabbed Tingwahr and drew him close, pointing to the horse. "In Fottengra I was warned. The high priest told me, beware the horse, the golden horse. I thought he meant Vorgus. I must have been wrong." He motioned for his men to crowd around him. "Listen to me! The horse is an evil thing. Be watchful and wary. This must be some kind of trick. It's an Ahhiyawan trick!" he shouted to the Trusians. In the excitement, no one heard.

The bravest of the Trusians were crossing the bridge for a closer look. The Thracians held back and mumbled among themselves.

"Do we get closer?" asked Tingwahr.

Though there was dread in him, he was drawn as if by irresistible fate.

"Yes."

No one knew what to make of it. A chariot went back up the plain to the city. The king was being sent for and the high priest. In the meantime they crowded around the feet of the great beast.

It was big, made of ship's timbers. It stood twice again as high as the wall. Tail and mane were golden, bedecked with captured Trusian loot. It was dark against the blue sky, ugly in spite of its trappings.

Dagentyr went forward and drove his dagger into its wooden leg, expecting it to give a demonic whinny and kick out, sending grown men skittering over the beach like children's toys.

"What are you doing?" asked a Trusian. "Let be. Do you want to anger the gods just when they have smiled on us? Do you want to defile the appeasement?"

Dagentyr twisted the blade in the wood and

wrenched it free again, bringing splinters with it. The man watched him with horror but said nothing further.

Now that the wonder of the horse was dimming, the realization came to them that the Ahhiyawa were gone. There were men standing in groups at the ocean's edge, looking out across the open water and joking. Their weapons were put away or held carelessly, as if the men were glad of the excuse to be rid of them. No sails were in sight. They had sailed away at night, as they had come. Dagentyr meandered from group to group with his men, listening to the talk.

"Cowardly dogs stole away with their tails between their legs, ashamed to be seen leaving in daylight." There was satisfied, derisive laughter from a tired, black-bearded man. His listeners agreed and threw pebbles out into the water, calling threats and abuse to the absent raiders. They were enjoying the joke. Dagentyr sensed their confidence, their overconfidence. It's when a man goes into battle high, overblown, that he gets the spear through the guts, he thought. Irzag's words ran in his head, and the metal tail and mane jingled flatly in the wind. He went to find someone to tell, someone who might listen.

Awunash was standing in his chariot, by the horse.

"It's a bad thing. You sense it too, don't you, Awunash?" said Dagentyr. The prince motioned for him to come closer.

"It makes no sense. I expected them to stay another winter. It's like a prayer answered, but I do not believe that it's free of consequences. Where does your suspicion come from?"

"From my homeland, a warning given to me by a priest to beware the golden horse."

"I have grown weary of priests and omens, yet . . ."

"Why have they left all the gold, Prince? Surely

it wasn't necessary. Let us kindle a torch and burn it. Strip it of the gold if you must, but burn it."

"We must wait for the king and Lakowon, the high priest. They will be here soon."

"It must be destroyed."

"I will tell Lakowon of what your priest told you. I'll let him know that we are uneasy."

"Look at your men. You can tell that they are drunk with elation. That too is a bad omen."

Awunash stepped slowly to the ground, grunted as his damaged hip took the weight, loosened his helmet strap, and giving his arms to his driver, sat down in the back of the car and gazed up into the shadow of the horse.

"Should we look too hard for deceit, Dagentyr, when lack of it means an end to our troubles?"

The king and Lakowon arrived in the king's own chariot. The priest's sons were with him, lean, austere youths, long-haired and simply dressed. They were promised to the priesthood and helped with the divining.

At first, Lakowon stared on the horse with as much wonder as anyone else and then composed himself to be stonefaced. He and the king walked around it. The king seemed pleased, relieved, like a man whose great suffering has been endured well and then rewarded. Tears came to his eyes all too easily now, and he wept as he gazed on the empty water. The golden mane and tail clanked funeral music.

There were much fewer men for council than there had once been, but they decided to hold one there on the beach. The men grouped into a great circle on the sand, around the king and Lakowon. Priasham's words were filled with rejoicing.

"We are a victorious people. We have persever—"

A party of scouts broke through the brush of the

hills and yelled to the men. They looked toward the interruption. In the scouts' midst was a man, Ahhiyawan by his clothes and looks. They had him bound, and when they got to the beach, pushed him down to fall whimpering in the center of the ring. The guard who held the cord spoke to the king.

"We found him hiding behind a refuse pile at the end of the beach. Says he was left by the Ahhiyawa as part of the appeasement, like the horse. They drew lots. He's a sacrifice."

The man crawled to kneel at the king's feet.

"He speaks the truth, Lord Priasham! Mercy! I am no friend to them." The king's face contorted in hate at remembrance of slaughtered sons.

"The gods have blessed us. There must be an offering of thanks. You, Ahhiyawan, will be the token of thanks for us!"

There was a hearty cheer from the men. The man's eyes showed fear, and he reached pitifully to touch Priasham's robe.

Dagentyr felt an ominous chill in his blood. Why would the Ahhiyawa leave all their gold and just sail away, as an appeasement? Who was the man? He rose to his feet.

"No, wait. Save him from death for the moment. Pardon, Lord King. I speak out of turn and with no standing, but some of the men here know me. My curiosity must be theirs also. Have the man speak of the horse. What is his explanation? Where are the Ahhiyawa? Is this treachery?"

"No treachery! I swear it, a gift, Priasham, nothing . . . nothing more, a gift. To your gods and ours, a show of appeasement for wrong. We wearied of their displeasure. Better to bear defeat as men than be cursed by the gods. That's what they thought, those who ordered the horse made. Aganon himself had a hand in it! Believe me and spare a man who brings you good news. Mercy, great ruler of Trusya, mercy."

Lakowon turned his head first to the man, then to the horse and shook it in doubt.

The nods of the men and their laughter made Dagentyr know that they believed the man. He stood silent, wishing there was something he could do to make them understand what danger there was in what Irzag had said. He tried.

"Men! Warriors of Trusya. I am not one of you, but my people have fought here as I have, and some have died. The horse is evil. In my homeland I was given an augury against a golden horse. Now the message's time has come." He indicated the horse with his gesture. "The omen has followed me across land and water. You must burn the horse!"

They grumbled to imagine the loss of their gold.

"No. There's a fortune there. It's our gold. Sit down, you backland barbarian!" they said.

"All right then! Take the gold. Strip it, but burn the thing afterward, here on the beach. Make the horse your burnt offering. Throw this man on the flames if you wish." The men muttered. He studied the man's face for a reaction.

"Don't burn me," was all he said. A guard kicked him in the ribs to shut him up.

Priasham turned to Lakowon.

"Consult the signs. I'll not rob the people of such a trophy for no reason. If we burn the appeasement, may we not anger the gods ourselves?"

"I will consult, but my heart already believes the warrior. I sense that he tells the truth as he knows it. An omen with such power is serious. We should listen to him."

"The horse is evil!" Dagentyr said it again. He could do no more. He sat down to the muttering and hissing as Lakowon's sons brought a goat to the ring and made the cut. Sitting in the front rank, Dagentyr could smell the fresh entrails. There was blood on the sand of the beach. Men sitting with their backs to the water could not help turning to look over their shoulders at the sea. There were no ships.

Lakowon puzzled over the signs and stood up after a moment. The men fell silent. He spoke. "The signs are bad. There is a warning in these entrails. The gods are warning us to be careful. The warrior is right!"

A loud grumbling greeted his declaration.

Priasham said, "Quiet. It is not for us to challenge the gods. Very well. Take the gold they have left us, our gold. Load it into the chariots. We will go home in glory. Up now."

They cheered and stirred themselves, falling on the horse like carrion birds. Lakowon looked at Dagentyr. There was uneasiness in his face.

The city. Dagentyr hoped that the messenger who took news to the king had not let the word slip. The people would be impossible to control if they knew that the Ahhiyawa were gone at last. Children might be running by the river, and hot, sweaty people would be filling jugs with sweet water and praising Trusian gods. Already the gates might be open, wide open.

Helani would be happy at the prospect of being able to get free of the walls, but would soon realize that her liberators and providers of excitement were gone, and she would spend her life in Trusya. No, she would not. She was nothing if not resourceful. She would think of a place to go and a way to get there.

Their weapons were lying on the sand. Like ants, they crawled and climbed over the horse, despoiling it of its gold. The work was light, gleeful. Tingwahr watched with a certain envy.

"Do we go and help them, Dagentyr?"

The men looked to him.

"No. The only help they'll get from us is when they put the fire to it."

They looked like hurt, greedy children, but they

obeyed him. It was too much for Awunash. He
helped to load his car with gold.

Even now the people would be rejoicing, running
perhaps, following the chariot tracks to the beach,
eager to glimpse the golden horse. The Trusian
warriors were making quick work of it.

"Hold!" someone yelled. "The captive says
there's treasure inside it, too. Break it open!"

They fell to it with battle-axes, and used spears to
pry the timbers loose. Holding on to the neck, held
by his friends, a man was gouging out a baleful
golden eye.

Open gates in time of war were dangerous.

The king stood in his chariot. Lakowon idled
aimlessly on the beach, a drab note in the happy
melee. His sons stood with him. The goat lay dead
in a bloody pit of sand.

A faint trumpet note, sharply cut off, touched
their ears. Some men, busy with the horse, did not
hear it or made themselves believe they did not,
and carried on with the work. Lakowon and
Priasham perked up. Awunash froze.

Dagentyr knew now that the gates were open. All
heads turned in the direction of the city. Above the
sandy hills, a silvery line of smoke ascended as the
first fires were set. Horror gripped the men. They
had fallen for the diversion. After hiding all night
on the eastern plateau, under shields covered with
grass and brush, the Ahhiyawa were finally in
Trusya.

"No! This is not possible! Lakowon, what do we
do?" Priasham was too stunned to go on. Awunash
stepped in.

"Quickly everyone! Get the gold out of the
chariots! Load as many men in them as you can.
Drive quickly to the city and do what you can. The
rest will have to follow on foot. Hurry! We may
already be too late to save it!"

The beach was nothing but men running every-

where. The horse was instantly forgotten. Gold lay
where it had been thrown. Chariots rumbled off. In
mute fury, the king pulled his dagger, stabbed the
captive through the heart and watched dumbly as
he squirmed and kicked sand. Footmen followed
the chariots in a ragtag mob, screaming laments
and curses. Dagentyr ran more slowly, at a steady
pace. The city was so far away. Panic-stricken men,
running with all their might, in armor, carrying
weapons, fear constricting their chests, were falling
by the wayside, spent, forced to rest. They beat
their fists into the ground and prayed for strength,
and the others huffed and puffed their way by them.

The lines of dust behind the chariots converged
on the city. Dagentyr knew that there was not much
they could do. A tongue of flame leapt above the
battlements, and the smoke darkened. It blew over
the plain. They could smell and taste it.

Cursing men loosened their armor straps as they
ran and discarded it, carrying only what they would
truly need to fight. Behind them, the plain became
a littered arsenal. Were they halfway there? The
chariots were already engaged. Dagentyr could
hear the screaming horses and men. From the
city, terrible noises were discernible—brayings,
screams, children's cries. The city's groaning
pierced pathetically through the savage noise of the
fighting, dying men.

Now it was the Trusians who would have to take
the city. Inside, the gate guards would be dead. No
warriors had stayed behind other than the royal
guard. He visualized them defending the corridors
of the palace, surprised, choking in the smoke,
being cut down by the raiders.

Dagentyr saw the Ahhiyawa heading toward
them. It did not take many to sack an unprotected
citadel; there were many left to fight.

Tingwahr called, "This is folly!"

He had thought of it, too. They were spread out

over a long stretch of plain in disorderly groups, sore, collapsed with panic, exertion, and heat. They could see nothing of the Trusian chariots, but those of the Ahhiyawa were thundering close. They heard a brittle crack as something inside the citadel collapsed with flame. It was over. It would be nothing but butchery. He stopped, called to the men to halt. They did, gasping and panting around him.

"Wait." He tried to wet his lips with his tongue, but there was no spittle. "The city's doomed. Look at it; look at us. The Trusians, they'll be cut up like dead fish. This is it. Gods know we've waited long enough for it. We don't owe the city anything, and we owe ourselves our freedom. We know we're not cowards. We break for it now!"

Their hesitation was momentary.

Tingwahr said, "It's now, the time we've waited for!"

"For home!" they cried.

"But where from here?" asked Tingwahr.

"Hurry across the plain, inland. Fight your way across if you have to. Head for the hills east of the city, and go as far as you have to to get away. Let no one stop you, not Ahhiyawan, not Trusian. Go now!"

"What do you mean? Where are you going?" Tingwahr reached up to grab his wrist.

"I'm going into the city. We all know there's unfinished work there. I'll meet you east of here. I'll find you. Don't worry."

"You'll be killed. Forget them!"

"No. Now go or we'll all be dead. You'll go your own way when you're home, but for now you'll do as I say."

Dagentyr turned away and made for the cover of the river growth. When he stopped to see if they had gone, Tingwahr was still there, then under his gaze, broke into a run across the plain.

Chapter 28

It was cumbersome dragging the shield through the underbrush, but he dared not leave it behind. He would be vulnerable enough, one man alone.

The fighting on the plain was taking place in scattered patches. Townspeople who had managed to escape ran away in all directions, seeking safety. A fleeing man and woman, faces smeared with soot, tumbled into the swollen river, swam like dogs, then heaved themselves up on the other side. They cast glances back at the city and went stumbling on toward the hills.

A false twilight fell over the plain as the smoke thickened. Dagentyr used it like a protective cloak, pushing ahead quickly when it was dense, halting crouched beneath the shield when eddies of air thinned it out. The cries of the city cut through it all.

His expectations were high but vague. Where would he find Helani in the middle of the sacking, in the palace? Would he have to fight her bodyguard single-handedly in order to kill her? Perhaps she would not be guarded at all or had already perished in the flames.

Amazingly enough, there was little activity near the gates. The fighting was farther out on the field or deep in the streets. His brow became speckled with sweat. He was close enough to notice the heat of the flames and hot stones. Under the lintel stone came sporadic groups of fleeing men and women, or warriors carrying loot and captives. An Ahhiyawan stood near the gate, waiting to take the next woman that came through. Dagentyr ran him through from behind and left him dead at the base of the wall. A heavy puff of searing smoke spilled out through the gate, and under its protection, he slipped inside the citadel.

Once inside he became confused. He would have to try the palace first, but which way through the streets was best? Two men, Ahhiyawans, brushed by him in the acrid haze without noticing him. Luck, he thought, and stripped off his Trusian helmet. He did not look Trusian. If the gods were with him, he might be taken for any other Ahhiyawan raider. His time was being spent dangerously. He decided that the quickest way to the palace would be best.

There were dead men in the streets, lying where they had been cut down. A few were warriors. Fewer still were Ahhiyawan. All had been trampled into the heaps of garbage from the hovels. He picked up a rag and held it over his mouth.

A crying girl pursued by a marauder ran hysterically up to him, and thinking he was Ahhiyawan too, screamed wildly. The other man had seen him. Dagentyr grabbed the girl's arm roughly to detain her, and forcing evil laughter, threw her toward the man. He took her, nodded brusquely to Dagentyr, sharing the joke, and started to move off. When he turned his back, Dagentyr reached around and cut his throat. The man's hold on the girl released, and he went face first to the street. The girl stared at him strangely before she ran down to the gate.

Dagentyr moved up the wrecked street to the

palace enclosure. He stuck close to the house walls
for some frail sense of security.

The smoke was getting thicker, the calls of the
men louder as he neared the palace. Why not; they
would have headed there first for the treasure and
spoils, and for Helani. He had to hurry even more.
A large party was coming down the alley. He
ducked through the low door of a small house
and held himself still until they passed, then he
went on.

Ahead was the enclosure and the gate to the
central courtyard. He stepped over a dead guard
who blocked the way and made immediately for the
women's quarters. The screams from that section
were lively. Two or three warriors ran across the
court. His luck held and, if they saw him, they
made no move to stop him. Flames were coming
from the roof of the main hall. The smoke was
blinding. Men were coming from the women's
quarters, herding the captives into the center of the
court. A rain of ashes and cinder began to coat the
ground.

He ran the short distance to the entrance to the
stairway and went up, taking two at a time. There
were loud voices coming from somewhere above.
An armed man appeared in the doorway to the
second floor and confronted him. Perhaps he would
not be fooled. No, Dagentyr could see that he was
not, for the man was coming down at him, his
sword raised to attack. As the man put his foot on
the step above, Dagentyr slashed through his knee-
cap. Going underneath the man's stroke, he lifted
him off his feet and flipped him over his back to roll
down the steps to the bottom. He did not stop to
finish him, but went up.

The door to Helani's chamber was ajar. The hall
was free of men. He crossed quickly and threw the
door wide with a wild push of his arm.

"I've come for you, Helani!"

"Dahguinteer!" she yelled out, and at first he saw

only her, lying on the floor at the foot of the bed.
The bedclothes and fur coverlet were aflame. She
looked more a cooking woman than a queen, dirty,
disheveled, hair singed, lovely skin streaky with
soot, eyes terrified. Then he saw the men. Before he
had time to strike out at her, they came at him.
There were three, one a well-armed lord.
Mensalakus, he thought. The others were ordinary
warriors. Springing to the side of the bed, he
grabbed up the flaming coverlet and flung it at
them. While the two fussed with the fiery bedclothes, Mensalakus wrenched Helani from the
floor and pulled her toward him, away from danger.
The two men were free and between him and the
door. She would not get the pleasure of seeing him
die for her as so many others had. If I can't kill you,
I'll at least rob you of that, he thought. He leapt up
to the bed and over it, making for the balcony. He
yelled back at her as he reached the doors.

"May you live long, enchantress. Enjoy a long life
filled with years of loneliness and boredom." There
was just time to see the eyes glare at him through
the ruined cosmetics, and then he was up over the
railing and dropping to the court. Stealth now was
purposeless. It was time to get away, save his life
and start the journey for home. Where was home?
Where could ships be had? Should they flee north,
south? Astekar knew.

The two men were shouting from the balcony,
pointing him out. His legs sped across the court to
the royal rooms, in time, he hoped. He had only
been to Parush's chambers once. It was the only
place he knew to look for the trader. Was it left or
right along the corridor?

There was a group of men lying in the hall. Slaves
mostly, he figured, killed as useless. One lay on his
back. Dagentyr thought he was dead, but the head
turned sideways, and he moaned. The legs kicked
out, smearing streaks of blood across the floor with

the heels. Astekar's eyes fluttered open for a moment and closed again.

The sight was shocking to Dagentyr. Astekar had finally found something which cool words and aloof expressions could not handle. Dagentyr went to his side.

"Trader! It's Dagentyr. Don't die yet. You must talk to me first. You know who I am, don't you?"

"I know you." His voice was faint. His lungs were barely forcing enough air for speech. Astekar's eyes looked not at him but up at the ceiling.

"Where do I go, trader? Which way is home? Where can I take ship? Speak to me, and hurry!"

"Through the Pillars . . . and north. No ships here."

"I know that!" He grabbed the dying face and shook it. "Where do I take ship? Which way do I travel to get a ship?"

"North and east to Wilusa . . . Millawanda perhaps, south to—" He gave no final convulsion, no shudder. The words just ceased. Dagentyr let the head fall back to the floor, muttered a curse, and made ready to dash back into the court.

"So that's your end after all this, trader, not one at my hands as I vowed so many times." With all that was taking place, there wasn't even any time to enjoy knowing that he was dead.

He moved to go, and heard his name called somewhere. On hands and knees, a stick-figure man crawled from the prince's chamber and beckoned weakly.

"Ruki," said Dagentyr. His sword arm longed to kill. "The gods have kept you for me. They've sent you along like my shadow that I might do what I should have done when I first saw you. They were right when they said that you were cursed; they didn't know how vile the curse was." While talking, he moved closer.

Ruki coughed out words of protest.

"No, please don't kill me. Listen to what I am going to say to you! Take me. You're going; you must be. Take me, too. I have value, and by all rights I am yours. I regret all that happened—" It was as far as he got before Dagentyr lifted the sword. "Don't leave me here!"

Dagentyr stopped. "That's what you'd hate worse than anything, isn't it? Deep in your heart that's the most awful fate, isn't it!" He knelt, grabbed Ruki's tunic, and butted the slave's head into the wall. "Being laughed at the rest of your life, given as a prize to anyone who made a good offer for you, singing song after song, story after story, maybe living through sack after sack, and with me gone your hate would be impotent, frustrating. It would have no object and would start to devour you. Is that what you would hate and fear more than anything else? Tell me!" He twisted his grip on the neckhole of the tunic and forced the weak, breathless words to be strangled out.

"Yes . . . I beg you."

Dagentyr stood up, released the tunic. Ruki sprawled on the floor.

"Then I'll give you that thing. Stay here, Ruki, and remember that I am the one who let you live."

He ran to the court doorway. He knew the Ahhiyawa were not through, that perhaps they would kill Ruki, but the moment's satisfaction had been enough.

"Don't leave me! I do not belong here!" The voice rang in the dead corridor.

The women had been taken away. The common men were fighting for the leavings of treasure. If none had seen him clearly before, he could again resume his role as one of them. The way to the palace gate was clear. Without a single glance to Helani's rooms, he rushed through and out to the street. Ruki's screams still echoed in the hallway behind him.

The northeast gate had been opened from the inside to admit attackers but was seeing little use. A last run of luck would see him out and due east, over the hills to safety. Horse noises came along the walls. The Ahhiyawa had found the royal stables. Whistling men drove the horses away from the fire and out the portal in a frightened, kicking mass to be rounded up later. Dagentyr waited until they were gone. It was a special moment. He said good-bye to the garbage- and corpse-strewn street and went at a dead run out onto the plain. He let the shield go. The regret that he had not seen more death melted away. One of the horses ran in front of him at a distance. He used it as his inspiration and ran like pursued quarry, no, more like the beast up ahead, like a creature that has been kept pent up too long, and finding itself unhampered, runs to be free.

Chapter 29

The pale, rose-colored glow in the west was Trusya. Like a clouded-over moon, it showed up red on the black horizon, and the scattered campfires in the night were its companion stars. Not all the people had lit fires, just the brave ones or the ones with weapons. The Ahhiyawa, Dagentyr knew, would not stray far inland. It would be a wonder, in fact, if they were still in the area at all. The people around their fires would be safe from them. There would be others, though, desperate men looking for anything they could find, eager to prey on anyone who came into their hands. From a distance, the safe glow of a fire could disguise death, so he let the night swallow him up and sat curled against the trunk of a tree to wait for daylight.

It was magic. The city's weight had been burned off his back. Cleansing fire had killed the painful memories. He felt totally relaxed. The feeling invited sleep, but that would be foolhardy. He made plans, to keep himself awake, and thought on what they should do.

When morning came, his feeling of well-being had vanished. He was tired, hungry, and sore. The

sun came up through a red smoke-haze. His whole
body smelled foul with smoke, and his skin was
grimy, speckled with ash. With first light, there
were people already beginning the slow, cautious
march back to the city, looking for what company
they could find, preferably armed.

His group, if they had made it, would be by one
of the campfires that remained, for they had no
reason to return. He was suddenly filled with fear
that his men had been killed and that there would
be no one waiting for him. The mountains lightened from purple, to blue, to green, as he went
round to the remaining fires, sword in hand. When
he stumbled at last into their midst, they were as
glad to see him as he was to see them.

"Dagentyr! The gods preserved you." Tingwahr
rushed to him and grabbed his hand. The others
stood up and made a ring around him. He was
aware of the warmth of their words and eyes.

"They did, and you." He looked at all their
faces. There were none missing. "And you too, all
safe."

"Koricus has a cut on the leg."

Koricus nodded. "It got close at the end there,
crossing the plain, but it's a small thing."

They gave him what food they had left. "I feel
like singing a song," he said, "one of the old warrior
songs of home."

They all laughed, and the laughter was easy,
loose, a gift shared between friends. They joked at
his black skin. He threatened mock reprisal with
his sword and joined them around the fire.

Tingwahr asked, "Is the business done?"

He stretched out on the cool earth. "Not as we
thought, but done, truly, and we are done with this
place."

His answer satisfied them. Even though they
were free, he was still chieftain. They talked easily
for a while, joked, then Dagentyr started a war

song, and they joined him until his voice grew soft, silent, and he fell asleep.

They had it in mind to live off the land but found that most of the time it was unnecessary. Where there were villages, they were given food, shelter, and directions. A band of eight armed men was a force to be reckoned with, and the villagers served them out of fear and in return for tales of Trusya. The headmen of the towns showed them courtesy and let them go on their way without hindrance.

The daylight travelling was warm, but the sharpest edge of the heat was gone. Their path led over the grassy plateaus, and the green-clad mountains receded. Evenings were filled with stories retold around the fire, exploits recounted and embellished. •

Rough-cut feelings of freedom urged them to travel long hours, and on the tenth day, Dagentyr said they would head due north and follow the seacoast to Wilusa. How much farther had that peasant told them last night? Five days' journey? They found the coast and saw fishing hamlets on the shore. Here, the welcome was more brusque.

"What are your intentions here?" the headman would say, knowing that no one could stop them no matter what their intentions were. "We've seen pirates in these waters not long back. Where are you from?" Their answer hardly ever satisfied. Certainly their weapons looked Trusian, but they themselves did not. In places, their reputation preceded them and villagers either ran to hide or assembled in front of their huts to see the band of giants from a strange place. The effect of their appearance was always the same; they got what they wanted. It boosted their spirits, and they became the men they had been before capture.

"How long?" Dagentyr asked the king of Wilusa.

He was a younger man than Priasham and a stronger one. The hair had not greyed with age, and he wore it as Hektu had. He shrugged and scooted his rump to a different spot on his chair.

"With the coming of next spring. I'll not let you sail till then. Your Ahhiyawa, they prowled the coast for a while. Even now we see unfriendly sails. Now that Trusya has fallen, who is to say that they will not come back, greedier, bolder now that their hearts have been inflamed. If Trusya could not withstand them, surely we cannot here in Wilusa." The king was right. It was not as grand a place as Trusya. The walls were not as formidable. It was not as populous. It was small, sleepy. The king would not budge from his position.

Dagentyr fumed. "Why will you prevent us?"

"Because I need you till the danger is past. Stay with us until next spring. Men like yourselves would be useful here in my service. I will give you gifts if you stay, fine arms, weapons. I will make you know your worth. When spring opens the seas, and I am sure the Ahhiyawa are gone, go."

Dagentyr saw the disappointment on his men's faces, but reluctantly, seeing nothing else to do, he agreed.

It was a time of feasting. Nights were passed away in wine and stories. The house singer sat dejectedly in his corner as they told what they had seen and done in Trusya.

A ship did appear, close in to shore like a lost wanderer. The men armed, and waited on the beach should it land, but it did not and glided back the way it had come. And then winter set in.

The wind whipping off the black water held ice in its hand, and the snow fell thickly and covered the land in white. There were no troubles. The season passed coldly but quickly. Wood was piled higher in the hearths and hot wine poured higher in the cups.

Cool spring came, and the skies cleared to the color of bright blue flame. Very soon, the ships were

uncovered and put out to fish and trade. They took
one headed south through the straits of Dardanu
into the Blue Sea.

The beach of Kiastu slipped by. It was inhabited
again. People used what they could find to build,
incorporating the Ahhiyawan wall. The road still
led to Trusya. The northerners were kept busy
pointing out the places where fights took place,
where Sarpedon fell. Soon it was far astern, and
they kept their eyes ahead to where they were going.

From Alasiya the ship took copper and left the
passengers to look for another way home. The
island was pleasant, drenched in warm sunshine.
The fine spring weather had brought out ships like a
swarm of new-hatched insects. There were boats
bound for everywhere. They made themselves understood as best they could and asked one persis-
tent question—west?

Weeks of journeying melted into one another and
became as one. Dagentyr's mind herded in all the
sights, and sounds, and smells, penned them up,
and he promised himself that he would never let
them go. There were countless fiery sunsets over
calm, dark waters, piles of copper ingots shining
red on the beaches of Alasiya, wild goats roaming
in and over the scarred jumble of ruins near
Knossus. They had walked to the wreck for something to do during the long wait on Crete when
there were no ships going farther.

The farmer who pointed the ruins out to them
said they were haunted, but they went anyway and
saw the weeds sprouting in cracks between neat
stones, and rainwashed pillars still holding hopefully to flimsy coats of bright red and blue pigment
as if there would be a future chance to stand erect
and dare to hold the roof of a proud palace.
Darkness drove them away. It was then that they
could feel the ghosts rising. Dagentyr wondered if
Ruki lay dead in some cold nook in Trusya's

interior, and if all the men whose death Helani had
savored could fill this empty place with life.

More and more days were spent along the beach,
asking if men were needed on ships bound west.
How odd it felt to be next to Ahhiyawans, for Crete
was an Ahhiyawan kingdom, and not draw sword.
As summer moved in, more ships came and went.
At last, they went also.

"From the northern lands, the far northern
lands, eh? Sailed before?" asked the captain.

"Yes," said Dagentyr.

"Look at you. You're all stout enough. And what
is it you will want in return—gold and weapons, I'd
say, isn't that what? No, I'm not able to give you
that."

"Just take us west, no more."

"What's this?" The swarthy man hopped down
from the prow of the ship, took off his pointed cap,
wiped his hand over his thinning hair, and replaced
the headgear. "Are you all touched? What kind of
men are you that you work for nothing?"

"We sail in exchange for where you take us. We're
bound for home. If you want good men to work,
you'll find none better. When you reach port on the
other end, you must find others."

"Ah, I'll bet there's trickery here somewhere."
Dagentyr sneered.

"Can you steer?" asked the Tyrian captain.

"Yes," said Dagentyr. "By the stars." There was
power in being able to say it. The learning would
now be put to use.

The man weighed the price against the risks.

"You're with me, then. With a lot like you I need
not fear attack. I wouldn't need men at all except
that my crew took sick, all of them, all but one or
two anyway, and me. It'll take the sea itself to do
me in."

When they sailed, they breathed their excitement

into the ship, and it seemed to fly. Crete was out of sight quickly.

"There you are as always," said Dagentyr to the star snake as night covered sea and sky. He could feel the steering oar bite into the sea, moving the ship where he wanted it to go. "Where are we bound?" he asked the captain.

"For the barbarian coast."

"Not through the Pillars?"

"Only an idiot would go through the Pillars."

"We had wanted to go north."

The Tyrian shrugged. "North is north whether on land or water. When we land, go north."

They would, he thought, as the wind hurtled the ship forward into blackness, and he would be grateful for the good fortune they had received so far.

Standing on the stern platform, he strove to re-create the scenes he had left behind in Fottengra. No matter that they might be painful or maddening and make his heart beat quicker with anger and wishing. The hurting thought came to him that nothing stayed the same; everything was inconstant.

He remembered her eyes. The pale eyes came back clearer than anything else. Saying her name was strange. It was tinged with Trusian accent that made her sound like another woman altogether, so long had it been since he had spoken it. He fought back the foreign drawl and spoke it clear.

"Kerkina. Star-snake, can you hear me? Kerkina!"

He had wakened the men in the belly of the ship, but when they looked sleepily at him, he just raised his head to the sky and let the wind tug through the strands of his beard.

Chapter 30

Long green forest shadows reached out to them. The air was seasoned with the smells of bark, pine resin, and moist leaves. There was rain on the horizon. The shriveled campfire smoked. Night parted company with the forest.

North had been their mutual goal, but the lands of Tingwahr and the others lay to the northeast, Fottengra somewhere to the northwest. He realized the time had come to go different ways. The days of hardship and rough travelling were behind them. Behind them too, days of good company, of men who understood each other, who shared a common place in life. Their paths now lay over different horizons.

"I said that I would keep no man from going when the time came and his fate was before him. You are sure the great river lies northeast?"

Tingwahr chose to speak for all of them.

"The men of the last village said that it does."

A heavy sadness bloomed in him that he knew nothing could dispel. "I know that you have to go. I'm glad that you too are free to seek your homes. It's a reward that we all have coming to us. It will be

an emptier trip without you, and I could wish that
we were going on together."

Tingwahr stepped forward. "It heartens us that
you could wish it. We have thought much since the
city fell, about our homes, and we have talked."

"All of us have talked together," said Cingetos,
walking awkwardly to the fore of the group. "We
have been our own village for a long time, and it
has been good. We have been fortunate. You have
been a good chieftain."

Tingwahr nodded. "You are our chieftain. A
warrior does not abandon his chieftain."

Cingetos elaborated. "If you become as good a
chieftain with your own people as you were with us,
you will be god-favored and renowned, and us
along with you. We were taken in battle. At home
we will be shamed. With you, we have not known
shame."

The men agreed vocally.

There were tears rolling down into Dagentyr's
beard. "Good men and warriors, all. With what
we've seen and done, we can do anything. We will
be kings among our people."

"The forests have never seen our like," said Tingwahr. Dagentyr took hold of Tingwahr's shoulders.

"Then surely, we'll be telling each other of our
deeds for many years, and our sons will tell their
sons of what we have done." He embraced
Tingwahr roughly and then each of the others.

They turned and started off together, swirling the
dawn mist. He waited until he could hold it in no
longer and called out at the trees. "We will be
kings!"

"Kings!" came the throaty cry, in unison, hidden
in the mist like a voice coming down through
clouded memory.

The sun burst up into the sky. They passed on
through the oaks, past the ancient and sacred
groves. Forest knowledge came back to them like
swimming to a fish returned to the water.

Dagentyr noticed each leaf, each different, musky forest odor. His mind became riveted to what he would find when he arrived at his destination.

They travelled openly but cautiously, staying in villages when they could, passing themselves off as a band of watermen lost, searching for the main trading band. They asked questions in every hamlet and were given information, directions, and at last, news of a violent, war-loving chieftain in the north, whose power was growing. He had driven out some of his own people, and they had moved away to another place.

Dagentyr heard the news with excitement and apprehension. Could it be Vorgus? Where were those who had been driven out? he asked, and was given an answer.

The journey north continued. Days passed. Dagentyr steered himself by vague instinct and by the stars as much as he could, and by an odd premonition. The forest lands wrapped around them, and then the country took on familiarity, like something he had seen or dreamed about long ago. A feeling compelled him to turn east, and it began to come back to him. The shape of the terrain jelled from his memory, and he recalled trails used when dragging a strange, twitching captive back home. He was driven on, up a remembered rise, no droning of bees, no loot, no companions, no Vorgus, just the same hill and the taste of rain on the breeze, and oddly out-of-place trails of smoke.

There was hesitation. His feet did not want to carry him up over the ridge. His courage faltered. There were many reasons a man should weep. He did not think he had one, yet he desired desperately to weep, and scream out his formless apprehension. Almost against his own will, he took the remaining distance running and stood on the top of the rise, looking down into the valley of the lake.

It was the same and not the same.

The surface of the lake was silver under a monochrome sky. Pastureland spread out as it had on the day he and Vorgus had struggled to kill each other. It was still beautiful but no longer unspoiled.

There was no grove. It had been chopped down. Cattle and goats and sheep were eating the grass, and men tended the animals. The smoke from the cooking fires sullied the air. A small, stockaded village sat where the grove had been.

Nothing stays the same, his brain echoed.

It came as a shock. He moved cautiously down the hill, staring at the things about him, trying to take it all in.

There was an armed lookout halfway down the slope who saw them coming and hollered the alarm. The herdsmen looked up in panic and began to drive the beasts to the palisade. Men rushed from the enclosure, swords drawn. The lookout braced himself, expecting them to attack.

"We will move slowly and go down to meet him," said Dagentyr.

Tingwahr looked skeptical. "Is this wise?"

"Do not draw your weapons. I think I know these people. I think we are home."

"But this is not Fottengra."

"It may be what is left of my Fottengra."

The guard confronting them called out.

"Stop! Who are you? Where do you come from?" Dagentyr gave his shield to Koricus, held up his empty hands, and went forward alone. He could see the man's mind working to place him as the warning was given again, "Hold, who are you?"

Dagentyr knew him. Beldigar was his name. The other warriors from the village were close. He braced himself for the words he had waited so long to say.

"I am Dagentyr, son of Ashak, of the village of Fottengra. I have come home. These are my warriors and friends, Beldigar."

It was done; the tension was released. The point

of the man's spear bit into the earth as his arm relaxed with the revelation.

"Dag . . . Dagentyr? It is you. I can see that now. I didn't know you. But how can you be here?" He turned to the others. "Hold! It is Dagentyr, Dagentyr!" The men squinted at him, talked excitedly, mouths opened in amazed recognition. "You escaped and were thought dead. Vorgus told everyone you were dead." Confusion was taking over. "The chieftain must be told. I must take you—" He stopped abruptly and put his arm out to Dagentyr. A smile came to his lips. "Welcome back, dead man. I say welcome back and do not even know where you have been."

"The tales will take many nights of feasting to tell." He took Beldigar's hand finally to prove to him that he was not a ghost.

He seemed reassured. "Come with me. I will take you to Targoth."

"Targoth?"

"Aye, he's . . . by Curnunos. Of course you know nothing of that. Targoth is chieftain here. Do you remember him and his brother, Sem?"

"How could I not remember them? My cousin Arvis and I called them friends." Their faces came back to him just as they had been at that final feast, filled with worry. He had ignored Targoth's warnings about power. He wondered what Targoth thought now that the village was his. "What is this?" He swept the view of the village with his hand.

"It would be too much for me to tell, and better that you hear it from Targoth, who knows more of it than I. There will be drink there, too. Could you use some? Have you come far?"

"Farther than you'll ever know. But what is this village? Are there others here that I know? There was a girl, Kerkina, daughter of Lokuos. Is she here?"

"Come with me before the rain arrives. You've

given me a good excuse to get in out of it for now. I was supposed to watch until sunset." Dagentyr's heart had stopped when Beldigar opened his mouth, for fear that he would say no. His teeth were clenched hard. "There is a Kerkina here. Lokuos is one of the men who came with us after Vorgus killed Clavosius."

"What?" His mouth dropped open even though it was something he had known would happen. The situation was clearer, but Targoth had much explaining to do, perhaps as much as he had himself. Beldigar had said that she was here. He looked over the hollow, seeking the auburn hair. His eyes darted everywhere, and he wanted to shout her name. He longed to yell that Targoth could wait. What use was there now in keeping his love for her a secret? So much had changed. Beldigar had mentioned nothing of Gertera. Foolish idiot, he thought, you've come home to your own land and people, and already she is constricting you again.

They walked into the hollow and up to the gates of the rude fortress. The gate guards looked at him strangely. One was about to say something to him but kept quiet. The hall was a puny thing. Beldigar announced loudly that they were going to enter, threw aside the door flap, and they ducked in.

Targoth stood in the middle of the room, putting on his war tunic. Sem was handing him his weapons, and his eyes stared in disbelief.

"Tell me of the alarm, Beldigar," said Targoth concernedly, and then turned to look at who had entered. He was still himself, immaculately shaved, but seemed self-conscious of what he had become. He was also deeply puzzled. "There is no need to tell me, Beldigar. He has not changed so much that I do not recognize him. But I am at a loss, Dagentyr. How are you here?"

"Dagentyr?" said Sem. "It's you back with us after so long? We thought you were dead." He came and slapped Dagentyr's shoulders. "It is Dagentyr!"

Sem had always been the outgoing one, Dagentyr mused, but some of his jubilation jumped to Targoth.

"Yes, yes," he chuckled at last. "There is so much that you must want to know. I don't know what to do or where to begin." Sem called to a slave for mead. The ice had been broken, so Dagentyr moved to the room's center and sat. "This is much for a man to think on," Targoth went on. He drew his last words out, convincing himself firmly of the fact. "Dagentyr is home."

The mead was in front of them. The fire had been stoked. Two full cups had been drunk already. A sweet taste coated the inside of his mouth, an almost sickening taste. He had become used to wine. The drinking of mead needed to be relearned. Targoth had begun to explain.

"It was over quickly. We woke one day and Clavosius and Galmar were dead. Vorgus proclaimed himself chieftain, and there were men who sided with him. As you can see, we are not many here. We decided that we would take our chances elsewhere, away from Fottengra and Vorgus. He would have us no longer. It has been hard. Guards must be maintained all the time. Vorgus steals our cattle. Melvaris, one of our women, was taken a month ago as she picked berries. We do what we can."

"Were there so many who supported Vorgus?"

"Enough."

"But why?"

Targoth shrugged. "Fear. He won them over by fear. Believe me, he is not feared without reason, and now he craves more power. The southern tribes know his name. Perhaps their children too have nightmares of him."

"Come, you exaggerate," Dagentyr said, pushing his cup away. Already the kernel of what they must do was coming to him. "Surely you see that we must attack him."

"You're drunk," said Targoth and sat up stiffly on his wolfskin.

"Drunk at the very least. Have you come back to us a madman?" Sem asked.

"Why madness?" Dagentyr said. "You would throw your hands up in amazement if I told you what I have seen surprise do. Will he expect us to attack him? No. That is his weakness. Trust this. I have seen walls as tall as trees topple because of it."

Sem broke in. "The walls of the watermen's city? Tell me more of them, and the men who live there, no, tell me first of the women."

"No, Sem. That will wait. I won't be distracted from this other purpose. I've burned with it these years. Vorgus must die. That is all that need happen for us to be victorious. No weight of numbers is necessary, just boldness and speed."

Targoth drummed his fingers on his goblet in irritation. "You've burned with it, but we've lived with it. We'd be crushed. You don't know what you're saying."

"Have you been sitting here becoming so cautious that you've forgotten that it is bravery that men take pride in?"

"No!" He bolted up and cast the goblet down. "We are as much men as we ever were, but I am chieftain here. Chieftains must think! You never did understand that."

Sem tried peacemaking. "Targoth. What kind of homecoming is due a warrior? Not this, certainly. Dagentyr, you're tired, and things have changed here."

"Things have changed with me, as well. I am back, alive. That should tell you that I know how to get what I want. Let Targoth think on that."

Desolate silence set in.

Targoth turned his back on Dagentyr and went to the fire. He said, "Gertera is here. I brought her when we left, out of honor for you."

Dagentyr stood up to leave. "I see." His head was whirling. If Targoth wanted thanks for that, he would not get it.

"On the morrow we must feast to celebrate this homecoming of yours. Many ears will want to hear of your journeys. I'm sure Herkin could do no better if he were here." Targoth's tone was more friendly but not apologetic.

Sem seemed to think that everything was healed. "Yes, Targoth. I will tell things. My head grows woozy." Only curiosity made him ask, "Where is Gertera? She stays with someone who has taken her in?"

"With the family of Lokuos."

"Impossible!" Kerkina's kindheartedness and guilt had overcome her. What had she been thinking of? What sort of thoughts was Gertera harboring toward the giver of her good fortune?

Targoth shook his head. "I'm sure they will let you in as well. Lokuos is a good man. He always favored you."

The mead sat even more uneasily in his stomach. He was speechless and made for the door, and fresh air.

"Gods welcome you back," called Sem.

The surprise he felt when he stepped out was even more overpowering than the mead. A crowd of people waited outside the chieftain's door. Beldigar had told the village, and news of him had spread. The whole village was there. The gate guards looked at him with definite recognition.

When they saw him, a hush fell. The mad rushing of his heart pumped away the effects of the mead. He stood there for a moment, then began to walk toward the gate. The villagers started a murmur, then a buzz, then a cheer. In a flash he remembered to look for two faces, his mind working along lines that it had not for years. He quickened his step to be among them and raised his arms to the gods as he went. His men surrounded him and shared his moment.

From the mass of people, two broke away, running, running at him. It was all going so fast. One of them, the dark-haired one, stumbled and fell to the ground, and then the one with the deep green eyes and russet mane arrived in his arms.

He wanted to pick her up and run with her, to where there was no village, no people, no Gertera. Kerkina had her mouth on his. Her arms sought what seemed a stranglehold as they fought to pull him closer.

Though he knew the fallen woman was coming near, he gave in to Kerkina's pleading fingers and lips. They were soft, salted lightly with tears. He forsook the crowd and sank drowning into her eyes, and the warmth of her skin.

She babbled, "I'm afraid that this will all go away a moment from now, and you will not be here and all these people will mourn for me and say that I went mad with grief and longing, and that the forest devils snatched up my soul and drowned it in the lake." Her hands clutched to anchor him to the spot. Time apart had destroyed her caution but suddenly caution had no meaning for him.

"You are the only thing that I came back for," he said. "To see you and have you here next to me, so close. In these years there were moments when I would have died willingly and even dishonorably for a bare instant of this, and now it can be always. And the old woman?"

She shook her head and began to cry. Her fingers stroked serenely through his hair. He pulled a tear-soggy wisp of hair from her eyes and smoothed it back. Over her shoulder he saw Gertera standing with the dirt still clinging to her dress. He knew her hands longed to stroke him too, but they were just clenched, white and ugly at her sides. Her mouth worked horribly between embarrassed smile and grimace of hate. Her eyes were Vorgus's, and Parush's, Ruki's, and every Ahhiyawan's who had come against him. He could do nothing but look at her while Kerkina sobbed against his chest. Pretense was something he had told himself he would dispense with if ever he returned. That had just been accomplished. Lokuos came forward, breaking the spell, to invite him to stay at their hut. Dagentyr released Kerkina to clasp her father's hand in thanks and friendship. Gertera stared at the ground.

The village had seemed not to notice the scene. Surprising, he thought. Perhaps they were so wrapped up in the diversion of his return that old suspicion and talk were unimportant. He didn't care. He would be master of his own household. Gertera would find that out to her dislike.

Lokuos was leading the way to his hut. People nodded to Dagentyr as he passed. Later, he thought, I will tell them of Trusya, but not now. Time is something I have in plenty. But he knew that was not true. Before there could be peace here with Kerkina and peace within himself, Vorgus had to be killed. His vow was only half complete.

The curious followed them a way, and parents leaned down to their children to say, "There is the man we told you the stories about. See? Isn't he just as we described?"

Dagentyr looked back at the chieftain's hut. Targoth and Sem stood in the doorway and saw all that went on. Targoth looked troubled and perplexed. Dagentyr thought, He does not know that the people are with me, or will be. He doesn't know that in my absence I have become chieftain; he will know it soon enough.

He took Kerkina's hand as they walked. Gertera came behind and smoldered like a dangerous fire. Not a word had been spoken or a touch given.

There was much he wanted to say to Kerkina, but with Gertera near, it could not be done. He pressed Kerkina's hand tighter. He felt her fingers close harder in mute answer. He did not look back.

Chapter 31

The knot of men that formed around him early the next morning stayed for most of the day. There was an occasional change of faces as some left and others came to hear. A cluster of children hovered at the door of the hut, eager to hear the stories and longing to be nearer the hearth where the fire burned, bathing the faces of the storyteller and his listeners in a mystic halo, but they were not allowed in. It was a time only for men, so the younger boys shivered in the rain and hung on to his words.

Dagentyr was aware of them, lurking wide-eyed at the door, but they were not his main concern. He resisted any temptation to embellish his stories for the children's sake. His words would lose the ring of truth needed for the convincing of men. He started at the beginning and told them, and the hut was never empty of people to listen. When someone new would come in, the others would say, "Dagentyr, tell about the fury of the big water for Evos, he's just come in. Tell it again."

He would. His listeners did not get bored. Lokuos had Iaris, his wife, see that there was refreshment for all who shared the roof of his hut and joined in the company. Lokuos sat back satisfied when Dagentyr spoke, for it brought him honor to have the traveller in his home. They spent the day drinking and questioning and eating food the women cooked. Not even when Kerkina's hand touched his as she handed him his refilled cup did Dagentyr's concentration waver. Had he really killed Molva? No? Then who, and why? He told them.

His warriors were all there with him. When he would come to an especially unbelievable event, they would nod and agree, giving credence to his tale. Having them there gave him stature, the air of a visiting chieftain, and that was what he wanted.

He told them the adventures of the years, but the horse he left out. It was not time for that yet, not until the night, with Targoth there, in the presence of the other warriors. It would be a tale he would try to weave to his own advantage. What had been a bad omen for Trusya would be a good one here, a useful one.

The hut reeked of mead, smoke, and seared meat. What his words could do to master men amazed him. Firelight sparkled in their attentive eyes. With every unfolding of a new episode, they were more caught up in what he had been through. In their eyes, he seemed to grow until his head brushed the thatch of the ceiling. No one doubted his words. They murmured, and exclaimed with their hands and arms, spilling mead on themselves. When each man went away, he left with visions of exotic things in his head.

"Will you tell us again at the feast tonight?" they asked.

"Yes, and I will tell you the strangest part of the story, for you have not heard the ending." He would make his move then.

When the sun went down, the men left and
Lokuos shooed the children from the doorway.
Tingwahr winked as they went away to the places
that had been given them.

There was time to rest and think before the feast.
He ached for a moment alone with Kerkina, but
she and Iaris and Gertera fussed, preparing their
evening meal and doing the chores of the hut.

His first night in the village had been torture.
With his eyes open in the dark and Gertera next to
him once again, he feared that this one thing would
never change, but she did not pester him. She made
no effort to touch him, and her body seemed to
radiate cold hate instead of heat. Lokuos had
thought no more than that she was a wife well
trained. Dagentyr knew that his miraculous return
would make it easier to take and wed Kerkina.
Gertera he would keep for his father's memory, but
it would not be the same as it had before. He was
ashamed that he had not asserted himself sooner.

Kerkina was at the loom. Iaris was seeing that the
animals were all in the forecourt. Lokuos felt the
need for sleep before the feast and was lying with
the coverlet pulled snugly up to his neck. Gertera
came and sat next to Dagentyr by the fire. She
pretended to stoke the embers, then kept still and
looked at his face. He turned to her.

"Truth has followed you home, Dagentyr," she
said.

"It was always there, but you never saw it."

"I see now, and worse than that, I feel it now."
She spit the words into his face but kept them low.
"This is the cruelest, most dishonorable— And
how was it last night, staying under the same roof
with her but sleeping with me. Did you sleep? I half
expected to hear the rustle of the straw as you
switched beds, and the stifled sighs and murmured
urgings." She had not forgotten when to stop. His

eyes had lit up with their old warning. His hand clenched as if to strike. She looked away into the fire. "I slept as I never have before, slept like someone dead, and maybe I was; my heart is dead. There was no fear of offending you, no worry that I might not be loved, no sick, gnawing hope, here." She put her hands to her stomach. "And so, I slept. I slept very deeply," she whispered.

"You have designed your words to hurt."

Kerkina cocked her head at the loom. Embarrassed, she stood. "I will see if Mother needs help with the animals." She left, new tears forming in her eyes, unable to stand the strain. Dagentyr acknowledged her leaving with a smile so she would not feel so alone. He turned to Gertera again.

"Why did your heart outlive Ashak? Did he not have possession of it? He thought he did." He did not want to disturb Lokuos, so he moved closer to her. She hadn't expected him to. She was afraid and put her arms in front of her face, fearing attack. "Out of all the times I threatened, I never once struck you."

"I would have been glad of your anger, your blows." She reached a seeking hand to touch his arm but drew back. "I would have been grateful for any kindness, any unkindness, just as long as it had been *something*."

He took her forearm in a gesture he hoped she would take for compassion. "Listen to this. The things I have done in the past I have done out of honor for Ashak. Whatever I do in the future, I will still keep honor for him, and you."

"You'll wed this girl. I'm no idiot. You did not know that I was not? Then why should you know anything about me; we are strangers."

"You insist on making the worst of everything. You only make yourself miserable. I'm not the same person that left here long ago. We were strangers before. It is even truer now. I have seen too much and realize that I must go my own way, do what is necessary, take what is necessary."

She narrowed her eyes. "And your wife is not necessary?"

"You are Ashak's wife."

"Was!"

"No, still are to me, always will be to me. There's nothing more to talk about. I have only meant this as a comfort to you, so you will know that you will always have a place."

Her face became red. Lokuos stirred in his sleep, and their talk was at an end. Gertera got up and set to work again. Dagentyr remained at the fire, thinking of the coming feast. All the first steps had been taken. This last, this break with Gertera, would prove to be the final unpleasantry. It was all an easy climb from here. The signs were good.

Kerkina caught him by the arm as he left the hut with Lokuos to go to Targoth's hut. He told the older man to go along, he would catch up. Her tight grasp conveyed her nervousness.

"We have had no moment together. I seem to feel that you mean to do things, things that will take you away and leave me without you once more. Do you wish me to be left alone to face Gertera's hate?"

"There are things I must do, but I will never be away from you for long again. I promise that."

A mild round of laughter came down to them from the hall. They would be waiting for him. She looked at him with a heart unconvinced.

"I received an omen against Vorgus once, or so I thought," he said, "but the omen was fulfilled in the land of the Trus—of the watermen. I'm a boat on the crest of a wave, and it is carrying me to shore. If I fall back, I will drown."

He kissed her. As he walked away, her figure looked small and helpless against the immensity of night. The star-snake glittered. It was all there in one picture—homeland, woman, guiding stars. What an omen this must be, he thought, and went in to the feast.

The men leapt up at the sight of him. All greeted him like brothers. "You've come at last. Come here and eat. Quick, give him mead so that he can start in. Finish your stories!"

He sat down. He and Tingwahr and the others were given the best portions of the meat. Targoth seemed aloof and unfriendly, but curious. Sem had caught the high spirit of the others. They were all eager.

He told it all again from the start. Those who had heard it before acted as though they had not. The slaves came and went, bringing meat and drink and feeding the fire. When the shouts of interest were heavy, Targoth looked like a man being swept away in a flood. It took much time to get through it.

Then he told them of the horse.

He told them in a rush, and before they had time to ask their stores of questions, he plunged along with his wave.

"This is what can happen again, here! We all know that Vorgus must die. We all want him dead. If we attack Fottengra now, we can use the ways of the Ahhiyawa. I have told you the reward of their cunning. The gods will be with us if we strike now."

They were stunned.

"Do we too make a horse?" said Evos.

"No, but we use surprise. Listen. When we first arrived, who did you think we were?"

"We did not know," said Beldigar. "You looked so strange, different."

"That is true."

Tingwahr whispered to Cingetos and gave a

questioning look to Drusos. They too were ignorant
of his plans.

"We looked like watermen," said Dagentyr.

"Yes!" Beldigar shouted. "That's it. It's been
long, yes, but your weapons, clothes, are all those of
the watermen."

"So then. We will *be* watermen. We have come
far telling the countryside that we were, and none
doubted us. Let me tell you the plan. We shall go
downstream of Fottengra, my watermen and I. We
will build rafts, take bundles with us, and then we
will sail up the river to the village. They will think
we are watermen; why shouldn't they? When
Vorgus comes down to meet us, I will attack and
slay him. While we take the warriors who have met
us at the river, you of this village will attack the
fortress."

"I do not understand," Sem said.

"You will have crossed the river at night and will
hide in the forest until the time is right. We will
strike together, twin blows like the thunder and
lightning. The gates will be open. It will be an easy
thing."

There was a hum of talk around the fire, men
leaning in to each other. He pressed them.

"What honor there will be in going home, as I
have received in coming here. I have told you of my
omen. Vorgus is not the golden horse, and I will kill
him when we meet. He is mine and Fottengra will
be ours again. You can share the glory or I can go
alone." Helani would be proud, he thought. "Men,
what do you say? Dawn can bring the start of
glory!"

Targoth shouted out, "No!" and came to his feet.
"What you would do is preposterous." He was
taken aback and stammered out, "It's useless.
What can we gain?"

"We can be the men of Fottengra again, like our

fathers, as we were meant to be." His story had stirred them up as he had wanted.

There were shouts of "Yes! I am for it!" Beldigar called a war cry. Sem was caught in the middle. Dagentyr stood to face Targoth.

"Who is chieftain here!" countered Targoth. "I say stay, fight if we are attacked. We're getting by in this place, on our own. You'd have us fight for the settling of your own personal battle."

"The need to fight is now. Hasn't he wronged you all? Surely he has or you would not be here."

"It is my right to say, to lead!"

"You who never wanted the chiefdom? How long have the rest of you yearned to fight back, to gain revenge?"

"Long! Since we were driven away!" came the answers.

"No!" said Targoth once more.

Dagentyr was ready. "If you were meant to be chieftain, then you will prevail." He drew his dagger.

The men hushed. Slaves made for the doors. Targoth's face hardened. Shocked faces stared at the two men and waited. Targoth looked into Dagentyr's eyes, knew the intent and purpose there, knew that the wave had washed over him. The others were caught up. He was alone. His eyes broke contact with Dagentyr's. He took two steps back, dropped his head, and went out of the hall.

Sem was devastated and got up, weeping, to follow his brother. Dagentyr raised his dagger in the air and said, "We leave at dawn!"

"Tomorrow!" they cried.

"We will be kings!" yelled his warriors. They looked at him in admiration, exultation. Tingwahr whooped wildly and shook his fist at the ceiling.

Dagentyr sheathed the dagger and went for his cup, hoping mead would heal the rip in his heart.

Targoth had been a friend. Sem had been a friend. Perhaps even Gertera had been a friend. His breaks with the past were coming quickly.

The others were up, calling out the war god's name, raising their cups to him, to the sky. The mead had lost its taste.

Chapter 32

It was daybreak and the men were armed and ready for the journey. When Dagentyr came to lead them away, Targoth and Sem were waiting with the rest.

"I'm no less honorable for anything that's happened. I go and fight with my people, and I follow who leads them," said Targoth. There was sad commitment and bravery in his voice.

"I'm glad, Targoth, and I am also sorry." He put a hand on his arm. Each knew that they had no other choice in their actions.

Kerkina and Gertera were in the group of people saying good-bye. Gertera's shawl was pulled up over her head like a hood, and her face was all black in the dawn light. It was all he noticed of her. He said, "Wait for me," to Kerkina, and then they were off, leaving only a few warriors to protect the village. There was a baby crying and a call of good fortune from the gate sentry, and they were headed toward Fottengra, east into the woods. The group of women and children saw them off in the drizzle and retired into the palisade until their return.

They went quickly, pressed by Dagentyr's energy and sense of impending victory. Each landmark on the way awoke new memories in him. This would be the true homecoming because it would fulfill the ends of fate.

It rained all during the two days of the journey. It rained even as they poled their new-built rafts quietly up the river. The sound of the water was soothing. It did not matter that Vorgus's followers would be twice their number. Dagentyr had returned miraculously. Was that not a victory over Vorgus in itself? How much more difficult could the raid be?

The village came into sight, and Dagentyr felt as though he had swallowed a rock. The herds were being tended in the fields. Smoke oozed from the roofs of the huts. It was sleepy and placid. Warriors would be lounging around warm hearths, not ready for war. Their gates were open. His dripping helmet plume fell by his cheek. His warriors held their large, distinctive shields in front of them where they could be plainly seen. A few of Targoth's men, pretending to be unarmed traders, clasped their weapons nervously beneath their cloaks.

Dagentyr shivered momentarily and looked at the men. "Remember, Vorgus is for me. Play the role of watermen as long as you can. Kill no one who might follow us if you can help it, only those who are firmly with Vorgus. When he is dead, Fottengra will be ours. Remember your purpose." He tried to look relaxed, tried to convey confidence. The plan was going well.

"Fight well, Dagentyr. We are with you," whispered Tingwahr.

He smiled back and it felt like the times before battle at Trusya. He nodded to them all.

The gate trumpet called from Fottengra. They had been seen. Herdsmen became alert, turned their heads.

Dagentyr lifted his arm, waved calmly, easily. He called a friendly greeting in Trusian.

The herdsman waved back. It was going well.

The trumpet blew its sad song out again. People were coming from the fortress to see, women, children.

Dagentyr waved again. "Raise your hand to them, Tingwahr."

Tingwahr smiled broadly and swung his hand back and forth slowly. "The luck of the gods is with us," he mumbled.

In spite of the rain, many people were coming to see their arrival. The more the better, Dagentyr thought.

The people at the gate stepped aside. A war cart was exiting the fortress.

Dagentyr's pulse began to race. This is it, Vorgus. You are the one I came to see. He was having difficulty staying calm. His hand opened, clenched, opened.

The chieftain was leaving the fortress with his retinue. More people were coming to the river.

"Slowly now," Dagentyr chided. "We must not arrive too soon; we could be recognized."

The chariot was moving down the slope. He could see the long yellow hair. A surge of elation ran through him. It would not be like the other times. Already it did not feel like the other times.

They were very close. Dagentyr had the men keep their heads down. The rafts bumped the shore. He shielded his eyes with his hands. The chariot had stopped. The chieftain was stepping out, moving to him, hands outstretched.

Dagentyr drew his sword. "Vorgus! It's me who's come to kill you, Dagentyr, son of Ashak!"

The men screamed their war calls and jumped from the rafts. Other men burst from the trees and ran to the palisade. The herders threw down their staffs, abandoned their animals, and ran for the fortress.

Vorgus hesitated before drawing his weapon. The

sword quivered in his hand. His eyes were shocked beneath the blond brows. Hate and recognition burned through the initial surprise. "You should have stayed dead, Dagentyr. This must be a blessing from the gods, for I will have killed you twice. There will be no return this time."

The accented voice came to him as hateful as any Trusian or Ahhiyawan drawl. He knew that in spite of Vorgus's bold words, the man was caught off guard, and then it was like all the other times. Vorgus made the first lunge.

Their blades met. Dagentyr felt Vorgus's momentum carrying him on. He rammed with his heavy shield, the way he had learned to fight at Trusya. Vorgus fell on his back.

He lunged, but the horse had rolled out of the way. Dagentyr swung down at him again and again, his cuts blocked as Vorgus scooted back on his rump till he could regain his feet.

"The omen about you is blotted out," Dagentyr grunted. He saw that Vorgus was weak and afraid.

The golden giant backed up, retreated, turning his head to see the carnage around him. The fortress discharged its people, but they had to run among the raiders to reach safety. Some were Vorgus's men, for Dagentyr saw them slain. A few recognized them as being from the lake and cried that they would help the raiders. There was no way that the gates would be closed in time.

Vorgus turned and ran for the gate. The men who had come with him to the river had been totally surprised. All were dead.

Dagentyr and his warriors pushed up the hill, meeting little resistance. Seeing that they would penetrate the fortress, the people were making for the woods. Sem shot one of the gate sentries with an arrow. Dagentyr saw that the other one had already been pulled down and killed. He lay crumpled in the supports of his raised platform.

Men came from the chieftain's hall and some of the huts. They fought them in front of the hall and through the streets. The battle sounds raged again in his ears, strangely muffled by the rain. There were cries of pain, surprise, anger. Unprepared, the men of Vorgus were falling or running.

Dagentyr fought his way to the hall and called again. "Vorgus!" He tore the door flap away violently and went in. Vorgus stood in the center of the hall, waiting for him. "Now, big man, your time has come. Your men are dead or have come over to us."

He attacked, swung down and felt his blade bite into Vorgus's hip, through meat and into bone. He pulled it free. There was a bright spurt of blood and a groan through gritted teeth. What shock Vorgus hadn't felt at seeing Dagentyr, he felt now. The leg with the severed sinews collapsed.

The sword was as light as a child's wooden toy in Dagentyr's hand. He swung it down.

Vorgus blocked, groaning in agony with each meeting of the bronze. He was gasping, frantically wiping the sweat from his eyes. The blade sliced into the top of his shoulder. He screamed.

Dagentyr knew the tide was taking him to shore. Any time he would land on it, as firm as rock. He was high with victory.

Knowing his time was almost done, Vorgus flung himself forward with all his weight, the blade up. The hip wound shot a last streak of red.

Dagentyr felt the point pierce his side below his rib cage and the blade slid up and in. His breath left him, driven out by hot, bronze fire. Muscle and flesh were ripped by the pitted, uneven edge. The scream came up from his guts and out into the air. What was happening? He dropped the shield, raised his sword with both fists, and drove it down into Vorgus's back, all the way through. The blade worked in Dagentyr's wound as Vorgus's grip loosened in death. The golden horse slumped with his face to the floor.

He could not regain his breath; it would not come. He stumbled to the door, pain searing him all the while. The fighting in the streets was blurred to him. Sounds were dim except for the rain. He stared at the sword still in him. What was running down his side—rain, blood? What had happened?

He did not know that he had hit the ground. All he perceived was fuzzy grey sky and a chill wind whipping across his face.

Eyes, unblinking, staring down passively at him, and he out through them at his life, seeing it through different shades as the eyes compelled him to. Different pairs of eyes, dark ones lined in heavy black; shaded, green ones; and these, suddenly grey and hard like Astekar's but not his, older, deeper, and a frowzy tangle of moustache somewhere beneath them.

In addition to the eyes, there was the pain, dull but constant and overpowering. He heard his breath rattle in and out of his chest and was aware that it was shallow; it left him aching for air, but he could do nothing. His body was leaden, sluggish, but it was warm. In the pain and confusion the warmth was a comfort. He moved his hand slowly over his middle and could not find the sword. It had been pulled, then. Exhausted by the simple movement, he felt the warmth coursing through him as if it came from inside.

Wondering if the eyes he saw were only in his mind, he worked to sit up and look about him. It took so much effort, so much. There they were, the grey eyes and the moustache, blurred and indistinct. They floated in darkness. The moustache bobbed up and down rhythmically as its owner's lips moved.

"It is Irzag, Dagentyr."

Irzag, he thought. Yes, I know who you are.

"You are in Fottengra. Do you hear me?"

He shut his eyes. His voice came out as a harsh whisper. Fire kindled in his vitals once more. "Yes," he said.

"You are in the chieftain's hut."

That made the surroundings more familiar. He let his head roll sideways. A blurred fire roared in the hearth. It felt good to be warm. It felt safe, like home. He was in Fottengra. The fur thrown across him was rich and thick. He hoped it was Vorgus's.

Irzag raised his shoulders as he sighed. "You have been in the ghost world for near three days. You are just now come back to us."

"And is the chiefdom mine?" Irzag blurred again. "Who rules?"

"Vorgus is dead. You rule here. Targoth has been chosen by the elders and warriors of Fottengra, in your stead for now."

"Am I dying?"

Irzag was silent for a while. "You are in the gods' hands. Many a man would not have survived at all. The omens are good. I am working magic for your recovery."

He closed his eyes. "He was the horse, then. It was him."

"My warning was a true one in more ways than one. I myself knew nothing of a wooden beast covered in gold. The men told me of your tale." Dagentyr sensed Irzag's hand on his shoulder through the fur. "Rest easy and well. Your own warriors guard the door."

The shuffle of feet told him that someone else had been admitted to the room. Irzag took back his hand and nodded to the person. "My chieftain, your woman is here for you." Irzag withdrew.

Dagentyr was pleased, at peace in defiance of the pain. Kerkina was here. They had arrived from the lake valley. It had all worked out. Vorgus was dead, the village was his, Kerkina would be with him. The warmth and comfort overwhelmed him.

A cool hand traced a line across his brow. A cold voice followed it.

"Poor husband." The pallet sank as she sat down upon it. "Are you to perform a final cruelty and leave me widowed and alone?" He opened his eyes and tried to speak. She prevented it by pressing her fingertips to his lips, harder than she needed to. "Shh. Don't speak. You are weak. Let me do the talking. Just lie still and listen. The gods have been good to me this day. They allowed me to see you alone before she could. The guards would not let her in, you know, but I am your wife and was admitted. Irzag has gone."

He tried to speak again or call out, but she pressed her hand down, bruising his lips upon his teeth. He felt threatened, but his mind was working so slowly. An attempt to lift his hand failed.

"Poor warrior, lost so much blood, and Irzag has given you an herb for rest." Her words were sickly sweet like mead. It was so much work just to keep his eyes open and look at her hazy face, shadowed, and back-lit from the hearth. "I travelled all this way, praying that you would not die. The people of the lake valley have returned to Fottengra. She came too, as I told you, and she prayed the same thing but for different reasons. Now she has lost. Why? Is that what you're trying to ask me?" She read the desperate movement of his lips and the struggle of his features. "Because I now have the courage." She ran her hands down under the coverlet, over his loins, his chest. She removed the hand over his mouth long enough to kiss him as she stroked, then she put it back again and drew the dagger from under her cloak.

"I have gotten pleasure from this meeting with you, more than all the other nights with you," she said as she pulled the blade across his skin, cutting his throat just beneath the line of his beard. When she had done, she touched a bloody finger to his lips in good-bye and walked to the fireside. Her cloak tail hissed along the floor. She sat down to watch the brief moments it would take him to die. Against the flame she was a formless thing of darkness.

He could not call out. Even in his stupor he knew it would make no difference. It was a laughable thought that he had at last given her pleasure. Kerkina was outside and the distance might as well have been as far as to Trusya.

The slash did not hurt much; there was not enough life left in him to feel it. Slow sobbing came from the shapeless lump at the fire.

He dropped his head to the side, or had it simply fallen because he could no longer hold it straight? He hoped he'd be remembered. Kerkina would remember him. Perhaps someday a wandering teller of tales from the forest would carry a word or two of him to distant lands. Ruki, if he were still alive, might hear of the tale and pluck a string to this moment.

A trickle of blood ran down the fur. Hairs that it touched wore individual beads of red like bright poppies. Each drop whispered as it hit the floor, forming a tiny, shining lake of red.